HEART OF THE VAMPIRE

THE COMPLETE BUNDLE

TASHA BLACK

13TH STORY PRESS

TASHA BLACK STARTER LIBRARY

Packed with steamy shifters, mischievous magic, billionaire superheroes, otherworldly alien mates, and plenty of HEAT, the Tasha Black Starter Library is the perfect way to dive into Tasha's unique brand of Romance with Bite!
Get your FREE books now at tashablack.com!

EPISODE 1

I n her dream, Drucilla Holloway stood barefoot on a cool stone floor, gazing out an enormous, arched window into the stillness of the dark summer night.

Stars dotted a velvet sky like a canopy of twinkle lights over the vast meadow below and the treetops of the forest beyond.

This was the setting of the hotel where she worked. She was sure of it. But in her waking hours, she had never seen it from above this way, at an angle that made it all look small and sweet, like a drawing in a book of fairy tales.

A cooling breeze swirled through the window, filling the room with the scent of roses.

Her dream-self knew that she was waiting for something.

But she couldn't remember what...

Footsteps rang out on the stone floor behind her, but she didn't turn.

He's here...

Her heart pounded in anticipation, and she closed her eyes against the rush of emotions that threatened to overwhelm her.

The footsteps slowed, and Dru could smell the cool, clean

scent of him. She could practically feel his touch, even before his arms slid around her waist, pinning her to him.

"Drucilla," he murmured into her hair, his dark voice sending shivers down her spine.

No one called her that. Even to her family, she had always been just plain Dru.

His lips trailed slowly down her jaw toward the tender place where her neck met her shoulder.

She moaned lightly, already shivering with need.

His mouth left a warm trail of honeyed sweetness wherever it touched.

Sensations washed over her in waves. Behind her closed eyelids, she saw roses blooming and withering, a forest growing taller, suns rising and setting so fast they seemed to strobe.

"Please," she whispered, not even knowing what she was begging for.

But no sound left her lips.

She tried again, desperate for him to hear her.

A strange sound erupted from her throat and she tried to move out of his grip.

But reality was bleeding in at the edges now...

DRU WAS VAGUELY aware that she wasn't really in the room with the stone floor.

She was held fast, not by the arms of her mystery lover, but by the threadbare quilts she'd been tossing and turning in. And the only roses were the ones on the wallpaper.

She sat up and ran a hand through her hair.

Soft, late-afternoon sunlight bled through the sheer curtains, catching the dust motes mid-waltz.

The light cast a warm glow around the room, but the actual temperature was practically frigid. The hot water in the radiators seemed to go tepid well before it reached her on the third floor of the old hotel.

She sighed, and half-expected to see her own breath plume in the chilly air. It was winter, and Dru had been dreaming of summer again.

She shivered and tried to shake the clinging feeling that something wasn't right.

A quick look around told her everything was in its place. Built-in bookcases flanked the window seat and lined the wall beside the bed. They were all overflowing with tattered paperbacks and assorted reference books - everything from *The Elements of Style*, to *The Unofficial Star Trek Cookbook*, to something called *Encyclopedia Vampirica*. The overstuffed chair in the corner was still just as covered in unwashed laundry as it always was. And her grandmother's ancient Smith Corona typewriter awaited her atop the antique desk, silently judging her for all the pages she hadn't written yet.

The thousand drooping roses on the wallpaper disappeared into the shadowy areas in the eaves, keeping watch over the whole scene, as if she were living in a creepy Victorian doll house instead of a "homey" Bed & Breakfast in the Pocono mountains of Pennsylvania.

But overall, the vibe suited Dru just fine. She was here to work on a horror novel after all, not get featured in *Better Homes & Gardens*.

Her stomach grumbled, clearly less concerned about the decor than the provisions.

She glanced at the clock - 4:30PM - time for breakfast.

Dru slid out from between the quilts, quickly pulling on a bulky sweater and a pair of well-worn slippers. She headed to the mini-fridge to grab some milk, and dumped the remainder of a bag of Fruity Dyno-Bites into a bowl that she was pretty sure was clean.

No matter how long she worked the overnight shift Dru still preferred breakfast foods as her first meal of the day.

The tiny kitchen of Hemlock House offered meals only at appointed, traditional times. In half an hour, Constance, the only cook, would ring the bell to announce that the dining room was open. Anyone willing to sit at the communal table could choose a plate of gray meat and even grayer potatoes or a half-hearted vegetarian option. Either way, the meal was served with a side of wacky conversation from the odd assortment of hotel guests, and a buttered roll.

Dru carried her off-brand sugary cereal over to the window seat and looked out the window as she ate. It wasn't as good as the real thing, but it turned the milk a startling shade of neon pink, which was a plus.

It had snowed an inch or two in the night. The expansive front lawn of Hemlock House was frosted with white, and the gigantic hemlock tree that had given the hotel its name looked like it belonged on the stage of *The Nutcracker*.

But the tire tracks on the circular driveway swooping up to the front door of the hotel ruined the magical effect. There was a shuttle bus that carried guests to and from the nearby town of Willow Ridge - the locals were really into the whole naming things after trees motif. Willow Ridge was only about a few miles down the mountain, but all the twists and turns in the narrow road made the trip take a half an hour, more if there was snow on the ground. In really bad weather, it was completely impassable.

Fortunately, there wasn't a big storm in the forecast anytime soon.

Chester Crawford, the groundskeeper, was the only one allowed to drive the shuttle, in any kind of weather. It looked like he had recently brought up at least one new guest, which was good. The old place could certainly use the business.

Dru was at Hemlock House this year in part because she had heard short term rental websites were dominating the Poconos.

If she ever wanted to give herself a working writing retreat at the quaint, possibly-haunted-but-not-really, hotel where her grandmother had worked in the sixties, it was now or never. Most of the smaller places were shutting their doors. She didn't think Hemlock House would be far behind.

And though the overnight shift was still rough on her now, she was sure once she was used to it, she would get tons of writing done. After all, there would be little else to do.

She finished her cereal, then rinsed the bowl and spoon in the sink of the small attached bathroom.

A quick shower and a few minutes of pawing through her small wardrobe had her dressed and ready for work.

But the sunlight had gone pink already.

"Come on, Dru," she told herself.

She had time to kill before she had to report for duty. She'd probably head down early and catch up with Hailey, but first, she was going to settle into some writing. She could knock out a few hundred words, if she was focused.

Dru sat down at the desk and faced off with the robin's-egg-blue Smith Corona, its single blank page full of wonder and possibility, like a layer of new snow before some shuttle bus comes along and screws it up.

Typewriters weren't exactly the most cutting-edge writing tool, and this one didn't even have a working '8' key, but the internet coverage was spotty in the mountains, and

Dru really didn't need the distraction of social media on her laptop anyway.

Plus, part of her hoped Nana Jane's typewriter would bring her luck, so that maybe she could build something from the snow, instead of just ruining it with her ugly tracks.

She absentmindedly ran her finger across the carved initials in the desk. *JA,* for Jane Anderson.

Nana always insisted she was quite the rebel when she was younger, and Dru had laughed her head off at that idea, not believing for an instant that her smiling Nana could ever be anything but what she was right then - a silver-haired lady puttering around in the garden, reading a never-ending stream of mystery novels, and burning all her ambitious baking experiments.

But here was plain evidence her grandmother had carved her initials into a desk, like a naughty schoolchild in a movie. And Nana had been twenty when she worked at Hemlock House.

This wasn't the first time Dru had thought of her grandmother's initials over the years. They were carved into the locket she wore every day, right next to a small piece of irregularly shaped crystal on a fine silver chain. The whole necklace had belonged to her Nana Jane. She had given it to Dru the year before she passed, when Dru was only ten, and Dru had worn it ever since.

She assumed it held some sentimental value to the older woman, since the hunk of crystal and the silver tag couldn't have been worth very much. Dru liked to imagine there was some grand, romantic story behind it, but her grandmother had never told her anything about where she got it.

The years had worn the surface of the locket so that the J-A engraving was barely visible, and Dru was guilty of rubbing her thumb over the letters herself whenever she was deep in thought.

She wished for the thousandth time that she could see Nana again. But that twinkly-eyed smile had disappeared from her life over a decade ago, and unless this hotel really was haunted, it wasn't coming back.

Dru wondered what she would even say to her grandmother's ghost, if such a thing were possible. She wasn't a big believer in that kind of stuff, but she had always had a good enough imagination to consider just about any possibility.

I'm walking in your footsteps, Nana.

And if she really wanted to make her grandmother proud, she needed to focus on getting some words on the page.

She cracked her knuckles dramatically, and placed her hands on the well-used keys. But the phone rang before she could type a single letter.

Dru jumped a little, still not used to the jangling of the old-fashioned landline. The double ring told her the call was coming from the front desk.

Hailey.

She grabbed the receiver.

"Dru," Hailey chirped before Dru could say hello.

"Hey," Dru replied.

"Listen, a ton of stuff came ahead for the Sapphire Suite," Hailey said. "Some of it is super heavy..."

"Are you asking for help?" Dru teased.

"Yeah, but I'm also offering soda and chips," Hailey teased back.

"I'm there," Dru said, hanging up and gathering herself to head down.

The guy who was supposed to arrive today to take the

Sapphire Suite must have big plans for his visit to the Poconos to be carting along so much luggage. Maybe it was photography equipment or something.

It made sense.

Helsing's Comet was due to be visible on Monday night, for the first time in almost sixty years. Hemlock House was the highest place around, so they were supposed to have a pretty great view, and the forecast was calling for clear skies that night. The hotel was expected to fill up on Sunday, as guests from all over came to see the comet. The guy checking into Sapphire was probably hoping to catch it with a telescope and camera.

Dru ran her thumb over the pendant around her neck, tracing the outline of her grandmother's initials one more time as she headed down the curved back stairs to help her friend.

D ru smiled as she caught sight of her friend.

Hailey stood just past the chestnut doorframe at the end of the first-floor hallway. The chandelier made the auburn highlights in her ebony hair shine. Hailey had a lot going for her - perfect dark hair, perfect dark skin, and a perfect dark, goth aesthetic that she was totally nailing today. But it was her almost impossibly positive outlook that had made them fast friends. Dru loved having someone like Hailey in her life, even if it meant listening to a lot of talk about fashion trends and makeup tips.

It only took one look at Dru to realize that neither of those things were very high up on her list of priorities. But Hailey wasn't discouraged by that at all. She seemed to view Dru as a challenge, like an old house that could really shine with just a coat of paint and good interior decorator.

And Dru was grateful for her input. After all, without Hailey, Dru might not even know that she was "an Autumn." Whatever that meant.

"Dru," Hailey cried, her beaming smile belying her

slightly annoyed tone. "I'm really glad you came down. Look at all this."

Dru had reached the foyer and glanced around. Hailey wasn't kidding about it being a lot of stuff. Two large chests and an enormous steamer trunk practically covered the faded Oriental rug by the fireplace.

"What do you think is in them?" Dru asked, her voice dropping to nearly a whisper, even though no one else was around to hear them. Somehow, she couldn't shake the feeling that they weren't alone.

The luggage looked old, practically antique. And there was something odd about the chests, a feeling she couldn't quite put her finger on, like they were... dangerous. But that was silly. What could be dangerous about a bunch of old trunks?

She was probably just tired from adjusting to her new schedule.

"No idea," Hailey replied. "But they kind of fit in around here, don't they?"

She wasn't wrong.

"Hey, maybe we can just leave them down here, in that case," Dru suggested, quirking an eyebrow.

Hailey let out a waterfall of laughter. Everything about Hailey was pretty, from her laugh to her hair, to her glamorous, goth outfits. Tonight she had her hair in two long braids, and she was wearing a black dress with a white collar. She looked like a sexy, Black version of Wednesday Adams.

It was no wonder that every guy, and most of the girls, that checked in on Hailey's shift couldn't help but flirt shamelessly with her.

In a way, it made Dru a little jealous, but it mostly just made her relieved. The last thing she wanted was any kind of romantic attention right now. Her last relationship hadn't ended well, and part of the reason she had come to the old hotel was just to get away from all that nonsense and concentrate on her writing in a place without so many distractions.

And when it came to deflecting unwanted attention, being in a room with Hailey was like wearing some kind of Harry Potter invisibility cloak.

"Come on, let's get it over with," Hailey suggested.

They each took one end of one of the smaller trunks.

"Dear God," Dru said as they heaved in unison.

It felt like trying to lift a trunk of wet cement.

"Man, I wish this place had an elevator," Hailey sighed.

After a lot of grunting and few close calls, they managed to get the trunk up the big foyer staircase, and down the hall to the Sapphire Suite.

"Here," Hailey said, in front of the door to the Onyx Room.

"I thought he was in Sapphire," Dru said.

The rooms in the hotel were all named after gem stones.

Back in her grandmother's time, there had allegedly been a jewel thief who hid his plunder in the hotel before disappearing.

And as if that wasn't enough, it had all happened on the same night that a multiple homicide at the hotel shook the little mountain town below.

Hemlock House had become a bit of a sensation after that.

And whether the rumors about the jewels he left behind were true or not, it was definitely good publicity for a hotel trying to make everyone forget it was the site of more than one murder.

For a couple of years, the place had been hopping with treasure hunters. But no one had ever found anything.

At this point, the world had moved on. And it was the general consensus that there probably had never been any hidden jewels in the first place.

But the cute room names stuck.

Which was good, because before that, they had very unsurprisingly been named after trees.

"The two smaller trunks go in Onyx," Hailey explained. "He booked both rooms."

That tracked. With all this stuff, their mystery guest would need the extra space.

Hailey used the skeleton key to open the Onyx Room and they half-dragged the trunk inside.

Dru moved to throw open the curtains in the darkened room, but Hailey put a hand on her arm.

"No, he wants it like this," she said. "Specifically requested that the curtains be drawn at all times."

"Weird," Dru said. Maybe her guess about photography had been correct after all. If he were developing film, he would want darkness.

They carried up the second trunk in silence, both of them panting lightly by the time they finished. Dru could feel the beads of sweat forming on her cheeks as she pushed her disobedient hair out of her face for the tenth time. Hailey didn't have a hair out of place, and the exertion seemed to have no effect on her, except to give her already radiant skin an extra glow.

Of course.

The third, and largest trunk was so heavy Dru nearly dropped her end.

"Holy crap," Hailey said.

"What's in this, a body?" Dru laughed.

"Too heavy to be a body," Hailey noted, rolling her eyes. "Why does this stuff have to come on my shift? Zander should be here. He's always trying to show off those muscles, especially when you're around."

Hailey shot her a wink and Dru furrowed her brow. That wasn't true, was it? Dru was notoriously bad about picking up on that kind of thing, but still, she would have noticed if Zander was into her.

Probably.

She decided that her friend was most likely just messing with her, and turned her attention back to the task at hand.

"In fairness, he's going to have to get it all back down," Dru pointed out.

Zander had the morning shift at the front desk, so all check-outs were on his time slot. Hardly anyone came or went on Dru's overnight shift. It was a small benefit.

After a short rest, and a mutual assurance that they were both empowered goddesses who could never be thwarted by something so mundane as luggage, Dru and Hailey wrangled the massive trunk up the stairs and deposited it in the center of the Sapphire Suite's huge bedroom.

The curtains were drawn here too, hiding the incredible view of the snowy mountains.

"This room is wasted on him," Hailey declared, eyeing the curtains.

"Can't argue with that logic," Dru said. "But more importantly, I believe snacks were promised upon completion of our little task?"

Hailey laughed. "Come on, I'll get your snacks."

They headed back down the stairs, and Dru settled in behind the desk in the foyer while Hailey headed for the hallway, and the vending machine.

Dru glanced over at the massive grandfather clock

before remembering the time didn't really matter. Being up all night had its perks. One of which was that she could indulge in all the caffeine she wanted.

Hailey returned, arms laden with cans and crinkly bags.

"Nice," Dru said, grabbing a Diet Dr. Pepper and a bag of salt & vinegar chips as Hailey dumped the rest of the feast on the desk. She knew all of Dru's favorites. Just like Dru knew that Hailey would much prefer an iced soy peppermint mocha with a double shot of espresso, but that wasn't exactly the kind of thing you could get from a vending machine at the top of a mountain.

Dru made a mental note to pick one up for her next time she went down into Willow Ridge for supplies.

"How was the beginning of your shift?" Dru asked, opening the soda and taking a sip.

"Boring," Hailey said. "Except for Agate."

"Who's in Agate?" Dru asked.

"Gorgeous guy," Hailey said, her eyes shining at the memory. "Tall, Asian, amazing hair, tight jeans. And his name, get this, is *Tyler Park*. Sounds like a movie star, right?"

"Nice," Dru said. "Who was he with?"

"He was alone," Hailey said, waggling her eyebrows. "Hey, if he calls down for anything tonight on your shift, let me get it?"

"Wow, he must be hot," Dru laughed. "Until what time?"

"Until one," Hailey decided. "A girl needs her beauty sleep."

Dru smiled. Hailey did not need beauty sleep. Hailey would be downright dangerous if she were any more beautiful.

"Noted," Dru said.

The front door flew open, letting in a draft of unwelcome cold air, followed by an even less welcome Howie Pembroke.

"Hey girls," Howie said in his nasally voice, wiping the snow from his smooth dark hair and smiling a little too widely at Hailey.

"Good evening, Mr. Pembroke," Dru and Hailey replied in unison, like they were addressing a substitute teacher. He always insisted that they call him Howie, which was precisely why they didn't.

Howie Pembroke wasn't much older than Dru, but he managed the hotel. It had been in his family for generations, since before the jewel-thief murders. His grandfather's old army uniform, complete with medals and an antique revolver that looked older than just about anything in the hotel, hung in the sitting room beneath the giant, taxidermized moose head that was known affectionately as Mr. Moosehead.

People around here really were terrible at naming things once they ran out of trees.

"Are we prepared for our guests?" he asked, with the usual manufactured enthusiasm.

"Sure are," Hailey replied brightly. "We just lugged all the trunks up to Sapphire and Onyx."

"Nice work," Howie said with another slick smile, as if he hadn't been watching from out front and waiting for them to finish before coming in so he wouldn't have to help.

Classic Howie.

"Well, I just wanted to check in," he said. "I thought we talked about that black nail polish before, Hailey."

Dru glanced down at Hailey's nails. They were so dark and glossy that it defied logic. Souls could be lost in them.

"These are navy blue," Hailey said, blinking innocently at him.

"Let's go with clear or pink polish from here on in, shall we?" Howie suggested with a smug smile.

"Sure thing, Mr. Pembroke," Hailey said so smoothly that Dru felt certain it was actually a murder threat.

"You're still on, right?" Howie asked Hailey.

"Yes," Hailey agreed.

"Okay, well there's a dead rabbit," Howie said. "On the north side of the hotel. Let's get that cleaned up."

Jesus. He obviously hadn't forgotten Hailey turned him down when he asked her out all those months ago. It was before Dru had come onboard, but Hailey had told her all about it.

Hailey's face went slack. Despite her embrace of the darker side of fashion, Dru knew that Hailey was pretty squeamish when it came to actual dead things. Dru once had to come all the way downstairs to remove a fly that had keeled over too close to the computer for Hailey to use it. She said she knew the dead fly was looking at her.

"I'll get it," Dru volunteered.

"Thank you, Dru," Hailey said, sounding relieved.

"Anytime," Dru said. "I'll probably head back up for a bit after, so I'll see you at shift change."

Hailey gave her that look that clearly said, *you're not really leaving me down here with Howie, are you?* And Dru returned the look with one of her own that said, *that's what you get for making me clean up dead stuff. Plus, I really need to get some work done on my book.*

At least she hoped that's what it said. It was a lot to fit into one look.

Dru grabbed a black trash bag from under the front desk, and her coat from the hooks by the main doors, and headed out with a final wave over her shoulder, but Howie was already busy explaining to Hailey how she would have to really bring her "A" game for the busy weekend ahead.

The door closed behind her, cutting off the sound, and Dru stopped for a moment to take a deep breath of the crisp air and let her eyes adjust to the relative dark. There were outside lights, that cast overlapping yellow circles around the building itself. But beyond that, the woods were just an inky black void. After a few years in the city, she'd almost forgotten what real darkness was.

Crunching through the inch of fresh snow in the shadow of the famous hemlock, Dru passed the abandoned wing of the hotel to the north side. She glanced up at the old turret with the arched windows and the horror writer in her half-expected to spot a shadowy figure staring back. As usual, she was disappointed to find only a single black crow, who took flight with a scolding squawk as she passed by.

There were tall tales that the thief's ghost haunted that wing. But it didn't take a detective to figure out that it was really shut down because of deferred maintenance. A few of the windows were boarded up, and the roof sloped at the center like a sway-backed pony. Paint curled off the shutters, as if it were trying to get away.

An ounce of maintenance saves a fortune in repairs. Dru's step-dad had announced this motto cheerfully on so many otherwise pleasant Saturdays when Dru found herself helping him clean the gutters or paint the porch deck instead of chilling out like a normal teenager. Back then, she hadn't appreciated the merits of being raised to be handy.

It was clear the Pembroke family could have used a couple of Saturdays with Stan Holloway.

She followed Howie's footprints through the new snow, and thought again about how easy it was to ruin something beautiful just by leaving your mark on it.

It was early for this much snow, but at least they wouldn't get pounded anytime soon. The blizzards in this part of Pennsylvania mainly came after the new year.

She sighed, and even that small sound seemed loud in the empty space.

Compared to her sublet in Philly, this place was silent, except for the birds and the sound of the wind in the trees. It wasn't so far away, but sometimes it seemed like it was on a different planet. The air even tasted cleaner here.

She turned the corner, and sure enough there was the tiny body of a rabbit laid out in the snow.

Howie's footsteps ended about where hers were now, so the poor animal was alone on a blanket of undisturbed white. The soft gray fur and long tender ears were sprayed with blood, which painted the snow around it in a Jackson Pollack-style splatter.

Dru wasn't the squeamish type, but something about the bright contrast of garish scarlet against the alabaster snow made her feel momentarily dizzy.

She took a deep breath and walked over, using the trash bag to quickly grab the unfortunate creature before she could get too skeeved out, and then turning the trash bag inside out around it.

The rabbit was so light it almost didn't seem possible. It must have been all fur and bones before meeting its untimely death.

She wondered vaguely how much a soul weighed as she carried the bag around to the back of the hotel. She had held the class rabbit in elementary school and was pretty sure it weighed more than this. Though she had been smaller then.

It was a mercy that it wasn't heavy. But it was also odd that it wasn't eaten. It wasn't terribly unusual to find a few feathers or bones, indicating a small predator had been enjoying a meal. There were plenty of hawks in the area, as well as foxes, and even the occasional bear. But what kind of animal killed a rabbit and then just left it?

She headed around to the back of the building and used her skeleton key to open the hatch to the basement.

Hemlock House sat atop a warren of underground tunnels. The local history held that the place had been part of the Underground Railroad, and then used again by the mob during Prohibition.

Howie had told them that a lot of them had been sealed off before he was born, and no one even knew where all the tunnels were anymore.

Now, the ones they still used were mainly just for storage. It seemed a little anticlimactic, after such a storied history, but Dru supposed it was for the best that they weren't really needed for anything important anymore.

She made it down the wooden steps and pulled the chain for the bare bulb that hung overhead. It flickered to life like it was angry that she disturbed it. Once she was sure it was going to stay on, she rounded the corner to the tunnel where they kept the trash. The bears and raccoons would get into anything that wasn't nailed down, so the tunnels came in handy for that, at least.

Her boots rang out on the hard-packed floor, and the air tasted stale and faintly musty.

She hurried through her task, tossing the bag with what used to be a rabbit into a large bin, and then jogging back to the stairs leading outside.

There was a way to get back to the lobby from the tunnels, but it was narrow, and Dru had always been a little claustrophobic. The idea of getting lost in the catacombs was unbearable.

She turned off the light and stepped outside, where the wind had begun to blow in earnest. She closed and locked the door to the basement, then headed across the back of the hotel to the servants' wing.

Lights were on in the solarium, making the glassy walls and roof look almost like a UFO with the yellow glow coming through a dusting of snow.

She walked across the sweeping brick patio and past the old Smoking Lounge for Gentlemen, now used as a Sitting Room for everyone.

At last, she reached the back door to the servants' wing and unlocked it. She jogged up the stairs and down the hall to her room. Hopefully, she could get a few words in before it was time to report for duty.

As the door closed behind her, she remembered that she had left her soda back in the lobby.

She grabbed another out of her mini-fridge. The one downstairs would keep until her shift. She cracked it open and took a long sip, letting the bubbles and fake sugar dance on her tongue for a moment before she swallowed, then sat down to face off with the typewriter.

All right. I don't like you, and you don't like me...

As long as she could remember, Dru had wanted to be a writer like Nana Jane. Or, maybe more accurately, like Edgar Allan Poe.

Now that college was over, and it was all in her grasp, she found herself struggling with writer's block for the first time in her life.

This spooky hotel was supposed to fix all that. It was isolated and creepy, and she would be up all night every night. What better conditions could there be for writing the Great American Horror Novel?

Dru noticed some flecks on the blank page. She must

have splashed some of her drink on it when she'd popped the top. That wouldn't do. She opened the lower desk drawer to grab some fresh paper.

Just as she bent to reach it, something crashed against her window from outside and she jumped, knocking over the rest of her Diet Dr. Pepper, and slamming her shin into the open desk drawer in the process.

Carmel-colored bubbles spread across the desk.

She had just enough time to grab the typewriter and move it to the bed before the low-calorie mess covered the surface.

Cursing quietly, she grabbed a t-shirt and used it to mop up the dark pool. At least diet soda wasn't sticky.

She strode to the bathroom and dumped the shirt in the sink. Sighing, she grabbed a towel and wet it a little, then headed back to the desk to wipe it down.

Thankfully, it didn't seem like she'd done any damage. She dried everything off with the part of the towel that wasn't wet and threw that in the bathroom sink, too.

"Laundry day soon," she mumbled to herself as she grabbed a sheet of paper for the typewriter and pushed the drawer shut again.

Only it wouldn't close all the way.

"Great," she said to herself, setting down the paper and trying to close the drawer with both hands.

It still wouldn't close the last inch. It was almost like something was stuck back there.

She had probably knocked something loose from the drawer above when she banged into it. Though she was pretty sure that drawer was empty.

Dru knew she should just ignore it and get back to her writing, or she would end up getting nothing done before her shift started.

Write now, fix the drawer later, that was undeniably the best course of action.

She crouched down to ease the drawer completely out of the desk, hoping she would be able to get it back onto the ancient tracks again once she had retrieved whatever was blocking it.

It was dark back there. She reached into the shadows, trying not to imagine something reaching back.

Her hand met something soft and skin-like.

She yelped and yanked her hand out.

"Come on, Dru," she chided herself.

She slid her phone out of her pocket and turned on the flashlight. In the shadowy recess behind where the drawer had been, there was a small, leather-bound book.

She reached in again and pulled it out.

The old leather was soft in her hands. It looked like some kind of journal. But of course, it wasn't necessarily old. New journals that looked like old journals were all the rage.

She opened it to a random page, wincing as the spine cracked.

The leather was still in good shape, but the paper was yellowed, and the glue had gone pumpkin-colored and dry.

She gazed down at the words on the page, and was greeted by what seemed to be a jumble of random letters, in a script that seemed oddly familiar.

Dru studied it for a moment, words and sentences coming into focus. But nothing she could understand. It definitely wasn't in English.

But it also didn't seem to be in any language she'd ever seen before.

She immediately started shuffling through the possibilities in her head.

So much for getting any writing done tonight.

3

———

Dru headed downstairs for her shift a few minutes before midnight, lugging the typewriter with her, and hoping Howie wouldn't stop in and complain that she was moonlighting.

He usually reserved his little pop-ins for Hailey's shift, and Dru was grateful for the relative peace, especially when she had work to do.

As she suspected, she'd gotten too ensconced in the strange journal to get much writing done, but it was putting her into a curious mood that she hoped would soon morph into inspiration.

Throwing a few of the words into an online translation program had brought up nothing, though she hadn't tried for long. The internet on the mountain was so slow it was genuinely painful at times. So it seemed the journal would stay a mystery at least a little while longer.

Hailey spotted Dru as she approached the front desk, and gave her a quick smile and a yawn before heading off to bed. Hailey was definitely not a night owl, and her light was usually ready to go out by the time Dru took over for her.

Dru wished her a good night as she put the journal and the typewriter down on the desk, then logged into the ancient desktop computer there. It probably dated back to the Clinton administration, but it had a wired connection, which made it the speediest piece of tech in the building. It wasn't much, but she typed in a web address and watched the machine chew on it for a full minute.

Hailey had stashed her drink and a few of the leftover snacks on a shelf under the long counter. Dru took a sip of her room-temperature soda and waited for her forum to load.

When she first decided to write a horror novel, she'd gone online to find writers' groups. But most of the users were chatting about sales and craft, not about actual horror.

A friend had given her a tip about an online forum for fans of a popular ghost-themed reality show. And while that forum hadn't yielded much, it had led her down a rabbit hole that wound her up in a forum for the defunct TV show *Ghost Getters*.

In the show, married couple Dan and Lily Getters had toured the country's most storied haunted houses with pseudo-scientific ghost-hunting technology, all while wearing tragically unhip '90s outfits. Though it was canceled after only two seasons, *Ghost Getters* had been elevated to the status of cult classic by both ironic and earnest viewers.

The forum Dru frequented was decidedly on the earnest side.

Once the landing page loaded, her username, Ghost-writer, popped up with a tiny typewriter icon, and she entered her password.

A reassuring ping from the computer alerted her that she was logged in.

It looked like two of the other regulars were active too.

Before she could scroll through what she had missed one of them was already typing a message to her.

TADSTRANGE:
Ghostwrɪter! You made it!

SHE SMILED AND TYPED BACK, fully aware that her feeling of contentment was just a trick of her endorphins, and that this didn't count as actual human contact, but not caring one bit.

GHOSTWRITER:
Sure did!

TADSTRANGE:
Any paranormal activity yet?

GHOSTWRITER:
Not unless you count a dead rabbit.

WRAITHGIRLI9:
Wicked!

TADSTRANGE:

That's definitely suspicious. Any unlikely drafts or doors slamming?

GHOSTWRITER:
Not yet. Just the rabbit.

WRAITHGIRL19:
#jealous

TADSTRANGE:
Maybe ActionPark will be on later. He has a copy of that book, I'm sure he wants to hear how you're doing.

ACTIONPARK WAS one of the more active members. He had a book about Hemlock House, probably self-published back in the '80s by a local historian, describing the hotel, the jewel thief and everything that had happened in the 1960s that put this place on the map of minor American ghost hotels.

It was likely the only remaining copy of *The Haunting of Hemlock House* in existence, and Dru would have gladly given a kidney for it.

Not hers, of course.

But there was no point asking ActionPark. He was a diehard ghostie, and the book would not be for sale.

The front door to the hotel swung open and a couple with a teenager poured in, laden with suitcases. The mother gazed at Dru with an expression of intense relief.

. . .

Ghostwriter:

I'd better get to work. Chat with you guys later.

She signed off with a single click that made a mockery of how difficult it had been to sign on, and jogged out to meet the family in the doorway.

"Welcome to Hemlock House," she said. "Let me get some of this for you."

"Thank you, sweetheart," the mom said, handing over a suitcase.

Dru organized all their luggage by the main staircase and then headed back to the computer to check them in.

"Let's get your room keys," she said. "What name is the reservation under?"

"Jeffrey and Jenna Wilder," the husband said, wrapping an arm around his wife.

He tried to wrap his other arm around his daughter, but she shrugged him off, focusing on whatever was playing in her ear buds.

"Sorry to come in so late," Jeffery offered. "We got caught up in traffic on the way to Willow Ridge."

"It was so kind of your caretaker to bring the shuttle down for us at this late hour," Jenna added. "Please thank him again for us."

Dru barely restrained a smile. Chester must have been absolutely thrilled to be woken up for that. She didn't doubt that she'd hear all about it in the morning.

Dru nodded and turned her attention to the computer as Jenna went up on her toes to kiss her husband, a little more passionately than Dru would have expected her to do in the circumstances.

The phrase, "Get a room," came to mind, but she supposed that was exactly what they were in the process of doing.

"Okay, you're in the Topaz Room," Dru said.

She grabbed the key from the board below the desk.

When she straightened, her breath caught in her throat for a second. A man had come in without her noticing. He was standing just behind the Wilders, staring her down with a strange intensity. He must have come up on the same shuttle.

She shivered a little, and turned back to the affectionate couple.

"Here's your key," Dru said, handing it to Jenna.

"Great," Jenna said. "And we should have a second room booked for Angie."

Dru frowned and rechecked.

"I'm sorry," she told them. "But there's only one room booked."

"Then can we add a second room, please?" Jeffrey asked politely. "We were hoping to get a little... private time."

Angie rolled her eyes. Dru figured her music wasn't turned up quite high enough to block that out.

Dru turned back to the computer and clicked through screens. Unbelievably, the man who had booked Sapphire and Onyx also had the Quartz Suite reserved.

"I'm so sorry," she said at last. "It doesn't look like we have any available rooms."

"Seriously?" Jenna asked. "I read that all these old places up here were having trouble booking guests."

So it was common knowledge that the Hemlock House's days were numbered. Interesting.

"The comet, baby," Jeffrey said quietly.

"Yes, there's the comet," Dru agreed. "And one of our guests seems to have booked a whole wing."

"Who?" Jenna asked, looking fascinated.

"Just some old dude," Dru said, shrugging. "No one special. I'll let you know right away if anything opens up. And in the meantime, your room does have a fold-out sofa."

"Oh baby, look. I did only book one," Jeffrey said, showing his wife his phone. "My mistake," he said, turning to Dru.

"Men, am I right?" Jenna said to her, winking.

"I'll keep an eye on the reservations in case we can get you an extra room," Dru told them.

"Thank you," Jeffrey said. "Come on, ladies."

"I'll help you up with your bags," Dru offered.

"No thanks," Jeffrey said. "We're fine."

"Okay," Dru replied. "When you get to the top of the stairs turn right, and the Topaz Room will be just ahead on your right."

They headed off and she ran a hand through her hair. She was alone with the next guest - not something that would normally have registered with her, but something about this man was slightly unsettling. Maybe it was just that he'd surprised her by slipping in without her noticing. That wasn't easy. Dru could usually hear that creaky old door from anywhere on the whole first floor.

"Can I help you, sir?" she offered.

"I'm sorry if I've caused an inconvenience."

The man's voice was deep and smooth as honey. His words took a moment to register.

"What do you mean?" she asked.

He smiled, and his blue eyes crinkled. There was a depth there, like calm water that you could get lost in.

He was handsome in a subtle way, tall and lean, with dark hair to his shoulders. She probably would have noticed the sexy vibe when she spotted him behind the Wilders, if he hadn't been staring at her in that intense way.

"I'm Viktor Striker," he said, arching an eyebrow. "The old dude who reserved all those rooms."

Holy shit.

"I-I'm so sorry, Mr. Striker," she stammered, thinking of his ancient belongings. She had just assumed, since they were so old...

But he wasn't all that much older than she was. At least Dru didn't think so. He was hard to get a handle on. She guessed he was most likely in his thirties.

"Please, call me Viktor," he said with a disarming smile. "I know it's unusual to book so much space. I just like to spread out."

She pictured him spread out on the bed of the Sapphire Suite, moonlight glinting in his dark hair.

"I'll get you checked in," she said, trying to shake the unprofessional thoughts.

"My belongings arrived before me, I expect?" he asked.

"Oh yes," she said. "We got those upstairs for you earlier. Don't worry."

"Not you?" he said, brows lifted again.

"Well, Hailey and I did it together," she said.

"Strapping girls," he said appreciatively.

She heard herself laugh as she bent to grab the keys to his rooms. Dru had been called a lot of things in her twenty-odd years, but strapping was a first.

When she straightened, she caught him observing her with serious eyes again.

Something flashed between them, like a storm at sea, and for just a moment, she felt herself drawn to him.

But he broke eye contact, and gave her another gentle smile.

"May I show you to your rooms?" she asked.

"That would be nice," he replied, his voice familiar somehow, deep, and almost rusty.

Dru stepped out from behind the desk and joined him at the foot of the staircase.

"After you," he said with a slight flourish.

For all that he looked like he might be in his early thirties, he did have a faintly old-timey air about him. She wondered if maybe he was some kind of antiques dealer. It would explain the trunks, and the manners.

She moved up the stairs, shocked at herself for feeling self-conscious about what she looked like from behind. He was just another guest, only a little more interesting than most.

She headed left at the top, and went to the door to the Sapphire Suite first, since it was the nicest room of the three. She slid her skeleton key into the lock and pushed the door open.

The curtains were still drawn, but the big trunk was in the corner of the room, its leather strap unbuckled. And there was a covering over the mirror on the dresser.

That was weird. No one should have been in here since she and Hailey carried everything up.

Most likely it was just Howie up here being nosy. But he should have at least refastened the lid to the trunk.

"It's a lovely room," Viktor said quietly.

She turned, plastering a professional smile on her face. If he'd noticed anything amiss with his belongings, he wasn't letting on.

"It's the nicest suite we have," she informed him. "Let's go check out the other two."

He smiled back and followed her into the corridor again.

Her hands shook a little as she opened the door to the Onyx Room. She was prepared for more of Howie's shenanigans, but thankfully, everything was just as she and Hailey had left it.

Viktor stayed in the doorway, watching her.

"Okay, let's get Quartz opened up," she said cheerfully.

The Quartz Suite was across the hall from Sapphire. She opened the door and saw the curtains were pulled back, revealing a sky full of stars.

"I'm so sorry about the curtains," she said, rushing over to close them.

"It's fine," he said. "You can leave it."

She turned back to him.

He was gazing at her in that curious way again. The starlight made his blue eyes bright.

"Let me know if you need anything," she said weakly.

"I will," he said, remaining motionless. "What's your name?"

"Dru," she said. "Short for Drucilla."

"Lovely," he said softly.

"Uh, thanks," she replied.

She felt an odd aversion to going closer to him, as if approaching would break the strange spell he had cast over her.

"I should get back to the desk," she said, overcoming her reluctance and heading over. "Here are your keys."

He put out his palm and she dropped the three sets into it, not wanting to risk touching him.

Get a grip, Holloway, she chided herself. *You're at work, not a seventh-grade dance.*

"I will see you again, Drucilla," Viktor said softly as she headed down the corridor.

Dru shivered again at his words, her heart beating just a little too fast. She couldn't quite tell if she was afraid, or aroused.

She was pretty sure she was both.

4

———

Dru wandered back down the stairs.

The lobby was empty again. The crackling of the fire and the hush of the wind outside were the only sounds.

She went back to the computer, and logged in the arrival times for Viktor and the Wilders.

Then she headed back to the Ghost Getters forum.

There were a couple of members on. Different time zones meant there was almost always someone online, even in the wee hours.

She figured it was a long shot, but maybe someone there could help with the journal.

TAD STRANGE:
You're back! See any ghosts?

BETHSMOM1972:
Hi, Ghostwriter, so glad you made it safe and sound. Did you

do a bedbug check? The newsman makes it sound like it's a real problem in vacation areas.

GHOSTWRITER:
 Hey guys, I'm good! Thanks for the tip, BethsMom. No ghosts yet but we had a weird guest. Does that count?

BETHSMOM1972:
 Oh, and don't take anything from the mini-bar. It'll be too expensive. You can normally get the same stuff from the kitchen for half the price.

DRU SMILED. BethsMom was so wholesome and obviously older than most of the other members. It sometimes seemed like she didn't belong in the group at all. But she was really into the *Ghost Getters* show, and true crime shows and podcasts too. Her knowledge was impressive.

GHOSTWRITER:
 Don't worry, BethsMom, I'm on duty - no drinking for me.

TRUTHS33K3R:
 tell us about the weird guest

GHOSTWRITER:
 He checked in after midnight.

. . .

TRUTHS33K3R:

could b a lot of reasons 4 that

GHOSTWRITER:

Yeah, for sure. But he had all these really old trunks sent ahead and he wanted all his curtains drawn even though his rooms have the best views in the place.

BETHSMOM1972:

What did he look like?

DRU FELT blood rushing to her cheeks, even though no one could see her or possibly realize she had just the slightest bit of attraction to the odd guest.

GHOSTWRITER:

Early 30s, maybe? Pale skin, dark hair to his shoulders, blue eyes, intense stare...

TRUTHS33K3R:

i dunno if that's really weird. seems like that place would attract a lot of ultra-pale wannabe spooky types

BETHSMOM1972:

Truthseeker might be right. This guy sounds like he's trying too hard.

. . .

TadStrange:

Keep your eyes peeled for someone trying too hard to fit in, that'll be your ghost.

Dru laughed. Truthseeker was the ultimate skeptic, but in this case, he was probably right.

Ghostwriter:

Point taken, guys. :) I also found a really old journal jammed in the back of a desk in my room.

TadStrange:
How old?

Ghostwriter:

Hard to say. But the pages are yellowed and the glue is all orange and cracked.

BethsMom1972:
What's written in it?

Ghostwriter:
I don't know because it looks like it's in another language.

TadStrange:
Could have the location of the hidden treasure ;)

. . .

GHOSTWRITER:
  Unlikely. But it would be neat!

THERE WAS a ding indicating another member had arrived.

ECTOCOOLR:
  Hey y'all! Guess who just watched the Jersey Devil episode?

INSTANTLY THE GROUP devolved into a blow-by-blow rundown of that episode of *Ghost Getters*, from the paranormal activity, to Lily Getter's pink Nirvana t-shirt and high-waisted jeans.

Dru followed along for a little while, but couldn't really get into it since she hadn't seen that one.

Truth be told, she hadn't really watched much of the show at all, other than a few clips on the internet since joining the group. She was most interested in the aspects of it that had stimulated its audience, which the users documented for her nightly.

And although she was getting a dose of it right now, for once she couldn't bring herself to take notes.

She signed off the forum and turned her attention to the typewriter instead. Time to get to work.

She had the setting for her novel figured out, and earlier today she had nailed down most of the character names. Now she was working through all their backgrounds.

It was amazing how much time she could spend writing without really writing. At this rate, she would still be night clerking at this hotel when she was as old as the Van Buren sisters that lived in the Amethyst room. And they had to be in their seventies, at least.

A particularly harsh gust of wind hit the hotel, rattling the windowpanes and causing the lights to flicker.

Dru shivered. And this time it was definitely out of fear.

You are not getting spooked, Dru Holloway, she told herself sternly. *This is part of the charm.*

The hotel was on top of a mountain. Of course it was buffeted by winds. Of course the electricity was at the mercy of the elements.

And of course she was going to lose her shit if the power went out.

D ru was finally in the zone, fingers clacking away on the keys of the old typewriter, when she heard someone cough.

She nearly jumped out of her chair.

"Hey there," a deep voice said.

She glanced up, already knowing who she was going to see.

Brian Thompson leaned his considerable form on the counter, a thick gold chain with matching gold cross dangled freely from the collar of a very large shirt that had one button too many undone. For such a heavyset man, he was extremely self-confident.

"How can I help you, Mr. Thompson?" she asked as politely as she could.

"People still use these things?" he asked, with a smile that was a little too wide as he leaned over the robin's-egg-blue typewriter. "I'm surprised it even works."

Dru leaned back instinctively, putting some distance between them.

Hailey had warned her that the guy in the Opal room

was always hanging out in the lobby for no reason other than to flirt, or at least to try to get a look down her blouse. But she also said he tipped very well, which was more that she could say for ninety percent of the guests she'd encountered. The very idea of tipping never seemed to cross most of their minds.

Still, she would rather go without tips than have to deal with some miscreant ogling her.

Thankfully, the miscreant in question had made a habit of sleeping through Dru's shift.

Until now.

"It works just fine, Mr. Thompson," she replied crisply. "What can I do for you?"

It wasn't entirely true. The typewriter was kind of a bear to wrangle, and the number eight key didn't work at all. But she wasn't about it tell him that.

"What can you do for me?" he echoed significantly, letting the words trail off as if he were mentally listing out dirty suggestions.

She buttoned her lips and turned her attention back to her typewriter.

"Hey, aren't you supposed to offer me a drink?" Brian snapped when he noticed he was losing her undivided attention.

"Would you like a drink?" Dru asked, a little too politely.

"As a matter of fact, I would," Brian said with another wolfish grin. "Why don't you get yourself one too?"

"I'm on duty, Mr. Thompson," Dru replied. "What would you like to drink?"

"I thought this place catered to guests," Brian said in a voice he probably thought was seductive. "And I want you to cater to me by having a drink."

Dru idly wondered how much it might damage a typewriter to drop it on someone's head. She suspected it would pull through just fine.

"Miss Holloway," another masculine voice cut in before she could respond. "I believe it's time for my tour."

Tour?

She glanced up to see Viktor Striker near the bottom of the stairs, surveying the scene below.

She wondered what it must look like, Brian Thompson leaning his bulk over her desk and her cheeks red with fury.

And here was Viktor, making up a fake tour to save her from having to deal with this idiot any longer.

A wave of gratitude swept through her and she jumped up from her stool.

"Yes, of course, Mr. Striker," she said. "Mr. Thompson, my apologies, but I have an appointment with another guest. There is self-serve coffee and tea in the dining room. Unfortunately, no alcohol can be served, except by a staff member."

"Hey," Brian began to protest as he turned from the counter.

"Good evening," Viktor said to him in a soft but steely voice.

Brian opened his mouth to retort.

Dru saw the moment he made eye contact with Viktor.

Whatever the big man had been about to say died in his throat, and Brian closed his mouth again and headed for the dining room without another word.

Dru turned to Viktor.

He observed her calmly, his expression less intense than before.

"Thank you," she said quietly.

He gave her a half-smile.

"We'd better get started on our tour before he comes back."

"Do you want a tour of the hotel?" Dru asked.

"There are trails in the woods, aren't there?" Viktor asked.

"For bird watching," Dru said, nodding.

"For bird watching," Viktor allowed. "I would like to see them. If it's not too much trouble."

"Of course," Dru replied. "Let me grab my coat."

It was a little odd to go out on the walking trails in the middle of the night, but it would be good to get some fresh air. And if she wasn't at the desk when Brian Thompson came out of the dining room, hopefully he would just give up and go back to his room.

She put the bee-shaped, wooden *Bee Right Back* sign on the front desk and grabbed her jacket from the hook by the door.

Viktor stepped forward to open the door for her with a flourish.

"Thank you," she said, stepping outside.

The air was cold and crisp. A million stars glittered above them.

Viktor moved to join her.

"It's always so lovely here," he said, looking out over the woods.

"You've been here before?" she asked.

He turned to her as if remembering that she was there.

"It's been a long time," he said with a smile. "Where are the trails?"

"Oh, right," she said. "This way."

They walked on in silence, across the lawn and toward the trees on the northwest side of the hotel.

Viktor gazed up at the ruined north wing, with its darkened tower, as they passed.

"No one stays there?" he asked.

"They say it's haunted," she offered.

He chuckled.

"I mean, clearly it just needs attention," she admitted. "It's an old building," she added, surprising herself with her urge to defend it.

"Old things do deserve attention," Viktor said cryptically.

She glanced over at him, but he chose not to add to his observation. Maybe he was talking about his luggage. Or her typewriter.

"The moonlight is lovely," he remarked.

He was right. The soft light sparkled on the crust of snow.

Dru's breath plumed in the air in front of her. She zipped up her jacket.

"How long have you worked at Hemlock House?" Viktor asked.

"Only about a week," Dru admitted.

"What brought you here?"

"I'm writing a book," she told him.

"Really?" he asked, eyebrows lifted slightly. "What's it about?"

"It's just fiction," she explained. "I thought this place might inspire me."

Dru kept the genre to herself. She wasn't ready for another condescending look when she told someone she was planning to write a horror novel. She'd gotten enough of that from the professors in her writing program.

"You're not secretly here to look for treasure?" he asked.

"No," she said with a smile. "How about you?"

"I just wanted to get away."

That was a non-answer. She stole a glance at him.

He wore a slightly dreamy expression. The moonlight made his creamy skin almost seem to glow.

"Do you walk the trails often?" he asked her.

"Not really," she said. "But I haven't been here long."

"So what do you do when you're not working or writing?"

She didn't bother to tell him that those were the same thing.

"Nothing, really," she replied.

"That's a shame," he told her. "You're young. You should take advantage of the chance to enjoy nature."

"Okay, grandpa," she teased.

He grinned at her.

"Yes, I know. You're all of twenty, so you know everything."

"As a matter of fact, I'm twenty-four," Dru replied. "And I don't know everything, but I do know that spending a lot of time in nature is not for me."

"Why not?" he asked.

"I'm accident prone, and I have allergies," she told him.

"Nothing to be allergic to at this time of year," he told her.

"True," she agreed, taking a deep breath of the clean mountain air.

"Do you live at the hotel?" he asked.

"Yes," she told him. "There's a section in the south wing for staff."

He nodded. "Does your room face the lawn or the woods?"

"Woods," she said. "It's really nice. I have a window seat and everything."

They had just reached the entry to the first trail.

"Okay, I'm going to get out my flashlight," she warned him. "It's very bright."

She slid the tactical flashlight out of her jacket pocket and clicked it on, focusing the beam on the trail.

Everything outside the beam's reach disappeared into darkness as they stepped under the canopy of trees.

It was hard not to think about the fact that whatever had killed the rabbit earlier today was somewhere in these woods. It was probably just a hawk, but still...

She found herself listening for unfamiliar sounds. But there was nothing but the hoot of owls and the singing of the night birds.

"Are there still treehouses out here?" Viktor asked.

"Observation decks, yes," she told him. "They're meant for birdwatching."

"I see," he said.

They walked on, the trail leading around a few curves and decidedly uphill.

It was cold, but it felt good to get a little exercise. Back in Philly, she had walked almost everywhere, getting her muscles moving every day without thinking about it. Even just a week behind the desk was having an effect on her. It was good to stretch out.

It also felt nice to spend time with Viktor Striker. The slight attraction she'd felt before was warming into something more interesting.

They had just reached a spot where the path curved around a massive oak, when there was a rustling in the undergrowth and a flash of movement nearby.

Dru let out a bit of a scream, really more of an embarrassing squeak, but managed to train the beam of the flashlight on the furry thing before its bushy tail disappeared completely.

"A fox," she breathed.

"We're not the only ones out for a late-night stroll," Viktor teased. "Are you okay?"

"Yeah," she said, distracted. "I guess that's him."

"You guess what?"

She turned to Viktor, remembering at the last second to lower the beam of the flashlight.

"There was a dead rabbit on the lawn earlier tonight," she explained. "That fox must be the culprit."

Viktor's eyebrows went up slightly. "I see."

"Though he didn't eat it," she went on. "Something must have scared him off."

Viktor nodded.

"Should we turn back, or keep going?" she asked. "The trail loops back around eventually."

"I hate to remind you, but do you need to get back to the desk?" he asked.

She winced. "Yeah, I probably should."

"Then let's turn back," he said with a sad smile. "Maybe we'll walk the whole trail another time."

"Sure," she heard herself say. "We'll do it in the daytime when you can actually see everything."

Frankly, she couldn't believe she'd made it this far without tripping over something. In the daylight, she'd have a much better chance of not embarrassing herself.

Viktor's smile faded, and he nodded tersely.

They turned around and headed back for the hotel.

Dru hadn't realized how far they had come, it was impossible to even see the light of the old building through the trees.

"How long do you plan to work here?" Viktor asked, after a moment.

"I'm not sure," she admitted. "I'm hoping to stay long enough to finish the book."

"Then what?" he asked.

"I don't know," she told him. "I haven't thought that far ahead yet, but I'll probably go back to Philly. I have an apartment there. It's small, but it's really nice. A friend is housesitting for me right now."

"Do you have a family?" he asked.

"My parents are out this way," she told him. "I grew up in the area. We see each other as often as we can, but they work, and I stay busy."

"Do you have a husband or a... boyfriend?" he asked.

She stopped in her tracks.

"I apologize," he said quickly. "I didn't mean to be familiar, and I assure you I'm not trying to woo you like that oaf back in the lobby. I was merely curious to know more about you."

"It's okay," she said. "You're just asking me a lot of questions."

"You remind me of someone," he said thoughtfully. "It makes me inquisitive. Forgive me."

"Who?" she asked.

"Someone I knew a long time ago," he said, and turned his attention back to the trail.

That was the lamest cover job for a flubbed pick-up she had ever seen, but at least he had enough respect for her to know when his attentions weren't wanted.

Only they might be wanted...

She jogged to catch up, scolding herself for thinking he was hot in the first place. What he was, was *odd*. And she was here to work, not to fraternize with the clientele.

Viktor was just so easy to talk to.

The path narrowed, and he let her lead the way, like before.

The warm yellow light from the windows of the hotel appeared between the branches of the trees.

For an instant, feeling that the goal was near, Dru let herself relax. Almost immediately, her foot caught on a tree root and she felt herself falling forward.

She flailed her arms, the beam of the flashlight strobing madly through the trees, and felt the instant when the last of her balance deserted her. There was nothing left to do but brace for the fall and hope she didn't break anything.

The next thing she knew, she was upright, strong arms holding her.

"Drucilla," Viktor murmured.

"God, how embarrassing," she muttered.

"Are you hurt?" he asked, his voice low with concern.

She could feel the hard muscle of his chest through the thin material of his shirt.

Some cavewoman vestige in her wanted to press herself closer. It was good in his arms. Safe.

She fought it back.

"Fine," she said, extricating herself. "I'm fine."

"Alright," he said, releasing her and leaving his hands up to show he was harmless.

"How did you catch me?" she asked.

"I was right in front of you," he laughed. "I practically couldn't help it."

She would have sworn he was behind her. But she probably just got turned around in the fall.

"Let's get back," she said, ready to put the incident behind her.

"Of course," he said. "You have your duties to attend."

Mainly, she had to try to stay awake and maybe write something. But she wasn't going to argue.

They walked back across the snowy meadow toward the front porch of Hemlock House.

She tried not to think about his arms around her and the odd sense of peace she had felt when he held her.

Lights were on in most of the windows and it should have looked welcoming, but the old hotel still loomed over them in an almost menacing way.

Dru repressed a shudder.

Yeah, this was the right place to be when writing a horror novel, not a romance.

D ru glanced up at the grandfather clock.

Her shift would be over in half an hour. Constance, the cook, was already banging around in the dining room, setting up the continental breakfast.

Dru turned her attention back to the daily audit. It was one of the night clerk's duties to log all the guests, payments received and other data. Oddly, Hemlock House still kept handwritten logs instead of a computer file, even though half the data on the log had to be copied down from the digital records.

The books were balanced for today and even better, Dru had finished up most of her character work for her book.

When Viktor had walked her back to the lobby, Brian Thompson had mercifully been gone.

And though she had expected to be distracted by the strange evening spent with her new friend, Dru found she was able to focus on her writing. The fresh air must have done her some good.

She had already taken the typewriter back up to her

room, just in case Howie decided to make an early appearance.

In half an hour, Zander would take over at the desk, and she could get some well-earned rest.

As if on cue, the front doors flew open and Zander strode in.

He was just as big and blond as he had been in high school. If anything, he was more handsome now, having gained a chiseled jawline and a little life experience in the six years since.

"Zander," she said. "You're early."

"I thought we could check the shift notes over breakfast," he said with a smile that made it seem like he had been caught in the act.

Hailey insisted that Zander had a crush on Dru.

Dru always figured his real crush was on Hailey, but the flush in his cheeks right now said maybe Hailey had been spot on.

Or maybe it was just from the cold outside.

Dru had crushed on Zander pretty hard back in high school. They had always been in the same advanced math classes, even though he was a bit of a jock.

It would be kind of amazing if she finally got the chance to date him because of an excursion back home.

"Sure, let's eat," Dru replied.

She closed up the audit book and slid it under the desk, grabbing the old journal to bring back to her room with her after breakfast.

They walked together the few steps down the corridor and left into the dining room, which was basically right behind the clerk's desk.

Small tables lining the walls housed a couple of cereal dispensers, coffee and tea carafes, pitchers of juice, a mini-fridge with milk and cream, and a huge basket of assorted, individually wrapped Tastykakes - classic Pennsylvania treats.

The massive dining table took up the center of the room. Hazel and Honey Van Buren were already firmly ensconced at the foot of the table, eating big plates of scrambled eggs and drinking steaming mugs of black coffee, like they did every day.

The Van Buren sisters lived permanently in the hotel, as far as Dru understood it. Their advanced age was offset by their high energy and near-constant, twinkly-eyed giggling.

At the end of their meal, each sister would customarily stuff a packaged cake and a piece of fruit in her purse. Then the two would link arms to go for a stroll through the solarium before their mid-morning nap back in the Amethyst Room.

"Good morning, Miss Van Buren and Miss Van Buren," Dru said politely.

"Hello, children," Hazel said, smiling up at Dru and Zander. It was clear she didn't remember their names.

"Good morning," Honey echoed.

Constance was behind the griddle station next to the head of the table.

Dru headed gamely toward her.

True to her usual grumpy form, Constance didn't even acknowledge her.

"Um, may I have some eggs?" Dru asked meekly.

Constance scowled at her and scooped a small portion of scrambled eggs on a plate.

"And some scrapple?" Dru added.

The cook threw a piece of scrapple begrudgingly on her plate.

"Thank you," Dru said, heading for the condiment table for hot sauce.

It always seemed like Constance didn't think the staff should get free meals. But it was literally part of the pay.

"Constance, this looks amazing," Zander exclaimed from behind her.

"Good morning, Zander," Constance said approvingly. "Eggs and bacon, right? Any pancakes?"

"Yes, please," he said enthusiastically.

Dru joined him at the table a moment later.

Zander's plate was piled high with food. Clearly Constance liked him.

Well, he was likable. Who could blame her?

"Oh my God, so good," Zander enthused around a mouthful of pancakes.

Dru smiled and took a bite of her scrapple.

She knew on some level that the way scrapple was made was gross. But the classic Pennsylvania breakfast meat was so good that she couldn't bring herself to care.

She hopped up to grab a glass of juice from the dispenser.

"Hey, what's this?" Zander asked.

She turned to see he was holding the journal she had set on the table between them.

"Whoa, I didn't know you liked cryptograms," he said, before she could answer.

"What?" she asked.

"My grandfather loves these things," he told her.

"I didn't realize that's what it was," she said. "I couldn't figure out what language it was in."

"It's not in another language," he said. "It's basically a code. You have to figure out the cipher and then you can solve it."

"Very cool," Dru said, nodding and trying not to snatch it back from him.

"Want me to try to solve it for you during my shift?" Zander asked. "I can bring it up to you when I'm done."

"Nah," she said. "I'll work on it myself now that I know what it is."

"It's pretty hard at first, there are a lot of strategies," Zander said, handing it over. "It would be a lot easier if you had a key. If you decide you want help, just let me know."

"Will do," she told him.

"So what's your plan for the day?" Zander asked.

"Well, I need to find Chester," Dru said. "There was a dead rabbit in the meadow earlier and Howie had me put it in the basement."

Zander nodded as he scooped up another big mouthful of food.

Chester Crawford drove the shuttle bus, but his real job was groundskeeper, and he dealt with the garbage. It didn't sit right with Dru to dump an animal carcass without giving him a heads up that it was there.

"We had a few new guests during my shift," Dru said, shifting her thoughts to the change of duty. "Jeffrey and Jenna Wilder are in Topaz with their daughter, Angie. They were hoping to book a second room, so if there are any cancellations, be sure to check in with them."

"Mmhmm," Zander said.

"And Viktor Striker is in Sapphire, Onyx and Quartz," she said. "He's interested in the birdwatching trails, but he got in really late, so I doubt you'll see him."

"What was his deal?" Zander asked. "Is he crazy old like Hailey said? Was he wearing a cloak or anything?"

"Weirdly no," Dru said. "I mean, he's kind of pale and he

sent a ton of heavy old trunks ahead, but he seems mostly normal. Not super old either."

"Weird," Zander said appreciatively, nodding with his eyes wide.

Dru knew she could have told him more, but she felt oddly possessive over the mysterious guest. For now, she liked that he was her mystery.

"I guess I should go find Chester," she said as she popped the last bit of hot-sauce-coated eggs into her mouth. "Are you okay to take over?"

"Go ahead," Zander said cheerfully, waving her on. "Stop down later if you get bored."

She waved back, then grabbed the journal and headed out through the solarium.

D ru stepped out of the dining room and headed for the door on the other side of the solarium that led outside.

The ceiling of the solarium rose swiftly into a glassy dome that came down on all sides, making guests feel like they were in a plant-filled bubble.

Ferns, figs, and leafy, flowered species Dru couldn't name made the air in the solarium oxygen-rich and fragrant. She was tempted to hang out in here a while. There were ornate metal benches scattered throughout the jungle-like room, and it was a great place to stop and just relax for a few minutes.

But what she really needed was to find Chester and then get some sleep.

The rear lawn was still cloaked in the blue of pre-dawn, and Dru had to wait for her eyes to adjust as she stepped out of the well-lit solarium and into the crisp snow.

The groundskeeper's cottage was behind the servant's wing, close to the edge of the woods. She had barely taken two steps in that direction when a noise from behind her brought her attention back.

Something was banging around in the basements.

The door to the catacombs that she had used for entry last night stood open. And something was clattering in there, the sound echoing off the wet stone walls.

Feeling a little bit like the idiot who gets murdered before the opening credits roll in a horror movie, Dru headed into the basement, pulling on the string that turned on the light.

If she had somehow left that door open last night and an animal had gotten in, it was her fault. She couldn't afford to lose this job after a week.

And most likely it was just Chester, getting an early start on his rounds.

The light from the single bulb was so dim that she decided to use her flashlight as well.

It can't be a bear, she told herself as the dimness of the basement surrounded her.

She was struck again by the musty smell of the place. It was as if the stone walls were sweating mold.

"Chester," she called out.

The name echoed off the walls, but there was no answer.

Taking a deep breath, Dru moved toward the sound of banging, the beam of the flashlight bouncing along the stone floor of the tunnel.

She passed an old shovel with a wooden handle leaned against the wall and grabbed it, switching the flashlight to her left hand. It would make a pretty good weapon, if necessary.

She was getting closer to whatever was making the noises.

"Chester," she called out again.

The echo back was a lonely sound. There was no reply, only more clattering and banging.

There was a turn in the tunnel coming up and it sounded as if the sounds were coming from the offshoot on the left. There was another light on down that way. Bears didn't use lights. But people answered when you called them. So what did that leave?

She put the flashlight in her mouth and clutched the handle of the shovel over her shoulder, like a baseball bat.

Her footsteps echoed in her ears, and she willed herself to walk quietly and hold her breath.

She jumped around the corner to surprise whatever was there.

She was greeted by a terrible scream.

Dru screamed too, causing the flashlight to fall from her mouth.

On its way down it, illuminated a very frightened looking Chester Crawford. The plaid hunting cap he always wore had half-slid off his head.

He stepped back, banging a built-in shelf behind him.

There was an odd scraping sound.

"I'm s-sorry," Dru stammered, bending to pick up the flashlight.

Chester pulled headphones from his ears and straightened his hat.

"What are you doing down here? And why do you have my good shovel?" His wrinkled face was furious, even his white hair looked spiky and angry.

"I'm so sorry," Dru said again. "I, uh, saw the door was open and heard noises and came to check it out."

"Hmph," Chester replied, holding his hand out for the shovel.

She handed it over, noticing that there appeared to be an even gap between the stones behind him.

"Hey, is that another secret passageway?" she asked, pointing to the space. "I think it might have opened when you hit that shelf."

"There are passages all over the place down here," he said irritably. "I don't keep track of them."

"Okay," she said, mentally regrouping. "I was looking for you anyway. There was a dead rabbit on the meadow yesterday. Howie asked me to throw it out. I brought it to the bins down here. But I just wanted you to know about it."

"Howie," Chester snorted.

At least they agreed on their opinion of Howie.

"I saw a fox in the woods last night too," she said. "I'll bet he killed the rabbit. So maybe it's better to close the basement door so he doesn't get in."

"Foxes don't want in," Chester scoffed.

"Anyway, sorry I scared you," she said, moving to leave.

"You didn't scare me," he retorted. "Just startled me, that's all. Next time, don't go sneaking up on people. You could end up getting yourself punched in the throat."

That was an awfully specific outcome, and she hadn't snuck up on him - she'd been yelling his name the whole time.

But Dru saw no reason to argue. Instead, she gave a little wave and headed back down the tunnel toward the reassuring dawn of the world outside.

8

Dru was dreaming again.

Knowing it must be a dream didn't change how hard the stone floor felt beneath her feet, or the warmth of the redolent air that swirled around her, filling her senses with roses.

She searched the stars for some meaning, but this world was the same as before - unchanging, and pretty as a picture.

Knowing what was coming next, she listened for the footsteps.

This time, when they rang out, she turned to see her mysterious lover.

The room she stood in was round, and lined with arched windows just like the one she had been gazing from. It was familiar, yet she was sure it was somewhere she had never been.

A tall, dark figure appeared in the doorway, moonlight glistening in the dark hair that brushed his wide shoulders.

Viktor.

He moved toward her slowly, a panther stalking his prey.

Dru felt herself go warm and soft. She was ready to be devoured. All she wanted was for him to touch her, to possess her.

"Drucilla," he murmured when he reached her.

She froze, transfixed by his deep blue eyes.

He reached out his hand and swept her hair away from her neck in a gesture so tender it resonated in her bones. He leaned in, cupping her cheek in his hand, those blue eyes mercifully closing at the last instant, freeing her to lose herself in his kiss.

The breeze swirled around them, lifting her hair, rustling in her dress, pulling her away from him.

"Viktor," she tried to cry.

But the wind was drowning her out, squeezing the sound back into her throat before it could reach him.

And she was cold, so cold.

His arms were disappearing from around her as the dream faded and the real world seeped back in...

DRU SAT UP IN BED, still breathless, and looked around the room.

She was alone, though the curtains moved slightly in the draft from the windows, letting in fragments of stark afternoon light.

Strange, it had all seemed so real.

And so similar to the dream she had woken up from last night. Before she had even met Viktor...

"Get up, Holloway," she groaned to herself. "You just need a better social life."

But she didn't deserve a better social life. Not yet anyway. She had to get this book written first. Her parents had worked their butts off to pay for her college, only to have to watch her get a Creative Writing degree. She knew she'd better make it worth their while, even if they would never say it.

The hot shower washed away the vestiges of the dream and brought with it the certain knowledge that she was out of cereal and had to go downstairs and eat dinner for breakfast.

At least she could check in with Hailey. That was always the best part of her day.

She dressed quickly, stuck the journal in her pocket, and headed out into the corridor.

She made it almost to the staircase when she heard something in the janitor's closet.

"Gert?" she called, opening the door.

But it wasn't the tiny but fierce housekeeper inside.

"Uh, hey," a man's voice said.

"Can I help you?" Dru asked, her heart pounding.

"Sorry," he said, stepping out into the light of the hallway. "Do you work here?"

"Yes," she replied.

He was tall and very handsome. His jeans hung low around his hips and a black t-shirt clung enough to show off his lean muscular form.

This must be Tyler Park, the hot guy in Agate that Hailey had been gushing over.

"I spilled some soda in my room, and I was just going to get something to clean it up," he said, looking embarrassed. "The girl in the lobby seems a little... high strung. I didn't want to disturb her."

Hailey was probably flirting madly with him and he was afraid to go down there. Dru didn't blame him. She didn't see how anyone could hold up under the weight of Hailey's full attention.

"It's fine," Dru assured him. "I'll take care of it."

"No, no, I insist," he said. "I'm the klutz that caused the problem, and I'm guessing you're not even on duty."

"You're right," she admitted. "I'm not."

She grabbed paper towels and a spray bottle of cleaner and handed them over.

"Just leave them right inside the door when you're done."

"You're a lifesaver," he told her earnestly.

"Don't worry about it," she said, making a hasty retreat before he got the impression that she was as flirty as Hailey.

On the way down the stairs, she bumped into Gert, who was also heading down, a massive bag of laundry in her small arms.

"Oh, hey, Gert," Dru said. "The guy in Agate said he spilled some soda. He really wanted to clean it up himself, so I lent him paper towels and cleaner."

"I was just in Agate," Gert said, her blue eyes stern. "There's no spill."

"Weird," Dru said.

Maybe Tyler had cleaned it up enough on his own before looking for products that Gert hadn't noticed.

But that seemed unlikely. Gert had the eyes of a hawk when it came to that kind of thing.

"I'll head back up in a minute to make sure," Gert assured her.

The woman was obsessive about cleanliness. Dru respected that, even if she couldn't sympathize.

"Dru," Hailey yelped from the desk below, grabbing her attention.

"Hey, Hailey," she replied as she moved to join her friend.

"Your beau left something for you," Hailey said, waggling her eyebrows suggestively.

For one moment she thought of Viktor, then realized Hailey must mean Zander. She felt her cheeks burning and was glad Hailey couldn't read her mind.

"Someone's blushing," Hailey announced.

Dru laughed.

"Who's my beau? Do you know something I don't?"

"I mean poor, innocent Zander Jenkins," Hailey said, "He only wants to love you and you never bother to notice."

"We were friends in high school," Dru said, shrugging. "That's all."

"A likely story," Hailey said.

She was wearing a stunning lavender crushed velvet jacket with tiny Victorian buttons that looked amazing against her beautiful complexion. Under the jacket she wore a silvery sheath.

"Hailey, I love the jacket," Dru said.

"I know, right?" Hailey said as if she couldn't believe her own luck. "My brother sent me this."

She spun around so Dru could take in the full effect, knee high leather boots and all.

"Amazing," Dru said sincerely.

"A person's clothing should reflect their sense of self," Hailey said. "You need to let me accompany you on a shopping trip so I can help you figure out how to tell the world who you are."

"I'm fine," Dru said, knowing she could never pull off Hailey's look.

"Really?" Hailey asked. "Because you're hella hot, but that outfit says *spinster aunt.*"

Dru looked down at her long plaid skirt and green sweater and knew her friend was right.

"I was going for *elderly school girl,*" she joked weakly. "But I guess you're right."

"I'm only teasing," Hailey said, putting a hand on Dru's arm. "You know that, right? I'd love to go with you on a shopping trip, but you're awesome just the way you are. And the green really works with your hazel eyes."

"So what did my beau bring me?" Dru asked, eager to change the subject.

"Oh, shoot, yeah," Hailey said, heading back behind the desk and emerging again triumphantly with a circular piece of paper in her hand.

Dru took it. The paper was sturdier than she had expected. It was made of the hotel's card stock.

One side had a pen and ink drawing of the hotel in its heyday printed on it.

The other side had two circles of letters and numbers.

"Looks like some kind of spy device," Hailey said dubiously. "Did he write you a love letter in a secret code?"

"No," Dru said. "But I found a coded journal. This must be for making a cipher."

"Sounds... complicated," Hailey said.

"It's pretty neat," Dru said, sliding the journal out of her pocket and sticking the cipher wheel between two of the pages before replacing it.

"Any action last night with the weirdo with the trunks?" Hailey asked.

"He came down once," Dru said, not wanting to share the whole story for fear that she would turn beet-red again.

"And?" Hailey asked.

"He seemed...normal," Dru offered.

Hailey nodded, her eyes narrowed.

"Do you know what Gert said?"

"What?" Dru asked, leaning in.

"She said that he's got a Do-Not-Disturb on Sapphire, but when she went into Onyx and Quartz the curtains were still closed and he had put sheets over all the mirrors."

That *was* a little creepy.

"What did she make of it?" Dru asked.

"Everything else in the rooms was neat and tidy," Hailey said. "She said it was like he hadn't even been in there. But she didn't like yesterday's sheets being over the mirrors."

"What did she do?" Dru asked.

"Took them down, cleaned the mirrors and put fresh sheets over them," Hailey said, her eyes sparkling with laughter.

"That woman is the ultimate in customer service," Dru said, genuinely impressed, even though she also wanted to giggle.

"That's our Gert," Hailey said.

"I met your hot guy in Agate a minute ago," Dru whispered.

"Is he coming down here?" Hailey asked, her hands automatically smoothing her already perfect hair.

"No, sounds like he's busy," Dru lied.

"Damn," Hailey said. "What did you think?"

"He wasn't that hot," Dru lied again, wondering if her lies were unethical. She didn't want to see her friend get hurt.

"No?" Hailey asked. "I've been here so long I have no context anymore. I wish we had a shared day off so we could go to Philly together and hit the clubs."

Dru shrugged. Clubs weren't really her thing, even though she lived in Philly. But they were never going to have a shared day off anyway, so there was no point in bursting Hailey's bubble.

"I'm gonna get some breakfast," Dru said instead.

"Okay, see you later," Hailey said, turning back to the game of solitaire she had open on the old computer.

9

D ru headed into the dining room.

Dinner wasn't due to begin for another fifteen minutes, but Constance waved her on to the steam tables anyway.

Thank God for small favors, I can't believe Constance is giving me a break.

The last thing she wanted was to have to wait until half the guests were here. Though he was harmless, she wasn't looking forward to seeing Brian Thompson again. And even the nice Wilders might want to chat.

Dru really just wanted some time alone with the journal and this cryptogram wheel Zander had made for her.

She grabbed a plate and piled it with roasted chicken and vegetables. The hot sauce wasn't out on the table and she didn't dare ask for it.

Instead she headed out to the solarium to eat at one of the benches.

She walked out into the glassy space and took a deep breath of fragrant air.

The sun was setting on the other side of the hotel. The

sky outside the glass was deep blue already, making it all but impossible to see anything outside.

Round globe lights on tall stems, like street lamps, made a natural path around the various beds and sitting areas.

Dru walked between the ferns to the corner that abutted the old Smoking Lounge. The small metal table and chairs tucked away in the corner would be a perfect spot to eat and work on the journal.

She set down her plate and slid the journal out of her pocket, placing it on the table as well.

The wear on the leather was more pronounced in the lamplight. She wondered again who it had belonged to and how old it was.

There was a shivering in the ferns, and she looked up to see that she had company.

"Hello, Drucilla," Viktor said.

He wore a white button down over jeans, his dark hair spilled over his shoulders. He looked more obviously handsome than he had last night.

Was he cleaned up after traveling, or was it the fact that she liked him that made him seem sexier than before?

His expression was pleased, but she sensed the tiniest bit of uncertainty too.

"Hey," Dru said. "How's it going?"

He smiled and indicated the chair opposite hers. "May I?"

"Please," she said. "But you should probably grab your dinner before all the good stuff is gone."

"I already ate," he said smoothly, joining her at the table.

Wow. She would have to rethink her stance on Constance cutting her a break tonight. Viktor must have eaten pretty early if she hadn't bumped into him in the dining room.

Why does everyone get special treatment but me?

"Penny for your thoughts," he said with a smile.

She gazed up at him, noticing again how handsome he was.

"Oh, I'm just feeling a little dreamy," she said. "I'm still getting used to sleeping during the day and being awake all night."

He opened his mouth like he was going to say something, and then closed it again.

"What?" she asked.

"My business keeps me up at odd hours too," he said.

"What do you do?" she asked him.

"Oh, a little of this and a little of that," he replied.

She blinked at him.

"Sorry," he said. "I guess that's not much of an answer."

"Are you in antiques?" she guessed.

"Why do you ask?"

"All those old trunks," she said.

"Clever girl," he replied, arching a brow. "Yes, I'm in antiques, real estate, some other investments internationally."

"So the international investments mean you keep weird hours," Dru realized out loud. "You have to be awake when they are so you can do business."

"How does your schedule work?" he asked.

"I work from midnight until eight," she explained. "I find it easier to sleep when I'm finished work and then get up around four."

"So you're awake only in darkness," he said.

"I get to see the sun go down," she said. "But I'm normally showering during that time."

He got a strange look on his face and she wondered if he was picturing her showering.

"You should watch the sunset first," he said. "Don't live in darkness."

"Well, it's not forever," she laughed. "But maybe I'll take your advice tomorrow."

"What's this?" he asked, indicating the journal.

"I'm not actually sure," she admitted. "I found it in the desk in my room. Zander thinks it's some kind of cryptogram."

"Zander?" he asked.

"Oh, that's the first-shift clerk," she told him. "You'll meet him if you're ever up in the morning."

Viktor took the journal in his hands and paged through. "So it's coded. Do you have the key?"

"No," she admitted. "But I've got a wheel to use for figuring it out."

"So we're looking for repeated letters, right?" Viktor asked.

"Yes, those are most likely to be substituted for common letters," Dru replied. "When we find them, we enter them on the wheel. But only after we're sure. And the wheel only works if it's just a shifted alphabet. Anything more complex than that would be tough to crack."

"This will take some time," Viktor observed.

"I've got nothing else to do until my shift starts," she said. Though it was a lie. She really should be writing.

It was just that the journal had captured her imagination. She was sure the contents would inspire her.

"May I sit beside you?" Viktor asked.

"Sure," she said, scooting over on the small bench.

He rose to join her, moving slowly as if he might frighten her away. The bench barely moved under his weight as he sat beside her.

She tried not to be overly aware of his big body and the lovely spicy scent of his aftershave.

But she found her heart was pounding anyway.

"Okay, I'll make a list on my phone," she said brightly, determined to focus.

They bent over the journal together and Dru did her best to focus on the pages of the old journal, no matter what else her body suggested.

10

D ru ran a hand through her hair.

"It's tricky," Viktor said.

He was still bent over the journal though.

She smiled. He was so eager to help her solve it.

So far, they had managed to rule out a few letters, but they were no closer to solving the mystery than they had been before.

It would be a painstaking process, she could tell that much by spending half an hour on it. But working on it with Viktor was fun.

And there was something so familiar about the writing. She had never seen anything like it before, but it was hard not to imagine its contents being meaningful in some way, or at the very least *interesting*.

"Dru," Hailey called out from somewhere in the solarium.

"Hey, Hailey, back here," Dru called back to her.

There was a rustling of leaves and then Hailey stood before them.

"Oh, hi," Hailey said, looking at Viktor in a surprised way.

"Viktor is helping me try to figure out the code for the journal," Dru explained.

"Nice," Hailey said.

"Pleasure to meet you, Viktor Striker," the man said, rising and offering Hailey his hand.

As she looked up at him, Hailey's expression went from suspicion to appreciation.

Dru felt an inexplicable little pinch of jealousy.

"Hailey Woods," Hailey replied, taking his hand without shaking, as if she expected him to kiss it.

"Is everything okay, Hailey?" Dru asked, hoping to break up this little hand holding session.

"Oh, yeah," Hailey said, dropping Viktor's hand and turning to Dru. "There's another dead animal, and Chester's not around, and..."

"I'll get it," Dru said.

"You're a lifesaver, Dru," Hailey sang. "Seriously."

"I know, I know," Dru said.

Hailey disappeared into the greenery again, ostensibly heading for the front desk.

"Hey, thanks for trying to help me with this," Dru said, reaching for the journal.

"It was my pleasure," Viktor told her, meeting her eyes.

She felt herself get lost in his gaze for a moment.

"Am I to understand that one of your duties has something to do with dead animals?" he asked, looking down at the journal again.

"Well, it's really the groundskeeper's job to clean them up," Dru told him. "But he also drives the shuttle, so he's on break right now before the evening rush."

"Is there actually a *rush* in the evenings here?" Viktor asked.

"Well, not really, but he has to make the shuttle run even if there's only one new guest," she amended.

"Cleaning up dead animals doesn't seem like a proper job for a young lady," Viktor said.

Dru laughed. "I'm not squeamish about blood. Though I don't love going into the catacombs."

"The catacombs?" he echoed.

"Oh, that's just my nickname for the creepy tunnels in the basement," Dru said. "The garbage goes down there until pick-up to keep the raccoons out of it."

"May I accompany you?" Viktor asked, standing and offering her his hand, as if she would need his assistance prying her lazy butt off the bench.

She took it anyway, and felt her heart thundering as she stood.

"Sure, but I have to grab a garbage bag," she said stupidly.

"Lead the way," he said, with a half-smile.

He let go of her hand and followed her down the leafy path and back out into the dining room.

"Here, Dru," Hailey said brightly, handing her two trash bags.

"Two?" Dru asked.

Hailey just wrinkled her nose.

Dru laughed and headed for the doors with Viktor trailing behind her. She grabbed her jacket and slipped it on, shoving the bags in her pocket.

Viktor held the door open for her, and she was struck again by his manners. He definitely wasn't East Coast born and bred like she was.

They stepped out into the cold night.

Snow flurries pirouetted slowly down like sleepy ballerinas. Yesterday's snow hadn't fully melted yet, so even the tiny flurries had a chance to add their bodies to the pale accumulation instead of melting instantly on the grass.

"It's unseasonably cold," Viktor observed.

"That's what they say," Dru agreed. "But it seems right that the mountains should have snow."

"The mountains," Viktor said with a smile.

"What?" Dru asked.

"I've traveled a lot," he replied. "These mountains feel a bit... worn down, more like hills."

"Oh, you're very sophisticated," she teased him, reaching down to grab a tiny handful of crystalized snow.

"Very," he agreed with a grin.

She launched her pathetic snowball and he ducked out of the way with ease.

"Drucilla, are you trying to initiate a snow battle with me?" he asked arching a brow.

"I don't think there's enough snow for that," she said lightly.

But he was already moving so fast it almost defied logic.

She had just enough time to snatch up another muddy handful of icy slush before he launched a perfectly symmetrical snowball at her.

It exploded when it hit her jacket.

"Oh, now you're in for it," she promised, pelting him with her own ammo.

He snatched it out of the air.

"Whoa," Dru said, putting her hands up and laughing. "Okay, I surrender."

"What are the terms of your surrender?" he asked.

"I, uh, won't throw snow in your territory," she offered.

"What about reparations?"

"Reparations?"

"Or at the very least, a gesture of good faith," he allowed.

"What would that be?" she asked, completely baffled.

"We'll think of something," he said with a smile. "Now where's your dead animal?"

Dru was thinking of quite a few things, but she wasn't about to say any of them out loud.

She pushed the thoughts away and pointed to the north side of the hotel.

They walked past the ruined north wing again. Viktor observing it thoughtfully, as before.

She was about to ask him if that wing had been in use when he was last here, but she spotted the animal in the snow.

Like the rabbit, this creature was out on the edge of the meadow, alone in a sea of white.

But its carcass was larger and even from here she could see the flame-red fur rippling in the breeze.

"It's the fox," she breathed.

Viktor nodded.

"What would kill a fox?" Dru wondered out loud.

The creature had startled her last night, but it was beautiful, even in death.

And more importantly, it was a predator.

What would kill a predator?

As they grew closer, she could see the scene was the same as with the rabbit. The fox lay motionless on the snow, flecks of scarlet blood on the pale ground beside it.

But the animal itself appeared untouched, as if it had been killed for sport.

It looked almost like a little dog, sleeping and dreaming of the big, wild woods.

She felt unexpected tears prickle her eyelids.

"Drucilla, what's wrong?" Viktor asked.

She shook her head, feeling very foolish.

"Give me the bags," he said softly.

She pulled them from her pocket and handed them over.

Viktor bent, and with a sorrowful expression, he quickly bagged the poor fox.

"Where do we go with him?" he asked quietly.

"This way," she said.

They headed around the back of the hotel.

There was a stillness in the night that felt fitting to their unhappy task. But Dru felt her mind whirling.

What would have killed a fox?

She caught movement at the edge of the woods out of the corner of her eye, but when she turned to look there were only trees.

"What is it?" Viktor asked.

"Nothing, I guess," she said, shaking her head. "I thought I saw something."

They continued around the back of the abandoned wing, and Dru led the way to the entrance to the basement, which was tucked between the abandoned wing and the solarium.

She slid the skeleton key out of her pocket and opened the door as Viktor watched.

Bracing herself, she headed down the stairs and into the darkness. She pulled the chain and the bulb seemed even more dim than usual. Somehow, it wasn't quite as scary this time, with Viktor as company, their footsteps echoing together on the stones.

"So the trash is kept down here?" Viktor asked.

"Yes," she told him. "But the whole basement is riddled with tunnels. It's legendary. Some of them were originally dug to help people hide while they were trying to escape slavery."

"The Underground Railroad," Viktor said.

"Exactly," Dru agreed. "And after that, they were used during Prohibition to hide the alcohol that got distributed by the mob to all the Poconos resorts."

He nodded.

"And finally, there was the jewel thief," she went on. "He supposedly left a fortune down here somewhere, before he disappeared."

"Do you believe it?" Viktor asked her.

She shrugged.

"There have been so many people here looking for that treasure," she said. "I mean, really, it's been like fifty years. I'd think someone would have found it by now."

She turned the corner to the trash bins and Viktor handed her the bag.

It was so light that it hardly seemed anything was in it at all.

"What?" he asked.

"Nothing," she said, tossing it into the bin. "We should get out of here."

"Agreed," he said.

They headed back down the tunnel to the stairs that would take them outside.

Viktor's presence beside her was comforting, even though she couldn't help but think about the weight of the three-story hotel above them, pressing down on the arched stone ceiling of the catacombs.

The tunnels were so narrow.

"Are you okay?" he asked.

"Sure," she said. "It will be good to get out of here."

"The building has stood this long. It's not going

anywhere now," he said with a half-smile, as if he had read her mind.

"Nonetheless," she said, speeding up to get to the steps.

As she emerged outside, she caught movement at the tree line again, but this time a person was silhouetted against the snow.

It was a man. He was standing near the groundskeeper's cottage.

"Hey," she waved.

He waved back and she headed over, Viktor in tow.

The man strode toward her as if to meet them in the middle.

She felt a little relieved when she saw the cameras hanging around his neck. He was obviously a tourist.

"Are you a guest of Hemlock House?" she asked the man, when they reached each other.

"Yes," he replied, nodding once.

He was short, with thick glasses and a shock of dark hair.

"I'm Dru Holloway," she said. "I work in guest services."

"Oscar Hawkins," he said. "Ornithologist."

"Nice to meet you, Mr. Hawkins," she replied. "Listen, you're welcome to explore the grounds, but don't let the groundskeeper catch you near his cottage. He doesn't like anyone over there, and he keeps some toxic items on hand for cleaning and fueling the equipment."

"Oh, wow, don't worry about me," Oscar said, hands up. "I wouldn't go near anything like that. The birds can scent it, and they won't let you get close. Even trace amounts can be fatal to avians."

"Got it," Dru said. "Just steer clear of the cottage and you should be fine. Happy birdwatching!"

He scuttled away, clearly not interested in making friends.

"Thank goodness," she said, turning to Viktor. "I guess that's who I saw walking around before we went to the basement."

"Do you get a lot of birdwatchers here?" he asked.

"Tons," she said. "Global warming has changed what's available to see in the region. The mountaintop is still a great spot to find Pennsylvania birds that aren't in other parts of the state anymore."

"Hilltop," he muttered.

"Please don't make me break our treaty," she teased.

"I wouldn't dream of it," he told her. "So what are your plans for the evening?"

"I need to lock myself up and get some writing done," she said. "Then I've got a shift at the desk. Should be interesting. We'll be full up because of the comet."

"I'll walk you to your room," he offered.

"Thank you," she replied.

They walked around the back of the hotel, past the solarium and to the backstairs that led to the servants' wing.

She wondered if he would walk her all the way up.

He opened the door for her, clearly intending to see her right to the door of her room.

She climbed the stairs ahead of him, suddenly feeling self-conscious. Had he asked her what she was up to because he wanted to spend more time together?

She would have said yes, but now that she had said so firmly that she needed to work, it would sound weird to change her story.

She reached her room and turned around.

Viktor stood a few inches away, his big body looming over hers.

She swallowed and glanced up.

His impossibly blue eyes were pale in the dim light of the hallway. He observed her hungrily, and she felt her heart rate speed up like she had sprinted the whole way in.

"W-would you like to come in?" she heard herself ask.

"Lock yourself up," he whispered, "and get some writing done. I'll see you later, Drucilla."

He turned on his heel and headed down the corridor toward the main stair before she could catch her breath.

11

D ru sat at her desk, hands on the keys of the old typewriter, as she gazed out the window and tried to spin her tale properly.

But it seemed as though her ghost story required a melancholy mood that she wasn't quite feeling at the moment.

It was that look in Viktor's eyes, and the strength of his arms around her in the woods the other night, giving her a sense of warm anticipation instead of the trepidation a spooky story required.

She ran her hand absentmindedly across the surface of the desk, feeling her grandmother's initials carved there. She'd been doing it habitually since she found them. Sometimes, it helped her focus.

Finally, her bedroom faded, and the world of the novel descended on her. She lost herself until the alarm on her phone went off, telling her it was time to head downstairs for her shift.

She stood up, stretched, and grabbed the typewriter and journal to take down with her, feeling good about making some progress. She left the room with a spring in her step and headed for the front desk.

"Hey, Dru," Hailey said before she could even get down the stairs.

"How's it going?" Dru asked.

"No, no, no," Hailey scolded her. "Oh, no. You're not getting away with that."

"Getting away with what?" Dru asked.

"Getting away with what?" Hailey echoed. "I don't know, how about getting away with noticing the weird trunk guy is secretly a hottie, and then hiding out with him in the solarium?"

"Oh, that's not—" Dru began.

"—and *then* taking him with you to clean up a dead animal," Hailey continued. "You might have convinced me you just bumped into each other in the solarium, but roadkill duty? That shit is reserved for boyfriend material."

Dru glanced around the lobby to make sure they were alone, and then felt a little silly about it.

"Nothing is going on with us," she said quietly.

Outside of the fact that I can't stop thinking about him, even when I'm asleep, apparently.

"So why did you have to make sure the coast was clear before you said that?" Hailey whispered back, arching her brows even higher. At this rate, they were going to end up jumping completely off her face.

Dru couldn't help but giggle.

Hailey's face broke into a warm smile. "I knew it."

"Nothing is going on with us, though," Dru protested. "That part is true. But, yeah, he is... hot."

"Yeah, he *is* hot," Hailey said. "Girl, lock that down before someone else does."

"You wouldn't dare," Dru said.

"What? *Me?*" Hailey laughed. "I would never hone in on your racket. But there are other women out there."

"Not here," Dru said.

There were a few female guests, but she was pretty sure there wasn't exactly a lot of competition. Unless Viktor was into married women, or geriatric sisters.

"Not here *yet*," Hailey corrected her. "But we've got loads of people coming in for the comet. All you need is one woman with a little initiative, and some big boobs and whammo, he's gone."

"Well, he's just a hotel guest," Dru shrugged. Though it didn't really feel that way. She felt... a connection. But that was too silly to say out loud.

"Just jump his bones," Hailey advised. "It'll be an inspiration for your book."

Could it really be that simple?

"Noted," Dru said. "How was your shift?"

"Boring," Hailey said. "No sign of Tyler."

Dru laughed.

"Well, I'm off," Hailey said. "Ciao."

"Ciao," Dru replied as her friend headed off.

She had just unpacked the typewriter and set the journal on the desk, when the front doors swung open.

A man appeared in the doorway, his wide-shouldered frame silhouetted by the porch lights. He wore a woolen overcoat, and she could see the crisp white shirt underneath, open just enough at the collar to show off a bit of his tanned chest.

Dru didn't think she'd ever met the man before, but something about his face was familiar. His head was shaved bald, so it was difficult to determine his exact age, but his solid jawline and the tiny crow's feet next to his gray eyes told her he was a bit older than she was.

He hadn't said a word, but somehow, she could already tell he was a man who was used to getting what he wanted. Maybe it was those steel-gray eyes.

"Welcome to Hemlock House," Dru said.

"Hey, there," he said, his tone more friendly than she expected. "I'm checking in."

"Here for the comet?" she asked politely as he set his suitcase down.

"Huh?" he asked.

"Oh, there's a comet passing soon," she said. "Some of our guests are here to see it from the top of the mountain."

"Yeah, I'm here for that," he said. "I just didn't hear you."

"What's your name, sir?" she asked.

"Johnny Smith," he said. "My girl called ahead."

She entered his info into the computer, then waited a few seconds for it to catch up.

"There you are," she replied. "You're in the Ruby Room. Since you didn't pre-pay, I'll need your credit card and driver's license, please."

"I'm paying cash," Johnny said, pulling a large money clip out of his pocket and peeling off bills to hand over. "I don't believe in credit cards."

Dru had never seen someone pull that much money out of their pocket before. There had to be a few thousand dollars folded into the clip.

"Good for you," Dru said, rethinking how old he must be. People in their thirties didn't say stuff like that.

"Here's your key," she said, grabbing it off the hook. "May I see you to your room?"

"I'm good, sweetheart," he said with a sly grin. "But here's a little something for all your help."

Without missing a beat, he took her hand in his, like he

was going to shake it. But instead, he passed her a neatly folded twenty-dollar bill.

When had he even had time to do that?

Before she had time to react, he shot her a wink and then jogged up the stairs.

Dru shrugged and slipped the tip into her pocket. She'd have to go into the register to break it down to smaller bills next time she opened it. The vending machine didn't take twenties.

What an odd man.

The more she thought about it, the more she was sure she'd seen him somewhere before. But she couldn't quite place him.

The phone rang and she grabbed it. It was already shaping up to be busier than most nights.

"Hemlock House, front desk," she said. "This is Dru."

"Hey there, it's Jenna Wilder, from the Topaz Room," a familiar voice said. "I was just calling down to see if there were any room openings."

"Let me check on that for you," Dru said. She knew there were no openings. There were sticky notes all over the front desk and computer begging for a spare room for the Wilders. The poor things really wanted privacy from that daughter. They certainly weren't having the romantic getaway they had planned.

She opened the occupancy program and clicked through, knowing what she would find.

"I'm so sorry, Mrs. Wilder," she said. "We don't have any openings yet. I have a note posted on the desk, so none of us will forget to call if anything becomes available."

"Thank you, Dru," Mrs. Wilder said, the disappointment coming through in her voice.

She hung up, and Dru did the same.

Though she meant to focus on her typewriter, Dru found herself examining the journal instead.

The non-words swam before her eyes, the graceful letters looking familiar and alien at the same time.

She ran her finger along the top of the desk absent-mindedly, but of course her grandmother's initials weren't here, they were only in her old room.

She tugged on her locket instead and ran her thumb over the letters *J-A*, comforted by their familiar scrawl.

Suddenly, the air went out of her lungs and she nearly leapt to her feet. She'd been looking for a key, but...

What if there was a reason the handwriting looked familiar?

What if the journal belonged to Nana?

What if I've had the key all along?

It was so simple that it couldn't possibly be right.

But the journal *had* been in her grandmother's old room. The initials were literally carved into the desk where the thing had been wedged.

Her hands shook as she tried to pull the cryptogram wheel out of the back binding of the journal where she had tucked it.

She spun the inner wheel until the *J* lined up with the *A*.

Then she bent over the journal and began to note each letter. She jotted the letter from the wheel over each original letter.

By the time she had gotten the first part of the first word she knew she was right.

J-a-n

She tried to remain calm as she followed the wheel to find the whole name written on the opening page.

Jane Anderson

. . .

"HOLY CRAP," she said to herself. "Nana."

Of course the handwriting was familiar. Nana had done all her professional writing on a typewriter. But there were a few of Nana's holiday cookie recipes jotted on index cards tucked into the cookbook at home. The perfectly balanced, loopy letters detailing her process for gingerbread and peppermint bark brownies were exactly the same as the letters in the journal.

And Dru had been carrying the key the whole time.

12

————

Dru was bent over the journal, lost in the process of methodically translating one letter at a time, when someone cleared their throat.

She looked up and nearly jumped.

Viktor was standing just at the other side of the desk. He smiled at her.

"How is your night going?" he asked.

"Fine," she said, closing the journal.

"You made some progress?"

"Yes," she said. "I found the key. Now I just have to decode it."

He stepped around behind the desk with her.

"May I?" he asked, indicating the other chair.

"Sure," she told him.

He sat beside her, so close their legs almost touched.

She fought the urge to lean closer.

"How did you figure it out?" he asked.

"That's the crazy part," she said. "My grandmother used to work in this hotel, back in the '60s. I asked if I could stay in her old room."

Beside her, Viktor stiffened.

"I know, I know it's so sentimental," Dru went on. "But I loved Nana Jane so much, and she's a real inspiration. Anyway, her initials are carved on the top of the desk in there, and it got me thinking. Sure enough, her initials are the key."

"So this is... her journal?" he asked softly.

"Yes," Dru beamed. "Isn't that amazing?"

He reached out and ran a finger down the spine of the little book.

"Look, I've already decoded the first couple of pages," she said, opening it for him.

"What does it say?" he asked.

"Well, nothing all that exciting," she admitted. "She started the journal when she started working here. So far she's mainly talking about the hotel."

Viktor leaned back in his chair.

"Amazing, right?" Dru asked.

"Are you sure you should be reading it?" he asked.

She glanced up, surprised.

His eyes seemed a brighter blue than before, he gazed at her intently.

"Why wouldn't I read it?" she asked.

"If that was written by your grandmother, maybe there are things in it that you don't want to know," he said.

"Not so far," she said. "And really, she's just keeping a record of her life here."

"But it was private," he went on. "Think about the kinds of things young women write in their diaries. Do you really want to read about your grandmother's romantic escapades?"

Dru laughed.

Viktor didn't.

"This was before she married my grandfather," Dru explained.

"And you think this makes it *less* likely that you'll read something you wish you hadn't?" he asked.

"Whoa," she said.

"It was the sixties, Drucilla," he said. "You have no idea what you might find in that book."

"I can't really picture her that way," Dru replied.

"If you want to keep not picturing her that way, I suggest you stop reading her diary," Viktor said.

He had a point.

She tugged her pendant and ran her thumb across her grandmother's initials.

Her initials...

"She wanted me to read this," she realized out loud. "She literally gave me the key."

"What do you mean?" he asked.

"It's her initials, *J=A*, I've been wearing the key to the journal around my neck all my life without realizing it." She lifted the locket up so he could see it.

Viktor leaned in and cupped the tiny locket in his palm.

She tilted her head to the side so he could read the faded letters.

But he wasn't looking at the necklace.

There was something like pain in his eyes as he leaned closer, his eyes on her lips instead of the locket.

"Dru, have you seen my key?"

Howie's nasally voice interrupted whatever might have been happening between them and Viktor stood suddenly, as if his chair were electrified.

"Uh, no, I haven't, Howie," Dru said, trying not to let her voice sound as disappointed as she felt.

Howie was forever losing his skeleton key, which was

super irritating, since he always wanted to borrow hers and then she had to track him down to get it back.

"Shit," he said, shaking his head and wandering off.

She glanced at the grandfather clock. It was awfully late for Howie to be wandering around. He must have wanted to get into the good guest snacks in the locked kitchen pantry.

"I'd better go," Viktor said, without making eye contact.

Dru watched as he disappeared back up the stairs, sorry to see him go, but a little relieved at the same time.

Whatever was happening between them, it wasn't for a place like the front desk.

She finished the rest of her shift uneventfully, taking occasional breaks from her writing to decode a little more of the journal. But it was a slow process, and Nana didn't seem to have much to say so far.

By the time Zander came in to relieve her, she was exhausted. She told him how useful his cypher wheel turned out to be, and he clearly wanted to hear all about it. But Dru was too tired to think straight, so she excused herself and headed to her room to get some rest.

13

I n her dream, Dru waited in the round room with the stone floor again.

Summery air swirled in her hair as she watched the arched doorway, her back to the pretty view.

She didn't care that it was a dream.

She needed to know why this kept happening. Where was she, and why did she keep meeting him here?

His footsteps were faster this time, setting an urgent pace.

"Drucilla," the words echoed through the chamber in his deep voice just as his familiar form appeared in the doorway, hair tousled and shoulders tensed. Hunger was written on his beautiful face.

He closed the door behind him, and she moved toward him, cursing her body for being so frantic for his touch.

Before she could reach him, he was suddenly illuminated.

A flash of white light washed out the shadows, over his face.

She turned back toward the windows to see a wall of fire burning through on all sides.

The flames were so bright they hurt her eyes.

She curled her body away, burying her face in Viktor's chest as he stood, immobile in the harsh light of the fire that would soon consume them both.

And it would consume someone else, too.

Because behind Viktor, the door to the stone room was creaking open once more, scraping against the floor.

Dru awoke in a cold sweat, her heart pounding.

The sound of the door scraping open hadn't been part of her dream. It was real, and it was still happening.

Someone was in her room.

"Hello?" she called out.

There was no answer.

But she was sure someone was there in the darkness.

She froze, eyes wide to let in as much light as possible, trying desperately to see. Her whole body was on high alert, but she couldn't sense anything.

Slowly, she reached for her bedside lamp and turned it on.

The light blinded her for a moment, and she cursed herself for not shutting her eyes first. Once they adjusted to the light, she saw only the familiar sights of the desk, typewriter, bookshelves, and laundry.

Dr u slid out of bed and tiptoed to the door.

It was still bolted from the inside.

She headed for the bathroom, still in stealth mode, grabbing a big glass paperweight from the desk on her way by, just in case.

She caught sight of her own movement reflected in the mirror as she stepped in, and barely restrained herself from smashing it with the paperweight.

Dru took a deep breath and drew back the shower curtain.

The tub was empty.

She wandered back into her room and ran a hand through her hair.

These vivid dreams were making her a little crazy - that was the only explanation.

"I've got to eat better," she said to herself.

It wasn't even noon yet. She knew she should go back to sleep, but there was no point. She was too amped up to sleep.

She showered and dressed quickly.

When she returned to her desk, Dru decided to work on the journal for a little while. She was still a little sleepy and didn't feel ready to write yet.

She reached into her bag, but the journal wasn't in the pocket.

Weird.

She grabbed the bag into her lap and rummaged around.

Nothing.

She closed her eyes and tried to remember the end of her shift. She could picture showing the journal to Zander when he came in to relieve her, and then sliding it into her bag.

That was this morning, right?

Maybe she was remembering wrong and she had left it at the desk. She was too tired to trust her own memory.

She headed downstairs to find out.

It was odd to see light filtering in through the stained-glass window at the landing. She hadn't been awake at midday in so long.

The hotel was bustling. Well, as close to bustling as Hemlock House ever really got. She could hear music and conversation behind some of the doors.

The Wilders were in the hall right outside of their room.

Jeffery had Jenna pinned up against the wall with his hips. She was moaning lightly and twining her arms around his neck.

Wow, they really did need some privacy.

She wondered why they didn't send their daughter out on an errand or something. But Angie was a teenager and probably too smart for that.

Dru tried to slip past them noiselessly but Jeffrey must have sensed her presence.

He pulled back from his wife, who made a little surprised sound and smoothed down her blouse.

"Sorry," Dru mouthed to her and kept going to the stairs.

She jogged down so as not to interfere with them anymore.

Zander was sitting at the desk, his wide-shouldered frame looked too big for the space.

"Dru," he said happily when he spotted her.

"Good morning," she said.

"Haha, I guess it is morning for you," he replied. "Did you swap shifts with Hailey?"

"Nah, I just couldn't sleep," she told him. "Have you seen that journal anywhere?"

"No," he said.

"Oh, I thought I might have left it down here when I showed you earlier," she said.

"Let's look," he offered.

She came around behind the desk with him. Together they checked the drawers, though she was very sure she hadn't put it in a drawer.

"Sorry, Dru," he said, popping up from under the desk where he was checking to see if it fell.

Suddenly, he was close enough to touch. Close enough to kiss.

"Hey, Dru," he said, his voice husky. "I, uh, was wondering if you might want to get dinner tonight. I could come back in before your shift and pick you up."

Wow. Hailey had been right after all.

Dru had longed for this moment since high school.

Now that it was here, she was shocked to feel annoyed instead of elated.

She backed up and cleared her throat.

"Maybe another time. I'm really worried about the journal, so I'm just going to retrace my steps."

She could see the disappointment in his eyes, but he didn't argue.

"Sure, thing," he said, nodding. "I hope you find it."

She found herself running back up the stairs, her feet carrying her to Viktor's rooms instead of her own.

She tapped on the door to Sapphire, feeling a little bad, knowing he was likely sleeping.

There was no answer, so she knocked loudly.

It occurred to her that he hadn't wanted her to read the journal, and now it was gone.

Surely, she was overreacting. He wouldn't actually *take* the journal just because he thought her reading it was morally ambiguous.

But it was too late - the idea had taken root.

She decided to knock on Onyx and then Quartz.

Nothing.

Before she could give up and go back to her own room, Dru spotted the housekeeper coming down the hallway toward her.

"Hey, Gert," she said.

"Someone's up early," Gert said brightly. "Or is it up late?"

"Feels like both sometimes," Dru replied, following in

the older woman's wake. "How's your shift going?"

"Oh," Gert said, sounding pleased and surprised. "So far, so good. Those poor folks in Topaz are really jonesing for some privacy though."

She paused to slip her skeleton key into Sapphire's lock.

"Oh the Wilders, yeah," Dru said, following Gert inside as casually as she could. "I caught them making out in the hallway today."

Gert clucked disapprovingly and strode over to the bed.

It looked purposefully mussed, but somehow not really slept in.

"How can anyone sleep without untucking the sheets all the way?" Gert asked, obviously not expecting an answer.

She threw the bedding into her wheeled bin and headed to the bathroom for towels.

Dru took advantage of the moment to look around.

The big trunk was still on the floor in the corner, and the closet had only a few items of clothing hung in it.

The surface of the desk was clear. There was no sign of the journal, and she couldn't really look without opening drawers, which she didn't dare do with Gert in the next room.

And there was no sign at all of Viktor himself. Was he really sleeping in one of the other two rooms?

Gert emerged from the bathroom with an armload of towels.

Dru knew she couldn't make enough excuses to follow her through all three rooms.

"Do you really wash all the towels every day?" Dru asked. "Some of those are still folded."

"Of course," Gert said. "It's the only way to be sure they're clean."

"What about in his other two rooms?" Dru asked.

"Them too," Gert said. "Though I can't see that he's ever spent any time in any of them except to put sheets over things. Weird guy. Seems like he could spare a room for the Wilders if he's not even using them."

It *was* weird.

Suddenly Dru felt desperate to find him.

"I guess I'd better let you get to it," she said. "See you later, Gert."

"See you," Gert said with a smile as she continued to fluff up pillows like her life depended on it.

Dru headed out into the corridor again.

The Wilders were gone now, presumably looking for a more private spot to enjoy each other's company.

Dru decided to check the solarium for Viktor.

After brushing off Zander, she didn't exactly feel like bumping into him again so soon.

She headed back to the servants' exit, and then down the backstairs. It was comfortingly dim back there, since there were no windows and just the one ancient light fixture.

She opened the door to the lawn and was momentarily dazzled by the brilliance of the sun on the snow.

The air was cold enough to be unpleasant without a jacket, so she turned right and entered the solarium quickly from outside.

Warm, fragrant air greeted her as she stepped in among the plants. Light filtered through the foliage, making her feel like she was in a palace in some fairytale.

Dru was struck again by how different the hotel was in the daytime.

A glance around made it seem that she was alone, but she wandered the paths between the plants to explore the nooks and crannies.

"Oh, hello, dear," Hazel Van Buren exclaimed in a pleased way, looking up from the game of checkers she was playing with her sister.

"Hello," Honey echoed.

"Hello, Miss Van Buren and Miss Van Buren, how are you today?" Dru replied.

"We're fine, child," Hazel said primly.

"You haven't seen an old diary around, have you?" Dru asked impulsively.

"I can't say that we have," Hazel said. "Did you lose it? I don't think you're old enough to have anything that could rightfully be called old."

"I did," Dru said with a smile. "It belonged to my grandmother. Would you let me know if you see it anywhere?"

"Of course," Hazel said.

"Of course," Honey echoed.

"Thank you, ladies," Dru said.

"You have a nice day, dear," Hazel told her.

"You too," Dru said over her shoulder as she headed for the door.

She stuck her head in the dining room and even the sitting room, but Viktor was nowhere to be found.

She went back the way she came, through the solarium and back outside, to get back to her room from the rear stair.

The snow around the back of the hotel was unbroken, except for a line of tracks leading from the groundskeeper's cottage.

That made sense, most guests going in and out would use the lobby to reach the trails. Only Chester had a reason to be out here.

Where are you?

She sighed, her breath pluming in the cold, clear air.

There was nothing to do now but go back upstairs and try to take a nap before her shift.

Though she had a feeling she wouldn't be able to sleep thinking about her missing journal, and her missing friend.

14

D ru woke up from a short, dreamless sleep feeling disoriented.

Her phone was playing its usual chime. She grabbed it and swiped it off, realizing she felt strange because she had only slept for a few hours, and she was fully dressed.

So much for thinking she wouldn't be able to get back to sleep without knowing where Viktor and the journal were. Apparently, she needed rest more than she needed answers.

She got up, stretched, and then freshened up.

It was almost eight, so too late for dinner from the dining room.

She left the typewriter behind for the moment, and wandered down to the vending machine as she searched for some change.

"Dru, where have you been?" Hailey yelled, spotting her from the lobby desk.

"Just grabbing something to eat," Dru said. "Want anything."

Hailey waved her off.

Dru selected jalapeño chips and diet Dr. Pepper from the machines and then joined her friend at the front desk.

"Where were you?" Hailey demanded. "It's been a super weird day."

"You didn't see an old journal down here, did you?" Dru asked.

"No," Hailey said. "Should I have?"

"I lost one, so I was just hoping," Dru said. "If you see it let me know."

"Sure," Hailey said.

"What was so weird about today?" Dru asked.

"Well, first of all Zander was mopey when I got here," Hailey said. "I've never seen him mope, have you?"

Ack.

She had a pretty good idea why.

"No," Dru replied, trying to hide her guilty expression by looking down at her hands.

"Oh, I see," Hailey said, eyebrows arched. "I can't believe you turned him down."

Dru shrugged. "I didn't, exactly."

"So you said yes?"

"I said maybe another time," Dru admitted.

"Wow," Hailey said. "Even worse than a no."

"How is that worse?"

"Because it means he has to ask you again," Hailey said. "And you probably still won't say yes. At least a no puts him out of his misery."

Dru sighed.

"It's that new guy in Sapphire, isn't it?" Hailey asked, managing to look a little scandalized and a lot delighted at the same time.

"There's nothing going on with us," Dru said.

"Well, fix that as soon as you can," Hailey said. "He was just down here looking for you."

"He was?" Dru asked.

"Twice," Hailey said.

Dru looked down sadly at her soda and chips.

"Go to him," Hailey said with a melodramatic flair. "You can eat your pathetic dinner later."

"You're right," Dru laughed.

"As always," Hailey acknowledged.

"And so humble," Dru teased.

"Careful, you wouldn't want anything to happen to your five-star meal while you're gone," Hailey said.

"Very funny, I'll see you in a little while," Dru said, heading for the staircase.

She was already knocking on the door of the Sapphire suite before she remembered to feel nervous.

Thankfully, it opened before she had a chance to chicken out.

Viktor stood in the threshold, one hand on the door, the other on the frame. He was shirtless, and his dark hair hung in front of his eyes.

"Where have you been?" he asked.

"I had a hard time sleeping," she said, trying not to look at the hard planes of his chest and his abs. "I can't find the journal."

"You lost it?" he asked, looking more dismayed than she would have expected.

"Apparently," she said. "I mean, it can't have gone far."

"Come in," he said. "I'll get my shoes on and we'll go look for it."

She stepped inside, trying not to feel guilty for having been in the room earlier without his permission.

Where had he been?

She couldn't ask him without letting him know she'd been searching for him.

He bent to put on shoes and the muscles of his back stretched taut like steel bands.

She forced herself to turn and look at his desk.

Unlike hers, which was covered in evidence of her absent-minded writer lifestyle, it was perfectly clear, with only a pen and a pad of paper in the corner.

His bed was still made with military precision, as if he hadn't even sat on the edge of it since Gert's visit this morning.

"Ready?" he asked, running a hand through his hair.

He had put on a shirt, making it easier for her to nod and head for the door like a sane person, instead of teaching him how to properly mess up a bed.

"I assume you checked at the desk, and in the stairs and corridor," he said.

"Yes, and the dining room and solarium," she added.

"Where else did you go?" he asked.

"Nowhere—oh," she said, remembering. "I took a bag of trash down to the basement."

"How did you get there?" he asked.

"Through the outside entrance," she said, not mentioning the fact that she found the inside path to the tunnels a little too claustrophobic to use.

They headed downstairs.

"Hi, kids," Hailey said with an obnoxious knowing look. "What are you up to?"

"We're looking for the journal, Mom," Dru teased.

Viktor was already at the front door.

"Outside?" Hailey asked.

"Retracing my steps," Dru explained, grabbing her jacket.

Viktor helped her put it on and she tried not to remember the feel of his strong arms around her.

He held open the door, and they stepped out into the night.

The snow had begun to melt during the day, but everything had frozen over again once the sun went down. The branches of the big hemlock out front were trimmed in ice that sparkled in the moonlight.

"Wow, it looks so cool," Dru said, gazing up at it.

"It's beautiful, but it's not good for the tree," Viktor said. "All that ice is heavy."

"That's too bad," she said. "I guess it will melt again tomorrow."

"This weather is strange," Viktor said. "It smells like more snow is on the way."

"It does, doesn't it?" Dru said, taking a deep breath of the cold air. "It would be awful if it snowed during the comet."

"Let's hope it doesn't," Viktor said. "Did you walk around the north wing to get to the catacombs?"

"You said *catacombs*," she said with a grin.

"I like your name for them," he told her. "It feels like the right way to describe those tunnels.

"Yeah, it does," she agreed. "And yes, I did go around the north wing.

Dru took a dep breath of the crisp air and remembered their first walk outside together.

"It's too bad I got up so late. We could have gone for another walk on the trails," Dru said as they headed past the abandoned wing. "Did you ever get to check them out on your own?"

"I've been distracted," Viktor said. "But maybe we can do it together tomorrow."

"Tomorrow is the comet," she reminded him.

"Oh yes," he said. "I suppose you'll be quite busy."

"Hopefully, the whole hotel will be busy," she said.

"Is it usually very quiet?" he asked as they approached the corner of the building.

"I've only been here a short time, but it feels that way," she said. "People just don't want to stay in an old-fashioned bed and breakfast anymore. They want privacy - a short-term house rental they can book on a website without talking to anyone."

"And so the world moves on," Viktor said thoughtfully. "Change is the only constant."

That seemed like kind of an intense thing to say. But he wasn't wrong.

As they turned around the edge of the north wing, Dru spotted a man in an orange coat coming from the opposite direction.

He was tall and dark-haired. As they approached, she recognized him as Tyler Park.

"Hello, Mr. Park," she said.

"Hello," he replied tersely, glancing down at the ground.

He was pretty good-looking, though it was more of a studied look than Dru normally went for - slicked back hair and jeans that looked like they were intentionally distressed. A small snag on the left sleeve of his jacket was the only imperfection.

That, and the way he was trying to avoid eye contact.

Poor guy. Hailey was such a flirt.

"What was that about?" Viktor whispered as they continued.

"Oh, that's Tyler Park, from the Agate Room," she told him. "Hailey is flirting with him so much it's probably stressing him out whenever he sees the female staff."

"You aren't flirting with him, are you Drucilla?" Viktor asked, stopping in his tracks.

"Of course not," she replied, feeling her face grow hot.

"Why not?" Viktor asked.

You. Because of you...

"Because I'm... not interested in him," she replied awkwardly.

Viktor's expression softened, and he reached his hand out gently, brushing her cheek with the tip of his finger.

"You're blushing, Drucilla."

She opened her mouth and closed it again, unable to think of a single thing to say.

He let his hand fall to his side.

"Come, let's search the catacombs."

They walked together to the basement entrance. He watched as she slid out her skeleton key and opened the door.

The usual musty scent greeted her as she descended the stairs with Viktor right behind her.

She activated the dim bulb overhead, then got out her phone and turned on the flashlight function so she could scan the floor ahead of them with it.

They walked slowly down the damp corridor, the only sound the echo of their shoes on the stones and the drumming of her heartbeat in her ears.

They made it all the way to the bins without any sign of the journal anywhere.

"Where else did you go?" Viktor asked.

"Just back up to my room," Dru said.

"Through the lobby or the backstairs?" he asked.

"Backstairs," she said.

"Let's go."

They headed back down the corridor and up the steps into the night.

"You really don't like it down there, do you?" Viktor asked.

"It always feels like those walls are closing in," she admitted. "It doesn't bother you?"

He shook his head.

She turned off the flashlight on her phone and relied on the moonlight and the soft light emanating from the solarium to search the ground on the way to the backstair.

"It's bright as day in there," Viktor said, looking thoughtfully up at the solarium.

"Yes, although it's very different in there in the daytime," Dru said. "I went looking for the journal in there earlier."

"What was it like?" Viktor asked.

"It was less mysterious," she said. "More cheerful - like something out of a movie, or a children's book."

He nodded thoughtfully.

"I'll bet the greens were greener."

"It was *so* green," she agreed.

There was a hungry look on his face that she couldn't understand.

"Maybe you can get up early one of these days and check it out with me," she suggested.

He nodded with a half-smile.

They had reached the backstair.

She pulled out her key again and opened the door, and they headed up the narrow staircase together in the dim light. It was hard not to think about how close he was, and the fact that they were going to her room.

Unlike the Sapphire Suite, Dru's room was mostly bed.

She opened the door and instantly wished she had cleaned up... well, ever.

"Sorry," she said. "I'm uh, still getting used to this schedule."

"You're the creative type," he said, observing the room from the doorway.

Ouch.

"Well, come in if you want," she said, turning back to survey her domain, such as it was. "I really don't think it's here though."

She heard him enter and stop.

"You carry this up and down with you every night?" he asked, looking at the typewriter.

"Yeah, I know a laptop would be easier," she said. "But it was my Nana's, so it's kind of special. Besides, I can't check social media on it."

"Focus is a dying art," he agreed, fixing her in his azure gaze.

His eyes looked pale blue again.

It must be the light up here.

"So you came up here," he said. "And you put your bag down with the journal still in it, as far as you know?"

"Yes," she said. "I put the bag down next to my bed."

He knelt beside the desk in the spot she had indicated.

"I already looked," she said.

"Humor me," he teased. "Wow, there's a lot of stuff back here."

He tossed her a tissue box and a dog-eared paperback.

Dru cringed, hoping he wouldn't find anything embarrassing. She seriously needed to clean her room.

"What's this?" he said softly.

A moment later, he emerged with the journal held aloft.

"Whoa, I can't believe it," Dru breathed.

"You must not have checked carefully enough," Viktor said, handing it over.

"Clearly not," Dru said. "I have no idea how it would have gotten that far back there, but I'm really glad you came."

He straightened up.

She had moved closer to take the journal. And when he stood, they were mere inches apart.

Viktor reached out slowly, as if she might run if he moved any faster, and slid her hair back over her shoulder.

Tingles of awareness spread from her neck down her spine.

"I like to see your face," he told her softly.

Heat washed over her, and though she felt incredibly self-conscious, she couldn't look away.

He bent and she closed her eyes, tilting her chin up for his kiss without a second thought.

But he pressed his lips to her forehead instead, leaving her reeling.

"I should let you get your writing done," he said, his voice husky.

He was out the door again before she could catch her breath.

15

———

Dru wandered down to start her shift, typewriter in tow, still feeling dreamy.

She liked Viktor, liked him a lot. He was hard to read, but there was something about him that was so *familiar*. It made being lost in the throes of attraction much easier to bear, even if she didn't know exactly where she stood.

"Did you guys find what you were looking for?" Hailey asked, blinking innocently at Dru.

Dru laughed.

"Yes and no."

"Ooohhh, tell me all about it," Hailey said.

"There's really nothing to tell," Dru said, sliding behind the desk with her friend. "We found the journal and then he kissed me..."

"Yesssss," Hailey interjected.

"On the forehead," Dru added

"Oh," Hailey said, taken aback. "That can be sexy though. What was it like?"

"I don't know," Dru said, retrieving her chips and Diet

Dr. Pepper from under the counter, so as not to have to make eye contact. "He pushed my hair out of my eyes, said, *I like to see your face*, and then he kissed my forehead."

"Nice," Hailey said, leaning back. "Classic older man move."

"What's that supposed to mean?" Dru asked.

"He doesn't want to come off as pervy, but he definitely wants to kiss you," Hailey said, with great authority. "*That* was his way of toying with the boundary to see how you would respond."

"Oh," Dru said, wondering if that could really be right. Hailey had clearly put in way more thought on the subject than she ever had.

"How did you respond?" Hailey asked.

"I, er, thought he was actually going to kiss me. I closed my eyes and everything," Dru admitted. "I probably looked like an idiot."

"Nah," Hailey said. "It means next time, he'll go for what he really wants. You passed the test."

"That makes me feel better," Dru laughed. "But I'm not sure it's accurate. He can't be that much older than me anyway."

"He *seems* older, though," Hailey said. "Don't you think?"

"Yeah, he does," Dru admitted. "But I'm sure it's only a few years."

"Well, you'll have plenty of time to think about it on your shift," Hailey said.

"Weird day got quieter as it went on?" Dru guessed.

"It did," Hailey said, grabbing her bag. "See you tomorrow, and text me if he makes a real move."

"I will," Dru laughed.

But she wouldn't really. Dru wasn't the type to kiss and

tell. Unless Hailey was right here to drag it out of her. She also wasn't the type to put up much of a fight with a friend.

"Ciao," Hailey said, and blew her a kiss on the way out the door.

"Ciao," Dru echoed.

Though she knew she should probably be writing, she decided to check in with the *Ghost Getters* message board instead.

After several excruciating minutes of getting the front desk computer online, she heard the ping of her avatar popping up in the room.

TADSTRANGE:
   Ghostwriter!

ACTIONPARK:
   Hey, ghostwriter, did you figure out the key to your journal?

GHOSTWRITER:
   Yes, it actually belonged to my Nana. Crazy!

ACTIONPARK:
   No way!?!?!?

BETHSMOM1972:
   That's incredible! Wasn't she there during the jewel thief thing?

. . .

GHOSTWRITER:
Yeah

TADSTRANGE:
wow

ACTIONPARK:
What does it say?

GHOSTWRITER:
Not much yet. I just figured out the code. But who knows?

BETHSMOM1972:
Keep us posted!

WORMULUS:
lily getters boobs 4ever

BETHSMOM1972:
Very classy, Wormulus.

UNCLEPETE58:
Easy Wormulus there are ladies present.

WORMULUS:

balls

WORMULUS SIGNED OFF 12:17AMEST

BETHSMOM1972:
Don't you wish we could keep certain people out?

UNCLEPETE58:
YES

A COMMOTION in the solarium distracted Dru from the board for a moment.

Two male voices were speaking in harsh, staccato tones.

It was hard to tell from the lobby, but it sounded almost like an argument.

GHOSTWRITER:
I've got to get some work done, just wanted to say hi.

BETHSMOM1972:
Keep us posted, GhostWriter.

SHE SIGNED off and slipped into the threshold between the lobby and the dining room. It was definitely an argument. She could hear the voices cutting each other off and growing louder.

These two men sounded violently angry - angry enough that it seemed like they might be about to hit each other.

"You know what?" One of them yelled. "Fuck you, Sullivan."

Sullivan? Was there a Sullivan checked in right now?

Drew thought about it, but was drawing a blank. Then again, she didn't have a ton of contact with the guests while working the night shift.

"No, fucking way you can talk to me like that," the other one shot back.

"*No, just fuck you, Sullivan. I'm done with you.*"

Dru didn't relish approaching them by herself. But there was no one else around. Of course, Howie never seemed to be around when anything unpleasant needed doing, Chester would be long asleep in his cottage, Gert and Constance were off-duty at night, and neither Hailey nor Zander would be back until their shifts began.

She had the sudden urge to go find Viktor.

Come on, Dru, she coached herself. *It's just an argument. You're a grown-up. You can break it up.*

She stopped and took a deep breath, then stepped into the dining room.

The solarium had gone silent.

Footsteps thundered toward her.

Before she could make herself scarce, Brian Thompson charged out of the solarium, nearly smashing into her on his way out to the lobby.

She gasped and stepped back, smacking her hip into the corner of the table.

"Ow," she said quietly to herself.

By the time she got back to her desk, Brian was long gone.

She hoped he was ashamed of himself. Who acted like that? And who had he been yelling at?

Whoever it was, they must have left through the exterior door of the solarium.

On a whim, Dru pulled up the guest log and began going through names.

HAZEL & *Honey Van Buren - Amethyst Suite*
   Brian Thompson - Opal Room
   Tyler Park - Agate Room
   Jeffrey, Jenna, and Angie Wilder - Topaz Room
   Viktor Stryker - Sapphire Suite, Onyx Room, Quartz Suite
   Oscar Hawkins - Pearl Room
   Johnny Smith - Ruby Room
   Paid Hold for H. Channing - Emerald Room
   Paid Hold for E. Tuck - Amber Room

THERE WERE no Sullivans anywhere on that list.

She shook her head and bit the end of her pen.

It was possible that the man Brian Thompson was arguing with hadn't left the solarium to go outside.

Maybe he was still there, or he had gone into the sitting room.

Suddenly Dru was as eager to lay eyes on the man as she had been anxious not to before.

You're bored, Dru, just get some writing done.

But the idea was in her head.

She put up the *Bee Right Back* sign, then slipped back into the corridor and headed to the sitting room.

A fire was crackling in the fireplace, but the leather chairs and tables were empty.

She stepped through the doorway into the solarium, soaking in the fragrant air.

It took a bit of looking through the trails of trees and foliage, but the solarium was empty too.

She went back out through the sitting room and into the corridor, figuring she would stick her head into the kitchen, just in case.

But before she made it to the kitchen, a big, familiar, male figure strode down the hallway toward her.

"Hey there," Brian Thompson said.

He stepped close enough that she had to press her back up against the wall to avoid his big frame brushing up against her.

"Sorry I almost slammed into you back there," he said, putting a hand on the wall behind her head. "You okay?"

"I'm fine," she said, moving to duck under his arm.

He grabbed her shoulder with his other hand, trapping her.

"You're a pretty little thing," he said. "I'll bet you get lonely up here at night on this mountain."

"Not really," she said. "I have to get back to the desk."

"Don't rush off," he said. "Let's get to know each other."

16

D ru felt her heart threaten to pound out of her chest.

"I have to go," she repeated.

But Brian was leaning close to her, so close she could smell the onions on his breath and feel the heat of his gut against her stomach. Light from the lamp on the hall table twinkled in the gold cross he wore.

Adrenaline crashed through her veins and she tried to twist her shoulder out of his hand.

But his meaty paw only clenched onto her more tightly.

"You're a feisty little thing, aren't you?" he asked, sliding the hand that was on the wall to grab her jaw.

Moving on instinct, Dru jerked her right knee up with brutal force into his crotch.

"*Fuck you, bitch,*" he choked, not letting go of her.

Frantic, she tried to wrest herself out of his hold, but he was too strong. She flailed her free hand until her fingers closed on the base of the brass lamp on the hall table. It was heavy, and would probably do some pretty serious damage when she slammed it into his head. Dru decided she was okay with that.

"Enough," a calm, masculine voice said from the end of the hallway.

Dru turned to see it was Viktor.

She released her hold on the lamp, shame and relief washing over her in equal measures.

"What do you want, weirdo?" Brian snarled.

"The lady has asked you to unhand her," Viktor said lightly.

There was a single instant of throbbing tension.

Then Brian let go of her so fast she stumbled.

Viktor was already at her side somehow, taking her arm.

"Are you okay?" he asked.

"I'm fine," she said, looking down.

"Do you want to alert the police?" Viktor asked. "I saw everything. I would be more than happy to provide a statement."

She shook her head, not wanting to spend one more minute thinking about it.

"This fucking place," Brian muttered, stomping down the hallway toward the lobby.

"Stop," Viktor said quietly.

Dru was amazed to the see the big man freeze in his tracks, then turn slowly back to them.

"If you so much as look at her again, the authorities will be involved." Viktor said. "And I don't think that would end well for you, Mr.... Thompson, was it?"

The man gave Viktor a confused look.

"Sure thing, buddy," Brian said, his old swagger back.

He turned and stomped away, shaking his head.

"Drucilla," Viktor breathed.

His eyes were pale blue, and his expression was hungry again.

Without thinking, she went up on her toes and pressed her lips to his.

He froze for an instant and then seemed to give in, kissing her back gently.

Everything about him felt right. Dru's senses were reeling. His mouth was warm and delicious. She instinctively pressed her form closer to his.

"Easy," he whispered against her mouth.

Somehow, even the word of caution thrilled her senses, and she had to fight herself not to wrap her body around his.

Viktor cupped her cheek in his hand and pulled back slightly.

"You'll drive me mad," he murmured.

She had no idea what he meant. If he wanted her, she was his for the taking.

Hailey was right, she needed this, needed him more than she could have imagined. A taste was not enough.

"Viktor," she whispered back, too stupid with wanting to make a coherent argument for herself.

"Come," he told her.

He lifted her in his arms, seemingly without effort, and carried her to the empty lobby and up the staircase.

Dru closed her eyes and rested her head against his chest.

He was so strong, his body firm beneath her cheek. She listened for the reassuring drumbeat of his heart, but couldn't hear anything because her own was pounding so loudly in her ears.

He opened the door to her room and stepped inside, closing and locking it behind them.

She felt a thrill of happiness.

He placed her gently down on the bed and sat beside her, leaving one arm wrapped protectively around her shoulder.

"I know you have to get back to work in a few minutes," he said. "But I think you should rest a little first. You've had a scare."

"I'm not scared anymore," she told him. "And it's after two in the morning. I don't need to get back downstairs yet. No one will need me for hours."

"Drucilla…" he began. But he didn't finish.

She would have sworn he wasn't interested, if it weren't for the way his body was curled around hers as if he were magnetically drawn to her.

He gazed down at her, his pale blue eyes hazy with need.

She held still, unwilling to make the next move.

"Drucilla," he said again, the word a surrender.

When he finally pressed his lips to hers, she felt herself almost swoon with the pleasure of it.

17

Dru held herself perfectly still as he kissed her.

Hailey must have been right. He was older than Dru thought.

Guys her own age wouldn't have hesitated to kiss her in the first place. And once they were kissing, it would have been a race to the finish line.

But Viktor kissed her slowly and carefully, as if she were breakable.

She felt her whole body grow warm under his touch.

After a time, he cupped her cheek in his hand, coaxing her jaw open with a light caress of his thumb.

When his tongue stroked hers, she nearly moaned.

He tasted like moonlight, and his slow pace made her feel as if he were trying to soothe her lust instead of inciting it.

It only made her more frantic.

She slid a hand up his chest and around his shoulder.

He grabbed her hand and brought it back to her lap, then pulled away slightly.

"I should go," he murmured.

Dru wanted to scream.

"You're not feeling yourself," he said. "You're excited over what happened."

"No," Dru moaned. "I want you."

He closed his eyes and looked away.

"Please, don't go," she whispered, feeling ashamed but unable to keep herself from begging.

"Lie down, Drucilla," he said softly.

"No, you can't leave me," she said.

"I won't leave you," he told her, meeting her gaze. "Just lie down."

Her heart soared and she leaned back onto the pillow as he stretched out at her side.

"Rest, my love," he told her, stroking her cheek.

She turned her head and pressed her lips to the palm of his hand. He hissed in a breath.

She met his eyes again and saw that he was battling with himself again.

Why don't you want me? What have I done?

But it was obvious that he wanted her. His eyes were pale as ice, and fixed on her mouth like he wanted to devour it.

He groaned and dipped his head to brush her lips with his again.

She closed her eyes, losing herself to the sensation.

Instead of deepening their kiss, he pressed his lips to her eyelids, her forehead, the shell of her ear.

She fought the urge to reach for him, and instead allowed him to explore her body with his mouth.

His hand was against her collarbone, his thumb pressed to the hollow of her throat.

She could feel her body coming to life under his touch.

He nuzzled her neck, inhaling her as if she were a fine perfume.

"So beautiful," he murmured, caressing her ribcage and the curve of her waist and hip.

She fought the need to arch her back, but she couldn't stop herself from trembling all over.

He cupped her breast in his hand almost reverently, skimming his thumb over the nipple, which throbbed in an agony of pleasure through the material between them.

"My God, Drucilla," he groaned.

She held very still as he unbuttoned her blouse.

First, there was cool air on her chest and then his hungry mouth was raining kisses on her chest as he slid a thumb under the cup of her bra, exposing one breast to him.

Dru clutched the sheets as he stroked the eager nipple.

When he lowered his head to lick it into his mouth, she moaned and arched her back in spite of herself.

He peeled back the other cup of her bra and lapped her nipple, teasing the other between his thumb and index finger and sending her into a tailspin of need.

Dru could feel him, stiff as steel, pressed against her hip. She longed to touch him, but was afraid to break the spell that held him tenuously close to her.

She whimpered, lost in unsatisfied need.

"Oh my sweet girl," he moaned in sympathy. His jaw was tense with his own need.

She closed her eyes against the onslaught of sensation.

He shifted on the bed, moving lower.

Then his hands were under her skirt, peeling down her panties, sliding up her thighs, pressing them apart.

She forgot to be self-conscious, spreading her legs wantonly for him and crying out as he fed on her breasts again and cupped his hand over her sex.

He pulled back from her breasts and looked into her eyes as he slid a finger against her opening.

Dru gasped and felt herself throbbing around his finger.

"God, Drucilla," he whispered, stroking her again.

Her hips trembled as the pleasure slashed through her.

He lowered his face to her neck, nuzzling and kissing her tender flesh as he sank his fingers into her heat.

Dru lost track of her own sounds as his thumb found her tiny pearl, massaging so slowly that she thought she would lose her mind.

The pleasure was building in her, a hunger so blinding it lifted her out of herself.

"Viktor," she cried out as ecstasy obliterated her.

She felt his teeth graze her neck and then she was falling, falling back down to earth and the bed where she trembled in the arms of this mysterious man who had become her lover.

18

D rucilla awoke just before dawn, feeling disoriented.

"I have to go, my love," Viktor said, stroking her cheek. "And you have to get back to work."

She shot out of bed, buttoning her blouse as she went. "What time is it?"

"Nearly seven," he said.

"Oh, Zander won't be in for almost an hour," she said, relieved. "I can't believe I fell asleep. Want to walk down together and have coffee?"

A pained expression marred Viktor's handsome features.

So, this was the end of their friendship - a one-sided one-night stand and then an awkward morning after.

Suddenly her chest ached. This hurt more than it should have, given the short length of time she had known the man. Desperately, she tried to force herself to tamp down her disappointment until she got away from him.

"It's okay, I totally get it," Dru said quickly. "I'll see you around."

"Drucilla," he said.

"I really have to run," she gasped, shoving her feet back into her shoes and grabbing her typewriter off the desk.

"Drucilla," he said again. Somehow, he had moved across the room and wrapped his hand around her upper arm.

"Last night was special to me," he murmured into her ear, sending a tingle down her spine. "I can't go with you right now, but it's not because I don't want to. I want to be with you always."

She couldn't help but smile at his words, and she felt his returning smile against her neck.

"I'll see you later, then," she said, more gently this time.

It made sense. He was a busy man. He'd probably missed out on a lot more work while spending time with her than she had by abandoning the empty front desk for a bit.

"Yes, you will," he said, pressing a kiss to her forehead.

Viktor walked out of the room, looking over his shoulder to wink at her as he disappeared down the corridor.

She turned back to her room, depositing the typewriter back on the desk so she could wash up before heading downstairs.

Last night had been incredible, but also unusual.

Dru wasn't the kind of person who got physical casually, certainly not with someone she barely knew.

But the connection she felt with Viktor seemed to defy their actual relationship.

She would have thought she was obsessed only because of the intense physical attraction, but what he had said this morning kept echoing in her mind.

I want to be with you always...

She felt the same, had felt it since their walk through the woods. Though she hadn't been ready to articulate it, even to herself.

Easy, Dru, she warned herself.

But it felt like whatever had been holding Viktor back in his feelings for her was gone now. And it was impossible not to let herself enjoy both the corresponding attraction and the tenderness she harbored for the man, even though she knew practically nothing about him.

"I'll just have to fix that part," she said to herself as she dragged a brush through her hair.

She grabbed her stuff and jogged downstairs to the lobby.

She pulled the *Bee Right Back* sign from the desk and had just settled in, when Zander came in the front door.

"Good morning," she called to him, her happiness making her forget that she was trying not to encourage him.

His face lit up and she instantly got the sinking feeling that he was going to ask her out again.

"Hey listen, Zander," she said, before he had a chance to say anything. "I was thinking about your question last night, and I just want you to know I would hang out anytime as friends. I'm kind of seeing someone right now, and I'm sorry I didn't say so yesterday. You just surprised me."

"Really, you were surprised?" he asked.

"Well, did you know I had a massive crush on you in high school?" she asked.

He shook his head, smiling in a very pleased way.

"Well, there you go," she said. "People surprise each other all the time. Have a good shift today."

"I guess you're right about that," Zander said in a way that made her think he might be the one guy in the world who was totally cool being friends after getting turned down for a date. "Anything interesting happen overnight?"

For a split-second she thought he somehow knew what she'd been up to.

Then she remembered that he was just talking about work. They always caught up on things during the shift change.

"Nope," she said. "Actually, Brian Thompson was arguing with someone in the solarium."

"Who?" Zander asked.

"That's the weird thing," Dru told him. "I never figured it out. Brian came storming out of there and whoever it was must have gone out the back door. I thought I heard him call the guy *Sullivan,* but there's no one here by that name."

"Weird," Zander agreed.

"Anyway, that was about it," she told him.

She decided not to mention how the rest of her little adventure with the big man went. Even though none of it was her fault, she felt slightly embarrassed by the whole thing. She wasn't sure if it was because of the way he'd acted, or the fact that she'd been about to brain him with a heavy lamp when Viktor had showed up.

"I'll keep an eye out," Zander told her.

Dru gathered her stuff and said goodnight.

She climbed the stairs, wondering if she would be able to sleep at all after her little nap with Viktor.

Hopefully, she could get some rest. Tonight was the night of the comet. She would need to have her wits about her.

Dru opened the door to her room and placed the typewriter back on the desk. Then she undressed quickly and slid under the sheets. Sunlight wafted through the windows and she closed her eyes and thought about Viktor's hands on her.

She drifted off almost immediately.

19

D ru woke at the usual time, feeling completely refreshed.

She sat in bed for a moment, replaying her evening with Viktor in her mind.

I want to be with you always...

She hugged herself and then hopped up, eager to see him again.

Once she was showered and dressed, she headed downstairs to eat.

It didn't hit her until she was almost in view of the front desk that she should have already put some thought into how much of her time with Viktor she was going to hold back from Hailey.

The trouble was, she *wanted* to talk about him, wanted to sing about him and knit a sweater with his picture on it and wear it everywhere.

Don't be a psycho, she advised herself.

But it was too late, she was smitten.

"Someone had a good night last night," Hailey said, waggling her eyebrows.

Dru's shock must have shown on her face. Was it obvious before she even spoke that she had *gotten lucky*?

"Zander mentioned that you told him you're seeing someone," Hailey said gently.

"Oh, right," Dru said.

"But I'm loving your vibe right now," Hailey said. "Come tell me all about it."

"There's not that much to tell," Dru said, heading back to the desk to set her stuff down.

"Like fun there isn't," Hailey retorted.

"Good morning, girls," Hazel Van Buren said brightly as the old woman passed the desk with her sister in tow.

"Good morning," Honey echoed.

"Good morning, Miss Van Buren and Miss Van Buren," Hailey and Dru chorused back to them.

"Big night tonight," Hazel confided with a wink.

"Yes, we're very excited for the comet, Miss Van Buren," Hailey said politely.

"Comet?" Hazel said. "I don't know anything about a comet. It's lasagna night."

"Lasagna night," Honey echoed happily.

"Oh yes," Hailey said. "Good stuff."

The ladies headed down the corridor, presumably to wait in the Sitting Room and be first for dinner.

"Tell me what happened," Hailey hissed.

Dru smiled and leaned on the counter. "Well, I guess you were right," she said. "He did want to kiss me for real."

"How did it happen?" Hailey asked.

"Oh my gosh, I almost forgot to warn you," Dru said, suddenly horrified at herself.

"What?" Hailey asked.

"That creep Brian Thompson also tried to kiss me last night," she said.

"*What?*" Hailey cried.

"He grabbed me in the corridor, and I don't know what he would have done if Viktor hadn't come along."

Most likely he would have learned what life was like with a brass lamp as a permanent part of his skull, but she didn't think that was a good thing to mention.

"Did you report him to the police?" Hailey asked.

"He didn't really end up doing anything," Dru said.

"You need to talk to Howie about this," Hailey said. "I'm here during the day when there are witnesses, but you can't be on duty alone at night if that guy thinks he can put a hand you."

"Pretty sure he doesn't think that anymore," Dru said with a wry smile.

"Why? What happened?"

"Well, first of all, I kneed him in the nuts," Dru said.

"Naturally," Hailey nodded.

"And then Viktor threatened to call the police if he got wind of him doing anything like that again," Dru said. "He seemed to take it pretty seriously."

"Props to Viktor," Hailey said. "But a guy that slimy will just make sure Viktor isn't around next time."

She was probably right about that.

"I'll talk to Howie," Dru said.

"Good idea," Hailey said. "So how did this unpleasant incident lead to you kissing Viktor."

"Well, Brian ran off, and then we were alone, and I just... kissed him," Dru said, realizing how weird it must sound.

"You did?" Hailey asked.

Dru nodded. "I know I must seem crazy, one minute I'm fighting with some deviant, the next minute I'm throwing myself at someone. But it just felt... right."

"I think it's awesome," Hailey said. "You know what you don't want, and what you do."

"Very true," Dru said.

"So how was it?" Hailey asked.

"Amazing," Dru said, envisioning it all again.

"That's great," Hailey said. "Now find out if he has a brother for me to date."

Dru laughed. "I have no idea if he's got a brother or not."

"Seriously?" Hailey asked. "What do you guys talk about?"

"He doesn't talk about himself much," Dru said. "He's always asking questions about me."

"An ideal man," Hailey said, nodding. "You did the right thing by kissing him."

Dru laughed.

The conversation was interrupted when the front door of Hemlock House flew open. A man stood in the threshold, arms outstretched, snow swirling around him.

"*Barren winter, with his wrathful nipping cold,*" the man cried. "*The icy fang and churlish chiding of the winter's wind bites and blows upon my body. I shrink with cold. What freezings I have felt, what dark days seen, what old December's bareness everywhere.*"

"Henry the sixth," Hailey said.

"Part two," he replied with a flourish and a half-bow, leaving the door open behind him.

Dru dashed over to close it as the man approached Hailey.

He was short in stature, but his personality seemed big enough to make up for it.

"Hugh Channing," he said. "Local actor and hotel patron. What's your name, my dear?"

"Hailey Woods," she replied. "Amateur fashion guru and

professional hotel clerk. I saw you in *Arsenic and Old Lace*, Mr. Channing. You were brilliant."

"Please, call me Hugh," he said, leaning on the desk, looking totally smitten.

Dru smiled. Hailey had such a way with everyone. Dru definitely would have stuttered stupidly at anyone with personality the size of Hugh's.

She watched Hailey check in their latest guest, and then went back to chat with her friend when Hugh was safely on his way to the Emerald Room.

"Did you know that he's the artistic director of The Three Blind Mice?" Hailey asked Dru.

"I had no idea," Dru admitted.

It checked out though. The Three Blind Mice was a nearby dinner theatre. From what she understood, they ran a brisk business with bland but copious food, and a steady stream of comedy and musical standards.

"You would think he headed up the Royal Shakespeare Company," Dru joked.

"Hey, making money from the arts at all is a pretty amazing feat," Hailey said.

"You're right about that," Dru said, feeling a little embarrassed. After all, no one around here ever saw her without Nana's typewriter. She'd be proud to get paid anything for her work, let alone make it into a successful business.

"Anyway, would you believe we only have one more guest coming?" Hailey asked. "Then I can finally paint my nails."

"Are you going to go with pink or light pink?" Dru teased.

"As if," Hailey said, rolling her eyes.

The door opened again, and two women came in, followed by Zander and a very grumpy looking Chester.

"Mayor Tuck," Hailey said. "Welcome to Hemlock House. It's an honor to have you here."

"My pleasure, dear," the mayor said with a smile.

The mayor was a middle-aged woman with a Jackie O. haircut and a smart little Chanel knock-off suit to match.

The woman at her elbow had short red hair and a camera around her neck.

"This is my staff photographer, Melody Young," Mayor Tuck explained. "She's here for some photo opportunities but she won't be staying. I booked a room for myself though, should be under Tuck."

"I've got the keys to the Amber Room right here for you," Hailey said. "Do you need help finding it?"

"Oh no, dear," Mayor Tuck said. "I worked here in high school."

Hailey grinned at her and the mayor gave a little wave and headed up the stairs.

"Weather is a mess," Chester said, leaning over the desk. "I'm *not* going back down tonight. I don't like the looks of it. I'll take the shuttle down to Manny's to get the chains on when it lets up."

"How am I supposed to get home?" Zander asked, walking up to join them.

"No idea," Chester grumped and stormed down the corridor, presumably to use the solarium door to get out to his cottage.

"Well, the guests are all here," Hailey said, shrugging. "And Howie's been in the kitchen nagging Constance for an hour. I guess we're fine."

"People are going to freak out if they can't see that comet," Dru worried out loud.

"Well, they already paid for their rooms," Hailey said.

"And maybe they'll drink more. That would make Howie happy."

Zander rolled his eyes.

Dru laughed. It was nice to have the whole desk crew here at once.

"Come on, let's get some dinner before the Van Buren sisters eat all the lasagna," Zander said, nudging her with an elbow.

20

D ru pulled the hood back up on her jacket, knowing the wind would blow it off again almost immediately.

It was just after midnight, and the snow had let up for the last few minutes, though the wind was still whipping the mountaintop.

Guests were clumped in small groups all over the snowy meadow, gazing up at the sky.

Although Dru was fairly certain no one could see the comet, everyone was in high spirits due to the drinks that had been flowing in full force after supper.

From six until eleven forty-five, the guests had sipped wine and mixed drinks, ready to rush outside around midnight to see the comet pass by.

Hailey was right, Howie was pleased with the uptick in drink sales. In fact, Howie was pretty pleased in general. He'd been strutting around, very self-importantly, spouting helpful facts about comets and other useful bits of information.

But it was good to see everyone having a good time.

Currently, Zander was flirting shamelessly with Hazel and Honey Van Buren, who could not contain their giggles.

Dru smiled at the three of them, sure Zander was making the sisters' day.

"Binoculars?" Dru offered, holding out the box she carried.

"Oh, we can't see anyway," Hazel said. "We're just happy to be part of the excitement."

Honey nodded.

"I'll take a pair," Zander told her.

She handed a set of binoculars over.

"Wow, your hands are so cold," he remarked.

"I forgot my gloves," she admitted. "I'll be okay."

She noticed Viktor leaning against the abandoned wing of the building and headed his way.

He was a guest, after all, she told herself, and he might like a pair of binoculars.

She was glad to spot him. He hadn't shown himself yet this evening. Dru had found herself searching for him, feeling restless to see him again.

"Drucilla," he said when he noticed her approach, his voice low and husky.

Instantly, she felt the blood rush to her cheeks.

"Hi, Viktor," she said, suddenly feeling shy. "Do you want binoculars?"

"No," he said, a half-smile drawing up his lips.

Oh God, I know what he wants.

She blushed even harder.

"Beautiful," he said under his breath.

"Have you spotted the comet?" she asked.

"I don't think so," he laughed. "It's snowing and there's cloud cover."

"Then what are you doing out here?" she asked.

"I thought I might find you here," he said. "I missed you. But I didn't want to interfere with your duties."

"It's going well so far," Dru admitted as she scanned the gathered crowd. "With the weather, I was afraid the whole thing would be a total Charlie Foxtrot."

"A what?" Victor asked.

"Oh, it's just something my grandmother used to say," Dru explained. "She was too much of a lady to come right out and call something a *clusterfuck*, but not quite enough of a lady that she didn't want to."

Viktor laughed, and the sound of it tickled her from the inside.

"My grandfather was in the army," she told him. "So he taught her all the codes they used on the radio. Like Alpha, Beta, Charlie for A, B, C. That kind of thing. Charlie Foxtrot was one of her favorites."

Viktor smiled down at her, and she couldn't help but smile back. He looked around, then took her hand.

"Drucilla," he said, sounding surprised. "Your hands are freezing."

"Oh, I just forgot my gloves," she said. "I'll be fine."

"Where are these gloves?" he asked.

"On my dresser," she told him. "Really, I don't need them. I'm sure we'll be done out here soon."

"I'll be right back," he said with a wink.

She watched as he disappeared toward the solarium, door, presumably to go upstairs and retrieve her gloves.

The mayor was standing in the pavilion, posing for the photographer, who could not possibly hope to be getting footage of the comet since there was a roof over the pavilion.

The mayor was smiling, her cheeks pink, and the photographer's laughter was bright, like a chiming bell.

They seemed to be enjoying themselves.

Jeffrey and Jenna Wilder were nowhere to be found, but Angie was leaned on a tree trunk with her headphones in, looking annoyed.

Dru figured the girl's parents were taking advantage of a few minutes when Angie would be out of the room comet-watching. Based on Angie's bored expression, she guessed they had less time than they thought.

Hugh Channing rounded the front of the hotel deep in conversation with Tyler Park, who looked like he wished he could escape.

Dru headed their way with the binoculars.

"And so, dear boy," Channing was saying, "a career in theatre might be a valid option for a person with your bone structure. And there will be no shortage of women waiting at the stage door each evening, I assure you."

Dru tried to hide her smile at the image of the women at the stage door waiting for Tyler. The Three Blind Mice had a decidedly older client base.

"Hello, my dear," Channing said, spotting her. "I was just encouraging my young friend to audition for our upcoming production of *The King and I.*"

"Oh, are you a singer, Tyler?" Dru asked politely.

"Nah," he said, shaking his head.

"Anyone can sing," Channing pointed out. "But we have a serious shortage of Asian actors at The Three Blind Mice."

Tyler blinked at him.

"Oh dear, is that racist?" Channing asked. "You know it's so hard to tell anymore," he went on, without waiting for an answer. "I just thought if I wanted a more diverse group of actors the way to do it was to put on a production they might be interested in auditioning for."

Dru bit her lip. He kind of had the right idea. Except that

no one had been *interested* in auditioning for *The King and I* since like 1950.

"That's cool, man," Tyler allowed. "But I really don't like being in front of people. Thanks, anyway."

Tyler strode out onto the meadow, leaving Dru to pick up the pieces.

"And another one bites the dust," Channing said cheerfully. "I won't get anywhere if I don't ask, right?"

"I guess not," Dru acknowledged.

"What about that delightful girl at reception?" Channing asked.

"You mean Hailey?" Dru asked. She was pretty sure Hailey would be very disappointed to be called a *delightful girl*. She made such an effort to look sexy with just a touch of scariness.

"Yes, that's the one," Channing said. "Do you think she would be interested in performing? I think a young, diverse ambassador could bring new vitality to the theatre."

So he was hoping Hailey would get butts in seats because she was hot.

He was probably not wrong.

And Dru actually suspected Hailey would love to perform.

"You should talk to her," Dru said. "I'll bet she would hear you out at least."

Channing took the last pair of binoculars from her box and lifted them to her in a sort of salute before heading out across the meadow, ostensibly in search of Hailey, whom Dru had last seen listening to Howie pontificate about the difference between comets, asteroids, and meteors.

Dru made her way to the front porch to drop off the box. She would finally be able to put her hands in her pockets.

"Hey, do you have any more binoculars?" a deep voice asked.

She nearly jumped out of her shoes.

She noticed a glowing red dot in the darkness in front of the hotel and then realized it was the end of a cigarette.

"Mr. Smith?" she asked.

"Yup," he replied. "I thought I'd come back here for a smoke break. Doesn't seem like a smoker-friendly crowd out there."

He was right about that.

"Sorry, I don't have any more binoculars," Dru told him. "But I'll bet one of the others will share."

The front door of the hotel burst open and Oscar Hawkins dashed out, looking alarmed.

"Hey, Mr. Hawkins, everything okay?" Dru asked.

He spotted her and his face went slack.

"Don't worry, you didn't miss it," she told him. "I'm out of binoculars but maybe someone will loan you a pair."

"Oh, I've got my equipment," he said, patting his bag. "I took a nap, and my alarm didn't go off."

"Lucky you woke up," Dru told him.

Oscar nodded and headed for the others.

Dru gave Johnny Smith a little wave and followed Oscar back out to the moonlit meadow.

She looked up at the sky. To save her life, she could not see any evidence that a comet was overhead.

The clouds were getting thicker, and snowflakes were beginning to drift down again.

"There you are," Viktor said, joining her.

He held out her gloves, and she took them with relief.

"Thank you so much," she said.

"My pleasure."

She couldn't help but notice that he wasn't wearing

gloves himself, and the jacket he had on wasn't even fastened.

The snow was really coming down now. So much for stargazing. Most of the guests began to head back in.

"Maybe we'll be able to see it better next time it comes around," Hazel pointed out cheerfully to Zander as they passed.

"Sure, Miss Van Buren," Zander said politely.

Dru was fairly certain that Hazel and Honey Van Buren would not be around in fifty-seven years to see that comet again. But she smiled at Zander and he winked at her on his way past.

"Who was that?" Viktor asked tersely.

"Oh, that's just the Van Buren sisters," she explained. "They basically live at the hotel. But they're early risers."

"No," he said. "The boy."

"Oh, uh, that's Zander," she said. "He works first shift at the front desk. We went to high school together."

She left out the part where Zander had asked her out, and where she had crushed on him for years. No need to complicate things.

"I don't think I like the way he looks at you," Viktor said, his eyes narrowed to indigo slits.

"Oh, we're friends," Dru said. "He's really nice."

Viktor pressed his lips together.

"I should get back in," she said. "I'm officially on duty."

"It's going to be crowded in there," he said.

"Yeah," she agreed. "Not usually a lot of excitement around here. This is a real party by our standards."

They headed around the north wing again.

The snow was falling harder now and faster, driving in with the wind. The side of the hotel had sheltered them while they were chatting, but this was blizzard-like.

"Oh wow," Dru said, but her voice was drowned out and whipped away by a wall of falling, blowing snow.

They reached the front porch just behind the others. Someone opened the door and golden light poured out as the first few guests went in.

A terrified scream rang out, loud enough to pierce the snowy air and chill Dru more than the cold could ever manage.

21

D ru's heart pounded and she pushed through the
crowd. Something bad had happened, on her
watch.

She was sure she had extinguished all the candles in the
dining room before heading out to join everyone. What else
was there to go wrong?

Viktor's hand was at the small of her back and he moved
with her, the crowd parting slightly for them, as if their
hurried pace gave them some kind of authority.

There were whispers and gasps from the guests gathered
around the lobby rug.

Dru finally made it through the crowd.

It took her a few seconds to process what she was seeing.

Brian Thompson's massive, lifeless body lay prone at the
center of the carpet.

She turned away, but not before she noticed the gash
across his throat, and the lights from the chandelier twinkling like stars in the pool of dark blood that surrounded
him.

Viktor's hand fell away from her waist. His face went slack with shock.

"Please let me through," Tyler Park called out. "I'm an EMT."

The crowd parted again, and Tyler moved to squat beside Thompson's head.

Dru couldn't bring herself to look, but she assumed he was checking his pulse. Seemed kind of late for that to her, but it was good there was someone here who had the wherewithal to do it.

"It's too late," Tyler said quietly.

A sound like a gunshot rang out, followed by a loud, metallic thunk.

She had barely registered the sounds, when the lights went out.

Dru swallowed a scream, but many others didn't.

One by one, small halos of light appeared as the guests pulled out their cell phones.

"Holy crap, it wasn't a gunshot," Hailey said from the darkness near the front window, obviously thinking the same thing Dru had. "It was the old hemlock."

All that heavy ice must have finally done it in.

Dru heard the front doors open, and everyone crowded out onto the porch.

The snow was blowing so hard now the air was just a sheet of white.

She could just make out the huge tree down across the drive. It had always seemed like a big tree, but she hadn't appreciated *how* big until she saw it lying across the driveway. Its length stretched from the center of the front lawn all the way past the south wing of the hotel and out of sight beyond. Even prone, it was nearly as tall as the hotel itself, though half its circumference was flattened by its own weight.

"It must have taken out the lines," Howie said. "We need the generator on. Where's Chester?"

"Does anyone have cell service?" Tyler yelled out from his position near the body. "We need to call the police."

Dru took out her phone, her hand shaking.

But she had no service.

The storm must have taken the cell tower out as well.

She turned to Viktor, craving the comfort of his arms.

But he was pale and trembling, his eyes gazing at something far away, as if he had seen a ghost.

Everything is fine, Dru told herself.

But it was a tough line to swallow.

They had just lost power and all communication with the outside world. And someone at the hotel had been murdered, by someone else who was trapped up here with them.

She was never going to get any writing done now.

***

EPISODE 2

D ru gazed around the lobby, taking in all the anxious faces.

They were snowed in at Hemlock House, with no way for anyone to come or go.

The power and phone lines were out, the cell tower was down, they were trapped with a group of strangers...

And one of them was a murderer.

The Van Buren sisters hid their faces in Zander's chest. Poor Hazel and Honey were too old and too sweet to find themselves in this mess.

Zander patted their backs awkwardly, the tension in his jaw giving away his own fears.

Melody Young, the photographer, was similarly patting Mayor Emily Tuck's back. The mayor herself reminded Dru of a fuller-figured Jackie O, with her startled eyes and Chanel knock-off suit.

Only Oscar Hawkins observed the scene with the same dispassionate expression he always wore. But that wasn't necessarily suspicious. Birdwatching required extreme patience and a placid nature, and birdwatching was why Oscar had come.

Johnny Smith stood in the corner, stabbing angrily at his phone with his index finger, as if threatening it would bring the cell tower back online. The huge, bald man in the tailored suit looked more frustrated than scared, but in Dru's experience men like that didn't like to show their fear. The fury could just be a cover for his real feelings.

Hugh Channing paced back and forth. As an actor and director, he was probably used to chaos, but this was extreme.

Tyler Park still knelt beside the body, looking lost. His EMT skills were of no use to the dead man, but he couldn't seem to walk away from his patient.

Behind the front desk, Hailey was trying the landline and the computer, but Dru didn't even have to ask how it was going. The dismayed look on Hailey's face was clear - all lines of communication with the outside world were down. They were on their own.

A clattering on the stairs drew everyone's attention.

Hazel Van Buren yelped out in fear and Honey yelped in reaction to that.

Cell phone flashlights strobed onto the stairs to reveal Jeffrey and Jenna Wilder, their clothing pulled on haphazardly, hair mussed as if they had been about to share some private time before chaos descended on Hemlock House.

"What's going on?" Jenna asked. "Is the power out?"

"Mom, God," Angie yelled out from the lobby below. "Button your blouse. This is a freaking crime scene."

"This is a what?" Jeffrey yelled.

"Okay, let's remain calm, everyone," Howie yelled out. "I need to go find Chester to turn on the generator. Who's coming with me?"

No one volunteered.

It suddenly occurred to Dru that until they figured this out, it wasn't really safe for anyone to be alone with anyone else.

She glanced over at Viktor.

He was standing in the far corner of the lobby, eyes still locked on the swirling snow outside, like the body on the floor was the last thing on his mind.

So much for wanting to be with her always.

"Come on, Zander," Howie yelled to Dru's co-worker, clearly too scared to walk back to the groundskeeper's cottage alone.

Zander let go of the Van Buren sisters, who looked like a pair of frightened sheep without him.

"Tyler, could you help Hazel and Honey to their rooms," Dru whispered to the handsome EMT.

"What?" he said, looking up as if he didn't recognize her. "Oh. Oh, sure, yeah."

He looked almost relieved to have something productive to do.

To their credit, Hazel and Honey went with him passively, trading one good-looking young male protector for another was apparently all in a day's work for the charming octogenarian pair.

When Dru turned back to the lobby, the door was just closing behind Zander and Howie and a hush had fallen over the room.

"A crime scene," Hugh Channing said suddenly, his voice ringing out with authority and a slight Southern accent Dru hadn't noticed before. "The child is right. That's just what this is."

In the pale blue glow of her phone, Angie rolled her eyes at being called a child.

"Our first step is to alert the local authorities," Channing informed them.

"No dice," Hailey piped up. "It's all down."

Channing considered for a moment, then continued.

"In the absence of the authorities, the responsibility falls to us," Channing explained. "We will investigate, but we must observe proper protocol at all times."

Channing strode over to the body.

"Our first job is to scan the scene for danger," he said. "A man has died. Do not move, but look around you. Does anyone see a weapon or anything else that could cause harm?"

The beams of cell phone flashlights leapt into motion.

After a few minutes it appeared that no one had found anything dangerous on the scene.

"Excellent," Channing said, clearly gaining confidence. "Next, I will need to record the name of the medical professional who examined the victim. Where is he?"

But Tyler had gone upstairs with the Van Buren sisters.

"I'll get his info for you from the log," Dru offered, relieved that someone was taking charge, even if she wasn't entirely sure he knew what he was doing.

"Very good," Channing said. "While you take that down, we'll move on to the next step - apprehending the suspect. Who did this? Was anyone present at the time of the crime?"

Dru heard the whispering as she pulled the paper log from the drawer, grateful for once that Howie made them keep an old-fashioned written record.

"No one stepping forward. Unsurprising," Channing said. "And no witnesses either? Well. We'll get to the bottom of it. Don't you worry. The next step is to secure the scene. No one move from where they are right now. We'll need photographs of everything just as it is. If you see anything out of place near you, call out to me and I'll come photograph it."

Dru slipped back out from behind the desk with a note pad and pencil. She had already taken down all of Tyler Park's info and marked it *Medical Professional (EMT)*.

"Take note of the weather," Channing advised her. "You can put it on the same note pad."

He was photographing the body. Each flash of his camera phone illuminated the grisly image of Brian Thompson's lifeless body, surrounded by a pool of blood.

Dru was grateful to have a reason to turn away and make notes about the snow storm.

The dead man had made unwanted advances on Dru when she was alone in the hotel corridor at night. He was a total creep. But no one deserved to die like that.

"Look at this," Angie called, shining the light from her phone onto the spatter of blood near the head of the body.

"Interesting," Channing agreed. "There is a small break in the pattern. That means that there was someone standing right here when the body fell. And that person is likely to have some of the victim's blood on his shoes."

"Or hers," Hailey added from behind the desk.

"Naturally," Channing added. "Now, if everyone would be so kind as to shine your phone lights on your shoes, we can have a quick look right now."

There were some glances exchanged, but for the most part, all of the phone lights swung down to highlight the eclectic collection of footwear present. Channing moved from one person to the next, taking enough foot pics to start a fetish site, but not finding any trace of the expected blood. Even Viktor moved from his spot at the window to offer his leather boots for inspection.

But Channing stopped short when he got to Johnny

Smith, who still stood off to the side, poking at his phone screen, but making no move to light his own shoes.

"If you would be so kind, Mr. ...?" Channing said.

"Smith," the man said flatly, meeting Channing's gaze, but making no move to comply.

There was a moment when Dru wondered what they would do if people just stopped cooperating. It wasn't like they had any real authority.

But then Johnny activated the light on his phone and aimed it at the ground near his feet. Channing snapped a pic, but the man's expensive Italian loafers were spotless.

There was an almost audible sigh of relief from the gathered crowd.

"Now then, do we have any witnesses to suspicious behavior of any kind?" Channing called out. "Did anyone see Mr. Thompson with someone in the last hour or so? If you saw something, by all means say something."

Dru made a mental note to mention last night's argument to Channing when things calmed down. It might be important, but it was embarrassing to yell about what you had seen in front of everyone. And after all, it had happened last night, and she hadn't seen the person he was arguing with.

And then there was the matter of her own encounter with the victim shortly after that. And Viktor's reaction when he'd come onto the scene. He hadn't exactly been pleased.

Dru pushed the thoughts aside for now. It wasn't like either of them was the murderer, so there was no point overthinking it.

"I will remain in charge of this case until the proper authorities can be notified and arrive on the scene," Channing went on, his Southern accent growing more pronounced. "If you find evidence, or remember something, do not talk with other potential witnesses or suspects. Come straight to me."

He walked over to Dru. He was clearly playing a part at this point, but it was working so far, so she didn't see any reason not to play along.

"At this point, we would normally identify a recording officer," he told her quietly. "But I think I've already found one."

He gave her notepad a significant glance.

"Will you lend us your efforts toward solving this heinous crime?" he asked.

"Uh, sure," she said, glancing over at Viktor, who had gone back to staring out the window.

She wished he were by her side right now. But he seemed to be staying as far away from the crime scene as possible. She supposed that was natural. She wasn't exactly enjoying it herself.

"You can go back to your rooms," Channing called out to the others. "But stick together in groups. Until we find out what happened, we have to take the attitude that every one of us could be in danger."

There were whispers of surprise and horror.

"What makes you an expert?" Jenna Wilder called out. She seemed more upset by the fact that her private time had been interrupted than she was by the body at her feet. "Aren't you that dinner theatre guy with the cart ad at the ShopRite?"

Behind her, Angie rolled her eyes so hard that Dru was worried she might injure herself.

Hugh Channing drew himself up to his full height, which was probably about five-foot-four.

"Yes, I am that dinner theatre guy," he said with great

dignity." But for my role in *The Perfect Crime*, I did a ride-along with the Willow Ridge Police Department. I am the only one here with first-hand experience in securing a crime scene."

"What, like a cat up a tree?" Jenna asked with a sneer.

"No, madam," he replied. "A serious crime that I do not wish to discuss. Now if you'll excuse me, I need to confer with my recording officer."

He turned on his heel and headed back toward the sitting room, and Dru was left with no choice but to follow him.

It was going to be a long night.

Dru trailed Channing into the sitting room.

He stood before the fireplace, which was mercifully still crackling, providing enough light for her to see his silhouette, and taking some of the chill out of the air.

"This is a nasty business," Channing said, pacing in front of the fire.

He sounded so much like one of the black and white Agatha Christie movies Dru used to watch with her Nana, that she had to stifle an inappropriate smile.

But she had things to tell him.

He might not be a real detective, but he seemed to know what he was doing, at least enough to tell the real police when they arrived.

"Listen, Mr. Channing," she said.

"Call me Hugh," he said, turning to her.

"Hugh," she said.

But she couldn't seem to formulate what needed to be said. Was she about to incriminate herself?

"Dru," he said quietly, "as the front desk clerk, I'm sure

you see a great many things. Anything, no matter how small might help us solve this case. There is nothing you can tell me that I won't be grateful for. Your forthright nature is why I chose you to be my recording officer."

Dru strongly suspected that he had chosen her because she had a notepad and a tendency to scurry when someone yelled for help. But she had to come clean, so now was the time.

"There are two things you should know," she told him.

"Then give me the pad for now," he told her. "You talk, and I'll make notes."

She felt a brief sense of relief that he would be looking down at the pad and not at her when she spoke.

"When I was on last night's shift, I heard the, uh, victim arguing with someone," she said.

"Who was it?" he asked.

"I have no idea," she admitted.

"What exactly did you hear?" Channing asked, looking up from his pad.

"I was at the desk and I heard two men arguing in the solarium," she said.

"Ah, so it was a man," Channing said, marking it down. "Very good. What else?"

"Someone shouted *Sullivan* more than once," she said.

"Is there a Sullivan staying at Hemlock House?" Channing asked.

"No," she told him. "I went through the whole log."

"Very good," Channing said approvingly. "Then what happened?"

"Brian came rushing out of the solarium," she told him. "He practically knocked me into the dining room table."

"I thought you said you were at your desk," Channing said.

"I was curious," she admitted, feeling her cheeks burn. "And the argument sounded violent enough I was also worried it might end in a fist fight. I thought I should check it out."

"Very wise," Channing said. "And your natural curiosity has given us clues we wouldn't have had otherwise. What else?"

"I went to the solarium, but no one was there, then I checked the sitting room," Dru said, then paused, uncertain how she could share the next part without getting herself into trouble.

It wasn't fair.

"Go on," Channing said. "Was someone there?"

"No," she said. "I headed back into the corridor to check out the kitchen and then Brian came back."

"Did he have anything with him?" Channing asked.

Dru was taken aback by the question.

"No," she said. "At least he didn't have anything in his hands."

"Think back," Channing encouraged her. "Try to picture his hands."

"Oh, I can picture them just fine," Dru said. "He, uh, he touched me."

She could see Channing lowering the notepad in the semi-darkness.

"Please explain exactly what you mean," he said softly. "You can take as much time as you need."

Dru took a deep breath.

"He came right up to me and put his hand behind me on the wall," she said. "He said he thought I must get lonely up on the mountain at night."

She closed her eyes, smelling his rancid breath again.

"I told him I had to go, but he grabbed my shoulder and then my jaw," she said.

In the darkness, Channing nodded sympathetically.

She was grateful to him for remaining quiet.

"I kneed him in the, uh, privates," she said. "I don't know if the police will find any bruising."

"Good for you, dear," Channing whispered.

"And then Viktor Striker came downstairs and told him if he caught him making unwanted advances again, he would report him to the police," Dru said.

"It was very brave of you to tell me this," Channing told her softly. "What he did to you must have made you feel powerless and angry."

"Yes," she said. "But I didn't kill him, if that's what you mean."

"It's not what I meant, but thank you for clarifying," Channing said. "What about this Viktor Striker. Would he be willing to kill to protect your honor?"

"I don't think so," Dru said. "He's very mild mannered."

"Plenty of criminals are," Channing observed thoughtfully.

"Nonetheless," Dru said. "I really don't think he had anything to do with it. And he was with me outside."

Except for the time he was inside, getting my gloves.

Dru decided to leave that part out.

Channing shrugged. "We'll get to the bottom of it somehow."

And though he was a little bit ridiculous, and a lot over the top, Dru suddenly thought that Hugh Channing really might figure this thing out.

"I'm glad you're here," she told him.

"We'd better get back out there, before they all panic," he suggested.

She nodded, and they headed back into the corridor.

"Oh," Hugh said in surprise.

Viktor stood, half-shrouded in shadow, just outside the sitting room door.

"Drucilla, you shouldn't be alone with anyone right now," Viktor hissed. "Not even this guy."

"A fair point, my friend," Hugh said, clapping Viktor on the shoulder.

Viktor winced and didn't respond.

Dru wondered how long he had been in the corridor.

But there was no time to waste on the question. Hugh Channing was sweeping back into the lobby with the two of them trailing in his wake.

D ru turned to Viktor when they reached the lobby again.

"Why were you lurking in the hall?" she whispered.

"You shouldn't be alone with anyone right now," he whispered back. "For all I knew, that little creep pulled you aside to murder you."

His eyes were flashing and his jaw was tight with tension. She had never seen him like this. He hadn't been this intense when he'd confronted Brian Thompson. Something had him on edge.

But she supposed a dead body was enough to put anyone off their game.

"Well, he wasn't," Dru said. "Channing seems like he's really making every effort to help."

Viktor shrugged.

"Are you... jealous?" she asked.

"Of course not," he retorted, loudly enough that Angie Wilder turned to smirk at them. "We shouldn't be whispering. It looks suspicious."

"Literally everyone else is whispering," Dru said, gesturing around the room.

"We need to think about what to do with the body," Tyler Park said as he came back down the stairs from depositing Hazel and Honey in their room.

"We mustn't disturb the crime scene," Channing said.

"Did you see the tree that's down over the driveway?" Tyler asked. "Do you know how long it's going to take for the authorities to get out here? They don't even know we need them yet."

"Volumes of evidence are contained in that corpse," Channing said.

Jenna Wilder let out a small gasp, presumably at the word *corpse*.

Jeffrey pulled her to his chest.

"Do you know what else is contained in that corpse?" Tyler asked. "Bacteria, bile, blood, and fecal matter, just to name a few things. As we speak, his body is cooling and stiffening, which will make it harder to work with each minute that passes. By morning, his skin will be marbleizing from the gases trying to escape. Blow flies will be using his body as a breeding ground, filling him with their maggots. And he will begin to stink. Soon, bloating from putrefaction will have his eyes and tongue protruding out of his face. Do you think he'll be more fun to move then?"

More than one of the gathered crowd looked a little ill at Tyler's words. Dru was glad to know it wasn't just her.

"Dear God man, there are ladies present," Channing cried.

Dru couldn't tell if Channing really thought that the women in the group had more delicate sensibilities, or if that's just what he felt the vaguely-southern gentleman detective he seemed to be inhabiting would say. She had to admit, his dedication to the craft was impressive. She might just have to go see one of his plays when this was all over.

"I think we should move him now," Oscar said lightly, raising his hand as if he were casting a vote about whether or not to have a picnic on the lawn.

More hands went up.

"Okay, okay," Channing said, throwing his own hands up. "Who would like to help."

All the hands went down.

"That seems about right," Tyler said, rolling his eyes.

"Gentlemen, step forward," Channing said. "This falls to us."

"Sexist," Melody said, handing Mayor Tuck her camera and stepping forward.

"Thank you, dear lady," Channing said to her.

"Don't mention it," Melody replied, rolling her eyes.

Angie Wilder snickered.

Jeffrey Wilder stepped forward too, giving his daughter a look that she studiously ignored.

Dru looked to Viktor.

He was pale and tense, but when he sensed her eyes on him, he stepped forward as well.

"Whatever," Johnny Smith said, and joined the others.

"I'll man the desk," Hailey offered. "In case anything comes back online."

"That should be sufficient," Channing said. "Dru, I'm sorry to ask it, but would you come and record the moving of the body for us."

"Record it?" she asked.

"Make note of anything you observe," he told her.

She took a deep breath and headed over.

"We'll want to roll him up in the rug," Tyler suggested. "That will be the easiest way."

"Won't it be much heavier that way?" Jeffrey Wilder asked.

"At least it'll keep all his guts in," Johnny said. "Probably."

"Would his guts have fallen out?" Jeffrey asked, looking a little green around the gills.

"I think what he means is that the blood and other loose body matter will stay with the corpse if we wrap the body in the rug," Tyler said.

"Yeah, sure," Johnny said. "It'll be like a burrito."

"Can we just do this?" Jeffrey asked.

"Of course," Channing said.

But of course they couldn't, because they had to figure out how to roll up the rug first.

Brian Thompson, obnoxious even in death, had fallen at an angle, which meant they would have to adjust him before rolling him up.

Tyler gamely took his head and shoulders and Jeffrey took his feet.

As Tyler lifted, the head fell backward, revealing the scarlet gash at the neck.

"Hey," Dru said. "Look at his neck."

"I'd really rather not," Jeffrey said in a pinched voice.

"No, not the wound," Dru said.

"What is it, child?" Channing asked her.

"His cross necklace," Dru told him. "It's missing."

"It probably came off when the attacker slashed his neck," Tyler pointed out reasonably.

"Then it should be here somewhere," Channing said. "Place him down again and let's find it."

The others begrudgingly obeyed.

Dru turned her back as Tyler and Channing shifted the body around looking.

"Roll him over," Channing called out.

Dru shivered.

"Nothing," Tyler said.

"We'll search his room for it," Channing suggested.

"He was wearing it every time I saw him," Dru said.

"Then this may be a clue," Channing said. "Well done."

Dru nodded, hating the feeling of so many eyes on her.

If it was a clue, then the murderer definitely knew it was her fault that it had been brought to light.

"I'll go on ahead and open up the catacombs," she said absently.

"You'll do what?" Channing asked.

"The basement tunnels, I mean," Dru said. "It's cold enough down there to preserve him somewhat. We can't put him outside, or the animals will get to him. And it will be easiest to get him down there if we go out the back way."

With a swirl of snow and a gust of wind, the front door opened and Howie entered, with Zander and Chester in tow.

"What's going on here?" Howie asked.

"We're moving the body to the basement," Channing said, as if it had been his idea all along. "It can't be allowed to decompose in here."

"That rug is an antique," Howie retorted.

"Perhaps you'd like to have a look at it?" Channing offered.

Howie stepped closer, took one look, and backed away quickly, waving his hands. "Go ahead, do what you have to do."

"I'll help," Zander offered.

Viktor stepped back immediately. "I'll accompany Miss Holloway to the basement to open up."

"Fine, fine," Channing said.

"I would help," Howie informed them. "But I need to... put Mr. Moosehead back up on the wall before someone trips on him."

He was obviously reaching with that excuse. The giant moose head had been down since before Dru started her shift. She assumed Gert must have taken him down to give him a cleaning.

But it didn't matter. Howie would only be in the way anyway. And someone should stay behind to watch over the other guests.

Dru grabbed her coat and headed out to the dining room and into the solarium with Viktor trailing behind her.

She had a weird feeling she couldn't place, the hair on the back of her neck was standing up.

You're in the middle of a murder scene. You were just privy to a very detailed description of decomposition. It makes sense that your Spidey-senses are tingling, she told herself.

But there was something else tickling her mind too.

"Slow down," Viktor said. "It's going to take them a few minutes to catch up. They haven't secured the body yet."

"Sorry," she said.

"You're understandably upset," he said gently. "This is frightening for everyone."

"You don't seem frightened?" she observed.

"I am, though," he told her. "I'm just better at hiding it. But I can't stand the thought of you being in danger. Please don't go anywhere without me, Drucilla."

"Aren't you even a little bit scared for yourself," she asked.

He smiled a bitter smile. "Let me focus on worrying about you."

She opened the door leading out of the solarium. A blast

of icy wind lifted her hair. The storm seemed to be intensifying. The world outside was just a blank sheet of white.

She ducked her head and headed out into the weather.

Viktor took her arm, and together they battled the driving wind and snow to get to the basement entrance. She slid the skeleton key out and opened the door.

For once, she was relieved to step down into the stony tunnels below.

Once she was out of the snow, she took a deep breath of slightly less cold, musty air.

"You're freezing," Viktor said, pulling her into his arms.

He felt so good, his arms strong and secure around her. She closed her eyes and basked in his presence.

"Oh, Drucilla," Viktor murmured, nuzzling her hair.

She felt her heart rate slowing and her body coming back to itself, comforted.

But there was a commotion at the threshold. The others must have managed to roll up the body faster than expected.

"Dru," Channing shouted.

"Right down here," she called back, heading toward the steps to guide them in.

Behind her, Viktor sighed.

Dru wrapped her coat around herself and followed the others up the stairs and back out into the storm.

It had been a little gut-wrenching to leave a person's body alone in the dark tunnels, wrapped haphazardly in an old rug.

But what choice did they have?

She tried not to think about the rats she sometimes saw in the tunnels. At least the body wouldn't be mauled by bigger animals.

Viktor wrapped an arm around her as they walked, but when they reached the solarium door again, he had to let go so she could walk inside.

She slowed her pace and let the others go back into the lobby ahead of them, not anxious to be surrounded by the stressed-out crowd again. But after a lap around the solarium, she realized she was going to need a little more time.

"I think I need to go upstairs and catch my breath for a minute," she told Viktor.

"Of course," he told her. "I'll come with you."

She went back to the front desk, but Hailey was nowhere in sight, so she grabbed the *Bee Right Back* sign. The guests could do without her for a little while.

"I'll take over for a bit," Zander said, moving to join them.

"You don't have to do that," Dru said.

"What else do I have to do?" he asked. "I can't get back home. I already told Hailey to go get some rest."

"Thank you," she told him sincerely. "You can use my room to shower and sleep and stuff until they open the road back up."

"Thanks, Dru," he said with a smile that looked tired, but genuine.

"Come, Drucilla," Viktor said impatiently.

She turned to him, noticing once again how brutally handsome he was. His dark hair was tousled from the wind outside, and his icy blue eyes seemed to cut through her like diamonds.

She headed for the stairs without a word, Viktor shadowing her.

The wide wood planks of the lobby floor looked pale and naked without the rug that had covered them for over a hundred years.

There would be no way to be in the lobby without remembering what had happened.

She headed down the darkened corridor, using her phone for light. It occurred to her to worry about what would happen when the battery died.

"Weren't they supposed to turn on the generator?" she remembered.

"I thought so," Viktor agreed.

They walked on in silence.

At last, Dru reached the door to her room.

"Listen, Viktor, I kind of want a moment to myself," she told him.

He looked uncomfortable, but nodded. "I'll be right here," he told her. "You don't have to worry."

"Thanks," she said, unlocking her door and slipping inside.

She tried to lock the door silently, but of course it made a crisp click when she turned it.

He had definitely heard that. She hoped it hadn't hurt his feelings.

She paced the floor, allowing all that had happened to wash over her.

There had been a murder, an actual murder, with blood and slashing and a dead victim wrapped in the lobby carpet. It made the horror story she'd been trying to dream up for her book seem a little silly.

And while Channing had them all busy collecting evidence and dealing with the body, no one was talking about the most urgent issue.

There was a murderer at Hemlock House.

The killer was guaranteed to still be among them, because there was literally nowhere else to go. No one could get in, or out.

And Dru was going to be a sitting duck down at the desk all night long.

She would be alone, in plain view of the landing and stairs above her, the lobby in front of her, the dining room and the corridor behind her, and the vending machine alcove to her right.

And she would be not ten feet from where the body had been discovered.

Meanwhile, she had no weapon to defend herself with, and no clue who the murderer was.

It could be the nice photographer lady. It could be the family man with the wife and kid.

It could be the weird guy who reserved three rooms, but didn't seem to sleep in any of them.

No, she thought to herself. *It can't be Viktor.*

But suddenly her mind was picking at the loose threads.

Viktor was so pale. She only saw him at night.

He's got international business to attend to.

He had strange, heavy trunks that traveled ahead of him.

He deals in antiques.

He had covered his mirrors and windows.

I would do the same if I had trouble sleeping during the day.

But other thoughts were suddenly crowding her mind.

She had thought there was something funny when she was out walking with him that first night.

She closed her eyes and pictured it - the snowflakes falling, her breath pluming in the air.

In her mind, she looked over at Viktor. His breath didn't plume.

She shivered and paced some more, thinking back to the time they had spent together.

She pictured herself eating dinner in the solarium and Viktor telling her he had just eaten. She had never seen him eat or drink anything.

But that didn't make him a murderer.

She thought of his reaction to the murder itself.

He was so shocked, so upset by it...

She could still see him, gazing out the window into the snow, looking despondent and horrified.

Had he been faking a reaction? And maybe playing it up a little, for the sake of the witnesses? Or had he just been overwhelmed in the presence of so much blood.

He had never told Dru anything about himself. He always turned the conversation to her.

What was he hiding?

She'd read enough horror novels to see how the pieces of this puzzle fit together.

No breath, no food, weird reaction to blood...

Take it easy, Dru, she told herself. *You can't really think that your boyfriend is a vampire. The throat was slashed, not bitten. The body wasn't drained. There was blood everywhere.*

But of course the slash could have been deliberately placed to hide two puncture wounds. Plenty of blood could have been missing before the fatal wound was administered.

And then there was the missing cross...

Weren't vampires afraid of crucifixes?

It hit her that there was a vampire book on one of the shelves by the window seat.

She scrambled across the room for it, slamming her shin into the side of the desk on the way.

"Ow," she moaned to herself.

"Drucilla?" Viktor called to her from the hallway. "Are you okay?"

"I-I'm fine," she stammered. "I just need another minute."

He knocked on the door.

She made it to the bookshelves and ran her fingers along the dusty spines.

Viktor was banging on the door now.

"Drucilla, I'm worried about you," he called to her. "Please let me in."

"I'm f-fine," she called back, scanning desperately for the book she wanted.

Finally she saw the thin scarlet volume, grabbed it, and shoved the *Encyclopedia Vampirica* into her bag.

She jogged over to the door, suddenly panicked about what to do next.

She didn't want to be alone with Viktor now that she suspected his secret.

But she couldn't exactly accuse him without endangering herself, or at the very least embarrassing herself.

She unlocked the door and opened it slowly.

"Thank God," he said with seemingly heartfelt relief. "What was that noise?"

"I bumped into the bed," she said, shrugging.

He smiled and his blue eyes crinkled. "I was picturing the worst, of course. Someone waiting to ambush you in your room, grabbing you, forcing you at knife-point to tell me that everything was okay."

"You watch too many movies," she teased, impressing herself with her ability to play it cool.

"Guess so," he said.

She still couldn't bring herself to go out into the corridor with him alone. She was just beginning to feel panicky again when she saw Mayor Tuck heading down the hallway with Melody the photographer.

"Mayor Tuck," Dru called out in a bright voice. "I wanted to ask you about that... thing at the last council meeting."

"The Aging-In-Place for Senior Citizens task force?" Mayor Tuck asked with a dubious expression.

"Yes," Dru said emphatically. "That's definitely the thing I wanted to ask about."

"I'm so glad you've taken an interest," the mayor said with a big smile. "Now isn't a great time to get into a big policy discussion, but if you want to give me your basic thoughts, I'll make a note of it. Though the best way to share your ideas is at a council meeting."

"Really?" Dru asked, slipping past a very confused looking Viktor to join the mayor in the hallway.

"Oh yes," the mayor told her. "That's how I got my start in politics, you know. I attended a couple of council meetings and fell in love with the process. Now, tell me, what are your thoughts on easing zoning restrictions for seniors?"

"I have so many," Dru began as they headed downstairs.

Dru managed to handle the conversation in a way that probably didn't impress the mayor, but hopefully didn't arouse her suspicion either.

"Well, it's an unusual stance, but I'll note it down, Dru," the mayor said when they reached the lobby. "Thanks for your input."

"Dru, there you are," Howie barked out.

"Sorry, Mayor Tuck," she said.

"Nice to speak with you dear," the mayor said, heading over to Melody, who appeared to be waiting for her by the fireplace.

Dru took off her coat and hung it by the front door. A battery powered lantern sat on the front desk, casting a beam of harsh light across the lobby, and darkening the shadows around it.

"Where have you been, Dru?" Howie asked.

"Sorry, Howie," she said. "I just needed a minute. Zander was covering for me."

"Well, I need you to get some food for these people,"

Howie said. "They're freaking out, and none of them will go to bed."

"I'm, uh, not a very good cook," Dru warned him.

"Oh for Pete's sake, I'm not asking you to make them a proper meal," Howie said, exasperated. "Just go to the kitchen and find some snacks you can bring out. Got it?"

"Yeah, sure, Howie," she said.

She headed for the kitchen with Viktor still at her elbow.

They would be alone in there, with all the knives.

"Hey, Zander," she called. "Will you give us a hand?"

"Sure," he said eagerly.

The three of them stepped into the darkened corridor that led to the kitchen and sitting room.

Dru held her phone out in front of her, wondering once again how long the battery would last, and what she was supposed to do when it died.

"Hey, didn't you and Howie go to find Chester?" she asked. "I thought he was going to turn the generator on."

"Oh, man, yeah," Zander said. "Chester was so pissed."

Dru could picture that.

"Turns out we don't have a lot of fuel around and the generator is *finicky*, according to Chester," Zander explained. "He's *working on her*."

"Holy crap," Dru said.

"So we won't have power again for a while?" Viktor asked.

"And when we do, we'll be using it sparingly," Zander agreed.

Dru placed her phone on the stainless-steel island so that the light made a wide circle on the ceiling and cast the kitchen in dim light.

"What do you think people want to eat right now?" she asked.

"We'd better not open the fridge," Zander said. "Don't want to let any cold out."

"What do you think, Viktor?" Dru asked.

She could see his surprised expression even in the shadows.

"Comfort food," he said after a moment.

"Chips and salsa," Zander agreed. "And cookies."

"The carbs will make them crash," Dru said.

"I think that's what Howie wants," Zander suggested.

Dru shrugged and the three of them gathered up the snacks in silence, placing everything on trays to carry into the dining room.

"Constance is going to flip out when she comes in and sees that we raided the kitchen," Dru said.

"Nah, she's super nice," Zander said.

"Tell you what," Dru said. "Let's tell her you did this by yourself."

"Sure, Dru," Zander said. "But I really don't know what you're worried about."

Dru led the way to the dining room with her phone as Zander and Viktor followed, each carrying a tray of snacks.

Zander put his tray down and stepped into the lobby.

"Snacks in the dining room," he announced and headed back to the big table to grab some sustenance for himself.

There were normally a few candles burning in the dining room for ambiance at dinner. Dru lit them now, hoping there was a good supply somewhere since they were clearly going to be needing them.

"Oh, thank God," Angie Wilder said, sauntering in and grabbing a handful of chips.

Others trailed in after her, digging into the junk food with relish.

Dru grabbed a plate and placed a couple of cookies on it.

Zander already had a mouthful of chips.

But Viktor was standing in the corner, watching her. When he caught her looking, he smiled. She walked over to him, grateful for a change to have so many people in the room.

"Here you go," she said, holding out a chocolate chip cookie.

No one could resist a soft-bake cookie with the chips gleaming in the candlelight.

"No thanks," he told her. "I just ate."

Dru gulped, her throat suddenly dry.

He definitely hadn't just eaten. She had been with him for hours now.

"Dru, what's wrong?" he asked, concern marring his handsome features.

But she heard a sniffling sound coming from the solarium.

"Someone's crying," she realized out loud.

She headed for the solarium door, with Viktor right at her elbow once again.

It was just her luck that she seemed to have ensnared the world's clingiest vampire.

Dru stepped into the solarium.

Even in darkness the air here was redolent of sunshine.

"Hello?" she called out softly.

"Dru?" Hailey's voice called back to her.

She slipped between the plants, back to the little table in the corner where she had studied the journal with Viktor what felt like a thousand years ago.

Hailey was sitting, her body curled in on itself as she tried to stop herself from crying. Apparently, she hadn't gone off to bed at Zander's suggestion after all.

"What happened?" Dru asked, wrapping an arm around her friend and holding her close.

Viktor stayed back a little, to give her some space with her friend.

"There's been a *murder*," Hailey said. "We need the police."

"They can't come," Dru reminded her. "You saw that tree. And it's still storming."

"There's not supposed to be a blizzard," Hailey sniffled.

"There hasn't been a blizzard this early in the season in Willow Ridge for a hundred years."

"It's going to be okay," Dru told her. "The snow will let up, then they'll clear the roads and get the cell tower up again."

"If this were a horror movie, I'd be the next one killed," Hailey said. "First the fat guy, then the hot Black girl."

"No one would dare kill you," Dru told her. "Look at your amazing outfit. You look like an executive monster hunter."

Hailey glanced down at her outfit and couldn't contain a small smile.

"We just have to be patient, that's all," Dru said.

"No," Hailey said. "We don't have to be patient. Our regular cell tower is down, but the one over in Lady of the Lake might not be."

"But we can't get down the mountain right now," Dru reminded her.

"We don't have to get down," Hailey said. "It's on the other side of the mountain, but if we hiked to the top, there would be nothing in the way of the signal from the valley."

"In the middle of a blizzard?" Dru asked.

"Sure," Hailey said. "Unless you'd prefer to stay warm and dry and *murdered.*"

Hailey had a point.

"Let's go," Dru said, making up her mind on the spot.

Hailey was right. It was better to do something, anything, than to just sit around and wait for the next bad thing to happen.

"Really?" Hailey asked.

"Really?" Viktor echoed, moving closer.

"Of course," Dru told them. "But we're sticking together. Agreed?"

"Of course," Hailey nodded.

"I don't know about this," Viktor said, touching Dru's arm.

"Do you have a better plan?" she asked.

"No, but this one seems dangerous," he said quietly.

"Not getting help when you're trapped with a murderer is pretty dangerous," Hailey said.

"Point taken," he replied. "I'm in."

"Dru," someone called from the hall.

They headed toward the door and found Channing poking his head into the solarium.

"There you are," he said. "I need my recording officer."

"I have another idea," Dru said. "Well, *we* have another idea."

"Go on," Channing said.

"Hailey and Viktor and I are going to hike up to the peak," Dru said. "We want to see if we can get a signal from the tower down in Lady of the Lake, on the other side of the mountain."

"That's not a bad plan," Channing said after a moment of consideration. "No splitting up though."

"No splitting up," Viktor agreed. "And if we're not back in four hours, send help."

"Agreed," Channing said. "God speed."

"I've got to get my coat," Hailey said. "I'll grab yours too, Dru."

"Uh, me too," Viktor chimed in.

"Perfect," Channing said. "I'd like to chat with Dru for a few minutes, anyway."

"Do it in the dining room," Viktor said pointedly.

Dru headed out in Hailey's wake before Channing could protest.

Did Viktor really think Channing was a danger?

It could be an elaborate cover for his own guilt.

"Are you really comfortable with this plan, dear girl?" Channing asked her gently. "I'm happy to pull you off the mission for necessary work here."

"I'm fine," Dru said, wondering if she was telling the truth. "I'm an experienced hiker, and it's really not that far."

"Good, good," he said. "When you return, we'll search the victim's room."

"You can do it now," she suggested.

"No, ma'am I cannot," he retorted. "Not without my recording officer. Anyone could be the guilty party. We want a proper record of everything that happens here, with more than one reliable witness."

"Hopefully, we'll be back soon," she said.

The others returned and Hailey handed over her coat.

"Thanks," Dru said, slipping it on. "See you later, Hugh."

Hugh Channing gave a funny little bow and stepped back into the corridor.

Dru led the way to the solarium's exit door that led to the patio.

The snow was still coming down hard and fast outside. She ducked her head down and walked into the wind before she had a chance to talk herself out of it.

Dru's thighs were burning and she was sweating and freezing all at once by the time they reached the peak that overlooked Hemlock House.

She was grateful that Hailey seemed to know her way around the trails. Dru had taken a hike or two since arriving, but everything looked different now under a heavy blanket of snow.

The wind and cold had prevented them from really communicating, other than to wave each other on during the long trek.

But now that they had reached their destination, it was time to make a plan.

Dru pulled her phone out, allowing herself just the tiniest bit of hope.

No bars.

And she was at less than 5% battery life.

"Let's all move around a little," she yelled through the wind. "We'll stay in each other's sight, but we can cover more territory if we spread out."

Viktor frowned, but Hailey nodded.

"Viktor, you go left," Dru told him.

He gave her an icy look, but moved slowly in the direction she had indicated.

"I'll go right, and Hailey you stay here but try going up and down the hillside a little," Dru said.

Hailey nodded.

Dru hiked to the right, raising her phone and checking her signal every few feet.

One bar flashed up very slightly, but disappeared just as fast.

She glanced back at Hailey and Viktor.

Neither of them seemed to be having any luck. It was really going to suck if they had braved the snow and come all this way for nothing.

She kept moving, trying not to look down into the snowy valley. In the deepening snow, it would be all too easy to lose her footing, so concentration was key.

A high-pitched sound emanated from Hailey's direction.

Dru turned and could make out that her friend was speaking with someone, screaming into the wind to be heard.

At the same moment, Dru's phone buzzed in her hand.

She looked down to see it was showing new messages from her chat group, which meant that she had service now, too.

Every instinct told her to head back to Hailey.

But she couldn't resist asking her friends to weigh in on Viktor. If she was quick about it, maybe she could get answers before Hailey was off the phone. She opened the site and took off her gloves, holding them in her teeth so she could type quickly.

.   .   .

GHOSTWRITER:

Only have a minute - power out, battery dying. Suspect mystery guest may be a vampire after all. Evidence:

- Sent heavy trunks ahead, arrived after dark

- Keeps all mirrors and windows covered

- Never eats or drinks in anyone's presence

- Never leaves his room until sundown

- Always disappears before dawn

- A man was murdered in the hotel and his crucifix is missing from around his neck

Thoughts?

TADSTRANGE:

How did you not lead with the murder?????

A MESSAGE POPPED up on her screen.

Low Battery: 3% of Battery Charge Remaining.

She dismissed it.

When the board was visible again, she could see three messages had been posted in quick succession.

BETHSMOM1972:

Are you okay, Ghostwriter?

WRAITHGIRL19:

That's a vampire, Ghostwriter

Mos def

. . .

TADSTRANGE:

100% a vampire. You know what to do now. We all know exactly what to do when faced with a real vampire.

SHE MOST CERTAINLY DID NOT KNOW WHAT to do.

TADSTRANGE IS TYPING...

DRU WAITED WITH BATED BREATH.

There was the ding of a new message, just as the screen went black.

"What are you doing, Dru?"

Viktor was standing right in front of her.

She jumped, nearly dropping the phone into the snow bank.

How long had he been there?

"My battery died," she gasped, fumbling her gloves back on.

"Well thankfully, Hailey got through and the police know what's going on here," Viktor said.

Dru couldn't bring herself to meet his eye.

Had he seen what she was up to?

He couldn't have, from that angle.

Could he?

"Hey guys," Hailey yelled, heading toward them. "They're sending a crew as soon as the road is clear. Help is on the way!"

"That's great, Hailey," Viktor told her. "We should head back."

She nodded and the three of them set off toward the hotel again with the wind at their backs.

Did he see, or didn't he?

He wasn't letting on if he did, and there was no way to know.

She trudged forward into the snow. At least the hike would be easier on the way back down.

8

D ru stepped into the hotel with a great sense of relief.

She had spent the whole hike back wondering if they would make it, or if she and Hailey would fall victim to Viktor's appetite.

Just make sure you're not stuck alone with him...

Surely, he wasn't really a vampire. She had been hoping that the people on the message board would tell her that she was crazy and there was nothing to worry about. She'd forgotten that most of the people on there were pretty intense. And they ate stuff like this up.

But she had to admit that the clues kept adding up in her own head until the tower of her sanity threatened to topple over.

She was dusting the snow off her coat and stomping her feet to dislodge it from her boots, when suddenly, Viktor's hand was on her shoulder.

She froze.

"I have to go, Dru." He leaned close, whispering into her hair. "I'll see you tonight."

She watched in silence as Viktor headed up the stairs to his rooms.

The lantern on the desk in the lobby illuminated the grandfather clock. It was nearly seven.

Of course he had to go.

The sun would be up soon.

Dru shivered.

"Are you okay?" Channing asked, approaching her, carrying a lit candle.

Thankfully, no one else was paying her any attention. Hailey was regaling the others with the tale of their walk through the driving snow and her heroic call for help. She seemed to be embellishing it a little, but no one was complaining.

"I'm fine," she said.

"You've been up all night," Channing said. "Can you stay awake another hour to search the victim's room?"

"I normally go to bed around nine in the morning anyway," she told him.

"How fortunate for me," Channing said. "You're the perfect recording officer."

It was easy to forget he wasn't really a detective.

She hung up her coat, and they headed up the stairs toward the Opal Room.

"Won't you need the key?" Channing asked.

"I've got a skeleton key," Dru told him, patting her pocket.

"Very interesting," Channing said. "Does every employee have one?"

"Yes," Dru said. "Well, usually. Howie was looking for his yesterday. He's always misplacing it."

"Very, very interesting," Channing said. "When we get to the room please note that down."

Dru didn't think it would be important. The murder had happened in a communal area. There were no locked doors involved. But she supposed it wouldn't hurt to write it down.

"So are we looking for anything special in his room?" Dru asked.

"We're looking for anything out of place," Channing said.

"Like what?" Dru asked.

"We'll know it when we see it," Channing told her.

They reached the Opal Room, and Dru retrieved her skeleton key and opened the door.

Before she could step inside, Channing put a hand on her arm.

"Let's wait here a moment, shall we?" he asked. "Let's see what we can observe from here, before we step inside and potentially damage the clues."

That was a good idea. Channing wasn't half-bad at this.

Dru looked into the room.

Brian Thompson had clearly not been a neat freak. The floor was strewn with various items, including two enormous pairs of boxers, three socks, and an open suitcase.

The bed was unmade, and she could see toiletries on the bathroom sink through the open door at the back of the room.

"Do you see anything suspicious?" Channing asked her.

She shook her head.

"Very well," he said. "I'll take some photographs now. After that, we'll make a thorough search."

"Shouldn't we wait for the police?" Dru asked.

"I thought the same thing earlier this evening," Channing said. "But it's still snowing, and there's still a murderer on the loose. We have a responsibility to solve this as quickly as we can, before someone else loses their life."

Dru nodded. His words were chilling, but he wasn't wrong.

"Do you have gloves?" Channing asked her.

"Only my winter ones," she said.

"May I borrow them?" he asked.

She handed the gloves over, and they stepped inside as Channing slipped them on.

There was a slight funk in the air, as if Thompson didn't bathe as frequently as he should, along with an undertone of some body spray clearly marketed at teenage boys.

"Let's begin in the near left corner and sweep right and back," Channing decided. "Do you have your notepad?"

"Yes," she said, jotting down what he had said before about Howie's skeleton key.

"Then we will begin," Channing said, placing the candle down on the dresser.

They worked their way slowly through the room, Dru noting each item as Channing examined it.

She wished they had electricity, or even a good flashlight. They usually kept a tactical flashlight by the front desk, but she was pretty sure Howie took it when he went to look for Chester. He probably still had it. It seemed like the type of thing Howie would hold onto during a power outage.

They continued the search, but didn't find anything unusual. Thompson seemed to have a taste for luxury that was evident in his toiletries, if not his clothing. But other than the mess, nothing seemed to be actually out of place.

After nearly an hour of looking over everything in the room, Channing finally made an actual discovery behind the bedside table.

"His phone," he said, breathless with excitement as he

bent over beside the bed. "It must have fallen back here. That explains why we didn't find it on him."

"Oh, that's fantastic," Dru said.

At least they knew the killer hadn't stolen it. And it might have some leads as to whether or not Brian Thompson had any enemies.

They leaned over the little device together as Channing pressed the button to wake it.

But the screen was locked.

Dru sighed.

"It's been a long night," Channing said. "We all need some sleep. Let's lock the room up and hit it again when we've had some rest."

Dru nodded, still looking at the phone. "Can I hang onto this?" she asked. "I'll try to figure out how to hack into it."

Dru could no more hack into a phone than she could the Pentagon, but it sounded like the right thing to say. Maybe Channing's enthusiasm was rubbing off on her.

"That would be marvelous," Channing said.

Dru slipped the phone into her pocket and they stepped out of the Opal Room.

"I'll walk you to your room," Channing offered.

"Thanks," Dru said.

The sun was shining through the stained-glass window on the landing, the colors saturating the small island of light in the darkness.

"We don't appreciate the light until we've spent some time in the dark," Channing said thoughtfully.

They set off down the hallway to the servants' wing. When they reached Dru's door, she pulled out her key once again.

"Keep your door locked," Channing advised.

"Of course," she said.

"I'll see you this afternoon then," he told her. "Thank you for your help."

"My pleasure," she told him.

"Really, do keep your door locked," he reminded her, handing her the candle.

She suppressed a shiver as she closed herself into her darkened room.

Alone.

9

D ru put on her pajamas and tried to get herself ready for bed.

The temperature was already dropping in the hotel. Without electricity to ignite the boiler, the only heat was coming from the fireplace downstairs.

Dru sincerely hoped Chester would make some headway with the generator soon. But she was too tired to worry about it right now.

She slipped on a fuzzy sweater over her pajamas and crawled into bed, exhausted to her core.

But sleep wouldn't come.

All she could think of was Viktor's icy blue eyes.

Is he, or isn't he?

She sat up and grabbed Brian Thompson's phone from her bedside table to distract herself.

Much as she wanted to believe she could figure out his password, the fact that her only real knowledge of the man began and ended with the info in the hotel check-in log made that seem pretty unlikely. Unless he was using his birthday or driver's license number, she was out of luck.

She tapped the screen to wake the phone and waited while it tried and failed to use facial recognition to unlock.

Facial recognition...

A horrifying idea occurred to her.

They didn't have a shot at his password, but they still had access to the man's face.

She would have to wait for Hugh Channing to wake up later in the day, because she absolutely wasn't going back into the tunnels alone.

Tyler Park's words over the body returned to her.

Soon, bloating from putrefaction will have his eyes and tongue protruding out of his face.

If she waited too long, facial recognition might not work anymore. Not to mention the fact that it was going to be a lot more gross to even try.

It's broad daylight, Dru, she coached herself. *Just go downstairs, scan his face, and come back up.*

She slid out of bed and pulled the dark curtain aside to look out the window.

The snow had slowed down enough that she could see the pink light of early morning reflected on the frosted meadow below.

She slid her feet into a pair of boots before she could change her mind, then headed into the hallway, locking her door behind her. The hall was silent, but she took the servants' staircase down the back of the wing anyway.

Stepping outside made her appreciate the remaining warmth in the hotel. The wind seemed to reach inside her and whistle right through her bones.

Dru made her way across the patio behind the solarium to the basement door as quickly as she could. A moment later, she was descending the steps into the catacombs, using the ambient glow from the face of Brian's lock screen for light.

Her own footsteps echoed off the wet walls and she shuddered, thinking about what might be outside the faint glow of the phone's light.

There were the real things - like rats and spiders.

And then there was her imagination, working overtime, envisioning a murderer around every corner.

Or worse.

Drucilla Holloway, you will not think about zombies.

But she couldn't help thinking about zombies. After all, she was going to find a corpse.

And this whole thing was starting to seem like a horror movie.

A nasty business, Channing had said.

Dru had nearly giggled at the cliched turn of phrase.

But Hugh was right. Everything about this business was nasty.

She was nearly at the alcove where the bins were kept, when it occurred to her to worry that Chester might have moved the body.

But as soon as she turned the corner, she knew it was still there.

The stench pierced the frigid air, filling her senses.

Just unlock the phone and get out, she told herself.

She stomped a few times, and then paused, wanting to give any rats that might have followed the scent of the body a warning she was coming, and plenty of time to flee.

Dru inched forward, until at least her feet nudged the carpet.

She pulled her sweater up over her mouth and nose and unrolled the carpet. It was harder than she expected, and her makeshift sweater-mask kept falling down.

Finally, enough of the body was revealed for her to do what she had come to do.

As Tyler had said it would be, the victim's face was marbleized. But his eyes and tongue were not popping out.

Dru held her breath and held the phone up to the face, suddenly frantic that there might not be enough light from the screen to show the face for recognition purposes. Didn't these things have special cameras that could see in the dark?

But when she turned the phone back, it was unlocked.

Quickly she went into his settings and turned off all of the lock features, aiming it at the man's face one more time for verification.

She turned the phone off and back on again.

There was no lock screen. She had full access now.

She slipped the phone into her pocket and began the job of rolling the carpet back up.

It seemed to take forever, but at last the body was hidden again.

She headed back down the corridor, eager to get out of the tunnels.

Somewhere in the darkness ahead, a door banged shut.

Dru froze in place.

Footsteps were coming toward her, as if someone had entered from the lawn and was headed toward the trash bins.

It's probably Chester, she told herself frantically.

But Chester had been up all night working on the generator. And the man valued his sleep.

She had just reached the little alcove where Chester had been working on the shelves the other night.

She ducked into it, hoping whoever was coming hadn't heard her.

The footsteps rang out, closer and closer.

Dru had a sudden epiphany. She had found that secret door when she was here the other day, maybe she could hide in it until the danger had passed.

She pushed the panel that she had discovered by accident, and heard the corresponding groan of stone sliding against stone.

Dru held her breath and listened, but the rhythm of the footsteps was unchanged.

She stuck her fingers into the open gap and pried.

A door creaked open and she tried to move into the hidden area behind. With the shelf partially blocking the entrance, it was a tight fit, and her jacket snagged on the edge for a second before she freed it, slipping inside, then pushing the door closed behind her all but an inch, not wanting to get trapped in the dark alcove.

She moved away from the opening and pressed her back to the wall.

There was another groan as the wall before her slid the rest of the way shut in the darkness.

Dru bit back a scream.

You're not trapped. There has to be another stone in here that you can push to get out, she told herself silently.

But her claustrophobia clutched her stomach with hard, icy fingers and sent sweat sliding down her spine, despite the cold.

It was impossible now to hear if the footsteps were growing closer. The stone blocked out too much sound.

Dru wasn't sure whether to scream at the top of her lungs for help getting out, or hide for fear of being discovered.

It would be just her luck to be rescued by the murderer and end up joining Brian Thompson in that carpet, waiting for the rats.

She closed her eyes and forced herself to focus on her breathing.

One hundred breaths in and out, and then you can look for the button.

Dru made it almost to fifty before she broke and tapped the phone for light.

She was in some sort of storage closet. There were a few empty wooden pallets on the floor and nothing else.

She pressed the stones all around the door she had entered but nothing happened.

Her hands began to shake, and she put the phone back into her pocket so as not to drop it as she scoured every wall in the room, pressing each stone, one by one.

What if it's not a single stone? What if it's some kind of combination?

She pushed the thought aside. Her heart thundered in her ears and there was a bitter taste in her mouth, like old pennies.

She worked her way around another corner to the back wall of the room.

A single stone moved under her hand and she nearly cried with relief. But when she slipped the phone out again, the wall was still in place.

Turning around, she saw that the *back* wall of the room had opened into a narrow corridor.

The stones were sweating, and she could only see a foot or two ahead in the weak light of the phone screen.

She turned on the flashlight feature, though she was afraid she would drain the battery.

There was still just a narrow tunnel as far as she could see.

The idea of squeezing into an even tighter space threatened to overwhelm her.

But what choice did she have?

Out of the frying pan, into the fire, she thought to herself as she set off down the tunnel.

At least the body was on the other side of the wall now.

She was pretty sure zombies couldn't activate secret doors.

10

Dru walked on and on through the dark, damp tunnel.

She had the sense that she was walking up an incline, but it could have been an illusion brought on by exhaustion and terror.

Surely, the hotel wasn't big enough for her to have been walking as far as it seemed she had.

But she had lost her sense of time and direction almost immediately. Her whole focus was on assuring herself that that walls weren't closing in, and she wasn't going to get stuck.

Dru dragged herself onward. There had to be a door soon.

She had put the phone in her pocket, and was tracing the walls with her fingertips to stay on track. The idea of running out of battery life while she was still in the tunnels was too terrifying to risk.

When her foot hit a stone wall in the darkness in front of her, she cried out.

The sound echoed eerily through the space and she

clenched her hands into fists to stop herself from breaking apart.

I'm trapped. I'm trapped. I'm trapped.

But while her mind was melting, her hands explored the wall.

Something was there, something wooden.

She pulled out the phone and took a look.

A rickety wooden ladder had been built into the wall directly in front of her. It clung to the stone surface and led up into the darkness.

I can't climb that...

But she knew that she would climb it.

"I feel like fucking Alice in Wonderland," she murmured to herself. "Except I'm going in the wrong direction."

The rungs wobbled a little, but it held up. She climbed on and on.

Suddenly, there was no more ladder when she reached up.

The wall above her ended, taking a ninety-degree turn and becoming more stone floor. Somewhere ahead, she spotted a sliver of light, and her heart rejoiced.

"At least I wasn't coming from the other direction," she told herself, shuddering at the idea of stepping over the edge and falling in the darkness.

She pulled herself all the way up to the floor above and turned the phone flashlight on.

Whatever came next, she wasn't going to stumble into it.

The corridor narrowed dramatically, until it scraped her shoulders and she had to turn sideways to keep going.

Breathe, Dru, breathe...

She turned off the flashlight and put it back in her pocket. If she dropped it at this point, she wouldn't be able to lower herself down to pick it up again.

The walls seemed to press in tighter as she inched along.

She wondered how tightly she would press herself in to get to that sliver of light. Would she wedge herself into the walls so tightly that she couldn't get out again?

Just as the terrifying thought threatened to consume her, the corridor widened again.

She moved faster, eager to get to the light and out of the tunnel.

Hopefully out.

Something crackled under her foot, but she didn't bother to investigate it.

She moved closer to the light that she could now see was clearly coming from under a door-shaped opening made of thick wood.

Thank God.

But when she pushed, she found the door was sealed.

"No," she moaned to herself.

Once again, she began pressing stones all over the walls. Nothing opened, so she went to the bottom stones and then finally the ones up higher than her head.

Her hand caught on a jagged piece of stone and there was a groaning sound.

Dru held her breath and watched the light.

Slowly, slowly the ancient wood slid sideways, revealing light so bright she had to cover her eyes for a moment.

When she opened them, the door was gone.

And she was standing in a stone tunnel that opened into her own bedroom.

Dru stood, gaping and horrified, until she heard a creak and another groan.

The wooden door was moving back into place.

Desperately, she flung herself to the floor of her room.

She turned to see one of the built-in bookcases slide back to cover the entrance to the tunnels.

As she clung to the floor, panting, she couldn't help thinking about her nightmare about someone being in her room.

She pulled herself up to a sitting position and pulled her knees up to her chest.

Had someone really been in her room?

Dru noticed a stray piece of paper stuck to her boot. It must have been the crinkly thing she'd stepped on a moment ago.

She retrieved it and smoothed it out to find that it was a receipt from the little coffee shop in town - a slice of lemon cake and an iced soy peppermint mocha, dated two days ago.

It hadn't been a dream after all.

Someone *had* been in her room.

11

D ru pulled herself to her feet and stood in the center of her room.

The once-familiar sloped walls were no longer cozy, the space didn't feel like home.

It felt like a trap.

Everything here was a trap.

The murder, the fallen tree, the snow, the hidden passage to her room, all of them kept her penned in and vulnerable.

And her feelings for Viktor were the biggest trap of all.

She closed her eyes, thinking of his intense blue gaze, the delirious pleasure of his body pressed to hers.

He's a vampire.

And he was probably in here spying on me.

But if Viktor had wanted to murder her and drink her blood, he'd certainly had ample opportunity already without having to sneak around.

And if he wanted to kill her, why did he look at her like he cared about her, like the sight of her caused him pain, but he couldn't look away?

It was time to get some answers.

Instinctively, she stepped out into the corridor, locking the door behind her.

Her feet carried her down to the second floor, toward Viktor's rooms. She could hear the voices below and feel the soothing warmth of the lobby fireplace curling up the staircase.

She knocked on the door of the Sapphire Suite once, to be polite.

There was no answer.

Without overthinking it, she let herself in using the skeleton key and closed the door behind her, knowing that Gert wouldn't be there to interrupt her search during the housekeeping rounds.

Dru walked slowly through the bedroom. The bed was made, the chair was empty.

The closet still held a modest array of Viktor's clothing.

The giant trunk was still in the corner.

She headed into the sitting room and the bathroom.

There was no trace of Viktor anywhere. But she still had the Onyx and Quartz rooms to check.

On the way back through the bedroom, she felt herself inexplicably drawn to the antique trunk. It was massive, the metal corners dented and scratched from years of heavy use.

The leather strap was still unbound.

Dru crept closer to it and extended her hand to touch the soft leather.

There was a loud buzz and she pulled back, stumbling over her own feet and nearly falling.

But it was only the sound of Brian Thompson's phone in her pocket.

She went from terror to elation in a heartbeat. The cell towers were up again.

But when she pulled out the phone, she saw it was only a low battery warning. There was still no signal.

Dammit.

She slid the phone back into her pocket and headed back to the corridor, locking the door behind her.

There was no point searching the other two rooms. She already knew she wouldn't find Viktor in either of them.

But she went through the motions anyway, knocking on the door of Onyx and searching the empty space, then doing the same with Quartz.

The dressers looked like ghosts draped in their sheets in the shadowy rooms.

But as she suspected, there was no trace of Viktor anywhere.

Whatever Viktor was, he was not available to her right now. She would have to confront him after dark.

If that meant what she thought it did, she needed to get some sleep.

This might be the only safe time to let her guard down.

The thought of lying down in her bed in a room connected to the catacombs was terrifying, but the hotel was overbooked already. There wasn't anywhere else to go.

She headed back to her room and surveyed the scene.

The bookcase needed to slide sideways to open. If she could shove something in its way, then no one could get in, and maybe she could get some sleep.

Unfortunately, it looked like the only thing in the room large enough and heavy enough to block it was her bed.

She locked the door behind her, then grabbed the thick wooden headboard and gave it a tug. The bed was heavier than she expected, the solid wood frame getting stuck on the rug and every loose or uneven floorboard - which was most of them.

A few minutes later, and after some noises that definitely would have made anyone passing by wonder exactly what was going on, Dru smiled with grim pleasure at her handiwork.

The bed was the perfect width to be wedged between the wall and the shelf.

This meant lying down with her back to the corridor. But she was so exhausted now that it felt imperative to lie down and rest her aching body, even if she knew she wouldn't be able to sleep.

She crawled under the covers once more and closed her eyes.

Don't think about Viktor. Don't think about the murderer or the snow or the tree or the tunnels...

Her body felt heavy. Her own warmth finally began to fill the blankets, draining the deep chill out of her bones.

She wondered how they would get Brian's phone charged up to search it tomorrow if the generator wasn't working. Maybe she could siphon power from someone's laptop if anyone still had any juice.

It seemed like a small problem compared to the problem of unlocking the phone. And she'd managed that all by herself.

Before she could stop her wandering mind, she thought of Brian Thompson's body again, grotesque and rotting in the rug down in the tunnels.

She rolled over, trying to erase the image and only thought of his body rolling inside the rug as she wrapped him back up again.

Think of something good instead, something that makes you happy.

But the image that came into her mind was a vision of Viktor's beautiful face as he cupped her cheek.

His words rushed back to her.

I want to be where you are, always...

"Please don't be a danger, Viktor," she whispered into her pillow.

The wind rattled the windows and she thought of the snow and the tree blocking them from the rest of the world, leaving her trapped.

But sleep took her anyway.

12

Dru woke to the sound of someone knocking.

For a hair-raising instant, she swore the sounds was coming from the tunnel beyond the bookshelf.

Then she came to her senses and realized that of course the knock was coming from the hallway.

She slid out of bed and made her way to the door, feeling totally gross in the pajamas she'd worn while wandering the catacombs.

Hugh Channing gave her a look as the door swung open.

"What?" she asked.

"You can't just open the door when someone knocks," he scolded her. "What if it was the murderer?"

"Point taken," she said. "Come in. Sorry I haven't showered or anything."

"I woke you," Channing said. "Forgive me."

"I needed to get up anyway," she said. "And I have a surprise for you."

"You do?" he asked.

She grabbed Brian's phone from her desk and woke it.

"You unlocked it," Channing breathed. "How did you work out the code?"

"I didn't," she said.

"You hacked into it?" he asked.

"I wish," she said. "I, uh, did something a little crazy."

Channing sat in her desk chair, setting his flashlight on the desk, as if he was ready to settle in for a good story.

And it hit her that she *had* a pretty good story.

But she didn't like thinking about the tunnel leading to her room, let alone telling someone about it. It almost felt like talking about it out loud would make it more real, and more likely that others would find out about its existence.

Someone already knows...

"What did you do?" Channing asked.

"Well, I saw that it also responds to facial recognition," she said. "And his body was right in the basement."

"My God, that's clever," Channing said. "But please tell me you didn't go into the basement by yourself."

"I didn't know who else to trust," she admitted.

"Next time, wait for me," he said.

"I was afraid the face would be all... that it might not work if I waited much longer," she told him, trying to keep the gruesome image at bay. "And you were asleep."

"Next time, wake me," he said firmly. "Did you find anything on it?"

She shook her head.

"By the time I got back. I was too tired. Why don't you have a look at it now? I need to shower and get dressed."

He was already poking the screen and scrolling.

She grabbed some clothes and headed into the bathroom.

The water was freezing. Without the boiler running, there was nothing to heat it. Under other circumstances, she might have just skipped it. But after her trip through the catacombs, she felt like she needed ten showers to even begin to get clean.

Dru showered as quickly as possible, her whole body shuddering with the cold by the time she got out.

She was shaking too hard to dress, so instead she wrapped herself in a giant fluffy bathrobe, and hoped her hair would dry before it formed into icicles.

Back in her room, Channing hadn't moved from the spot where she'd left him.

"Find anything?" she asked, climbing back into bed and wrapping blankets around herself so she could try to thaw out while they talked.

"I think he was here for the treasure," Channing said, looking up at her with wide eyes.

"Really?" Dru asked.

It didn't feel right. Brian Thompson gave off an air of having money, not the kind of guy who had to go on a goose chase for rumored lost treasure. And he didn't seem like the amateur historian type either.

"There are tons of messages back and forth with a woman," Channing said. "She must be the girlfriend. He writes to her constantly."

"Poor girlfriend," Dru said, thinking of the body in the basement.

"Maybe she dodged a bullet," Channing said.

Dru thought of the night Brian had pinned her to the wall and tried to touch her.

"Right," she agreed.

"But he's also got several email messages here to a guy called Conner, who he calls *Cuz* in some of the emails," Channing explained. "Brian keeps telling this Connor that he hasn't found what he's looking for yet."

"So he was here for the treasure," Dru said. "I guess a lot of people come here for that. It's a fun idea."

"It feels like he isn't just here to look," Channing told her. "He expected to actually find it. He was *relying* on it."

"What do you mean?" Dru asked.

"When I go back further in these messages with Conner, I see him saying he's tired of not having money. He's unhappy, he doesn't like this lifestyle, that kind of thing."

"He didn't look like he was hurting for anything," Dru said thoughtfully.

"Everyone wants more than they have," Channing said dismissively. "But you're right, we shouldn't be surprised that anyone visiting this hotel is interested in treasure. But there's something else that is much more concerning."

"What?" Dru asked, forgetting how cold she was and leaning forward.

"When he signs the messages to Conner, he signs them with a different name," Channing told her.

"What name?" Dru asked.

"Nicky," Channing said.

There was another loud knock on the door.

"Grand Central Station," Dru said, sliding out from under the warm blankets and back into the frigid room to get the door.

Channing opened his mouth to say something, most likely to repeat his earlier warning about not blindly opening doors for murderers, but he was too late. The door was already open before she had time to consider.

And Viktor stood in the threshold.

His wide shoulders took up most of the frame as he stared down at her hungrily.

Dru stood before him, her shivering ceased as the heat between them threatened to combust her.

He could be a monster...

But whatever he was, she was drawn to him, pierced by his pale blue eyes and ready to submit to whatever hunger inspired his expression.

"Oh, hello there," Channing said brightly.

Viktor blinked and looked up, his eyes moving back and forth between Channing and Dru.

Belatedly, Dru realized what it must look like.

"Hugh came by just now to see if I had unlocked Brian's phone," Dru said quickly. "We're discussing the case."

"Good to see you, *Hugh*," Viktor said, in a tone that made it clear it was not, in fact, good to see him at all.

"I'm going to bring this downstairs with me," Channing said. "It's dreadfully dim in the dining room, so I can turn down the brightness and not waste batteries while I read some more about our late friend."

"See you down there," Dru said.

Viktor merely nodded in Channing's direction, not taking his eyes off Dru.

She suddenly remembered she was wearing nothing but a bathrobe. She could feel the blood rising to her cheeks.

She heard the door close behind Hugh Channing on his way out, leaving her alone with Viktor.

A shiver went down her spine, and she wasn't sure if it was fear or desire.

But she suspected it was both.

13

Dru looked up at Viktor, transfixed by his azure gaze.

"What was he doing in your room?" Viktor hissed, eyes flashing.

"We were looking at Brian's phone," she retorted.

"How do you know you can trust him?" he asked.

"How do I know I can trust you?"

"What is that supposed to mean?" he asked.

She shrugged.

"You're practically naked," he groaned.

The sound of his voice poured through her like honey.

"Viktor, I have to talk to you," she said, trying to shake the onslaught of lust. It wouldn't do her any good to fall back into his arms before she found out the truth.

He nodded, his fierce blue eyes narrowed.

"I have to ask you something," she said.

Suddenly the room felt too small and his body too big. Her thoughts were scrambling, and she wanted to do anything but confront him.

But of course, she wasn't really supposed to confront him. That would be dangerous.

She was supposed to use her wits to back him into a corner so she could figure it out without having to embarrass or endanger herself by saying it.

The plan had seemed so sensible when it occurred to her. Now she wasn't sure.

"What do you want to ask me?" Viktor asked.

"Did you know that there's a secret corridor from the catacombs that leads straight into my room?" she heard herself say.

She watched his face.

His eyes widened and he scanned the room, but his gaze did not linger on the bookcase. Though maybe he was too clever to give himself away so easily.

"You moved your bed," he noticed.

"You used that secret entrance," she said, pointedly not answering the question. "You were in my room while I was sleeping."

"Drucilla, I wasn't," he said sadly.

"Someone was," she said.

"You aren't going to sleep in here anymore," he said. "It's not safe."

"The hotel is full," she said. "*Someone* booked three rooms."

"I'll un-book one of them," he offered.

"You snuck into my room while I was sleeping," she said. "And you won't even admit it. You betrayed my trust, and I want to know what you want with me."

"It wasn't me," he said quietly.

"Yes, it was," she said.

"Why would you think it was me?" he asked.

"Who else would want to sneak in here?"

"It... it couldn't have been me," he murmured, looking out the window into the moonlit night.

She let his words hang in the air.

"Because you can't go out in daylight?" she heard herself ask at last.

Dru, you weren't supposed to confront him...

"I care for you, Drucilla," he said, turning back to her. His expression was tortured. "I want to protect you."

"You sent your things ahead," she said softly. "Ancient trunks so heavy they could be filled with anything, like dirt to sleep in."

He turned away from her again.

"You never eat. I never see you in daylight," she went on. "You covered up all your mirrors and windows."

"What are you saying, Drucilla?" he said pleadingly. "Think about what you're saying."

"You said that the person who came into my room in the daytime *couldn't have been you*," she said. "Why is that?"

"Because I only want to protect you."

"Then tell me the truth."

"You already know," he said quietly.

"Tell me anyway."

He walked to the window, resting one hand against the frame so that his body was silhouetted by the moon outside.

Moonlight kissed his chiseled jaw, leaving her weak in the knees. In spite of her trepidation about what she was waiting to hear, Dru couldn't help admiring his inhuman beauty. She was helpless in its wake.

"It was a long time ago," he said at last, his voice rough. "I was on my way home from the shops. A man cornered me in an alleyway. I thought he wanted to rob me."

Dru held her breath.

"Instead he slammed me into a brick wall and bit down

on my neck, tearing my flesh and feeding on my blood as if he would never stop," he went on. "When he finally let go of me, I collapsed into the dirt of the alley knowing I was dying. But instead of leaving me to find my peace he said, '*You're a pretty one,*' and pressed his wrist to my lips, making me taste his essence."

He turned back to her.

The floor seemed to drop out from under her.

She'd been the one to suggest it, but it couldn't really be true.

Could it?

"The hunger washed over me like poison," he went on. "It is a pain that cannot be assuaged."

Dru was frozen in place, terrified.

She had suspected and made her case, all the while convinced in the reasonable part of her mind that she had to be wrong.

"I lost everything," he went on. "My family, my career. I isolated myself. I raved and fought against the darkness."

His face was drawn in agony now. And though she knew what he was, it was impossible not to feel his pain. It pulsed in the air between them, like another soul in the room.

"I fight my hunger, every day," he told her. "I feed on lesser creatures," he said softly. "I avoid human blood and human company."

"The fox," she breathed. "The rabbits."

"It's horrible, I know," he said sadly. "But when I kill those animals, I can stave off the need for human blood."

"Stave it off?" she echoed.

"I cannot survive forever without it," he said, looking down as if ashamed. "But I can go long enough that I need it only once a year or so. And there are civilized ways to find it."

Blood banks. He must rob blood banks. She'd read a pretty good horror story about some vampires doing that kind of thing.

"This is why I've been alone for so long," he said quietly.

"You're trying to do the right thing," she said.

"I have endeavored to live this second life without harming others," he said. "When I couldn't avoid company, I have tried to behave with discretion."

Dru's heart threatened to beat out of her chest.

"But my heart is drawn to yours, Drucilla," he said. "I cannot bring myself to stay away, even though I know I should."

She pictured his arms around her, his mouth on her.

"This is why you didn't want me to touch you," she realized out loud.

"It was the first time any other hunger has obliterated my senses," he told her. "I was afraid of losing control."

She nodded slowly.

"You put together what I am, Drucilla," he went on. "And I am glad, because I want you to know the truth. You should be frightened of me. I'm a monster."

She opened her mouth and closed it again.

"I am a monster, but I will never hurt you," he told her.

She gazed into his beautiful eyes.

"And I was not in your room," he said. "Do you believe me?"

She found herself nodding slowly.

Against all odds, she *did* believe him.

"Then please also believe me when I tell you that I had nothing to do with that man's death," he went on. "Someone here killed him, and that person is still on the loose. A murderer is among us, and now you tell me that someone has been in your room."

He paused and bit his lip, emotions battling on his face.

"Drucilla," he said, "I understand that your feelings for me have changed. I'm a monster, but let me be your monster. Let me stay close so that I can keep you from harm."

Her monster.

Dru liked the sound of that.

14

D ru closed her eyes, trying to call back her common sense.

But when she opened them again, she was still standing in front of a man she had come to care about.

Not a man...

"Drucilla, say something, please," he murmured.

He lifted a hand toward her and then let it drop again by his side, as if realizing that she must be frightened of him.

But no matter how much she knew she should be, she realized that she never had been. From the moment she'd met him, she'd felt a connection, and she couldn't deny it any longer.

The pain in his eyes was more than she could bear.

She moved to him slowly, lifting her own hand to touch his cheek.

He closed his eyes and leaned into her touch.

She lifted her other hand, cupping his face between her palms.

"Drucilla," he murmured, eyes still closed as if the emotion would break him.

"I don't care," she whispered.

He opened his eyes.

"About what?" he asked.

"About any of it," she said. "I need you, Viktor."

His arms were around her in a heartbeat as he pressed his lips to hers. His movement was lightning fast, as if he had been hiding his true speed from her until now.

She had just enough time to twine her arms around his neck before he lifted her in the air and deposited her on the bed.

"Drucilla," he moaned into her hair, sweeping his hand down to loosen the tie of her robe and expose her to the cold, candlelit room.

She watched his expression as his eyes raked down her body and saw tenderness and lust in equal measures.

His face was at her breast, as suddenly as if she were watching a film with missing frames.

She felt the softness of his mouth close over her nipple and the pleasure licked through her like a flame.

He flicked his tongue and circled her other nipple with the pad of his thumb.

The sensations sizzled and Dru arched her back and cried out, need setting her on fire.

He growled and nuzzled her belly, nudging her thighs apart as he trailed kisses down her body.

She howled with need, lifting her trembling hips to meet his mouth.

"My God, Drucilla," he groaned.

Before she could beg, he gave her what she craved.

Dru felt herself almost lift off the bed with the pleasure of his tongue caressing her, slowly at first, and then with such speed his dark head seemed to blur between her thighs. His touch was quick, but light, just enough to send her over the edge with pleasure.

The the rising tide lifted her, then broke her into shimmering pieces.

But Viktor didn't stop.

15

Dru was splintering apart with pleasure. The climaxes were coming so fast she could hardly tell where one ended and the next one began.

She tangled her hands in his dark hair, trying to pull him away before she disintegrated completely.

Viktor only growled and sent her flying again.

"Enough," she whimpered as she came down from another dizzying high. "Please."

She felt his mouth slowing on her sex, with long, soothing strokes of his tongue.

"Beautiful girl," he murmured against her belly as he crawled up to lie beside her, pulling her close.

She snuggled in, letting his clean scent wash over her, as she tried to catch her breath. She felt like she was filled with warm honey, tingling and sweet all over.

Viktor pressed his lips to her hair. She could feel the steel length of him pressed to her hip.

Lust shot through her again, stronger than before.

She rolled over slightly to stroke him with her hand.

He pulled away so fast her hand caressed only the air.

"Drucilla," he said warningly.

"I want to touch you," she told him. "I need you."

He paused as if torn, but when she reached for him again, he caught her wrist easily in his hand.

"Please," she whimpered.

"Oh, Drucilla," he murmured. "Don't you see that you can't?"

She buried her face in his chest, embarrassed that she couldn't control herself enough to make this easier for him.

He let go of her wrist and she slid it up to his chest, stroking him lightly.

"That's so good," he whispered, his eyes closed as if he were in ecstasy. "It's been so long since anyone has touched me like that. I'm afraid of what might happen."

She leaned back slightly and caressed his rough jaw and the silk of his hair.

"Do you ever have to cut your hair?" she asked absent-mindedly.

He laughed gently. "No," he told her. "I don't have to shave either."

She slid her hand back to his chest. Even through his shirt she could feel the solid planes of muscle. She stroked his pecs and allowed her hands to slide down to his abs.

He put his arms behind his head and relaxed.

The room was cold and quiet. There was nothing but Dru's breathing and the slight hush of her hand skimming across the fabric of his shirt.

She felt such peace, even as the tension in Viktor's body grew. He never opened his eyes, even as his cock strained for her hand.

He could do this, she was sure of it.

She lay her head on his chest again and ran her hand

slowly down his right hip, melting inside as she saw his cock twitch in anticipation of her touch.

She slid down slightly, loving the feel of his abs under her ear.

"Drucilla," he whispered.

"It's okay," she crooned.

When she brought her hand back up again, she allowed the tip of her finger to trail along his length.

Viktor groaned but he didn't move.

Emboldened, she slid down further still, and nuzzled him through his clothes.

His hands gripped the sheets, knuckles white.

She smiled and kissed the tip of him through the fabric as she stroked his length with an open palm.

"No," he roared.

Suddenly she was being pulled into the air and pinned on her back.

She gasped and he sealed her mouth with a brutal kiss, his tongue invading her mouth as he held her down.

When she tried to pull back for a breath, he released her and sat back.

"Viktor," she murmured.

He smiled at her lazily and she could see his canines were just a little too long. His eyes were so pale that they were nearly white.

He turned his head away a second before a loud knock sounded at the door.

16

"Just a sec," Dru yelped, scrambling out of bed to get dressed.

By the time she had tugged on some clothes, Viktor was standing beside the bed, looking unruffled.

He observed her curiously.

What could he be thinking?

"Dru?" Channing called, banging on the door again.

She rushed over and opened up.

"It's time for interviews," Channing said excitedly. "I need my recording officer."

"Of course," she said. "Let me grab my notepad. Or should I use the typewriter?"

"Notepad is best," Channing said. "The typewriter will make them nervous."

He stepped inside. "Oh, hello," he said, turning to Viktor.

"Hello," Viktor replied.

There was a beat of awkward silence while Dru grabbed her stuff.

"Let's go," she said brightly when she had everything in hand.

Channing seemed a little troubled.

She guessed it was because he hadn't expected Viktor to be included.

But Dru understood that she couldn't really ask him to leave her side.

Let me be your monster. Let me stay close so I can keep you from harm...

She would not deny him that.

It was quite possible she wouldn't deny him anything at all.

Though he seemed quite willing to deny himself.

A shiver of lust at the thought of touching him went through her and she had to force herself to get out of her own head.

Beside her, Viktor was smirking, as if he was reading her thoughts.

Wait, vampires can't read thoughts, can they?

Viktor, if you can hear me, nod your head.

Nothing.

She made mental note to ask him about it later anyway, then scowled at him and headed into the hallway with the two men in tow.

When they reached the lobby, she could see that many of the guests were waiting by the fireplace.

"I can't believe they didn't all heed the summons," Channing muttered to himself.

"What do you mean?" Dru asked.

"I asked them all to report to the lobby for questioning," Channing said. "Some of them denied my authority."

Dru couldn't blame them for that.

"But my authority isn't what's important," Channing

went on. "The sooner we take statements, the more people will remember. If we wait for the police, valuable testimony could be lost. And the longer we wait, the more the guests will speak to each other, which will influence their stories."

"You have a point," Dru admitted.

"Besides," Channing added. "As an actor, I am a dedicated student of human nature. Being observant enough to imitate is a hard-earned skill. I intend to use it to help solve this crime."

"A worthy cause," Viktor agreed.

Dru couldn't tell if he was teasing Channing or not.

But if he was, he was doing it subtly enough that Channing wouldn't notice.

"Thank you, friend," Channing said in a gratified tone, and gave a little bow. "Now, let's see, oh, Miss Van Buren and Miss Van Buren, we can't have you waiting around. Please join us in the sitting room."

The sisters giggled and each took one of his arms.

Dru and Viktor followed them into the sitting room.

Channing fussed over the ladies for a few minutes, making sure they were cozy on the sofa, asking if they needed hot tea and generally putting them at ease.

By the time he sat in the leather chair opposite the sofa, the two of them were positively beaming at him.

"Drucilla, Viktor, please have a seat," he said, indicating the two smaller leather chairs near the writing table. "Ladies, Drucilla is here to take notes so that I don't lose a precious word of your helpful conversation."

He didn't say what Viktor was there for, but the sisters didn't seem to mind.

"How long have you lived at Hemlock House?" Channing asked, sitting back comfortably.

"Oh, we've been here almost forever," Hazel said.

"Forever," Honey echoed.

"I know a gentleman never asks a lady her age," Channing said with a wink. "But in this case, dates are important - at least dates in general."

"It was the nineteen-sixties," Hazel said with a dreamy look in her eyes. "A long, long time ago."

The sixties? Dru knew the sisters had been at the hotel a long time, but she wasn't expecting it to be that long. If they were there in the sixties, they might have crossed paths with her grandmother. How had she never thought to ask them about that?

"My word," Channing said. "You know this place like the back of your hand."

"Better than the back of our hands," Hazel said with a grin.

"So tell me," Channing said. "Did you notice anything about the victim that might help us solve this case? Anything at all, no matter how small, would be a help."

"I hate to say it," Hazel said. "But he was not a mannerly man."

Channing's eyebrows went up and Dru was secretly impressed. He already knew from her own story that Thompson was anything but mannerly. But he was allowing Hazel to spin her own tale.

"Can you elaborate?" he asked her.

"Well, it's a shame to see them back around again after so many years," she said in a hushed tone. "That element is no good."

Them?

"What do you mean by *that element*?" Channing asked.

"Oh, you can always tell," she said confidingly. "It's the attitude, like they're better than everyone else and always in a hurry. And always tipping everyone, just to show off."

"Fond of showgirls and jewelry," Honey said suddenly.

"Right you are," Hazel said, patting her sister's arm.

Dru's mouth dropped open. She had never heard Honey initiate a statement before.

"You remembered how it used to be," Honey added, nodding to Viktor as if he could confirm.

He blinked at her and Dru looked back and forth between them.

Suddenly Honey looked confused, as if realizing that the thirty-year-old man across from her could not have been at the hotel more than fifty years before.

But Drew knew better.

Could he have been here then?

She'd never asked him how old he really was.

"The mob," Channing realized out loud, bringing Dru out of her thoughts. "Are you implying that Brian Thompson was in the *mob*?"

"Oh yes," Hazel said, speaking for both sisters again.

"How could you tell?" Channing asked.

"Well, he wasn't dressed for it," Hazel admitted. "But he started every conversation by looking over his shoulder, same as they always did."

"So there were men from the mob here before?" Channing asked.

Dru knew enough about the history of the hotel to know it had old ties to organized crime that went all the way back to the days of prohibition. There were little snippets about the hotels storied past scattered around. It was supposed to be part of the charm.

But it was suddenly less charming than it had seemed when it was all part of the distant pass.

"Yes, there certainly were," Hazel confirmed. "Would

you like to know a little about the history of Hemlock House?"

"I would love nothing more," Channing said.

Hazel settled back in her seat and took a deep breath, clearly enjoying the attention as the rest of them leaned in.

"When Honey and I first arrived, we were young girls," she said. "Like you, dear."

Dru smiled and nodded to her.

"We were meant to stay for a short time," Hazel said. "Our parents wanted us to marry, and hoped we would find eligible young men who would be here for skiing."

Channing nodded, smiling.

"But we didn't want to get married," Hazel said, her eyes twinkling. "So we never met anyone, and our stay here was extended."

"No man could tame you," Channing said.

"I should hope not," Hazel retorted. "At any rate, though it was meant to be a nice hotel, that element was already here."

"They used the tunnels," Honey said.

"That's right, dear," Hazel agreed. "The tunnels were built as part of the Underground Railroad. But in Prohibition times, they were used to smuggle rum. The remote location between Philadelphia and New York made it a perfect spot. The Irish mob was all over this place. And they kept using it for their stolen goods and other sundries even after Prohibition was over."

"Until *that night*," Honey said.

"Until that night," Hazel agreed.

"What night?" Channing asked.

Dru knew they had to mean the night with the murders, the night the jewel thief disappeared.

But Channing seemed determined not to influence their story.

"There was so much blood," Honey said softly, shaking her head.

"It was the night of the... *murders*," Hazel mouthed.

"You were here during that time?" Channing asked.

"It upsets my sister to talk about it," Hazel said, patting Honey's hand. "But yes, we were here. And whatever you heard about it, doesn't begin to reflect how bad it was."

Channing nodded, rubbing his jaw.

Dru figured he was giving her time in case there was more she wanted to say. She glanced over at Viktor to see if he was as impressed with Channing as she was.

But he was staring at Hazel Van Buren, as if hanging on her every word.

"The bodies were spread across the lobby floor, like in that Scarlett O'Hara movie," she said quietly. "And the blood... They kept finding it everywhere afterward, in the carpet, on the ceiling, in the chandelier..."

"On the s-staircase," Honey whispered.

Viktor was on his feet suddenly, walking to the window and looking out across the rear lawn and into the trees of the hillside beyond.

"That's enough of that, dear," Hazel said, wrapping an arm around her sister. "At any rate," she said, turning back to Channing, "after that night, those bozos stayed away. And when things got back to normal, it was better here, quieter."

"So the clientele changed once that element disappeared?" Channing asked gently.

"Oh, yes," Hazel said. "And the staff, too. Most of the old staff left not too long after that ugly business."

"But you came back," Honey said, squinting in Dru's direction.

"No Honey," Hazel corrected her. "That's not right. But there was a girl who was the spitting image of you, dear."

"Was her name Jane Anderson?" Dru asked, already knowing the answer.

"It *was*," Hazel said with a wide smile.

"That was my Nana," Dru said.

"She was always banging away on the typewriter too, dear," Hazel said. "We should have known. She was a fine woman. She used to say Honey and I were the only thing holding this place up."

"Who's that?" Honey asked.

"Sweet Jane from the front desk," Hazel told her. "That's Drucilla's grandmother. How is she, dear?"

"Oh, she's fine," Dru lied. She simply didn't have the heart to tell the ladies that her Nana was dead.

Viktor spun around and fixed her in his piercing blue gaze, and she felt momentarily guilty.

Did I even tell him my Nana was dead?

"I'm going to turn the conversation back to the present now, ladies, if I may," Channing said.

Dru listened and took notes as he walked them through the events of the past few days.

But it was hard not to picture her Nana, sitting beside them, reminiscing.

17

Dru stood up and stretched.

Channing had finished interviewing the Van Buren sisters and then insisted they all take a break. He headed into the dining room, most likely to indulge in some of the cereal that was always out on the counter.

It was funny to picture the pretend detective eating colorful sugary cereal out of a paper cup between interviews.

But he probably had the right idea. She was feeling hungry herself.

She glanced up at Viktor, wondering suddenly if he was hungry too. It had been days since the last time she'd collected the fallen body of a small animal. And he'd said himself that those were really enough to stave off his hunger forever.

She wondered how long it had been since he'd really fed.

"Penny for your thoughts," he said softly.

"Are you hungry?" she asked.

He winced. "I'm fine."

"You're not fine," she said.

"Let's stretch our legs," he suggested.

There was no point extending this conversation, especially since they couldn't have it freely in a public space.

"Let's go out on the porch and look at the snow," she suggested.

"Of course, Drucilla," he said, smiling indulgently.

They headed down the corridor.

The lobby was half empty now. The others must have given up on waiting around, since the Van Burens were being interviewed for so long.

"Where are you kids going?" Hailey asked from the desk.

"Just grabbing some fresh air," Dru told her.

"Don't do anything I wouldn't do," Hailey suggested, waggling her eyebrows.

That still left a pretty long list.

Viktor smiled and gave Hailey a nod.

Dru pulled on her coat and looked back at Viktor as she opened the lobby door. A blast of icy wind greeted them. It was almost enough to discourage her from going outside.

But the moonlight shining on the snow was so pretty, and the open air was so tempting after so long in the stuffy hotel.

She stepped outside and took in the view.

Things had changed since the last time she and Viktor had taken a walk.

"Wow," she murmured.

He put his hand on the small of her back and she leaned back against his shoulder.

The landscape appeared softer, snow smoothing over the angles, leaving curves in its wake.

The forest looked shorter, but she knew it was just an

illusion because the deep snow made the ground look higher than it was.

And the fallen tree in front of the hotel appeared even larger than before, with so much snow on top of its toppled body.

"What's that?" Viktor asked.

"What's what?" she replied.

"Do you hear that?" he asked.

She listened closely until she heard a faint, high-pitched warble from the direction of the fallen hemlock.

"Is that a bird?"

"I think it's trapped," he said, striding off the porch and into the deep snow.

She trailed behind him. The snow was up to her thighs, but she was too curious not to follow.

Viktor trudged to the far side of the fallen tree.

She could hear the throaty cries more easily as she got closer.

Viktor was already digging through the snowy branches. They were near the base of the massive old tree, and some of the branches at that point were big enough to be trees in their own right.

"Be careful," she warned him.

"We can't just leave it," he said.

She followed, trying to hold aside smaller branches to make it easier for him to look.

"I think I see him," Viktor said suddenly, and climbed into the snowy limbs, working his way up toward the trunk.

The tree shifted, and a mini-avalanche of snow began to slide down around them. The wood groaned from the sheer weight of it all.

"Get back, Drucilla," he called to her. "That branch isn't stable."

The groan turned into a cracking sound as the weakened branch began to splinter.

"Get out of there," she yelled back. "You'll be trapped if it breaks."

She had a brief vision of Viktor trapped beneath a massive tree branch until the sun came up.

"I almost have him, Drucilla, just go," he cried back to her.

Reluctantly, she moved back, holding her breath for fear that something would happen to Viktor. She didn't like the thought of not having him around.

Several long minutes later, he reappeared on one of the thicker limbs, about six feet off the ground.

His face was covered in scrapes and his clothes were most likely ruined, but he wore a victorious expression.

He'd taken off his coat, and held it in a bundle, tucked against his chest. As he got closer, Dru could see that there was a very confused raven swaddled in the ball of material.

"Can you take him so I don't jostle him when I jump down?" Viktor asked.

She jogged back over, then reached up and gingerly took the bundle from him.

The bird lifted its head in alarm, but settled in again when she pulled him into her chest like Viktor had been holding him.

Viktor leapt down and landed like a cat in the snow beside her.

"Did he scratch you?" she asked, looking at the lines on his face.

"No, no, these are from the tree," Viktor said. "This little guy seemed to know I was there to help."

"What's wrong with him?" Dru asked, looking down at

the bird. His feathers were velvet black with an iridescent gleam.

"I think he has a broken wing." Viktor said sadly.

"Can we help him?" Dru asked.

"I think so," Viktor told her. "I've helped injured birds before. We just have to tape his wing and keep him calm and warm for a while."

To be a *monster,* Viktor certainly had a soft side.

She glanced up at his handsome face and saw that the scrapes had disappeared.

"What is it?" he asked.

"Your... your face," she said.

"Oh," he said, looking downcast. "Yes, I'm difficult to hurt."

He was clearly worried about what she must think of him.

"That's amazing," she said honestly, reaching up to stroke his cheek.

The raven cawed at her and she pulled back.

"Sorry," she said to the bird. "Let's get you inside. It's very slightly less cold in there."

Viktor laughed and put an arm around her as they moved through the deep snow to the hotel. It was a little easier going back, since they had forged a bit of a path on the way out to the tree.

"Why don't you go on up to your room," he told her when they reached the porch. "I'll see if I can find a good box for him."

"That's a good plan," Dru said. Her clothes were cold and wet. And if they hung out in the common spaces, everyone would want to look at the bird.

Without working electronics, she suspected the guests and staff were bored enough to get excited about almost anything. And she could already hear Howie lecturing her about bringing a wild creature inside the hotel.

Viktor held open the door as she approached.

Dru strode in and headed right for the staircase, making it to the upper corridor and down the dark hall toward her room before anyone noticed what she held in her hands.

18

W hen Dru reached the door to her room she had to shift the raven slightly in her arms to grab her key.

He made a soft scolding sound.

"You're okay, buddy," she told him. "We're going to get you settled in."

She pushed open the door and almost tripped on a sheaf of papers on the floor just inside. Someone must have slid them underneath the door at some point. She wondered if it was something from Channing about the case.

Not wanting to disturb the bird again, she stepped over the papers and across the room, where she pulled an empty drawer out of her dresser.

She set it on the bed and placed the coat and raven inside.

It was too big for him to feel cozy. Whatever Viktor found would be better. But at least this allowed her to go check out those papers and get changed.

She scooped the papers up and shut the door. She lit a jar candle on her desk that was supposed to smell like a mountain breeze, but really just smelled like laundry detergent, then came back and sat on the bed next to the bird in its makeshift nest.

The top page had a handwritten note:

DON'T TRUST HIM. *He's been lying to you about everything.*

THAT SOUNDED PRETTY DRAMATIC. But she supposed they were in a pretty dramatic situation.

She studied the handwriting, but it wasn't familiar.

She turned over the first page and gasped.

It was Nana's journal.

Someone had taken a picture of the first page and printed it out.

She flipped through the rest of the pages. It was all here.

In the excitement of the storm, the murder, the secret passageway, and the realizations about Viktor, Dru had forgotten all about the journal.

But whoever had photographed it clearly hadn't.

The first page was just as it had been when Dru last saw it, with each word carefully deciphered above the original word in her handwriting. But now, the later pages had been decoded as well.

And those deciphered words stood out in blue ink against the black and white image of the journal. Whoever had taken these photos had put in the time to translate the rest of the coded entries.

She paged through, stopping at random entries.

.   .   .

THE SUNSET last night was especially beautiful. Both Miss Van Burens were playing chess in the solarium and I wished I was a painter instead of a writer. There was something about the pink light moving through the greenery on their dark hair, their colorful dresses and the black and white of the chess board.

DRU SMILED. How funny that she had skipped right to a section with familiar faces.

THE NEW GUEST is very charming. He stood at the counter and asked me all about the hotel and about my life here - so many questions. I wondered why he arrived so late at night, but I didn't ask. It's one thing for a guest to ask me questions, but I'm sure I should allow the guests their privacy. He is very handsome. His name is Michael.

DRU SMILED. It was strange to think of someone flirting with her Nana, especially someone who wasn't Grandpa Frank. But she had been young once, and apparently looked enough like Dru that the Van Buren sisters noticed it.

I HAVE MADE a new friend in Michael, and it seems that he never sleeps. When the rest of the hotel is resting, he keeps me company on my long night shifts and asks me about my writing and my family.

    It's good not to be alone all the time, but I have to remember that Frank is at home, getting ready to go serve our nation at war.

    If it weren't for Frank, I'm sure I would have a terrible crush on Michael. But thankfully I keep my wits about myself, and

Michael is a very proper person. When I told him about Frank, I could see the sadness in his eyes, but he was respectful.

So it seemed Grandpa Frank was already in the picture. That made sense - she knew they had married young.

The more interesting part was that Michael was beginning to sound familiar.

A shiver went down her spine as she thought of Viktor keeping her company on her own night shifts.

I got a paper cut today and Michael was so distraught about it. He ran out of the lobby and found me a bandage. His face was pinched like he was disgusted. He must be afraid of the sight of blood.

Dru shuddered and paged forward a bit.

He's so gorgeous with those bright blue eyes and his long dark hair. I have to remind myself I'm only here to write, and that I love Frank.

Of course Michael is too much the gentleman to ever initiate anything now that he knows I'm spoken for. But in another life... who knows? It's so exiting to imagine all the possibilities.

Beside her, the raven cawed anxiously.

Dru realized at that moment that someone was opening the door to her room. She was so engrossed in the journal she had missed the footsteps. And she must have been too curious about the pages to remember to lock it.

She had just enough time to shove the papers down behind her before Viktor appeared in the doorway, his smile barely visible in the flickering light of the candle on her desk. He didn't carry his own light, but she suspected he was much better at finding his way in the dark than she was.

"Look at that, you already made him a house," he said approvingly, looking at the bird in the drawer. "But this one will be more snug for the little guy. And I snagged some towels from my room."

The raven was hardly a little guy, but Dru was too taken with Viktor's concern for the creature to care about that detail.

He strode over, and she scooted to the side.

"What's all that?" he asked, indicating the stack of papers behind her, mercifully face-down.

"Oh, just some scratch paper," she lied. "I thought we could line the box with it."

She wasn't exactly sure why she lied. But she wasn't ready to talk to Viktor about the contents of the journal just yet.

Don't trust him. He's been lying to you about everything.

Were they talking about Viktor? Did someone else at Hemlock House know his secret?

"Great thinking, Drucilla," he said, giving her a warm smile.

He took the pages and placed them at the bottom of a large shoe box, then placed a small hand towel on top.

Dru tried not to sigh with relief.

"He seems very comfortable with you," Viktor said. "Do you think you could hold him while I tape his wing?"

She nodded and eased the raven into her arms once more.

The large bird submitted patiently, for which she was grateful. He had a long, dangerous looking beak. If he had wanted to hurt her, he could have done so, and easily.

There was a stretching sound as Viktor ripped off a section of black electrical tape.

He could hurt her too, effortlessly.

Why must I love everything that is dangerous?

He stuck the tape on his thigh and reached out very slowly for the bird.

The raven ruffled its feathers but remained still otherwise, allowing Viktor to manipulate the injured wing.

Dru watched as he folded the wing gently against the raven's body and wrapped a bit of cloth around it to hold it in place.

"Now I can tape it over the cloth," Victor explained. "So we won't pull off his feathers when the tape comes off.

Dru watched in silence as Viktor performed the operation so swiftly his hands seemed to blur.

"Speed is an advantage of my, er, condition," he said, quirking a brow at her.

Dru had noticed that earlier.

She felt the blood heating her cheeks as she remembered how he had used his speed to send her into a frenzy of lust.

"Should we put him in his new box?" she suggested.

"Of course," Viktor said, looking a little disappointed.

She was being weird, and she knew it.

But how was she supposed to act when it seemed that he had been lying to her. Or at least leaving out a very important truth.

Have you been here before? Are you Michael?

She gently wrapped a fresh towel around the raven, and then eased him into the new box on top of the deciphered journal entries.

"I'll just put him by the window where he can feel safe, and see outside," Viktor suggested.

"Sure," she said, watching him place the box on the window seat.

The raven settled in, its dark eyes on the woods outside.

Dru hopped up before Viktor could return to the bed. She needed a moment to collect her thoughts.

19

Dru grabbed a dry pair of pants and rushed into the bathroom to change and wash her hands. She was sure that was the right thing to do after handling a wild animal.

For about the hundredth time, she wished she had access to the internet to look it up. She was beginning to get a feel for what it must have been like for her Nana, when people actually had to just know stuff, and she wasn't a fan.

When she came out, Viktor went in to wash his.

But of course he didn't have to worry about avian flu or whatever it was she was hoping to avoid.

He was invulnerable. He wasn't going to die from some weird disease.

As far as she knew, he wasn't even alive.

"Is everything okay, Drucilla?" Viktor asked as he came out of the bathroom.

"You said you try to avoid people," Dru said. "Why did you come here?"

"I had business in Philadelphia," he told her.

"That's almost two hours away," she said.

He walked over to the window and looked out over the trees.

"I had a happy memory here, once upon a time. I couldn't resist coming back."

He turned back to her and smiled, the light of the candle dancing in his blue eyes.

"Something was calling me back here," he said softly. "I didn't know what it was, until I got here and realized it was you."

"Viktor," she said. But she couldn't bring herself to ask him.

"I have waited generations to find you, Drucilla," he said, kneeling at her feet.

She waited for him to tell her about her Nana, to admit why he was drawn to her immediately.

And maybe even to help her understand why he had seemed familiar to her from the moment she had spotted him in the lobby just a few days ago.

But he only pressed his lips to her hand.

She felt desire rising in her chest. It was as if now that he had touched her once, she was more sensitive to him.

This was an addiction that would only grow until it destroyed them both.

He turned her hand over and brushed the inside of her wrist with his lips.

"There's a bird cage in the abandoned wing," she blurted out.

He lifted his face, his eyes hazy with lust.

"A bird cage?" he echoed.

"For the raven," she said. "We could get it cleaned up for him. So he doesn't try to fly off before the wing heals."

"Of course," he said, standing.

His expression was hard to read.

She grabbed her candle from the desk and headed for the door, but turned back when she didn't hear his footsteps behind her.

Viktor was gently picking up the box with the bird in it.

"We shouldn't leave him alone," he said.

She nodded and they headed out together and down to the second floor.

"Are we going to my rooms?" he asked as they approached the door to one of his suites.

"Not quite," Dru explained. "There's a sealed door just beyond your rooms. It's pretty well-hidden behind the wallpaper. We're less likely to be spotted entering there than if we went in from downstairs."

When they reached the end of the hall, she set the candle down and reached up to feel along the wall.

At first glance, it appeared to be just that, a solid wall.

But her fingers found the crevice and she was able to peel back the wallpaper enough to reveal the edge of a door.

"Amazing," he whispered.

She picked up the candle again and used her key to unlock the entrance to the passage beyond.

There was a blast of cold air as the door swung open.

Dru stepped into the soft light of the abandoned wing with Viktor on her heels.

It took her a moment to realize why it was brighter in the frigid space. The roof was rotted out on this wing to the point that the moonlight was pouring in through sections that acted as jagged skylights.

Snow lay in uneven drifts on the floor, sparkling and obfuscating the topography of the hallway that felt like an upside-down version of the one they had just come from. Wallpaper peeled down the sides, curling like the wings of a gigantic bird.

In the recesses the snow hadn't reached, the wooden floor rippled and rolled, swollen from years of unchecked rain.

"Drucilla, is this safe?" Viktor asked quietly.

"Just watch where you step," she suggested, moving forward.

She had no idea where this vein of strength and bravery in her was coming from. If she was being honest with herself, she knew she was probably running, quite literally, from what she had just read in the journal.

But the task at hand was too precarious to dwell on that. If she didn't focus, she was going to end up getting hurt.

She kicked some snow aside to clear a path to the staircase on the other side of the first two abandoned guest suites.

Fortunately, there was no snow on the stairs, which meant that they weren't as water-damaged as the floorboards in the hallway.

Dru clung to the railing with one hand, though she recognized how silly that was. The railing was as likely to be rotted out as the stairs.

Her other hand clutched the candle.

She stepped gingerly down on the first tread.

It held her weight easily, and her confidence rose swiftly as she made her way down.

Four steps from the bottom, there was a thunderous crack, and she felt her foot going through the wood before she had time to react.

Viktor's hand was under her ribcage instantly, holding her upright.

She clung to the railing, which swayed, but didn't give, and managed to pull her foot out of the rotted tread.

"I'm okay," she whispered.

He let go of her, but stayed close.

She stepped down into the main corridor.

It was wider than the one above, and opened in an elegant archway into the former ballroom. The surrounding woodwork revealed a hint of its former glory.

"This way," she whispered, heading for the ballroom.

Back in the early days of the hotel, this had likely been a popular spot for country dances and concerts. If Dru closed her eyes, she could almost picture the dancers whirling around the polished floor.

But nowadays, people didn't come to the mountains for dancing.

She scanned the rest of the room.

It was full of the cast-off junk that Hemlock house had accumulated over so many years. There were pieces of furniture in various states of disrepair, as well as several dusty paintings that had probably hung in the main rooms at one point, but had been replaced. In the far corner, under a small, stained glass window, Dru spotted an overturned bust of what she assumed was a female angel. The heavenly woman in the statue was completely naked, and *very* well-endowed. Dru wondered if the angel would even be able to get off the ground with that kind of baggage. It was pretty easy to see why it wasn't on display somewhere more prominent. It wasn't exactly what Howie would call *family friendly*.

Dru kept searching until she found what she'd been looking for. On a collapsing table next to the doorway, sat an ancient metal birdcage, the bars formed of vines of metallic ivy, so that it looked less like a cage and more like a piece of decor.

"That's very nice, Drucilla," Viktor whispered, clearly on edge. "Let's get back now."

She felt it too, the same anxiety about this haunted space.

But then she spotted the window seat on the other side of the room, flanked by built-in bookshelves.

Her own room had a similar window seat, but this was a much more glamorous version. And there were still books on the shelves.

"I just need to see what the books are," she whispered to Viktor. "I'll only be a minute."

"I'll go with you then," he said. "But let me hold your arm, I don't trust these floors."

They walked across without incident.

The books were leather bound showpieces - just reprints of the classics. Nothing interesting. Although she wasn't really sure what she'd been hoping to find.

Through the window, which had been boarded over, she could just see glimpses of the rear lawn and the groundskeeper's cottage at the edge of the woods.

"Ready to go?" Viktor asked.

She nodded.

Viktor handed her the raven wordlessly, and took the giant cage.

They made their way gingerly back into the hall and up the stairs, careful to avoid the rotten fourth tread.

Dru tried to keep her mind on the task at hand, and away from the thousand questions chasing each other around her mind.

20

Dru stepped back to admire their handiwork.

They had put the birdcage into her bathtub when they returned, and then taken turns cleaning it and rubbing the metal dry with a towel.

Now it sat on the window seat in the moonlight, looking good as new.

"What do you think, Edgar?" Dru asked the raven.

"You really can't call him Edgar Allan Crow," Viktor said, not for the first time. "He's a raven."

"I'm sorry, but I said it and it stuck," she teased. "We can just call him Edgar. No one needs to know the rest of his secret name."

Edgar ruffled his feathers and settled into his shoe box, showing no interest in his new house.

"We'll only put him in there if we have to leave him alone," Dru decided. "I hate to lock up a wild thing."

Viktor smiled down at her as if she had said something wonderful.

His eyes were a sweet sky blue and she lost the thread of what she had been thinking about before.

A loud knock on the door broke the spell.

She blinked out of her semi-trance and headed over to open it.

"Your friend, Hailey, has just made a discovery that blows the lid off of everything," Channing said excitedly. "Come with me."

He headed out again, not even waiting to see if she would follow.

She turned back to Viktor, who shrugged.

She held Edgar's box close to her chest as they followed Channing down the stairs to the second floor, and then through the corridor toward Brian Thompson's room.

"Is that a real bird?" Channing asked.

"Yes, Viktor rescued it from the tree," Dru said.

"Be careful," Channing said. "I hear they can carry diseases."

"Noted," Dru said.

"And look at that vicious beak," Channing added, sounding a little apprehensive.

"He's fine," Dru said, cradling the bird protectively. "He has a hurt wing."

There was no time to argue, because they had reached the Opal Room.

Hailey was already inside, her eyes sparkling.

"Hey," Dru said.

"Hey yourself," Hailey replied, looking elated. "Whoa. Is that a bird?"

"It's a raven with a broken wing," Dru explained.

"Seriously?" Hailey asked. "We're snowed in with no power and a murderer on the loose, and you decided it would be a good time to play nursemaid to a hurt bird?"

"I can't play around on the internet, so my social schedule's wide open," Dru teased.

Hailey rolled her eyes.

"Tell them what you discovered," Channing said to Hailey, smiling with anticipation.

"There's something interesting about Thompson's clothes," Hailey said importantly, pulling a jacket out of the closet, seemingly at random.

Dru leaned in, trying to see if there was anything noticeable about the jacket. It was dark gray, similar cut to everything she'd seen him wear already.

"This is from the Cole & Sons J.C. Penney line, fall of last year," Hailey said.

"Okay," Dru said.

"Now look at this one," Hailey said, whipping an Oxford shirt out of the closet. "Same thing, J.C. Penney, last fall."

"How do you know?" Dru asked.

Hailey raised one eyebrow.

"Okay, okay, you're getting ready to start your own fashion empire," Dru conceded.

"Where do you think this one came from?" she asked, pulling out a wool sweater.

"Last fall, J. C. Penney?" Dru asked.

"Yep, Cole & Sons again," Hailey said.

"Are you sensing a pattern?" Channing asked triumphantly.

"Is this true of every single item of clothing he has?" Dru asked.

"Everything here," Hailey said. "Same line, same season."

"What does this mean?" Dru asked.

"It could mean a lot of things," Channing said.

"Like what?" Dru asked.

"Maybe he lost a lot of weight and bought himself a new wardrobe," Hailey suggested.

"Maybe he gained a lot of weight and bought new clothes," Channing offered.

"Could have been a new job," Hailey said.

"Wouldn't he have kept his old pajamas?" Channing asked.

"Maybe he had a house fire?" Dru ventured.

"A house fire," Channing said, nodding. "Very good. That's an excellent guess. And along those same lines, a tornado or hurricane is a possibility."

"Could be lost luggage if there's an outlet mall around here," Hailey said.

"But wouldn't there be tags on some of this?" Dru asked. "He's only been here a few days."

"True," Hailey said.

"At any rate, it's a fantastic clue," Channing said. "And I never would have noticed on my own."

Hailey gave a funny little bow and they all clapped.

"You know what's odd?" Dru said thoughtfully. "Hazel and Honey mentioned his clothes too."

"Seriously?" Hailey asked. "Those two ladies are on point."

"Well, they didn't notice the season," Dru said. "But Hazel said he wasn't dressed the way he should be to be in the mob. I guess he wasn't flashy enough?"

"You think he's in the *mob*?" Hailey squeaked.

"It's one theory," Channing allowed. "Please don't share it."

"Sorry," Dru offered.

"My lips are sealed," Hailey said, pretending to zip her lips. Her eyes were still wide above her closed mouth.

"So if he's in the mob, why would he have all this new, cheap, unfashionable clothing?" Dru asked. "It is unfashionable, right Hailey?"

"Oh, without a doubt," Hailey said.

"It could still have been a fire or an act of nature," Channing said.

"Or it could have been an act of man," Dru said, realizing.

"What?" Channing asked.

"What if he's in witness protection?" Dru asked. "What if he was going to testify against someone, and they moved him into a new life, and that's why all his clothes are new, but cheap?"

It was a wild notion, but the pieces fit.

Channing stared at her in wonder.

"I mean, it's kind of an over the top idea," Dru admitted. "But it would explain the clothes and the behavior - maybe even the murder, if someone had a score to settle form his old life."

She started mentally running down the list of guests for possible mobsters. Or maybe that was the wrong direction. Maybe it was a civilian that he'd crossed in his mob days, someone looking for revenge.

"What would he be doing traveling if he's in witness protection?" Hailey asked.

"I have no idea," Dru admitted.

"No one else here seems like they would be in the mob," Hailey said.

"Brian didn't seem like a mobster to us either," Channing said. "This is an excellent theory."

They were all staring at her and smiling in admiration.

Dru began to feel embarrassed.

"I guess I'd better get down to the desk," she said.

"Sure," Hailey said. "Zander is covering for me right now. He'll be glad to see you."

Viktor had been leaning against the wall. He straightened and moved to Dru's side.

"He's been covering a lot," Dru said.

"Well, he's used to going home and having a life," Hailey said. "Unlike the two of us."

"So true," Dru said. "See you later."

She headed downstairs with Edgar Allan Crow, Viktor following close behind.

21

A few hours later, Dru pushed Gert's cart down the corridor, allowing the peaceful silence of the sleeping hotel to wash over her.

It was about five in the morning, and she had only a few more hours of her shift to go.

It had been a busier night than usual. The guests were finally feeling less frightened and more frustrated.

Without Gert or Constance, they had been a whole day without fresh towels and hot meals.

And the wind continued to blast the hotel with freezing air slipping in through every charming drafty window and doorway. The heat of the fireplaces was barely enough to keep the edge off.

And without internet or any kind of outside contact to distract them, the guests were going a little stir-crazy.

Dru had spent half her shift working through the dwindling piles of clean laundry. Now she was delivering bundles of fresh towels. If the generator didn't come on soon, they were going to run out within the next day or two.

Gert would have died if she had known Dru was

wadding up the towels and shoving them in plastic bags to hang on guest doors instead of folding them into swans with military precision.

But Dru was doing her best, and that would just have to be enough.

It wasn't fun, but it was nice to stay busy. It helped her not obsess over Viktor, who was waiting for her back at the front desk.

Had he known her Nana?

Was there something between them? Something that had drawn her into his arms.

Something that made her dream of him even before he arrived.

"Don't be ridiculous, Dru," she muttered to herself as she hung a bag of towels on the door of the Topaz room for the Wilders.

She crossed the landing toward the northern end of the occupied wing.

Viktor's three doors were grouped here, away from the others.

Why had he chosen these three rooms that were up against the abandoned wing and across the landing from the other rooms? Or was there no real reason? Maybe she was just overthinking things.

Dru started to hang a bag of towels on his door and hesitated.

No one was around.

And Viktor was at the desk for her, watching over the raven while she dropped off the clean laundry. She'd managed to convince him to let her out of his sight for a few minutes since everyone was sleeping.

Quickly, she slipped out her skeleton key and slid it into the door before she could change her mind. She stepped inside and closed it behind herself, afraid someone might wander into the hallway and notice her.

Leaning back against the door, she tried to figure out what she was doing. She had searched the room already, and there was nothing here. Some clothing, those ancient trunks, and that was all.

But she stepped further inside anyway. Holding her candle high to dispel some of the gloom.

She breathed in his clean scent and gazed over the room.

It was the same as before - sheets draped over the mirrors and windows like ghosts, a few items hanging in the open closet, and the creepy trunks.

Last time she was in this room, she had checked the closets, the drawers, all the surfaces.

She hadn't checked the bed.

Most people wouldn't hide anything in their bedding.

But most people slept in their beds.

Viktor didn't sleep in his bed. She wasn't sure where he slept, though she was pretty sure it had something to do with the trunks. But she was sure it wasn't the bed.

Before she could lose her nerve, she ran to the bed and began stripping it, setting the candle on the bedside table.

She pulled off the pillows, but there was nothing strange underneath.

She didn't find anything under the comforter or the sheet, but of course nothing would be there. Gert would have come across it while changing the sheets.

She eyed the mattress.

It was enormous. She was pretty sure she could get it off the bed, but was afraid she might not be able to wrestle it back on by herself.

But she was already sliding her hands under the mattress, heaving it up and pushing with all her might.

At first, she thought her efforts were in vain.

But when she lifted the fitted sheet from the box spring, she spotted something beneath.

Her hands shook a little as she reached for the plain, brown paper.

What am I even looking for?

She pulled out a manila envelope. It was unmarked.

She looked around, feeling silly for doing so. She was obviously alone in the dark room.

She carried the envelope over to the dresser, along with the candle, and pulled out the contents. A few pieces of paper slid out.

The first two pages seemed to be a profile of someone. There was a name at the top *"Little" Nicky Costello*.

She scanned the page and saw a rundown of crimes, spanning from burglary to solicitation to rape. Between the crimes and the name, it all sounded like something out of a mob movie.

Hurriedly, she flipped over the pages of the profile, and gasped when she saw what was underneath.

It was a black and white mug shot of a very familiar face - a face she had just used to unlock a phone screen - a face that had pressed close to her own, smelling of onions and cheap cologne - a face that was currently decomposing in a rolled-up rug a few floors below her feet.

Viktor...

Why do you have a picture of Brian Thompson in your room?

But she already knew why.

The man she was falling in love with was obviously a murderer.

22

Dru worked on autopilot as her mind raced.

She slid the papers and the picture back into the envelope and placed it on the box spring. She pulled the fitted sheet on top, yanked and tugged the mattress back into place, then grabbed the candle from the dresser, and stepped back out into the corridor.

There was no one in the hall. No one had seen her go in or out.

Viktor was probably the only other person awake in the hotel at this hour.

Vampire. He's a vampire, not a person.

She took a deep breath and tried to pull herself together.

She knew better than to confront him.

But each time she closed her eyes she could see the pool of blood surrounding Brian Thompson.

What if it hadn't all been there? How would anyone have known if some of it had been missing?

And the gaping slash across the throat could have easily been made to cover up the appearance of two little holes...

"Drucilla?" Viktor called softly from the bottom of the stairs.

She startled, then tried to pull herself together.

"Coming," she called back, moving to the landing.

He stood below, his blue eyes pale and worried.

He didn't look like a murderer. He didn't feel like one either.

But Dru knew too much at this point to believe her instincts.

She paused at the top of the stairs, not wanting to go to him, but afraid to do anything that would tell him she had seen the file.

"Are you okay?" he whispered.

"Fine," she said, forcing herself to descend and bring herself closer to him.

Scared as she was, it was impossible not to notice how he drew her to him.

In the cold light of her new knowledge, she tried to pick the feeling apart. Why was she pulled to him?

But it defied logic.

The attraction she felt wasn't purely physical. It wasn't sympathy or fascination.

He was familiar. Even now, he felt like *home* to her shivering soul.

She made it to the bottom step, and he reached out to touch her arm.

"Drucilla," he murmured. "What's wrong?"

"I was in your room," she heard herself say.

He stiffened, pale blue eyes narrowing slightly.

"I found the file," she whispered.

He didn't murder her for it. He didn't even get angry.

He just let his hand drop from her arm.

"Why, Viktor?" she asked. "Why would you kill him?"

"I didn't," he told her. "I know it's hard to believe, but I did not kill that man."

She blinked at him, slowly realizing that the one she shouldn't trust was herself.

Because, despite all odds, she truly wanted to believe him.

"Let's go someplace private to talk," he said. "I want to explain."

She shook her head slowly. "No, I won't go anywhere alone with you."

The hurt in his eyes cut her heart, and she stood before him bleeding.

"Can we talk in the sitting room?" he asked.

Here in the lobby someone could be close enough to hear them without their noticing. The sitting room was removed, but if she screamed, she might still be heard. And it was a public space.

It made sense.

She nodded and he smiled, hope lighting up his face.

He gestured and she led the way down the hall past the lobby and the kitchen to the sitting room, where she chose a chair near the fireplace.

Had they really only been in here a few hours ago, listening to Hazel and Honey?

It felt like a lifetime to Dru.

Viktor lowered himself into the chair opposite hers.

"I'm going to be honest with you," he told her. "Even if it means you will think less of me. You deserve the truth."

Dru watched silently emotions warred on his face before he continued.

"I came to Hemlock House to kill Brian Thompson," he said.

Dru gripped the arms of her chair.

"But I didn't kill him," Viktor said with a sigh. "Let me explain."

She nodded, feeling more stupid for sticking around with each passing moment.

"I told you before that I can feed on animals to stave off my need for human blood," he said.

She nodded.

"But I can't fully live without it," he went on, looking down at his hands. "Once every year or two, I have to feed on human blood. And my time is past due."

She bit her lip. She did remember him saying that. *Stave off*, not quench. And she had chosen not to ask the obvious follow-up question. She hadn't wanted to know.

"I choose my targets carefully," he said. "The lowest of the low. Rapists, murderers, people who bring nothing but misery to the world. Little Nicky Costello was one of those people. I could have killed him for what he did to you alone. Can you imagine how many other women he has assaulted? How many women do you think there are whose stories don't even appear on that report you found, because they're afraid of his connections? Or because they disappeared before they ever had the chance?"

Viktor rose from his chair and began pacing.

"Nicky had connections to the Irish mob. But he was too much of a loose cannon even for them. He became a liability. When he realized they were planning to cut him off, he agreed to testify against another mobster in exchange for immunity. He was placed in the witness protection program. You were correct about that. It was very clever of you."

He smiled proudly, then his face grew dark again.

"Can you imagine?" he asked. "A monster like that was going to spend the rest of his life in peace, protected by the federal government. The whole idea of it makes me sick."

He stopped pacing and turned to Dru.

"I have rules, Drucilla. One is that I never kill in anger, which is the only reason Costello made it past that night I caught him with you."

She turned in her seat to watch him warily.

"Another is that I do my homework," he said. "I've been tracking Little Nicky Costello for months. And when I found out he was coming here, I knew the time was right. This place was calling to me anyway. I had to come."

He stopped and knelt before her.

"But Drucilla, I never would have killed him in that way, leaving a frightening mess and a mystery behind," he said. "I brought the file to leave with his body, all of which I would have tucked away where no one would find it by accident. I planned to give an anonymous call to the police after I left, so they could discover it in the woods. They would have assumed his past finally caught up to him. Which would have been true, in a way."

She shuddered at the idea.

"I know it doesn't change what I am, Drucilla," he whispered pleadingly. "And it won't change your feelings. But I want you to know that I didn't kill him. But it was only because I didn't have the chance. Someone else got to him first."

"What does it matter?" she wondered out loud. "You're still a killer."

"I am," he agreed.

"It's in your nature," she said.

"It didn't used to be," he told her. "Even now, it disgusts me."

She gazed into the fire. It was dying. Unless someone added fuel soon, it would sputter out. Her heart was feeling the same way.

"What happens if you don't have human blood?" she asked.

"I get my warmth from the blood of the creatures I consume," he said. "You've noticed I'm not cold, like the vampires in the fairytales?"

She nodded.

"When I go too long without feeding, I become cold too," he said. "And the longer I go between human feedings the more animals I have to consume. Eventually, they are not enough."

He pressed his lips together, as if struggling to continue.

"And there are other concerns as well," he said.

"What concerns?"

"If I go too long without human blood I weaken," he said.

"Will you die?" she asked.

"I don't know," he told her. "That's not my worst fear."

She couldn't imagine what would be worse than that.

"Losing my humanity," he said, answering the question she hadn't yet asked. "Losing my empathy, losing myself to the hunger. That is what I fear most of all."

His words hung in the air.

She couldn't find the words to answer.

"If that happened, I would feed indiscriminately," he went on after a moment.

"Would feeding bring your humanity back?" she asked.

"I hope not," he admitted. "Because if it did, the guilt would be worse than death itself."

His beautiful face was rent with pain.

She reached out a hand to stroke his jaw in spite of herself.

But his hand was around her wrist before she could touch him.

"This won't work, Drucilla," he said flatly. "I can't live in your world without putting you in danger. It was stupid of me to even entertain the notion."

"Viktor," she breathed.

"I don't want to leave, but we don't belong in the same story," he said, his voice rough with pain. "The sun will be up in a few minutes. I'm going up to rest. When I wake again, I'll leave."

"Where will you go?" she asked.

"Far away," he said. "Far enough that you can't find me. Far enough that I can't bring my curse down on you."

"Please," she heard herself say.

She felt his lips brush her forehead and the breeze of his movement, as he disappeared into the darkness.

Dru sat alone on the leather chair, watching the fire die as the navy blue of pre-dawn seeped into the black sky outside.

23

D ru was still sitting in the chair when the last lingering flames in the fireplace finally winked out.

By then, the pink of dawn was rising in the east, behind the sitting room. Warm amber light seeped in through the big windows, casting a surreal glow around the stillness of the empty room.

Dru sighed and stood up. It was time to get back to work, time to try to put one foot in front of the other. And step one was getting the fire going again.

There was still plenty of wood inside, which was a relief. She grabbed a few logs from the rack and arranged them over the embers in the fireplace. Then she reached into the bin where there they kept the old newspapers for kindling, removing a few sheets and crumbling them into tight balls to wedge beneath the logs.

But something on the final sheet caught her eye.

There was a picture of the man she had known as Brian Thompson.

Little Nicky Costello Testifies While Mob Looks On, the headline read.

She scanned the article and it seemed to corroborate all that Viktor had said. Brian Thompson - Little Nicky Costello - had agreed to rat out his mob buddies in exchange for immunity.

She looked back at the picture and her mouth dropped open.

This couldn't be right.

Brian Thompson's wasn't the only face she recognized. There was another familiar guest in the background.

Johnny Smith.

In the picture, Johnny wore a black suit and stood in a line of angry looking men at the back of the courtroom. But she would have known his bald head and wide frame anywhere.

He was in the mob, Johnny Smith was in the mob.

Which meant he had reason to want Brian Thompson dead.

He must have been the other half of the argument she'd overheard. Johnny Smith was the one Thompson had called Sullivan.

Dru might have just solved the case.

And there was no one around to tell. She couldn't even call the police.

Think, Dru, think.

A plan started to form, and she sprang into action, jogging out of the sitting room and up the stairs to grab Brian Thompson's phone from her room, the newspaper still clutched in her hand.

Once she had the phone she came back down, pulled on her coat, and headed out the front door and into the cold morning air.

Snow still blanketed the meadow, the fallen tree, and the woods beyond. Sunrise tinted the icy landscape pink.

All she had to do was get through the snowy meadow into the woods where it wasn't as thick, and then hike up the hillside to find a signal, like she had done the other day with Hailey and Viktor.

The phone still had a charge. If there was enough battery life left to make a single call, she could let the police know about Johnny and Little Nicky.

She stepped out onto the porch and took a single step before she realized her mistake.

A figure stood next to the fallen tree, cigarette smoke swirling in a column above his bald head.

"Good morning, lobby girl," Johnny said with a thin smile.

She tried to cram the paper under her coat, but it was too late. He had obviously seen it.

"I see you're aware of my fifteen minutes of fame," Johnny said lazily nodding at the newspaper. "Where are you headed?"

"Just to get some fresh air," she lied. "But it's really cold out, I think I'll go back in."

She stepped backward.

Johnny moved as fast as a snake.

Before she knew what was happening, Dru found herself looking down the barrel of a gun.

"I think you're going to get that fresh air after all," Johnny said, standing up straight, cigarette hanging out of the corner of his mouth. "Come down here, and let's get to know each other."

Every instinct told her to run.

There was still some distance between them. He might not necessarily hit her. But Johnny's hand was steady, and his eyes were cold. He didn't strike her as the kind of person who missed.

And what would she do even if she got inside? She would still have to wake the others.

The only person in the hotel who would even consider protecting her from a man with a gun would be asleep in a trunk of grave soil by now.

"I know you think you can run," Johnny said, flicking his cigarette into the snow with his free hand. "Did you know that the bullet in this gun moves at twenty-six-hundred feet per second? It will go through you as easy as tissue paper."

Dru sighed and lifted her hands, letting the newspaper flutter to the porch floor.

"Good girl," he said. "Come see Johnny."

Each step felt like she was walking through wet cement.

When she reached the bottom of the porch steps, he waved her onward with the gun.

"Come on, come on," he said. "Moving slower won't change anything."

She moseyed anyway, making a show of trying to walk through the deep snow.

She gazed into the face of the man who was about to kill her, wondering if there was some way to figure him out, some perfect thing she could say that would unlock her hopeless situation.

But his face was calm and knowing.

He had surely killed before her and he would kill after her too.

She was nearly in his waiting arms when she heard the door to the hotel open behind her.

Johnny's eyes got bigger.

"Oh, this just gets better and better," he said. "Is this your boyfriend?"

She turned away from him without thinking.

Johnny locked his arms around her, and she felt the cold metal of the gun pressed to her temple.

"V-Viktor," she stammered.

Viktor stood on the porch, enveloped in shadow, his pale blue eyes seeming to glow.

"Let her go," he said, his dark voice cutting through the frigid air.

"Oh, I don't think so, loverboy," Johnny said. "I know you're not into her for her brains, but I'm sure you'd rather not see them splattered into the snow."

Viktor met her gaze for a moment, and she felt the sorrow there.

He was powerless to help her. There was an uncrossable ocean of sunlight between them.

His eyes shifted to Johnny, and he took a single step forward.

24

D ru tried to shake her head, but Johnny's hold was too tight.

"No, Viktor," she moaned. "Go back inside, call for help."

But he was already moving down the steps. He slowed when he hit the wall of sunlight, but he was still moving almost too fast to see.

The bite of the metal gun barrel disappeared from her temple.

There was a terrible blast, and Viktor staggered, then collapsed in the snow.

Dru was reminded momentarily of the first rabbit she'd found out here, helpless in a splash of red and white.

She'd been right. Johnny wasn't the type to miss.

"Come on, sweetheart," Johnny barked, dragging her toward Viktor. "I've gotta make sure Romeo is dead before we figure out what I'm gonna do with you."

She knew Viktor was more than human, but there was so much blood, and so much sun.

His body was motionless, face down in the snow. Smoke

had begun to rise from him, swirling up toward the brightening sky.

If the bullet hadn't killed him, the sunlight soon would.

"Is he on fire?" Johnny rasped, letting go of Dru with one hand to flip the vampire's body over.

Smoke lifted from Viktor's lifeless face, blurring his pale blue eyes like a mirage.

"What the actual fuck?" Johnny said in wonder, leaning over him and inadvertently blocking the sunlight.

Viktor blinked.

Then everything seemed to go in slow motion.

Before she could draw a breath, Viktor was standing, and punching Johnny so hard that his feet left the ground before he landed in a heap, his gun tumbling into the deep snow. He grabbed Dru as the front door to the hotel swung open.

Channing stood on the porch, staring. He must have been drawn out by the gunshot.

Dru felt Viktor's arms around her, and they dragged each other to the safety of the porch.

By the time they reached the shadows, Viktor was collapsing.

His skin was so pale, so very, very pale.

"Viktor," Dru sobbed.

Zander burst onto the porch, breathless.

"Don't let him get away," Channing said, motioning to Johnny, who had just begun to stir.

"He's dangerous," Dru warned. "Be careful."

Zander dashed off the porch and Dru turned her attention back to Viktor.

"Let's get him inside," Channing said quietly.

They each put an arm around Viktor and carried him in.

"To his room?" Channing suggested.

"Yes, please," Dru said.

It was too late. She knew already that he couldn't come back from this.

As they carried him upstairs, she thought about what he had been through - a gunshot, sunlight, so much pain.

And he was hungry.

An idea began to form in the back of her mind, but she wasn't sure it would work.

When they reached Viktor's rooms, Channing helped her place him on the bed of the Sapphire Suite.

Viktor's big body was sprawled out on the pale comforter. Even in his weakness he projected such strength.

"Leave us," she panted.

"Are you—" Channing began.

"*Leave us*," she spat. "Help Zander with Johnny. He's the killer. Get the newspaper off the porch and read it. Don't come back up here, no matter what."

She heard him pull the door shut behind him as she crawled into the bed.

"Can you hear me, Viktor?" she asked him as she peeled off her sweater.

"Drucilla." His whisper was hoarse, but he wasn't gone yet.

"Hold on, baby," she crooned. "Hold on, I've got you."

She unclasped her bra and placed it on top of her sweater.

The room was freezing.

She leaned back and pulled Viktor's head to her breast.

He was cool to the touch.

"It's time to feed now," she told him softly, sweeping her hair out of the way of her neck.

"Drucilla, no," he moaned. "Go away."

"I'm not going anywhere," she told him. "You saved my life, and now I'm going to save yours."

"No," he whispered.

"Yes," she said.

"It's not what you think," he murmured. "It's more than just food."

"Don't be stupid," she told him.

"It will bind us to each other," he told her. "We'll always be connected. If I manage not to kill you."

They had just broken things off.

Now she was going to be connected to him forever.

But none of that mattered. She was sure of it. This was the right thing to do.

"Just do it," she told him. "You're not going to kill me."

"How do you know?" he asked.

"Look, if I have to go find a knife and slice myself open and force feed you, I will," she told him. "Otherwise I need you to bite me. Now."

His expression wavered and she felt unshed tears stinging her eyes.

Whatever he was, he was already a part of her. They had been drawn together from the beginning. They would always be connected, no matter what.

"Please, Viktor," she said, closing her eyes. "Please."

She felt him lightly nuzzle her neck, and a shiver went down her spine.

Dru braced herself for the pain.

But the pain of his teeth sinking into her tender flesh was pleasurable, too.

Warmth washed over her, and she was filled with a sense of wellbeing.

Viktor groaned, the sound of his relief awakening her cells, filling her with a shimmering of desire.

She pressed herself closer to that hungry mouth.

He gripped her tighter now, his arms growing strong again, and warm.

Dru felt her body responding to his.

They had fooled around before, but this was something different, something darker and deeper. Something primal.

She tangled her fingers in his hair, pulling him in.

She could feel part of herself inside him now, pulsing, hot and exquisite. Behind her closed eyes she saw roses blooming and wilting, a thousand moons waxing and waning, until they seemed to strobe.

The universe was opening itself to her now and she yielded to it, taking it all in.

"Viktor," she whispered, moaning as she touched the face of the sun.

"Enough," he roared, tearing himself off her.

Dru swooned, her eyes still closed. The loss of his hot mouth at her neck left her swooning.

She opened her eyes, stretching languidly.

Viktor stood over the bed, his tangled hair falling in front of eyes as blue as the frozen lake.

His skin almost seemed to glow, and his presence was somehow even larger now.

Everything about him different, though she couldn't put her finger on a single thing that had changed.

He was still tall, lightly muscled, and handsome with long, dark hair.

But this man before her could never fit into the line at a crowded hotel. Charisma and raw power emanated from him, leaving her feeling a little dazed.

This man would always be spotted instantly, set apart from anyone else in the room with those denim blue eyes and the haze of brutal confidence that hung around him.

"Go, Drucilla," he said, looking away from her. "Put your clothes on and go."

"Viktor," she murmured.

"Go, before I change my mind," he snapped.

She dressed quickly and dashed to the door, unable to resist his command.

There was a creaking sound behind her and a sudden waft of loamy air.

She turned back to see him opening the largest of the trunks.

"Go, Drucilla," he intoned.

And though his deep voice slid through her seductively, she obeyed, closing the door behind her.

25

D ru took a few more steps down the hall, feeling so light that she had to look down to make sure her feet were still on the ground.

She clung to the railing as she lowered herself onto the first step.

Much as she hadn't wanted him to stop, Viktor was right. He had taken enough to leave her fuzzy around the edges.

The morning light was bleeding through the sheer curtains in the lobby, crawling over the pale area of the wooden floor where the rug used to be.

Dru took another step down.

There was a metallic thunk, followed by a loud rumble, and everything went white.

She closed her eyes and lowered herself to sit on the step, wondering if this was an effect of the blood loss.

Am I dying?

But when she opened her eyes again, she saw that what had blinded her was only the light from crystal chandelier that hung from the ceiling over the lobby.

The power was back on.

She pulled herself back to her feet.

Clinging to the railing, she moved down the steps.

No one was in the lobby to appreciate the chandelier or the clanging of the radiator pipes heating up.

She opened the front door to the whine of electric saws and a deeper rumbling.

A road crew must be out there, removing the tree.

And they must have brought fuel for the generator - that was the rumble.

Footprints in the snow led from the fallen tree around the abandoned wing of the hotel.

She knew she should go inside and get some juice or a cookie.

"Officer Wagner, Willow Ridge Police," someone called to her from the vicinity of the fallen tree.

She turned back to see a police officer climbing toward her.

He was tall and broad-shouldered, with military-short, blond hair. Big sunglasses protected his eyes from the glare of the snow.

"Thank God," she breathed. "There was a murder here, and we know who did it."

"Is everyone safe?" the cop asked, his tone surprisingly calm.

"No," Dru said. "The killer is still here."

"Where?" the cop asked.

"I-I'm not sure," Dru admitted, looking toward the empty spot where she'd last seen Johnny Smith. "But I know one of our staff was chasing him. And the footprints lead that way."

She pointed out the path and the officer took off without another word.

He didn't want her to follow, that much was clear.

But Dru hadn't spent days as a recording officer and then been taken hostage just to sit around while a killer was being brought to justice.

She followed as fast as she could, stepping in footprints left by him and the others so as not to wear herself out.

When she reached the back of the hotel, she could see Zander, Channing and Chester gathered outside the groundskeeper's shed as the officer approached.

"Stand back," he yelled to them, one hand going to the handle of the gun at his hip.

"He's trapped inside," Zander said helpfully.

"This is the Willow Ridge Police," the officer bellowed. "You have five seconds to come out with your hands over your head."

Dru kept moving toward them, eager to see Johnny led away in handcuffs.

But there was no sound or movement from the cottage.

"Five," the officer called out. "Four... three...two...one."

She had nearly reached the cottage when Officer Wagner kicked in the door, gun drawn. She held her breath, but there was no sound or movement from inside. The cottage was eerily still.

Officer Wagner stepped inside and flicked on a light switch.

Dru had never been in Chester's cottage before. Now she saw it was made up of a small room with a neat kitchenette and a living space large enough for a cot, an easy chair, and a television.

On the far wall was a built-in bookcase, next to something large and black.

No. It was more like a shadow.

Officer Wagner stepped inside and shone a flashlight at the shape on the wall.

But it wasn't a shadow. Dru could see now that it was an opening. It was shaped like a curved doorway, and lined with stones that formed a path that disappeared into darkness.

The catacombs.

Johnny had escaped into a secret tunnel.

"I'll be damned. I never knew there was a tunnel out here," Chester remarked. "I thought they were all in the basement."

Dru staggered backward and turned, tracing the horizon with her eyes. The forest was dark and imposing all around them, and the hotel loomed above. So many places to hide.

The killer could be anywhere by now.

***

EPISODE 3

Dru stood frozen, feeling the world around her spinning out of control.

Everything that had been charming about the Victorian hotel and the snow-covered grounds now seemed menacing to her.

It turned out that even the groundskeeper's cottage had an entrance to the underground tunnels beneath the hotel. And now the murderer had escaped down into them.

The forest all around gave cover, if Johnny had made it that far. If not, the nooks and crannies of the old hotel would provide ample hiding spots. And the rumble of the generator that was now powering the place would cover the sound of quiet footsteps.

The killer on the loose had every advantage.

And Dru was a sitting duck.

A hand closed over her shoulder.

She gasped, and then realized it was only Hugh Channing, the local theatre director, who up until now had been the amateur detective in charge of the case.

"Sorry I scared you," he said. "It's just that we need to talk."

"Sure," she said, swallowing and willing her heart to stop pounding in fear.

"Walk with me," he suggested.

She glanced back at Officer Wagner, who was conferring with Chester and Zander.

"I feel like we should stay with the group," she said.

"We won't go out of their sight," Channing offered. "But I don't think you want to discuss this in their earshot."

Dru turned back to him.

His expression was wary, but serious.

"Fine," she said, wondering what he could possibly have to say that she didn't know already.

The killer is mad at you, because you figured this out?

He was about to kill you before we ran him off?

Your life is in danger?

Dru was well aware of all those things.

"I know about Viktor," Channing said, throwing her completely off balance.

"Wh-what about him?" she hedged.

Maybe Channing just meant that he knew she had been seeing Viktor. There was probably some policy to stop staff and guests from fraternizing.

"I know...what he *is*," Channing said, his voice dropping.

Dru's heart dropped to her stomach.

"I don't know what you're talking about," she said coldly, breaking eye contact.

"I saw the way he moved when he went to help you, and what happened to him in the sun. And I stayed outside his door after you shut yourselves in," Channing said quietly. "I wanted to make sure he was going to be okay. He shouldn't have been okay. He was very badly wounded."

"I don't know what you think you saw—" Dru began.

"I'm going to be starring in a musical version of *The Lost Boys* next fall," Channing said. "You can't fool me. I've already been doing my research."

"What do you want me to say?" Dru asked. "What you're suggesting is ridiculous."

"I'm trying to say that I know he's a good man, in spite of being... *you know*," Channing said. "He risked his life to save yours. I saw it."

Relief flooded Dru's veins.

"You know he didn't have anything to do with Thompson's murder," she said quickly.

"Of course I know that," Channing told her. "But things are going to get intense now that there's a real officer of the law here."

Dru nodded, feeling deflated.

"I wanted you to know that I won't reveal his secret," Channing told her. "And if there's anything I can do to help you, let me know."

"Thank you," Dru said earnestly, though she doubted there was anything he could do to help.

"I wonder if he would chat with me after all this blows over," Channing said dreamily. "His input might give me a real edge at the Lakey Awards this year. I've been nominated and denied seventeen years in a row. They say I'm the Susan Lucci of the Poconos regional theatre."

"Let's hope this is your year," Dru said, wondering how he could think about anything beyond getting out of this hotel alive.

They had stopped about halfway between the abandoned wing of the hotel and the groundskeeper's cottage, and Dru could see that the others were heading their way.

"Hold up," Officer Wagner called.

She and Channing stayed where they were as they approached.

"Let's try to stick together," Wagner said sternly.

Dru nodded like a chastened child.

"Happy to, Officer," Channing said.

"Good," Wagner replied. "I see people are beginning to wake up." He nodded toward the hotel.

Sure enough, Dru could see lights were turning on. It must be eight by now and people would have been waking up anyway, but the roar of the generator and the lights going back on would have woken them regardless.

Not to mention the gunshot.

"We're going to gather everyone together," Wagner said. "And we're going to get to the bottom of this."

"Get to the bottom of what?" Dru asked. "We already know what happened."

"Do we?" Wagner asked, turning to her.

"Brian Thompson, the man who was murdered, was in witness protection," she explained. "His real name was Little Nicky Costello, and he testified against the mob. Johnny was in the mob too. He had every reason to kill him for squealing."

"That's an interesting theory," Wagner allowed. "But it sounds like the only thing you have to support it is a grainy newspaper photo and a little imagination."

"We had no power and no access to the internet," Channing put in.

"My partner and I will look everything over," Officer Wagner said. "You'll help us with access to the hotel records, Miss Holloway?"

"Call me Dru, and sure," she replied. "I'll help in any way I can."

"Excellent," Wagner said, nodding crisply.

He set off cheerfully toward the hotel, the others trailing in his wake.

It was going to be a long day.

But at least she would have something to keep her mind off her imminent murder.

Dru stood in the hotel lobby, watching the guests file down from their rooms. Zander was back on duty at the desk, and she didn't envy him his task.

"We want to check out immediately," Jeffrey Wilder told Zander anxiously.

Jenna and Angie, his wife and daughter, stood behind him. Jenna put her arm around Angie and Dru was amazed to see that the teenager was frightened enough not to shake it off.

"I'm sorry, Mr. Wilder, but the road isn't clear—" Zander began.

"No one can leave," Officer Wagner said. "This is still a crime scene."

"Not this again," Oscar Hawkins said as he walked past them to find a seat at the fire.

Dru noticed that Oscar had his camera with him, even though she doubted he was planning to go bird-watching when there was a killer on the loose.

"What did he mean by that?" Officer Wagner said.

No one answered.

"What did you mean by that?" he asked Oscar.

Oscar shrugged in a *don't-look-at-me* way.

"After the murder, we tried our best to collect some information," Dru offered. "We didn't know how long it would be until the police came."

"What kind of information?" Wagner asked.

"We took a lot of photos of the crime scene," Dru said. "And we asked everyone what they had seen and heard. I took notes."

"I see," Wagner said, nodding. "I'd like to see these pictures and notes. But first we need to have a little talk."

He clapped his hands together loudly, and the room quieted.

"This hotel and its grounds are officially a crime scene," he said loudly. "That means no one can come or go for the time being. We're going to get to the bottom of this. But for now, I'm asking each of you to go to your rooms and lock yourselves in until you hear from me that it's time to come out."

There was a communal groan at that.

"This is for your safety," Wagner said. "I will interview each of you later. My partner is still supervising the crew removing the tree, and it looks like that is going to take some time."

"Some of us are hungry," Tyler Park said loudly.

On the other side of the lobby, Dru's friend and fellow desk clerk, Hailey, grinned. She had a pretty obvious crush on the outspoken snowboarder.

"The young man at the desk will see to it that rations are brought to your room," Wagner said. "Any questions?"

Hailey looked a little disappointed at that. She probably wanted to bring Tyler his *rations*.

"When can we leave?" Melody Young asked. The local

newspaper photographer was standing beside Mayor Tuck, her arm around the mayor's curvy waist in a protective gesture.

Dru realized she probably wasn't the only one who had found romance at the snowed-in hotel.

"You can leave when we get to the bottom of this, and not before," Wagner said sternly. "Do I make myself understood?"

Young nodded, with a perturbed look on her face.

"Okay then," Wagner said. "Off to your rooms, all of you. Someone will be around with food shortly."

Dru watched as the guests shuffled off to their rooms.

"Show him the crime scene photos I took," Channing told her, handing her his phone.

"Thanks," Dru replied, taking it.

He nodded and gave her a significant look as he headed upstairs. She had no idea what it was about.

It was odd to watch the man she had begun to think of as a detective turn back into a regular guest now that the police were here. It seemed like he should be the one down here, explaining everything to Wagner.

She took a deep breath and approached the front desk.

Hailey arrived just before her.

"I'm also a desk clerk," Hailey said to Wagner. "Hailey Woods. I'd be glad to help with the meals." She smiled up at him.

Hailey's striking, goth beauty had always seemed almost magical to Dru, and she expected Wagner to fall instantly under her co-worker's spell.

"Excellent, Miss Woods," Wagner said, not seeming to notice Hailey at all beyond her offer of service. "Take the young man with you. Stick together."

"Yes, sir," she said.

Hailey gave Dru a look as she and Zander headed for the kitchen.

"Now, Miss Holloway," Wagner said, indicating the two easy chairs by the fire. "Let's have a seat."

Dru joined him, feeling nervous, though she had done nothing wrong.

"I'd like to hear everything, beginning with the night of the murder," Wagner said. "And please don't leave anything out."

"I don't have my notepad with me," Dru said. "So I don't have any notes on what everyone said."

"I don't care what everyone said," Wagner said dismissively. "At least, not yet. I want to know what you remember."

"Okay," Dru said. "Well, it was the night of the comet."

"What comet?" Wagner asked.

"Helsing's Comet," Dru said. "It's been all over the news. You can see it well from up here, so the hotel was full."

"I see," Wagner said, noting it down.

"It was my shift, so I was outside handing out binoculars," Dru went on.

"Who else was outside?" Wagner asked.

"Well, everyone," she replied. "I mean, not *everyone*, I think Mr. and Mrs. Wilder were... in their room."

It was probably best to leave out what she assumed they were doing.

"That's the man who wanted to leave just now?" Wagner asked, eyes narrowed.

"Well, yes, but they didn't hurt anyone," Dru said. "They just wanted some alone time."

Wagner raised an eyebrow.

"They meant to reserve two rooms," Dru explained.

"One for them and one for their daughter. But they mistakenly reserved only one."

"So you believe the Wilders were having sexual relations in their room during the murder?" Wagner asked, his pen hovering over his notepad.

"Please don't write that down," Dru said, feeling miserable.

"Miss Holloway," Wagner said.

"It's Dru," she told him.

"Dru," he allowed. "This is a murder investigation. Every detail, no matter how small or embarrassing, is important."

She nodded, pressing her lips together.

"Who else was missing?" Wagner asked.

Dru thought back.

"Their daughter was outside, so were the mayor and Miss Young," she said. "And Howie, Zander and Hailey, of course."

"You mean Howard Pembroke?" Wagner asked.

"Yes," Dru said.

Wagner noted everything down carefully.

"Who else was outside?" he asked when he was finished.

She thought back.

"Hazel and Honey Van Buren were there," she said, "They're the ladies who live permanently in the Amethyst Room. They were with Zander."

He wrote it down.

She tried to picture the hotel log in her mind to account for each guest. He would probably ask her to pull it out in a minute anyway.

She told him about Hugh Channing asking Tyler Park to be in *The King and I,* and she let him know about Oscar being one of the last ones out, saying something about oversleeping.

She hoped she wouldn't have to tell him about Viktor.

Viktor had been outside, but he had gone in to grab her gloves for her. That might raise some suspicion.

"What about the victim?" Wagner asked. "Was he outside at all that night?"

"Not that I remember," Dru said.

"And Johnny Smith?" Wagner asked.

"I did see him outside," Dru told him. "But he was around the front of the building, near the lobby, smoking."

"This was after everyone else was out?" Wagner asked.

"Yes. Wait, no," Dru corrected herself. "Oscar came out while I was talking to Johnny."

"What were you talking to him about?" Wagner asked.

"Binoculars, for the comet," Dru said.

Wagner wrote it all down.

She hoped she hadn't forgotten anything, or remembered it in the wrong order. But she didn't see what the big deal was. They knew exactly who the murderer was, and he was still on the loose somewhere nearby.

"Who discovered the victim?" Wagner asked.

Dru thought back but wasn't sure.

"We all sort of went inside at once when the storm picked up," she explained. "It was just a big mass of people rushing inside. There was a scream when someone discovered him - maybe Mayor Tuck? And then all of us discovered him."

"How did you determine that he was deceased?" Wagner asked.

"One of the guests, Tyler Park, is an EMT," Dru said. "He took his pulse and told us he was dead."

Wagner nodded.

"So you say that you took photographs of the crime scene and questioned everyone?" Wagner asked.

"That was Hugh Channing's idea," she said. "He played a detective in a play once, and had done some research at that time. He said we had to make sure the scene was safe and then record as much evidence as possible without anyone moving or interfering with anything."

"Very good," Wagner said, eyebrows raised. "What did you find?"

"There was a break in the blood spatter," Dru explained. "We thought maybe someone's shoe had gotten in the way. But we checked everyone's shoes, and they were all clean."

"Interesting," he said, making another note. "Anything else?"

"Not much," Dru admitted. "But we did take tons of pictures of the victim before we moved him."

"I'll need to see the body," Wagner said. "Where is it?"

"We, uh, wrapped him in the rug that used to be right there," Dru said, pointing at the bare floor. "And carried him down to the catacombs. It's cold down there."

"Very good," Wagner said. "We'll take a look at that shortly. And I'll want to see the photos."

"They're here, on Channing's phone," Dru said, handing it over.

"So you questioned everyone," Wagner said, taking the phone but not checking it. "I'll want to see the notes as well, but did anything of interest come up?"

"Not really anything about the crime itself, but Hazel and Honey, the two ladies in the Amethyst Room, they had noticed something about Brian," she said. "And, wow, about Johnny too, now that I think about it."

"What's that?" Wagner asked.

"They said they hated seeing *that element* back at the Hemlock House," she said. "They said something about not liking to see *them* back here. Of course at the time I was only thinking about the victim, but I wonder if they noticed something about Johnny too."

"What did they mean by *that element*," Wagner asked.

"They meant the mob," Dru said. "They were here back in the sixties when all that was still going on."

"How did they know the victim was in the mob?" Wagner asked.

"They said he was always tipping people and always looking over his shoulder," Dru said, realizing it sounded weak.

Wagner frowned and nodded at the same time, writing it all down.

"Then Channing and I searched the victim's room and found his phone," Dru said, feeling a little squeamish about sharing the next part.

"Were you able to open it?" Wagner asked.

"I, uh, had to get creative," Dru admitted.

"Meaning?" He gazed up at her with interest.

"I went into the catacombs and did face recognition using his corpse," she said, hoping that wasn't a criminal act.

"Very smart," he said. "Probably wouldn't have had much time to do that either, what with decomposition. Anything useful on the phone?"

"Messages saying he was here for some kind of payday," Dru said. "And we noticed he signed some emails *Nick* instead of Brian."

"Mmm," Wagner nodded. "Channing still have the phone?"

"Nope, I've got that one, too," Dru said. She pulled it out of her pocket and handed it to him.

"It sounds like Channing was heading up the investigation," Wagner said. "Why do you have all the phones?"

"Channing just gave me his before we sat down," she explained. "In case you wanted to see the pictures."

"And the victim's?" he asked.

"Well, like I said, I was the one who figured out how to unlock it," she reminded him. "And then I guess I just kind of held onto it."

"Did you use it for anything else after your initial search?"

"Almost," she told him.

He raised an eyebrow, clearly expecting her to elaborate.

"I was in the sitting room early this morning," she explained. "I was using newspaper to fuel the fire. And the one I grabbed happened to have a cover story about the mob case. I saw Brian on the cover. And I also saw Johnny."

Wagner nodded.

"My own phone battery is dead, and the generator wasn't on yet," Dru said. "But Brian's phone had a tiny bit of juice left. So I grabbed it and headed out to hike the hillside like Hailey and Viktor and I did before, so I could try to call the police again and share what I had learned."

"But you didn't," Wagner said.

"Nope," Dru replied. "I never had a chance. As soon as I got outside, I saw Johnny was out there smoking again. And he saw the newspaper I had in my hands. He knew that I knew."

Wagner was scrawling furiously.

"H-he held up a gun," Dru said unsteadily. She had done her best not to think about it. "And he told me to come to him."

"And you went?" Wagner asked.

"Yeah," Dru said. "I was afraid to run."

Wagner nodded.

"Then the front door to the hotel opened and I turned to

see who it was," Dru said. "That's when Johnny grabbed me and put the gun right to my head."

She touched her temple, which was still tender from the pressure of the metal barrel.

"Who was it?" Wagner asked. "At the hotel door?"

"Viktor Striker," she replied. "One of the guests."

"What did he do?" Wagner asked.

"He told Johnny to let me go, but he wouldn't." She swallowed hard, not anxious to remember the next part. "Then Viktor charged at us, and Johnny shot him."

"A man has been shot?" Wagner asked, looking up.

"Yes," Dru said.

"Is he in danger?" Wagner asked. "I knew there was a gunshot, but no one said there was an injured person."

"He's going to be fine," Dru said, realizing her error. She wasn't even sure if Viktor still *had* a wound after she fed him. That had kind of been the whole point. What was she going to say when Viktor showed up without a scratch on him?

"Can he corroborate your story?" Wagner asked.

"Of course," she said. "But I'm sure he's resting now. He's in some kind of international work, so he sleeps during the day."

She looked around the lobby. Sunlight was streaming in every window. There was no way he could talk with Viktor right now.

"I need to interview him before he forgets anything," Wagner explained. "I'm sure he can wake up for a few minutes for something this important. He can't have been in bed that long and with all the excitement, I doubt he's even asleep. In my experience, gunshot victims tend to be traumatized, no matter how minor."

"Oh," Dru said, utterly unable to come up with one good reason why they couldn't go see Viktor.

"Come on, let's go check on your knight in shining armor," Wagner said, winking at her as he rose from his chair and gestured for her to lead the way.

D ru led Officer Wagner up the staircase, her mind reeling.

If Viktor didn't come to the door, would he kick it in like he had the door of the groundskeeper's cottage? If he did, would he be suspicious not to find Viktor there? Would he check the trunk?

Viktor isn't suspected of anything. Wagner won't kick in his door.

Will he?

"Which one?" Wagner asked her as she paused in the hallway, trying to think of any excuse.

She pointed toward the Sapphire, Onyx, and Quartz rooms, wondering if she could slow him down by taking him to the other two rooms first.

But that was ridiculous, it was still morning. She couldn't keep him distracted until dark with some kind of Scooby-Doo doors and hallways gag.

"This one," she said, indicating the entrance to the Sapphire room.

Wagner tapped on the door. "Mr. Striker, this is Officer Wagner. I need to ask you some questions ab—"

The door swung open and Channing slipped out, wearing a white lab coat and looking like some kind of enraged pharmacist.

"How dare you disturb this man?" Channing demanded in a harsh whisper. "He is under my care."

"This is a police investigation, sir," Wagner said. "We need his cooperation."

"He'll speak with you when he's rested and not before," Channing scolded.

"He may need serious medical attention," Wagner said.

"The wound was minor, but he was shaken up," Channing retorted. "I've given him something to relax his nerves, so he'll be out for a little while. When he's feeling himself, I assure you that we'll call for you."

"Did you want to go see the body?" Dru suggested to Wagner.

She definitely didn't want to see the body again. But she hoped the offer might be enough to distract him.

"Very well," Wagner said, looking frustrated. "But I'll be back to speak with him as soon as he's up."

"Of course, sir," Channing said.

Wagner turned and headed down the stairs. His pace beating a staccato rhythm on the steps.

"Thank you," Dru mouthed to Channing.

Channing smiled delightedly, giving her a deep bow.

Dru grinned and headed after Wagner before he could notice she wasn't right behind him.

"That was Tyler Park, the EMT?" Wagner asked.

"No, that was Hugh Channing," she said, before she could stop herself.

"I thought you said he was...an actor?" Wagner asked, stopping in the lobby to look at his notes.

"Who can really make a living as a full-time actor these days?" Dru ventured, hoping it was enough.

"I see," Wagner said, and made a note. "Which way to the *catacombs* as you call them?"

"I usually go out through the solarium and enter from the back," Dru said.

"There's no access from the first floor?" Wagner asked, looking surprised.

"Oh, there is," Dru told him. "But there are so many tunnels that I prefer to go the most direct way."

She didn't want to talk about the fact the narrow tunnel from the inside was too much for her to handle sometimes.

"Wouldn't want to get lost down there, eh?" Wagner asked.

Dru shook her head. Once was enough.

"I remember touring this place in elementary school," Wagner said. "Underground Railroad and all."

"Me too," Dru said, grinning. "And I guess the mob used it to move alcohol during Prohibition."

"And to move stolen jewels, according to legend," Wagner said. "You get a lot of treasure hunters up here?"

"I've only been here a few weeks, so I'm not sure," Dru admitted.

They had reached the solarium, where she took him out through the door and into the snow.

The sky was clear and bright now. She wondered if the sun would have a chance to melt everything before it froze again overnight.

It had been a while since she'd been awake at this hour.

Dru slipped out her skeleton key and opened up the basement entrance.

A faint odor of decay greeted her right away.

"This won't be pretty," Officer Wagner said. "You don't have to come with me."

"I'll get you in there," Dru offered. "The tunnels wind and branch off. I want to make sure you find him."

"Here, then," Wagner said.

He was offering her a clean handkerchief.

She didn't even know they made those anymore.

"Thanks," she said.

"As soon as we locate the body, you'll leave me to do my work," Wagner said.

"Agreed."

They stepped down into the catacombs.

The awful, almost fishy scent overwhelmed the usual damp odor. Dru was grateful for the handkerchief, she pressed it to her nose and started off for the area with the bins, Officer Wagner by her side.

By the time the right branch was in sight, she was struggling not to gag.

She pointed and he nodded.

As he headed for the body, she turned and jogged for the light of the door back outside.

The tunnel seemed to stretch longer as she ran. After a few moments, she had the illogical feeling that she would never make it out.

But then she was jumping up the steps and flinging herself into the cold, fresh air.

Dru leaned against the wall of the hotel, panting.

She wondered if Wagner wanted her to wait for him. He hadn't expressly asked her to do so, but he seemed to be using her as a kind of tour guide.

The sun was bright in the sky, and she really ought to be sleeping.

But she was pretty sure sleep wasn't going to come, no matter how tired she felt.

Dru decided to wait for him, at least for a few minutes.

Her mind went almost immediately to Viktor, as it always seemed to do lately.

She closed her eyes and felt his mouth at her neck again, felt her life-force enter him, even as he owned her flesh with his mouth.

The sensation had been so unusual, so unexpectedly sensual.

She wondered if it made him crave her too.

Or maybe for him it was nothing more than nourishment, and a bond he formed to his prey, keeping it willing...

She had definitely been willing.

But he didn't want to be with her. He had told her he couldn't exist in her world.

No matter what he said, he saved my life.

She saw him bolting into the sunrise, his own life-energy pouring off him in shimmering, burning waves as he ran for Johnny.

Johnny.

Her eyes searched the horizon as the thought brought her back to her senses.

Johnny could be anywhere. Why was she standing out here alone?

The sound of heavy footsteps, moving fast, echoed from the catacombs behind her.

She gasped and turned to find Officer Wagner coming out to join her.

"What were you doing out here by yourself?" he asked. "I thought you were going back inside."

"I-I thought you might need me," she said.

He studied her for a moment. "What shift do you normally work?"

"I'm the night clerk," she said. "Midnight to eight."

"You should be sleeping by now, shouldn't you?" he asked.

She shrugged.

"Who's on duty now?" he asked. "The muscular guy, or the pretty Black lady?"

"Uh, Zander," Dru said. "The guy."

"Alrighty then," Wagner said. "Go to bed. I'll find Zander if I need anything."

"Thanks," Dru said.

"Are you okay to get up there on your own?" he asked.

"Wagner," someone called before she could answer. They both turned to find an older, uniformed gentleman with a white beard and mustache stepping out the door of the solarium and coming to join them. He was heavyset and shorter than Wagner, with twinkling eyes that reminded Dru of her Grandpa Frank.

"I see you found a pretty girl to talk to, eh Wagner?" the man asked, and then laughed at his own joke. "Left me to watch the crew while you took in the local talent, ha!"

Dru smiled in spite of herself. He was clearly just trying to break the ice.

"Miss Holloway, this is Officer Clemens," Wagner said.

"Pleased to meet you, dear," Officer Clemens said, giving her a Santa Claus-like smile.

"Miss Holloway was just leaving," Wagner said. "I'll fill you in while we check out the tunnels."

"Very good," Clemens said, giving Dru a little wave.

She headed into the warmth of the solarium as the officers talked about visiting Hemlock House before on an elementary school field trip.

D ru felt exhaustion descend on her like a heavy blanket the moment she opened the door to her room.

The past few hours had felt like a lifetime, and it was later than she normally went to bed. The shadowy rose-wallpapered space felt sheltered and dreamy in the late morning light.

The heat was back on, the comfort only adding to her drowsiness.

She checked to be sure her bed was still blocking the bookshelf from sliding open to reveal a secret door into the catacombs.

When she was satisfied that it was, and that her phone was on its charger, Dru collapsed into bed, fully dressed.

She closed her eyes and gave in to the pull of sleep, which came on so quickly it felt like the room was spinning around her as she sank into sleep.

Immediately she was falling, falling...

In her dream, Dru landed soundlessly on her feet, the scents and sounds of the forest filling her senses.

She was hungry, so hungry that the pain of it clawed at her from the inside. But instead of heading back to the hotel to find a snack, she held perfectly still.

There was no need to breathe, her body merely paused.

All around her, the denizens of the night forest revealed themselves.

She could hear the light tap of a squirrel's heart beat and the frantic thrum of a bird's.

Too small...

A light snow fell all around her, and she heard each tiny flake land on the leaves and branches, saw the crystalline perfection reflect in the moonlight in a spectrum that included colors she had never noticed before.

She waited.

Time had a different quality here. It stretched and bent. She had no idea how long she remained in statue stillness. Minutes? Lifetimes?

She discovered her quarry at last, not by sensing the creature itself, but by the other animals' reactions to it. One by one heartbeats sped and tiny feet scampered into nests and burrows.

Then the predator's scent filled her senses, and she felt the frenzy of her hunger solidify, turning her vision ruby red.

When she moved it was as if the forest around her slowed in her wake. She flashed through the underbrush, delirious with hunger as she grew closer to her prey.

Enticing, scarlet blood pulsed through its body - enriched and fortified by the other creatures it had consumed. She could *smell* it, the salt of the plasma, the tangy spice of the platelets, which would course and spin in a chase of their own long after she had drunk her fill, making her own body effervescent for a time, as if that life were her own.

Its heartbeat lubbed slowly in comparison to the smaller creatures she had sensed.

Dru flew into the meadow, and it was in her field of vision at last. She staggered mentally, even as she felt herself carried inexorably forward to her target.

The sensations she was experiencing weren't just unfamiliar. They actually belonged to someone else.

I'm Viktor. This is Viktor's memory...

The fox froze in place, as if it knew something was very wrong.

She was moving so fast that its flame colored fur lifted slightly at her approach.

The thrum of its pulse set off a chain reaction in her body, and she felt her canine teeth lengthen and slide downward.

There was a twinge of pain, but then her mouth was filled with saliva and her hands were plunging into the silken fur, grasping the creature before it even had time to fully realize she was there.

Her teeth sank effortlessly into warm flesh.

By instinct, she hit the unfortunate creature's jugular on the first try, as she'd done a thousand times before. Blood jetted against the back of her throat, and she might have gagged if she actually needed to breathe.

She felt her whole body coming back to life, as if she were a cold, dry sponge being soaked in warm water. She imbibed that life through every part of herself, her throat, her stomach, her nasal linings. It brought wild pleasure to every surface it touched.

The fox finally remembered to struggle, but it was far too late for that. Each kick of its hind legs sped more of the glorious feast down her throat. Her eyes rolled back in her head and she gloried in the sensation of warmth and satisfaction.

Visions of lush meadows full of rabbits, and the warm sun reflecting in the perfectly smooth surface of the lake flashed through her mind and she feasted on the creature's memories as well as its life force.

Too soon, the fox grew light in her hands.

She let its desiccated form drop to the snowy ground and sailed away from it, feeling a twinge of guilt even as she knew it was better this way. Better than gorging on her own kind.

But then again, humans hadn't really been her own kind in a long time.

Something else called to her, and she paused again, stone still, waiting, her heart shot through with anticipation.

Another pulse coursed through her.

If the fox had excited her senses, it was nothing compared to this.

This new heartbeat pounded at a rhythm that woke her soul, if she still had one. This was hundred times, no, a thousand times more intense than hunting the fox.

She could already taste the exquisite bouquet of the blood, the heady perfume of the creature that held it, pale and wide-eyed.

Everything in her body hummed with the need to protect this human.

She closed her eyes and saw the subject of her wild need painted in her mind.

Still inhabiting the body of Viktor, Dru's dream-self was shocked to see the image of her own face.

Viktor's memories of her flashed past while she was still reeling - images of herself standing behind the desk, positively radiant in Viktor's eyes, the thrill of her pulse visible to him through the honeyed skin of her pale neck.

She saw herself, saint-like and glowing in his eyes, sunlight emanating from her hair so pure he could taste it, her smile like rain in the desert.

Was this really how he saw her?

Something like love but more frightening enveloped them, binding him close to her.

Another hunger sizzled under her borrowed skin and urged the throbbing of Viktor's ghostlike heart.

Twin urges threatened to tear them to pieces.

I need to stay with her, to protect her always.

I have to leave her, my very existence is a danger to her.

She felt his battle to restrain himself, the tightness in his chest as he fought to circle in her orbit without crashing himself into her as his body and soul demanded.

Church bells rang as he gazed into her eyes.

The bells grew harsh as her image faded.

Dru awoke to the jangling bell sound of her phone alarm.

She sat up in bed and looked at the window. The last rays of the sun were still visible in the afternoon sky.

But Viktor would be awake soon.

A delicious shiver went through her at the thought and she hugged herself, trying to shake the dream and slip back into reality.

Half an hour later, showered and dressed, Dru headed downstairs to find something to eat.

"Holy crap, you missed so much," Hailey called to her from the desk.

"I'm kind of starving, can you hold that thought?" Dru asked.

Hailey rolled her eyes.

"Go ahead. Though how you can eat at a time like this, I have no idea."

Dru laughed and headed for the dining room.

There was still no Constance, and the whole place was pretty much on lockdown.

But the cereal, bread and toaster were still out from breakfast. Dru made herself big bowl of sweet cereal and a couple of pieces of buttered toast and poured herself out a big cup of apple juice.

She carried her meal back to the lobby and sat at the small table in front of the fireplace. Though the heat was on again she was still drawn to the fire. It felt like she might never be warm again.

Hailey came over and sat down right away.

"You eat," she said. "I'll catch you up."

"Thanks," Dru replied around a bite of toast. "So what's going on?"

"Okay, I'll start with the hotel," Hailey said. "As you can tell by the fact that it doesn't sound like an F-15 is landing outside, the power is back on and the generator is no longer needed."

"I hadn't noticed that, actually," Dru said. "But now that you mention it, it's pretty nice."

"Agreed," Hailey said. "The tree is out of the way. There are giant logs all over the place on the lawn, but it's possible to get up and down the drive now."

"Even better," Dru said.

"But here's the bad news," Hailey told her. "No one is allowed to go in or out until the police are finished. And they're taking their time."

"Really?" Dru asked, feeling a little hopeless.

"Channing said you figured the whole thing out," Hailey said.

"Yeah," Dru told her. "Only because I came across that newspaper. But I guess they still have to investigate."

Dru wasn't about to say it, but she'd wondered about just how lucky she'd gotten by finding that article. Was it really luck, or was there something more going on? She knew the rumors about the old place being haunted. What if someone, or something, had wanted her to find that paper?

But she had enough going on just dealing with mobsters and vampires. There was no need to bring ghosts into the mix.

"You're a real Nancy Drew," Hailey commended her. "I'm sure they'll find what they need to support your theory, and we'll all get some hot food again."

"That would be nice," Dru said, looking down at her half-eaten cereal. "And technically, we're both Nancy Drews. I never would have looked twice at that newspaper if you hadn't turned us on to the whole witness protection thing by noticing Brian's clothes."

Hailey gave her a little nod of acknowledgement and then stole a piece of her toast.

There was really only one question on Dru's mind.

"Did they find Johnny?" she asked quietly.

Dru was pretty sure Hailey would have told her right away if the man trying to murder her had turned up. But she was going to hold out hope as long as possible.

Hailey shook her head, sadly.

"Is the internet back up again?" Dru asked, trying not to show her disappointment.

"Yes," Hailey said with her mouth full of toast, looking delighted that Dru had asked. "I was saving that excellent news for last."

"Thank God," Dru said. "I kind of left my monster hunter group at a rough moment."

"Oh yeah?" Hailey asked.

Crap.

Dru trusted Hailey with her life, but she couldn't bring herself to start a conversation about vampires.

"Just, you know, the murder and everything," Dru said weakly.

"Sure," Hailey agreed. "Do you want to hear about everyone they've been questioning?"

"Did you sit in?" Dru asked. "Did they make you take notes?"

"Nah, I'm nobody's secretary," Hailey teased. "But I could see everyone going in and out of the sitting room from here. Crazy stuff."

The last of the pink sunset was draining from the room, leaving the windows deep blue. Dru lost the train of Hailey's description as a sensation of lightness filled her being. It was followed by a gentle tug, as if a rope were tied around her heart and someone was flicking it playfully.

"Oh," Dru said, standing.

"You okay?" Hailey asked, looking up at her.

But the tug was replaced by a steady pull.

It felt like she was at the bottom of a swimming pool with her lungs full of air, the pressure building, pushing her upward.

Viktor.

She could feel his presence enveloping hers with a warm insistence.

"Where are you going?" Hailey asked, her tone slightly whiney.

Dru realized she was ascending the stairs, without having consciously made the decision to go.

"I-I have to go," she murmured.

Viktor is awake.

Dru was on the landing when Channing spotted her on his way down the corridor.

"Dru," he called to her delightedly. "You're awake."

"Hello," she said, trying to focus on him even as she felt herself drawn toward Viktor's rooms.

"We've got internet access again," Channing said, jumping right in. "And the police have access to their records, of course."

"That's great," Dru told him distractedly.

"First of all, you and Hailey were right," Channing said. "Brian Thompson was in witness protection. He was really Little Nicky Costello the whole time."

Dru nodded.

"What about Johnny?" Dru asked.

"They seem to have a lot of guys scouring the woods, but so far no sign of him," Channing said, shaking his head sadly. "I'm sorry, Dru."

"Do they believe us that he's Johnny Sullivan?" Dru asked.

Channing shrugged. "Trouble is, we have no photos of the guy who was here. He paid cash, used a different name. All we have are eye witnesses, which they said are notoriously unreliable."

"Drucilla."

Viktor's voice shot through her, and she turned on her heel and walked away from Channing without another word.

"I'll, uh, see you later, Dru," Channing said somewhere behind her.

The hotel had disappeared. There was no corridor, no, floor, no ceiling, no one and nothing existed but Viktor's dark voice.

From the darkness of the doorway to the Sapphire Suite, bright blue eyes glowed, fixed on Dru.

As she approached, the shadow detached itself from the door and snatched her up in strong arms.

She closed her eyes and felt the rush of the air around her as he swept her into the room. The door slammed behind them and her feet touched the ground again.

She opened her eyes to find that she was standing at the foot of his bed.

Viktor loomed over her, danger flashing in his azure eyes.

He reached for her slowly, so slowly, and stroked her cheek.

She leaned into his touch, sighing out a breath she hadn't realized she'd been holding.

He acted so quickly the air around him seemed to blur. She couldn't track his movements, but she felt his hands on her.

An instant later she stood before him naked, her clothing on the floor at her feet.

Viktor gazed at her in rapturous wonder for one blinding instant, and then he was on her.

She closed her eyes and tried to hold onto herself under the onslaught of his violent kiss.

She didn't know if he wanted to feed on her again, or if he would make love to her.

She didn't care which, but he had to do something. She was empty, yawning open inside. Dru felt like a blank page, waiting to be written on.

Viktor was still dressed, his clothing abrading her tender flesh as he kissed her cheeks, her eyelids, her forehead, and then dove into her neck to nibble her hungry flesh.

Dru heard a low moan and realized it was coming from her own mouth.

Suddenly her back was slammed into the wall and Viktor was pressing his steely body against hers, his hands moving over her breasts, teasing and tormenting her.

"Please, Viktor, please," she whispered.

He knelt instantly, licking her nipple and then half her breast into his mouth, while he toyed with the other one with his hand.

Dru's hips were shivering as she arched her back into his mouth.

Viktor groaned.

She felt his other hand sliding up her thigh and a jolt of pleasure went through her in anticipation.

He groaned again as he pressed his finger inside her.

She was so ready for him. There was no pain, no hesitation as she jogged herself shamelessly against his finger.

He kissed down her belly, then grabbed her hips with one arm, pulling her forward so that his mouth could join the hand that teased her.

His tongue was velvet heat, moving at the speed of light.

The pleasure was so intense it was almost like pain. In her confusion, Dru struggled against it, and he pinned her more tightly.

Fireworks lit behind her eyes, exploding in colorful magic in time with her body. Dru was shimmering, flying.

No, she was being carried.

She opened her eyes to find herself in bed, Viktor standing above her, his clothing abandoned.

He looked like a god. Though the power was back on, his room was lit only with candles, their flickering glow highlighting the topography of his powerful body.

In place of the tortured expression he often wore, he exuded confidence. In spite of his still pale coloring, he was bristling with a healthy glow, he looked *vital*.

Me. That's me inside him, my blood, my life-force, illuminating him.

The idea sent another lick of desire through her and she reached for him, desperate to feel his arms around her again.

D ru gasped as Viktor pounced on her.

He pinned her to the bed with his hips and stared down at her. The expression on his beautiful face was close to fury, but she knew he was just wild with lust.

The powerful line of his jaw was mesmerizing. She lifted her hand to trace it. Before she could touch him, her wrist was pinned to the bed beside her head.

"Careful, Drucilla," he hissed through clenched teeth.

The sibilance seemed to stimulate her skin and she shivered beneath him, desperate.

He pressed his lips to hers and she tasted him once more.

Visions appeared behind her eyes.

She saw herself, delicious and vulnerable, pinned like a butterfly for his pleasure.

She saw him inside her, moving quickly, wrenching screams of pleasure from her, throwing his head back and howling with ecstasy.

She saw the black of the night sky, studded with diamond stars and felt their hands joined together.

"Yes," she pleaded, unsure of whether he was showing her these things on purpose, or if she had invaded him with her blood and these thoughts were stolen.

"Look at me."

She opened her eyes obediently.

He fixed her in his gaze, and she felt him press the heated steel of himself against her swollen opening.

The pleasure was so intense that she tried to close her eyes again.

"Look at me, Drucilla," he said, ceasing his movement until she did.

Lifetimes passed as he slowly entered her, every millimeter of movement setting off sparks inside her.

"Viktor," she moaned when he was finally seated fully inside her.

His eyes were hazy with pleasure.

It was suddenly easy not to close her own. She was so eager to watch his expression grow desperate with hunger.

He groaned and began to move.

Pleasure filled her from the tips of her toes to the follicles of her hair.

She felt her own pleasure, and his as well, sensations echoing back and forth like a hall of mirrors, lifting her too quickly.

She cried out as he slid a hand between them to thrum rapidly against her clitoris as he howled with the pleasure.

She could feel herself clenching him like a fist, his cock jetting in wild ecstasy at the same time as her own climax tore through her, a forest fire burning everything in its wake.

At last, the storm was over, and he curled himself around her and nuzzled her neck.

"Drucilla," he whispered.

Dru felt a peace she had never known before.

"You are mine now," he whispered into her hair, inhaling her so that she tasted her own scent.

She placed her open palm against his chest.

As she drifted into sleep, she wasn't sure if his chest was warming her hand or the other way around.

8

D ru awoke in a darkened room to a sense of loss.
She tried to press herself closer to Viktor, but
he was gone.

Panic shot through her.

She opened her eyes and sighed in relief when she saw
he was still in the room.

He stood beside the window. He had uncovered it, and
the sheet lay across the chair.

Viktor wore a pair of jeans and nothing else. The moonlight suffused his pale torso and shone in his dark hair, so
that he looked like a fallen angel.

Even his expression was mournful.

"Viktor," she murmured.

"My love," he replied, turning to her, his eyes caressing
her.

"What's wrong?" she asked.

"I was just watching the flashlights moving in the
woods," he said. "The police are looking for answers."

"I'm curious too," Dru admitted.

"But you already know who killed the man," Viktor said, a crease appearing in his forehead.

"Something's bothering me though," Dru said. "Why was Costello here? Why was Sullivan here? They weren't comet-watching, or looking for a quiet getaway. What was the big payday?"

"Does it matter?" he asked.

"What if there's still something else going on?" she replied. "What if we're still not safe?"

There was a blur and a breeze, and then he was holding her again.

The clean, masculine scent of him was intoxicating.

"You will always be safe," he told her. "You are mine now. I will protect you."

But who will protect me from you?

"I'm still curious," she said instead.

"Ah, now that's different," he said, sitting up. "Should we investigate?"

She smiled at his enthusiasm. "Yeah, let's investigate."

"Where do we start?" he asked.

She thought back to everything that had happened since killer and victim had arrived.

"Someone deciphered my grandmother's journal," she said, watching closely for his reaction. "They slid the pages under my door."

A fleeting emotion slid across his face and echoed in her own chest - flashing bright like a penny falling into a pool and then disappearing in the depths.

"And neither one of those guys seemed like they were big readers," Dru continued. "So it must have been one of the other guests. Who do you think it could be?"

"I don't know," he said, getting back out of bed and grabbing his shirt off the bedside table.

She watched him put it on and button it up.

Whatever she had felt, or thought she'd felt just now, he was trying to hide it from her.

Was there something in the journal that he didn't want her to know?

Was he Michael?

She thought back.

When the journal was lost, Viktor was the one who had found it behind her desk.

What if that had just been sleight of hand?

He was capable of inhuman speed. It would have been easy for him to take the journal and return it...

"Did you decipher the journal?" she asked him directly.

"No, Drucilla," he told her, his face snapping to hers, his eyes slightly widened in surprise. "Why would you think that?"

"No reason," she said, shrugging. "You were afraid for me to read it. I thought maybe you swiped it, deciphered it to be sure there was nothing in it that would upset me, and put it back."

"To protect you?" he asked.

She nodded.

"Interesting," he said. "Would that have been okay with you?"

"It would have been understandable," she said.

"Well, it didn't happen," he said.

He was telling the truth, she was sure of it.

"I think I'd like to read the whole thing," she said. "I never had a chance in all the excitement. Maybe there's some reason it was taken."

"Sure," he said lightly and bent to pull on his socks.

Was he indifferent? Or was he avoiding her eyes?

"I'm just going to clean up and get dressed," she told him. "And then we can go check some stuff out."

She got up, grabbed her clothing, and headed for his bathroom.

She was amazed to find that her clothes were entirely intact. He had removed them from her so swiftly that she had assumed they would be damaged. But there wasn't so much as a missing button.

Well, it's obviously not the first time he's done that.

She tamped down that thought and readied herself as quickly as she could. When she came out Viktor was leaned against the wall, waiting.

"Hey," she said.

"Hey, yourself," he replied, pulling her close for a kiss.

The world around her disappeared for the second time in a single night. Dru felt her whole body fill with warmth.

But Viktor pulled back slightly. "You want to do some sleuthing before your shift begins, right?"

"Y-yes," she said, trying to remember what it was that had seemed so important a minute ago.

"Why don't you go grab the journal pages?" Viktor asked. "I'll clear off my desk and we can spread out here."

"Sounds good," she said, still gazing into his eyes.

He chuckled and stroked her cheek with the pad of his thumb.

"Go on, Dru," he said. "I can't have you resenting me later for seducing you when you could have been crime solving."

"I know you're teasing me, but I really do want to read the journal," she said, pulling herself together and taking a step back.

"Pity," he said, arching an eyebrow.

She laughed and headed for the corridor, while her resolve still held.

The bond between them was strange and new. It felt good to remove herself from him just for a moment, to confirm that she still existed in his absence.

At the same time, she felt the lack of him yawning open inside her, like her heart was being stretched around an iceberg.

Never let a man own you, Dru. Always hold something back.

Her mother's advice was useless here. She wasn't sure she could hold anything back if she tried.

She had just reached the door of her own room when Channing came huffing and puffing up the back stairs.

"What's going on?" she asked him.

He pulled her into the stairwell and looked around feverishly, as if someone might be listening.

"They're coming for Viktor," he hissed. "I couldn't hold them off any longer. They want to question him. They want to check his *medical condition.*"

"Shit," Dru said.

"We have to warn him," Channing said.

They stumbled up the staircase and into the hall toward Viktor's suites. But Officer Wagner and his partner, Officer Clemens had come up the main staircase and were already knocking on the door to the Sapphire room.

Dru held her breath.

Viktor would think it was her. He would come to the door unprepared.

She had no idea what would happen if he had to submit to a medical examination, but she was pretty sure that the lack of a bullet wound would be the least of his worries.

She closed her eyes and tried to speak to him through

their bond, to warn him, unsure if that was even something she could do, but too desperate not to try.

It's the police, Viktor...

But she felt nothing. It was as if the thread between them had been pulled too taut with the physical distance.

She watched helplessly as the door swung open.

Viktor appeared in the threshold, his left sleeve pushed up to reveal a large bandage around his forearm.

"Good evening, officers," he said, looking back and forth between them.

"We'd like to ask you a few questions, if you're feeling up to it," Officer Wagner said.

"Of course, gentlemen," Viktor said. "I expected you would be by. I'm very happy to cooperate."

"We'll just step inside, then," Wagner said.

Viktor stepped back to welcome them, and they disappeared into his room. Wagner closed the door behind them.

"He's very smart," Channing said softly. "The bandage was a good touch."

"True," Dru said.

They stood there a moment more. Dru wished she could hear what was going on behind that door. And she had a feeling Channing felt the same.

"Let's go downstairs," he said. "We can't have them come out and find us here."

"I have to get ready for work," Dru told him.

"See you at the desk, then," Channing told her with a little wave.

She headed into her room.

Edgar Allan Crow greeted her with a light squawking sound.

"Hey bud," she crooned. "Want a snack?"

She was pretty sure that in the wild he would eat live prey, but that was beyond what she could summon.

She pulled a sleeve of crackers out of her bin of supplies, and opened the cage, pulling out the shoebox where Edgar rested.

The raven fluffed out his feathers a bit, but showed no signs of aggression.

She sat on the bed and placed the shoebox next to her.

"Here you go," she told him, breaking a cracker in half, and offering him one piece.

Edgar snatched it up like she might change her mind.

"You *are* feeling better," Dru said.

He made quick work of the first half, so she offered him the second.

He let out a joyful caw and snapped it out of her fingers.

She smiled in spite of herself, and hopped up to get the water bowl from his cage. It had been propped up on a book so he could reach it without moving.

He thrust his beak into it and threw his head back to swallow as she watched.

After three more crackers and another drink, he fluffed himself up and went promptly to sleep.

She made a mental note to try to figure out what else to feed him, and how long to keep the splint on his wing.

Now that the internet was on again, she was anxious to dive back in.

But for now, she had another mystery to solve.

She popped into the bathroom, washed her hands, dried them, and then came back out and pulled the journal pages out of her desk drawer, where she'd stashed them after retrieving them from Edgar's box.

She wasn't sure why her first instinct had been to hide

them from Viktor. But he knew about them now, so there was no need to keep them hidden away.

There were so many pages. Dru was curious about who had been so eager to translate them, but also grateful. As much as she was hunting for clues, she also wanted to treasure this stolen memory of Nana.

"Even if I find out something I didn't expect," she reminded herself softly as she spread the pages out on the bed next to the sleeping bird.

9

An hour later, Dru was deep into the journal pages. They described Nana's life at the hotel in the sixties, which was surprisingly not all that different than Dru's life at the hotel now.

There were staff that she liked and didn't like, favorite meals in the dining room, and then there was Michael.

The mysterious guest had caught Dru's eye the last time she'd perused the journal. He worked at night, and slept during the day, and his dark good looks reminded her enough of Viktor that the whole thing had her wondering if it was possible that Viktor had been here back then.

She should have just come out and asked him about it.

But part of her felt like she shouldn't have to.

If he was at Hemlock House back then, if he actually knew her grandmother, shouldn't he be the one to tell her that?

At least it seemed like the relationship never went anywhere. From what she read, Dru sensed that Nana appreciated Michael's charming personality and good looks, but she was already dating Frank, Dru's grandfather, who was getting ready to serve in the Army.

It felt like a harmless crush.

And honestly, there wasn't much going on in the journal outside of the musings of a young girl. Dru wasn't sure what she'd been hoping to find, but it looked like the whole journal was going to be a wash.

Dru had nearly reached the end of the pages when she came upon another section about Michael.

WELL, it happened.

Michael has asked me to go for a walk with him.

Of course I've walked around with him plenty of times, but it's never been planned. We're friends, and that's all. We just happen to be awake at the same time, which throws us together.

But this is different. I'm sure of it.

I'm so happy, even though I feel torn when I think of Frank. Frank is a good man.

But there's something about Michael that feels a little bit like destiny.

DRU FROWNED. That was certainly a twist.

But this wasn't like reading a novel. She *knew* what happened in the end. Nana married Frank and they lived happily ever after.

The next entry was dated that same day.

THE WHOLE HOTEL IS BUZZING.

Eddie "Diamonds" McCarthy just checked in. He used a different name, but we all know it's him. The other girls told me he's a famous thief, and rumor has it that he brought some of the goods with him from the Manhattan jeweler's row break-in last week.

I normally don't like the idea of criminals being here. But this is more like having a celebrity in the hotel. There was even a piece about him in the New Yorker.

I haven't seen him yet, but Mary Ellen said he tipped her a twenty and a pair of opal earrings this morning when he checked in.

I'm jealous about the money, but we all know he stole the earrings.

Anyway, I can't wait for my "date" with Michael tonight. Only a few more hours...

DRU FLIPPED the page and realized she was nearly at the end. There was only one more short entry.

I WAS WRONG ABOUT MICHAEL, so wrong.

I'm never going to see him again.

There's a treasure right under my feet and I know it probably makes me seem crazy, but I'm not going to touch it. I want my normal life back.

Maybe one day I'll come back. The key will be over the uniform, if I ever change my mind. The treasure will be safe under the pillars of Hemlock.

Until then, I'm going back to the simple life I planned. Frank is waiting to make me happy, and I'm going to try my best to deserve him. He's a wonderful man. Thank God it's not too late.

. . .

"Whoa," Dru murmured, going back to the part about the treasure.

There it was, clear as day, along with a clue.

The key will be over the uniform, if I ever change my mind.

Of course she thought immediately of the antique army uniform that was currently hanging in the sitting room.

She hopped up and carefully lifted Edgar Allan Crow's shoebox to bring him downstairs with her. She hated leaving him alone, and her shift was starting soon. If she found a real clue to find the treasure, she might not have time to come back up for him.

When she threw open the door to the corridor, Viktor was standing in the threshold.

"H-hi," she stammered, his proximity washing over her in sweet waves.

"Hi," he said.

"Is everything okay?" she asked, remembering why he hadn't been there to help her look over the journal. "What did they ask you?"

"Nothing I couldn't answer," he told her.

"Did they insist on getting you treatment?" she asked.

"No," he said. "Everything's fine. Where are you and Edgar headed in such a hurry?"

"I found a clue in the journal," she told him. "A clue about where to find the treasure."

"What was the clue?" he asked.

"It said that the key was over the uniform," Dru told him.

"Captain Pembroke's uniform," Viktor said, his eyes lighting up.

"Exactly what I was thinking," Dru said.

They set off together for the main stairs.

It was nearly midnight, but the presence of the police

and the power being back on seemed to have infused the place with energy.

Hailey was at the desk chatting with Tyler Park, who seemed to be returning her enthusiasm.

Jeffrey and Jenna Wilder sat in the chairs by the fireplace, reading, while Angie leaned against the wall, nodding her head in time with whatever was playing in her ear buds, and looking out the window.

Hailey gave Dru a nod as she went past with Viktor in tow. As if to say, *Look at us, with our gentleman callers.*

Dru nodded back and headed down the corridor for the sitting room.

On the way, they passed Oscar Hawkins, chatting with Melody the photographer, and the mayor over a snack in the dining room.

Mercifully, the only people in the sitting room were Hazel and Honey Van Buren, who appeared to have nodded off over their respective books. The ancient sisters looked like a Norman Rockwell painting, leaning against each other on the sofa by the fireplace, paperbacks dangling from their hands.

The uniform was exactly where it always was, in its place of honor over the small games table.

Above it, was Mr. Moosehead.

Could the clue be inside Mr. Moosehead? It would be such a pain to try to get that thing off the wall to look. And an even bigger pain to put it back up...

"Oh my God," Dru murmured.

"What is it?" Viktor asked.

"Someone's already been here," Dru said.

"What do you mean?" Viktor asked.

"The moose," Dru said. "He was on the floor. Chester

was so mad that he had to put him back up. Someone already took it down to look for the key. We're too late."

A wave of disappointment washed over her, snuffing out the fire of enthusiasm she'd felt on the way down.

"The person who deciphered the journal," Viktor said.

Dru nodded.

Someone had stolen her journal and deciphered it.

But if they had already found the treasure, then why give her the deciphered pages?

They must have hit a dead end.

Maybe they weren't too late after all.

They must have thought she would have more insight, since the journal had come from her family.

"The key wasn't in the moose," she breathed, stepping back out into the hallway. "Whoever gave me the pages is expecting me to figure it out. Which means they're going to be keeping an eye on me."

Viktor moved closer, as if instinctively trying to protect her.

Dru glanced around at all the people nearby.

The Van Buren sisters were still snoozing lightly in the sitting room.

In the dining room, Oscar, Melody and Mayor Tuck were chatting as they munched on cereal.

Tyler, Hailey and all three Wilders were in the lobby, relaxing.

But one of them wasn't doing what he or she seemed to be doing.

One of them was watching Dru.

A shiver went down her spine at the thought.

But she wasn't about to let it stop her.

10

B y two in the morning, things had calmed down a bit downstairs and Dru was feeling more like herself.

The guests had all trailed off to their rooms, except for Viktor, who was keeping Dru and Edgar Allan Crow company at the front desk.

"I guess I should drop off the clean towels at everyone's doors," Dru said. "Do you mind keeping an eye on Edgar?"

"Of course not," Viktor said. "But I can come with you if you want."

The offer was tempting. Knowing someone in the hotel was watching her was spooky enough, not to mention that there was still no sign of Johnny.

What if he was the one who had deciphered the journal?

But no matter how hard she tried, she just couldn't picture the big man hunched over any kind of book for that long. It had to be someone else.

And Viktor wouldn't always be around to act as her body guard. From dawn to dusk each day, she would be on her own.

"Nah, I'm good," Dru said, sounding more certain than she felt. "It'll only take a minute, and everyone's asleep."

He nodded, but his blue eyes were concerned.

"Really, I'll be right back," she promised.

She grabbed the bags of towels and jogged upstairs.

Edgar made a bleating sound as she left.

"I'm coming back bud," Dru sang out to him over her shoulder, gratified that she had a connection with the creature.

She headed all the way down to the servants' wing and then made her way back, hanging bags of clean towels around door knobs as she went.

It was incredibly quiet, even the sound of her footsteps was swallowed up by the thick carpet.

As she drew closer to the mayor's room, she heard the sounds of a television coming from somewhere nearby.

She hung a bag on the mayor's door, but before she could move along, the door opened.

Melody stood in the threshold in a pair of flannel pajamas large enough that they were clearly the mayor's and not her own.

"I'm so sorry to have disturbed you," Dru said softly.

"You didn't disturb me," Melody said. "Who could sleep with all that racket next door."

She wasn't wrong The TV really was louder than it needed to be. It seemed to be emanating from Tyler Park's room.

"I'll just ask him to keep it down," Dru said.

"Thanks," Melody said with a tired smile, grabbing the towels and closing the door.

Dru hated being a rule enforcer, but it was the middle of the night. Tyler should understand that sound would carry in the old building.

She knocked lightly on the door and waited.

There was no answer.

She knocked louder, trying to be heard over the TV, without waking up the whole hallway by banging.

Still nothing.

Something about the voices on the TV show sounded familiar, but she couldn't place it.

Why wasn't he responding?

With everything that had been going on, it didn't take her mind long to start moving in a dark direction. He could be hurt in there, or worse.

After another round of knocking with no results, Dru got out her skeleton key.

"I'm coming in, Mr. Park," she called out as she opened the door.

The lights were on, but the room was empty.

She quickly scanned the room, preparing herself for another body.

But she found something else entirely. Against the back wall, beside a gigantic bookshelf, was a huge opening, lined with stones.

Another passage into the catacombs.

Dru stepped back, shocked.

"...so thanks for joining us for another great episode of *Ghost Getters*," a familiar voice on the TV said.

She glanced over, taking a minute to realize what she was seeing.

Tyler had been playing an episode of the old show.

Feeling more than a little creeped out, she headed over to turn the TV down. But when she arrived at the dresser, something else caught her eye.

Tyler's messenger bag was open on the floor.

And a copy of *The Haunting of Hemlock House* was poking out.

Dru staggered backward as the pieces came together.

Tyler Park was part of her chat group.

ActionPark. Tyler *Park.* It was right there. How had she missed that?

Dru had always assumed the user name was a reference to that death trap water park in New Jersey.

Tyler was here for the treasure, not for snowboarding.

And he had been following her.

He had probably been the one that had used the tunnels to get into her room.

Dru fished around in her pocket until she come up with the drink receipt she'd found in the corridor behind the secret door in her room - A slice of lemon cake and an iced soy peppermint mocha. It hit her that it sounded an awful lot like Hailey's order. But that didn't make sense. Why would Hailey be sneaking into her room?

Dru noticed an indentation on the paper she hadn't seen before, and turned it over. As soon as she did, it all made perfect sense. There, on the back, was a phone number she recognized, right below where Hailey had scrawled her name in big, loopy letters. She must have used the receipt to give Tyler her number.

So Tyler had been the one in the passage.

Dru had a fleeting memory of running into him when she was headed for the catacombs with Viktor the other day.

Tyler had been coming from the opposite direction. He hadn't wanted to make eye contact. She assumed he was just trying to avoid Hailey.

But there had been a tear on the shoulder of his otherwise pristine coat - right in the same place Dru had caught her own jacket when she discovered the tunnel in the cata-combs that led back to her room.

She turned to the door, determined to run, but froze in her tracks instead.

The noise of the television must have drowned out the sound of Tyler returning.

He stood in the doorway that led out to the hall, blocking her path of escape.

Dru stepped back, half stumbling on his messenger bag, her back to the TV, her voice caught in her throat.

Tyler stepped inside, closing the door behind him.

11

Dru stood paralyzed, her heart pounding.

Tyler stared her down, his eyes burning with intensity.

Viktor was downstairs, just out of earshot.

Her only defense was a good offense. She doubted she could take Tyler in a fight, but she could at least let him know how she felt about him.

"You're ActionPark," she said accusingly, pleased that her voice rang out with righteous anger instead of fear.

He only kept glaring at her.

"You snuck into my room while I was asleep," she went on, furious now that she was actually confronting him. "You stole my grandmother's journal."

To her surprise, his shoulders dropped and he sighed, breaking eye contact.

"Listen, Dru," he said without much conviction. "The info about the passage into your room was in the history book, it's not some big secret."

"So you think that makes it okay to come into my room

without my permission and steal something from me?" she snapped.

"We should work together," he told her. "You have the journal again, and I have *The Haunting of Hemlock House*. Together, we can find the treasure."

"You came here, knowing who I was, and you didn't bother to tell me who you really were," Dru said. "You're a total creep, and there's no way I would ever work with you."

"Look, I've been digging into this for over a year," Tyler said, sitting down on the edge of the bed. "There's more to it than you know. There's a quiet listing on this little commercial real estate site. I think they're selling this place to a developer. He's going to knock it down to put a ski lodge up here. I just couldn't stand by and watch it happen, knowing the treasure is hidden somewhere in this building."

So this must be why all these people were here. The pieces began to click together in Dru's head.

If Tyler was here because he heard the place was being torn down soon, then the mob guys were here for the same reason. If the place got bulldozed, they would never have another chance to find the treasure. Brian must have known it was a risk coming back to his old haunts, but he also knew he was running out of time.

"What would you even have done with it?" Dru asked him. "You don't look like you're hurting for anything."

The room was peppered with high end electronics and name brand clothing.

"Well, it started out because I was interested in the ghosts," Tyler explained. "But the more I researched, the more I realized the ghost stories were made up."

Dru resisted the urge to roll her eyes. Of course the stories were made up. They were about ghosts.

But I'm in love with a vampire.

Dru shook her head to clear the crazy thought.

She wasn't really in love with Viktor, was she?

And why was *that* the most unbelievable part of it?

"I think the mob started those ghost stories," Tyler was saying, unaware of Dru's mental gymnastics. "They wanted to keep people away from the hotel while they searched for the lost jewels."

"Seems like it backfired on them," Dru pointed out.

"Yeah," Tyler agreed. "The ghost stories definitely made this place more popular. According to *The Haunting of Hemlock House,* the place was so popular for a while that the mob had to stop using it. Too many people were here searching the place with a fine-tooth comb for ghosts and lost treasure. It wasn't a great place to stash drugs or cash anymore."

"I guess the *Ghost Getters* episode was the nail in their coffin," Dru said.

"Well, by then the mob was long gone," Tyler said. "But yeah, it would have been."

Dru nodded.

"Dru, I know I don't have any right to ask you this, but what really happened this morning? Were those guys really in the mob?"

This morning.

Had it really only been this morning that she'd been held at gunpoint?

It felt like Viktor had feasted on her blood and showed her his true self a hundred years ago.

"I'm sorry," Tyler said. "I'm sure you don't want to talk about it."

"Yes, they're mob guys," Dru told him. "The victim was in witness protection. The murderer was here to look for treasure, but he recognized the victim and killed him for turning on the mob. It's pretty cut and dried."

"Then why was one of them going to kill you?" Tyler asked.

"I figured out that the killer was Johnny Sullivan," she said. "But he caught me before I could tell anyone. He held me at gunpoint, but I'm fine now."

"But he's still out there," Tyler said, with a frightened look.

"Yeah, and he's probably still looking for the treasure," Dru pointed out. "So I don't think we should be looking for it."

Tyler nodded sadly.

"How did you know I was in your room?" he asked.

"The tear on your jacket the other day," she said. "And I think you dropped Hailey's phone number. But I didn't put it all together until I saw *The Haunting of Hemlock House* in your bag. And heard the *Ghost Getters* on your TV. What were you thinking?"

Tyler's face fell.

"I know it seems dumb, but that chat room is basically my life. It's gotten me through some pretty dark times. The people in there know me better than my own family."

"You must not be very close with your family," Dru said.

"It's true, I'm not," he agreed miserably. "I'm so sorry for not being honest with you, and for taking your journal. Please don't tell the people in the group what a jerk I am. And I hope you can forgive me for being such a weirdo, but I understand if you can't."

Dru opened her mouth and closed it again.

He seemed genuinely sorry. And she wasn't really in the mood to be adding anymore enemies to her list. A week ago, she didn't even have a list.

"Give me the book and I'll call it even," Dru said, indicating *The Haunting of Hemlock House.*

He had the audacity to look torn.

"Let me make a copy for you," he hedged. "The original is priceless."

"So was my peace of mind," Dru told him flatly. "Besides, you got to read my grandmother's journal, so it's only fair."

Tyler handed over the book, his head down in defeat.

"Thanks," Dru said.

"Don't mention it," Tyler said to the floor.

Dru rushed out of the room before he could change his mind, or wonder why *she* wanted the book after she had just told him it wasn't safe to hunt for treasure with Johnny Sullivan on the loose.

12

D ru had nearly reached the staircase when she heard the raised voices.

She paused on the landing to see the mayor and Officer Wagner facing off in the lobby.

"You know who did this," the mayor said "You have witnesses. You can't hold the rest of us without cause."

"I'm not holding anyone," Officer Wagner said. "The door is unlocked, go ahead and leave if you want."

Mayor Tuck's eyes widened.

"But," Officer Wagner continued, "you should know that I've impounded the shuttle. So have fun walking down the mountain."

"Why are you doing this?" Mayor Tuck asked, her voice cold with fury.

"I'm doing my sworn duty," Wagner said. "I'm protecting the public."

"By trapping us on top of a mountain with a murderer?" Mayor Tuck asked.

"Well, I didn't say I was protecting *you*," Officer Wagner

said. "I don't know which one of you is the murderer. But I do know that if I don't let anyone go, I'm definitely not letting the murderer go."

"But you *know* who the murderer is," the mayor repeated in an exasperated tone. "Do you really think I had anything to do with it?"

"We have no evidence to back up your theory," Officer Wagner said. "Just two shaken eye witnesses and a wet newspaper. For all I know this is a *Murder on the Orient Express* scenario."

Someone cleared their throat directly behind Dru's ears and she was so startled she nearly fell down the steps.

She turned to see Howie Pembroke standing right behind her.

He wore satin pajamas under a ridiculous smoking jacket, like a mini Hugh Hefner in training.

"I see there's been a disagreement," he said loudly, in a voice that sounded like a bad imitation of a black and white movie star. "Why don't we discuss it like civilized people over a nightcap? Join me in the sitting room."

Dru glanced at Viktor, whose blue eyes twinkled with mirth.

"No thank you," Mayor Tuck said, turning on her heel and marching toward the stairs.

Dru jogged down to the lobby to get out of her way.

Behind the desk, Edgar Allan Crow screeched out a raspy greeting.

"I don't drink on duty," Wagner said, looking embarrassed. "Sorry to disturb you, sir."

"Nonsense," Howie said. He glanced up at the staircase and saw the mayor had disappeared. "Women, eh?"

"I've got to get some sleep," Wagner said, scowling, and headed up the stairs as well.

Howie glanced over at the desk.

Dru belatedly realized she shouldn't have been so obviously watching while he got humiliated by the hotel's most prominent guests.

"Is that a pet?" Howie hissed at her, his eyes narrowed.

Dru felt Viktor's fury rising up in her own chest.

"It's an injured raven," Dru said, quickly. "Not a pet."

"Get it out of here," Howie snapped.

She felt Viktor's anger coil like a whip.

"I've taken it in," he said lightly.

"We have a no pets policy," Howie said.

"It's not a pet," Viktor said. "It already lives here."

"What the hell are you talking about?"

"It lived in the abandoned wing of this decrepit hotel," Viktor said. "Until your half-dead hemlock dropped on it."

"That hemlock was in excellent health," Howie growled. "A perfect specimen. And you can't keep a wild bird in here. It's a health hazard."

Viktor's face went still and Dru felt the air go out of the room.

Even Howie stepped back slightly.

"Are you really asking the one guest who is paying list price for half the rooms in this place to endanger a living part of the Pennsylvania wildlife?" Viktor asked, his blue eyes glittering dangerously.

For a moment, Howie met his gaze.

But there was something about Viktor now. Something wild and dangerous. Something glittering and formidable.

Howie stepped backward, dropping his face in shame.

It just wasn't shaping up to be poor Howie's night.

"Keep it away from the other guests," he muttered as he headed back up the stairs.

He stopped when he reached the landing and turned back, as if gathering his courage.

"And *don't fraternize with my staff*," he cried.

Dru watched in awe as Howie turned on his heel and marched up the stairs, his silk smoking jacket flowing dramatically behind him.

13

A few hours later, Dru sat beside Viktor as they pored over *The Haunting of Hemlock House.*

Viktor's arm had been around the back of her chair, and she could practically feel his protective instincts enveloping them both. She wasn't sure whether to find it endearing or frustrating.

This alpha side of Viktor hadn't been as evident before he fed on her blood. Now, she was almost afraid of what he might do if he perceived that she was in actual danger. It was a good thing for Tyler that Viktor hadn't been around a few hours ago when he had cornered her in his room.

She wanted to tell Viktor that she could take care of herself.

But she also wanted to melt into his arms and drag him upstairs like some kind of cavewoman. It was kind of satisfying to be in a relationship with someone who wanted to destroy your enemies.

"What is it, Dru?" he asked.

She glanced up to find him studying her with a half-smile.

"Can you actually hear my thoughts?" she asked.

"No," he told her. "But I can feel your emotions now. They are not subtle."

She felt her cheeks burning, but she maintained eye contact. Drucilla Holloway was no delicate flower.

"Let's focus on the book," she said. "There's treasure to be found."

"Of course," Viktor purred. "But this book seems rather silly."

The book was definitely silly. It was nothing but a run-down of all the classic ghost stories and urban legends of rural America, thinly adjusted to fit into the Hemlock House myth. It probably sold well to tourists, and the author's mother, but it felt like practically no real research had been done in its writing.

Tyler Park thought it was priceless, but Dru would have described it as worthless. She had half a mind to return it to him.

The only cool thing about the book was the collection of photographs of the hotel, all taken around the time of the crime.

Dru had already scanned the photos, but she hadn't spotted her grandmother in any of them. They seemed less like candid shots, and more like pictures for a brochure, documenting each room and its amenities.

The kitchen had been put forth as extremely modern, with its wall of stainless-steel appliances. And even the furniture in the Gentlemen's Smoking Lounge was newer in the picture.

"Wait," Dru breathed. "Let's go back to the part with the pictures."

Viktor obliged, flipping to the photo section.

"Which room did you want to see."

"The Gentlemen's Smoking Lounge," Dru said. "I want to see if the uniform was in the same spot back then."

"Great idea," Viktor said as he turned the pages to a black and white image of the sitting room.

Everything looked very similar to modern day. And the uniform was right where it had always been.

But in the picture, there wasn't a moose head over the uniform.

In its place was a familiar bust of a very well-endowed naked woman. It was pretty easy to figure out why it had been removed once the room was no longer just for men.

"Holy crap," Dru whispered.

"That's not a moose head," Viktor said.

"I think I've seen that bust," Dru said. "It was in the abandoned wing."

Viktor glanced at the grandfather clock.

It was almost seven in the morning. The sun would be up in half an hour.

"Why don't you go to bed," Dru suggested. "I'll check it out and catch you up tonight."

Viktor was on his feet in a rush of air.

"No," he said firmly. "You're not going anywhere alone. We go together now, or we wait until tonight and go together then."

"But—" Dru began.

"It's out of the question," Viktor said. "Johnny's still out there."

Dru pressed her lips together.

"Come on, we'll go now," Viktor said. "If you know where it is, then it should only take a few minutes."

She got to her feet, resisting the urge to yell at him that he wasn't the boss of her.

Realistically, he was one hundred percent right. It didn't

make sense for her to explore the abandoned part of the hotel alone right now. Johnny was still around somewhere. And the last time she'd spent five minutes away from Viktor, she'd wound up in a confrontation with Tyler.

"Come," he said, taking her hand and giving her a smile.

She knew he was only encouraging her for surrendering, but it was impossible not to feel a surge of satisfaction of his approval.

They headed upstairs, past his rooms, to the section of wallpaper that could be peeled away to reveal the door to the abandoned wing.

The hotel was silent. Soon, the bodies would begin stirring, but for now, the corridor was still cloaked in silence.

Dru held up her phone flashlight, while Viktor pulled the paper aside and opened the door.

The smell that greeted them was mustier than she remembered, with a sweet, cloying undertone. It reminded her of the odor in the catacombs, where the carpet-wrapped body was still decomposing. She hoped Officer Wagner could get someone to dispose of it soon, or the rotten smell was going to permeate the entire hotel.

"Watch the last step," she reminded Viktor as they entered the darkened corridor and headed down the creaky stairs.

When she got to bottom of the stairs, she noticed it was actually the last two treads that were gone. She must have done more damage than she thought when she'd almost fallen through. The gap reminded her of a smile with some missing teeth, and a cold draft drifted up from the dark, open space.

She steadied herself for a moment, then jumped over the missing treads to land on the more solid floor below.

Viktor followed, skipping the damaged portion with ease, and landing with surprising grace on the floor.

Once he joined her, Dru made her way forward into the ballroom, shining the flashlight around until the beam landed on the upturned sculpture of the anatomically improbable angel.

It was exactly where she remembered, in the far corner of the room, just beneath the small stained-glass window. It sat, wings down, breasts lifted toward the ceiling, the nipples pointing upward like the peaks of two circus tents.

It was definitely the sort of decoration that wouldn't go over well with the modern clientele.

"Got it," she said, heading over, the floor creaking angrily with each step.

"Careful," Viktor said, following.

She crouched to examine the bust, but there was nothing special about it as far as she could see.

She turned it over in place. Though it had looked like marble in the picture, it was definitely plaster. But it was still very heavy. There didn't appear to be anything out of the ordinary with it. It seemed solid, and she couldn't feel any seams.

"Can you step back with the flashlight?" she asked Viktor. "I want to look at the floor around it."

He stepped back and slowly panned the light around the area.

There was plenty of dust and debris, but nothing resembling a treasure, or even a clue.

"I guess it's something to do with the bust itself," she said.

She lifted it up, to bring it back with them so that she could examine it further in her room. The sun would be up soon, and Viktor was starting to look a little nervous. She didn't want to waste any more time.

She carried the heavy sculpture back to the stairs, Viktor following behind with the light.

The jump up looked a little tougher, but it was only two stairs.

She turned back to Viktor, but he had stopped to examine what looked like an antique sliver mirror.

Dru faced the stairs again, and without overthinking it, she tightened her grip on the angel's wings and leapt across the gap.

But the weight of the bust and the force of the jump proved to be too much. There was a deep, trembling groan, and then the squeal of splitting wood as Dru felt the tread give out from under her.

She tried to grab anything for purchase, but it was no use.

The angel fell out of her hands, and she was falling, falling.

14

D ru wasn't sure how far she fell through the darkness, but she landed hard on her ankle, which twisted under her weight with a sickening crack.

Before she could react, something heavy fell on top of her, pinning her down and making it hard to take a breath.

Pain shot through her ribs, and she felt the bones grinding against each other as she took a shallow breath.

"Drucilla," Viktor roared from somewhere above.

"Viktor," she moaned, unable to raise her voice above a whisper.

Her voice echoed slightly.

She tried to look around but it was too dark. Only the faintest light shone down from the hole she had fallen through.

She closed her eyes and tried to use her other senses.

The sickly-sweet smell had grown much stronger.

A heavy thing pinned her to the cold stone floor.

She slowly reached her free hand up to touch it. Her fingers brushed against splintery wood.

She sensed light and opened her eyes again.

Viktor was shining the flashlight of her phone down from above.

She blinked and looked around.

She appeared to be in a small, stone lined cavern. It had to be part of the catacombs.

Her fall must have snapped a rotten joist in the floor, which was now resting on her broken ribs.

The angel bust must have smashed to smithereens when it fell. The whole cavern bottom was covered in white powdery dust and chunks of plaster. Even through the pain, part of her hoped she'd spot the key they had been hoping to find. But there was nothing like that among the debris.

She managed to turn to the left and would have screamed, if she could have drawn enough breath.

Johnny Sullivan sat beside her, almost close enough to touch, his body bloated and stiff, his neck twisted at an impossible angle.

That explained why the hole in the stairs was bigger than she remembered. Johnny must have tried to hide out in the abandoned wing, but gotten a nasty surprise instead.

"Drucilla," Viktor called out again.

"He's dead," she hissed with the last of her strength.

"Drucilla, come where I can see you," Viktor called back to her.

"Pretty sure my ankle is broken and there's a rotten joist on me," she moaned. "I can't go anywhere."

"Drucilla, please be very, very still," Viktor said.

That wasn't going to be an issue, since she couldn't move, even if she wanted to.

Dru looked up, trying to see his face past the beam of the flashlight.

Instead she saw another split joist about five feet up.

Hanging directly over her head.

She froze, afraid that if she moved even an inch, it would all come tumbling down. No wonder Viktor wanted her to be still.

"Drucilla, I need you to listen to me," Viktor said in a calming tone. "Close your eyes and listen to my voice."

A sense of peace washed over her, and she obeyed.

"If I try to get out of here to get help, the movements could drop that beam," he said. "And that's not a risk I'm willing to take. If I try to come down there, the same thing could happen."

Her mind struggled against the sense of wellbeing he was projecting onto her. If he couldn't get help and he couldn't help her himself, what was he saying?

But a small part of her knew, had known from the moment she felt the beam crush her chest.

"You have to go, Viktor," she whispered. "The sun is coming up soon. And I'm not going to make it anyway."

"Your blood saved my life," he told her. "And now mine will save yours."

"I don't want- don't want to be..." she trailed off, it hurt too much to speak.

"You won't be," he assured you. "I'll give you just enough. It will heal your ankle and give you the strength to get out from under that beam."

There was another groan as the joist above her sank a few more inches.

"Yes," she whispered.

"Open your mouth, my love," he whispered.

She tried to look up at him, but again was blinded by the flashlight, so she closed her eyes, and opened her mouth.

The first taste was a bitter spice that made her cough,

blasting her shattered ribs against the beam so that she moaned in pain.

"Easy, Drucilla," Viktor's voice was low and crooning. "Try again."

She opened her mouth again and this time it went down easier.

She could taste the bitterness, but also a rich note of honey and an oaky flavor that reminded her of communion wine.

She swallowed it down greedily, feeling her body greedily soak the life force.

Drucilla was suddenly feeling better. As a matter of fact, she felt fucking fantastic. Every cell inside her was coming to life.

"That's enough, Drucilla," Viktor said at last.

"More," she moaned.

"I promised I wouldn't change you," he told her. "But you should be strong enough now to move that beam. Just do it slowly, so you don't jostle the other one."

She considered the situation. It still seemed outlandish to imagine that she could move that hunk of wood.

But if she could, she would want to roll sideways to get out from under it without disturbing the one on top.

That would mean going right onto Johnny Costello's dead, disgusting lap.

"In for a penny," she muttered to herself.

"Drucilla?" Viktor called out.

"Nothing," she said. "I'm going to try."

She closed her eyes and envisioned it. The beam suddenly being made of cardboard, her body rolling to the side.

I have literally nothing to lose.

She braced her palms against the joist and pushed.

Unbelievably, she felt the splintery wood shudder and then move slightly. She pushed a bit harder, and then rolled with everything she had the moment it was off her.

She landed in Johnny Costello's dead arms, and neither the stench of his corpse nor the groan of the joist as it settled on the floor could rob her of a sense of elation.

"Good girl," Viktor told her. "Can you stand?"

Her ankle was broken.

But even as she had the thought, she could feel that it wasn't broken anymore, and her ribs had knitted back together as well.

She put her hands against the stone walls to be sure, and then pulled herself up.

Viktor was down on his belly, leaning over the hole. He put her phone beside him and reached his hands down to her.

She was up high enough now to see soft light beginning to pour through the stained-glass window overlooking the staircase.

The ballroom was on the east side of the hotel.

"Viktor, the sun..." she said.

"Give me your hands."

She obeyed as quickly as she could, praying that the rest of the stairs wouldn't give out under their combined weight.

But then his strong hands wrapped around her wrists and she was sailing upward and into his arms.

He cradled her against his chest, and they stayed there for a moment, holding each other on the dusty stairs.

"Viktor," she murmured into his chest, "we have to get out of here."

Light was beginning to pool on the landing near the window.

She wrenched herself out of his strong arms. The power

of his blood was already fading. She could feel the effort it took.

"Slowly, Drucilla," he told her as they got to their feet.

Suddenly, the staircase seemed to stretch upward indefinitely. Any part of it could fall out from under them.

"No," she said. "Quickly, I think."

He nodded and she took his hand.

She shot away from the spot where they stood, feeling fleet as a deer compared to her normal speed.

Then Viktor took off and she thought he would yank her arm off her shoulder.

She was fast, but he was so much faster.

The treads groaned and cracked, like an icy pond melting on a warm spring afternoon.

One moment Dru was running, the next her feet went out from under her.

She thought at first that she was falling again, but then she realized Viktor had taken her into his arms.

A second later, they were up the stairs and back in the hallway of the main wing of Hemlock House, standing just outside of his rooms.

He placed her down and they went into the room together.

Dawn was glowing through the sheet over his east-facing window.

"We can't keep doing this," Dru said softly. "Every time we're together, you almost get toasted in the morning. I'll be the death of you."

"It'll be worth it," he said, giving her a roguish grin and throwing open the trunk.

It was hard to think of him shutting himself in. She wondered if he was teasing to distract her from the strangeness of it.

"Don't do anything crazy, Drucilla," he told her. "My blood protection will wear off in an hour or so. Keep yourself safe. I'll see you at dusk."

"Thank you, Viktor," she told him, realizing that what she meant was *I love you.*

She turned on her heel and fled before she could hear his response.

After all, he couldn't read her thoughts, but he could read her emotions.

And they were not subtle.

15

D ru was relieved to find Officer Wagner and tell him about Johnny Costello's body in the tunnels beneath the ballroom.

Wagner asked for very specific info on where the body was, and she told him about the collapsing stairs in the abandoned wing, warning him that it could be a dangerous job.

Then Wagner barked at her to sit in a chair in the lobby by the fire and wait for him to come back so that he could take a statement.

Dru sat by the fire for what felt like a lifetime.

Edgar Allan Crow rested in his shoebox in her lap, while Dru re-read her grandmother's journal pages to stay awake.

The morning light from the windows hurt her eyes. She could still feel Viktor's energy dancing through her. He'd said it would fade within the hour, but she wondered if she would still feel a heightened connection with him when it did.

"Dru, are you okay?" Zander asked when he arrived to take over desk duties.

She looked up at him, squinting against the harsh sunlight.

"Yeah," she said. "It was kind of a rough night."

"Did you dye your hair?" he asked.

She shook her head. That was a weird question.

"Funny," he said. "It seems brighter today."

She glanced down at her hair. The red was definitely deeper and more pronounced. Was that another side effect of the blood Viktor had used to revitalize her?

"It's probably just the light," she offered weakly.

"Sure," Zander said. "You can go to bed if you want. I'll come get you when Officer Wagner is ready."

"I'm good," she said. "It can't be much longer."

As if on cue, the two policemen appeared atop the stairs, lugging a body bag, which meant that Wagner was probably done with the crime scene and ready for her.

Zander nodded and sat down in the chair opposite Dru.

Hazel and Honey were coming in from their early morning walk as the two cops got to the door with the body bag.

"Oh dear, what's this?" Hazel asked.

"Will you please move out of the way?" Wagner said, in a grumpy way.

"My goodness," Hazel said in a wounded tone, pulling her sister inside and closer to the window seat, out of the way of the police. "I much prefer that gentleman detective to this new one, don't you, dear?" she asked Honey.

Honey nodded.

"What are you talking about?" Wagner demanded.

But Hazel and Honey Van Buren had already made a beeline for the cold breakfast Zander had set up in the dining room.

"What are they talking about?" Wagner asked Dru and Zander.

She shrugged, trying not to smile. Hugh Channing certainly had a way with people that Wagner lacked. Too bad he wasn't a real detective.

"I'll be right back to talk to you," Wagner told her.

"Okay," she said. "I'll be right here."

She must have dozed off for a moment in the warmth of the fire, because she awoke to the sound of an excited conversation around the front desk.

Now that they had finally found the killer, Wagner must have released the shuttle bus.

Half the guests were gathered around the desk as Zander worked to check them out.

"But what was the outcome?" Jenna Wilder was asking.

"It sounds like they found the murderer's body," Zander said.

"Then who killed him?" Jenna asked.

"I think it was an accident," Zander said with a shrug.

"You *think*?" Jenna asked. "Well, we can't leave without finding out for sure."

"*I* can," Jeffrey said, handing Zander his credit card. "This has been fun and all, but we'll check the papers. Take care of yourself, kid."

"Thanks," Zander replied as he gave them the final receipts.

The Wilders stumbled out with their suitcases.

"Wicked crow," Angie muttered to Dru as she passed.

Dru didn't bother to correct her. The teenager wouldn't be able to hear her. She was wearing her ear buds as always, rocking out to who knows what.

Mayor Tuck and Melody Young were next.

Dru noticed that Melody looked a little downcast, as if

maybe she would have liked to be snowed in with the mayor for just a little longer. She hoped they had a chance to continue their relationship when they got back to town. But life was complicated, especially in politics.

Dru's thoughts drifted back to Viktor.

The whole lobby was sunny now, but the light no longer hurt her eyes. She glanced down, and her hair was its usual color again, brown with a russet tone.

Until this morning she hadn't let herself look too far into the future with Viktor.

But it was hard not to recognize what different creatures they were when she had spent an hour or two enjoying a hollow echo of his powers.

Could there ever be an equal relationship between an immortal with superhuman powers and appetites, and a plain young woman who had most likely used up twenty-five percent of her limited time on the planet?

She would grow old and die, and Viktor would remain always the same. There would be other women, other adventures, whole lifetimes ahead of him.

The thought was like a poison, seeping through her heart.

"Dru?" Officer Wagner said, approaching her at last.

"Hey," she said, shaking herself out of it and sitting up straighter in her chair.

Edgar Allan Crow made a soft scolding sound and reassembled himself in his box.

"Does the bird have anything to do with what happened this morning?"

"No," she said. "We rescued him from the fallen tree."

"By 'we' do you mean yourself and Viktor Striker?" Wagner asked.

She nodded, biting her lip.

"Was he with you this morning when you found Costello?" Wagner asked.

Shit.

She didn't want to lie to the police.

But Viktor wasn't exactly available to be questioned.

The only witness was Johnny Sullivan. And he was dead.

"I fell into that cavern by myself," she said. "It was so scary."

Wagner nodded and began to take notes.

"Well now that we've located the suspect," he told her, "I can tell you that you did a good job keeping everything under control and documenting the scene. We found a pair of shoes in Sullivan's room that showed blood spatter consistent with the pattern you observed near the body."

A good job.

Hugh Channing was going to be thrilled at the glowing review.

16

An hour later, Dru dragged herself up to her room. The sun was bright, even through the drawn curtains, and she felt hollowed out inside. She placed Edgar Allan Crow's box in the old birdcage and closed it. The inky bird was sleeping so hard he didn't seem to notice.

She missed Viktor. It didn't seem right that she had to sleep here alone while he was locked in that trunk.

After a moment she made up her mind and headed back into the hallway.

Mercifully, she made it down to the second floor and over to Viktor's wing without bumping into anyone.

She slid the skeleton key in place and opened the door.

The room felt vacant.

The sheets over the windows fluttered slightly as she closed the door.

She could feel his presence here, faintly.

She curled up at the foot of his bed, close to the trunk, and sank into sleep almost immediately.

In her dream, the world was brighter again, the colors more vibrant.

She was seeing things through Viktor's eyes again.

She looked around.

Viktor was here in the hotel, standing on the landing that overlooked the lobby. The colorful rug was back in its place at the center of the room, where it belonged. But something about the place was off. Maybe it was just the experience of seeing it through his eyes.

Below, at the front of the lobby, was her own russet head. She leaned against the desk, one hand toying with the keys of the old Smith Corona.

No.

It wasn't Dru at all.

It was Nana Jane.

That was why the place looked off. The decorations and furnishings were largely the same, but she was seeing them when they were still new, long before they became the mood-setting antiques she knew them as.

Dru felt Viktor's heart pound as he watched the woman from above, drinking in the color of her hair, the delicacy of her skin.

He watched Jane like he revered her, but he did not dare to love her.

He knew it was wrong to stand here. In a moment, he would go downstairs, and they would take the evening stroll they had talked about.

Viktor was torn.

He knew there was a man called Frank, who would be serving in the Army. He knew that this man loved Jane.

If not for Frank, he would never have asked her to walk with him. He would have endured the curiosity and admiration he felt for her. Jane was kind-hearted and smart. She deserved a normal life.

But jealousy had stayed his good sense, and now he would torture himself by spending time alone with her, maybe more than that.

Perhaps he could impress her with the riches he had saved from his service to the Irish mob.

He did not care for the brutish bosses, but they paid handsomely and there were so many hired killings, so much blood flowing freely...

When he traveled here from the old country, they took him in, asked no questions, as long as he played his part in their vengeance.

Movement from below caught his eye.

A short, blond-haired man was holding Jane from behind, his arm wrapped around her neck.

It was Diamonds McCarthy, the jewel thief.

Fury began to fill Viktor's chest and he had to force himself to breathe in cool air. He'd never had any patience for the man, always strutting around like he was some sophisticated cat burglar, when in reality, he was nothing more than a smash-and-grab thug.

"Wh-what are you doing?" Jane stammered.

"Sorry, doll," McCarthy said. "But I know you saw my stash, and we can't have you squealing about it."

"I... what?" Jane asked, sounding terrified.

"You were in the wrong place at the wrong time," McCarthy said. "What were you even doing up there?"

"P-please let me go," Jane moaned. "I don't know what you're talking about."

McCarthy pulled her in tighter.

Viktor couldn't contain his fury any longer. He let the

rage take control in a way he hadn't done since he was a fledgling, unable to rein in his all-consuming bloodlust.

He flew down the stairs, so fast the hotel lobby went past in a blur. Dru was watching the events through his eyes, but she couldn't process everything as quickly as Viktor was able to. She was barely able to follow his impossibly fast actions.

He ripped McCarthy off of Jane before the thief even knew he was there.

There was a muffled shriek and then nothing but the gurgle of McCarthy's blood pouring down Viktor's parched throat.

"Viktor," Jane whispered.

But she sounded so far away, so small compared to the hugeness of his pounding body, awakening at the well of life under his hungry mouth.

Three metallic clicks came from the corridor between the desk and the kitchen.

Viktor let McCarthy's limp body fall to the floor at his feet.

Jane cowered behind the desk as three more mobsters emerged from the shadows, guns drawn, looking like something out of a movie that Dru's stepdad would watch.

"Jesus, Viktor, what the hell?" One of the Murphy brothers rasped.

Viktor was on the man in a flash, snapping his neck without bothering to drain him.

"Seamus?" the other man asked, as if he wasn't sure if his brother was dead or just resting limply on the carpet.

Viktor sank his fangs into the second man's neck before he could figure out what had happened to his friend.

But there was no time to enjoy the meal.

The last man, Calvin O'Connor, was running straight for Jane, and he was a nasty piece of work.

Viktor threw the second Murphy brother to the ground, still bleeding, and flew straight to Jane.

O'Connor was looming over her as she trembled. He was a massive man. And Viktor had seen his mean streak at work firsthand.

But he was no match for Viktor after a double feed.

He launched himself over the desk in one leap, latching onto O'Connor's jugular before his feet touched the ground.

He drank deep as the big enforcer's struggles faded.

At last he let go, sated, and felt the mountain of a man collapse at his feet.

Jane was frozen, just inches away.

O'Connor's swiftly draining body had been the only thing between Jane and Viktor's murderous mouth.

She stared up at him, pale and horrified.

"Jane," he whispered.

He could feel the blood congealing on his face and clothing.

He was a monster, he knew that, but he had never felt the true weight of it until it was reflected back to him in her eyes.

There was the click of another gun behind him.

"Run," he told her.

His last glimpse of her was her hair in motion, flying behind her as she ran out through the dining room.

He prayed she would make it to safety.

Then he turned on his heel and made short business of murdering every last one of the bastards who might chase her.

When it was done, the lobby was littered with bodies.

Viktor stepped into the restroom and washed his face and hands.

He could not look in the mirror.

But he knew what he would see if he did. He would be gazing into the eyes of a murderer, a man who had made a good woman run in terror.

Never again, he promised himself as he stepped back into the lobby.

I will never give anyone a reason to look at me like that again.

Viktor turned and walked out the front door without looking back.

It was the middle of the night.

By the time anyone noticed the carnage at Hemlock House, Viktor Striker would be long gone.

17

Dru awoke in semi-darkness, the only source of illumination the pink sunlight that bled around the edges of the sheets covering Viktor's windows.

Viktor...

She had been seeing his memories in her dream, that much was clear.

But had he shown them to her voluntarily, or had she taken them by sharing his blood, or coming close to him to sleep?

It didn't matter.

Viktor Striker was responsible for the Hemlock House murders.

Dru was in love with a man who had coldly and efficiently killed a whole room full of people, without even blinking.

And he could do it again, anytime he chose.

Her phone alarm began to go off.

She grabbed it to turn it off and slipped out of Viktor's

bed, eager to get out of the room that held nothing but secrets and sadness.

Dru headed up to her own room to shower and dress, trying hard to think of anything but Viktor.

Her unfinished novel was stacked on her desk next to the Smith Corona. Maybe she would never finish it. After the events of the last few days, it suddenly seemed less important.

Her time at Hemlock House might turn out to be a waste. No novel, no boyfriend. She had never even found the key to the treasure, even though her grandmother had left her a clue.

Nana Jane would have agreed the whole experience was one big Charlie-Foxtrot.

Dru let the hot water of the shower pound down on her skin, wishing it could wash away her sense of defeat.

When she was dressed and ready, she headed down to the dining room with Edgar Allan Crow, hoping a good meal would give her the strength she needed to think.

She paused on the landing to take in the scene below.

Hailey and Zander were sitting at the lobby desk, Hailey's dark head leaning into Zander's golden one, the two of them speaking in low voices and giggling.

She smiled at the idea that the two were flirting. It was so wholesome, so...*normal.*

Her own feelings for Viktor were anything but wholesome. He had a history with her grandmother that he had chosen to hide from her. Not to mention the fact that he was a cold-blooded killer.

And as much as she cared about him, missed him, even now, maybe it was all too much.

But they had shared blood.

Dru wasn't sure if it would even be possible to run far

enough that Viktor couldn't find her through the bond that stretched and throbbed between them.

In the lobby below, Hailey giggled again. The sound was pure happiness.

Dru found herself smiling, in spite of her own troubles.

Zander and Hailey would make a great couple. Zander was hot and super nice, and Hailey was Dru's favorite person in the whole world.

Hailey glanced up, as if Dru had said her name out loud.

"Hi," Dru said, smiling.

Hailey's expression was suddenly guilty.

Oh, God, she was probably worried that Dru might have some claim over Zander because of that old high school crush.

Dru tried to give her a *this-is-awesome-go-for-it-sisters-before-misters* look before Zander could glance up.

"Hey," Hailey replied happily, clearly having gotten the message. "Somebody's up early."

"I thought I'd grab something to eat," Dru said. "I can't seem to write today."

"Wow," Zander said, putting his arm around the back of Hailey's chair and smiling up at Dru. "So the indomitable Drucilla Holloway is finally too freaked out to hit the keys, huh?"

Maybe it was the stress, or maybe she'd just been too focused on looking for secret keys to think about the ones that had been right in front of her.

Right in front of her...

The words tumbled around in her head.

Surely it couldn't be that easy...

18

D ru ran back up the stairs, not looking where she was going, and flung the door open when she reached her room.

The warm glow of the late afternoon sun filled the space, making it feel as if the roses on the wallpaper were coming to life, watching and waiting to see if Dru had figured out the clue at last.

She sat down at the typewriter and took a deep breath.

Her grandmother had been a fan of the NATO phonetic alphabet. She had a few key phrases she had taught to Dru, mostly so that she could curse while remaining ladylike. *Charlie-Foxtrot* was their favorite, especially since it always earned a disapproving look from her mom.

It had been a long time since Dru had thought about the rest of that alphabet.

If not for Zander's remark, she might never have remembered.

In the NATO phonetic alphabet, *Uniform* stood for the letter "U".

She studied the typewriter.

They key is above the uniform.

Above the "u" key was the "8".

It was the only key on the sturdy old machine that didn't work. It was the reason she had to write out all of her chapter numbers.

Hands shaking, Dru wrapped her fingers around the "8" and tugged gently.

Nothing happened.

She tried again, wiggling as she pulled.

This time the button popped off in her hand, revealing the arm below.

Something was affixed to it.

She reached inside and worked at it with a fingernail until it popped loose.

It was a tiny package, wrapped in paper.

She carefully unraveled the tiny bit of paper, which scrolled out, smaller than the fortune in a fortune cookie.

Almost there was penned on it in her grandmother's neat script.

Inside the bit of paper was a tiny key.

Dru flipped the paper over, but there was no mention of where the key should be used.

The key itself offered no clues. It was delicate, silver, and unmarked.

She sat back, fingering the edge and trying to think.

Maybe if she went back to the journal, she could figure it out.

She placed the little key in her pocket and grabbed the deciphered journal pages, flipping through until she reached the section about the treasure.

. . .

THERE'S a treasure right under my feet and I know it probably makes me seem crazy, but I'm not going to touch it. I want my normal life back.

Maybe one day I'll come back. The key will be over the uniform, if I ever change my mind. The treasure will be safe under the pillars of Hemlock.

THE PHRASE "under the pillars of Hemlock" had seemed symbolic to Dru when she first read it. She had taken it to mean that the treasure would be safe at the hotel.

But what if Nana Jane had literally meant *under the pillars*. The wide front porch had a line of slender columns. Could something be hidden under them?

She picked up the raven's box and headed downstairs again, flying past Hailey and Zander who were still at the desk, and Howie, who was reading the paper by the fire.

"Dru, what's going on?" Hailey asked.

"Nothing," she said as she pulled on her coat. "Just have to look at something."

She was out the front door before they could question her further.

Once again, the snow outside was stained pink by the setting sun. Piles of wood from the cut-up hemlock tree lined the sides of the driveway.

Tomorrow, Constance and Gert would be back, and the hotel would return to business as usual.

Dru ran to the closest pillar and knelt on the chilly porch floor to examine the base, placing Edgar Allan Crow's box on the porch floor beside her.

The wood of the column was affixed directly to the floorboards. She couldn't see a way to slide anything underneath.

She moved on to the next one, running her fingers along

the far side since she couldn't see it, feeling for some kind of seam or keyhole.

Again, nothing.

She had just scooted over to the third pillar when the front door of the hotel opened.

"Hello, dear," Hazel Van Buren said kindly. "Did you drop something?"

Dru smiled up at the sweet ladies. They had been here all this time, through so many unpleasant incidents. They had been here before Nana arrived and would probably be here after Dru left. And they were endlessly positive.

"Oh, hello, Miss Van Buren and Miss Van Buren," Dru said, smiling at the twin fixtures of Hemlock House.

Suddenly her heart skipped a beat.

Not fixtures.

Nana Jane had told them herself that they held the place up.

Like pillars...

It couldn't be.

"I'm looking for something," she said carefully. "Would either of you know of a lock that this key might open? Maybe something in your room?"

She pulled the key out of her pocket and held it up.

The silver of it glimmered in the strange afternoon light.

The ladies bent obligingly to examine it.

"No, dear," Hazel said straightening up. "The keys to this place are mostly larger antique models, and so lovely too. We don't have anything like that in our room."

"Unless it's for the door under my bed," Honey said brightly.

Dru and Hazel turned to Honey in shock.

"There's a door under your bed, dear?" Hazel asked her sister.

Honey nodded with a pleasant smile.

"Would it be okay for me to check that out?" Dru asked.

They waited, but Honey appeared to have nothing further to say.

"Of course, dear," Hazel told her. "But it will have to be a bit later. We always take an evening stroll. And after that we have a regular date with the chess board in the solarium. Shall we say seven o'clock?"

"Would it be okay for me to let myself in and check it out now?" Dru asked. She felt bad for her impatience, but she wasn't sure she could wait that long.

"Oh certainly, dear," Hazel said. "Let us know what you find."

"Let us know," Honey echoed.

"Yes, of course," Dru said, already on her feet with the bird box in her arms, dashing back inside. "Thank you!"

19

Dru reached Hazel and Honey's room and used her skeleton key to gain access. She was immediately greeted by the scent of mothballs and cinnamon.

To her left, a small table and chairs had a view from the only window. On the table was an aging lace doily with a bowl of potpourri at its center.

To her right, twin beds flanked a single dresser. Each bed wore a pink comforter with a matching pink dust skirt, and a painting of an angel hung between them.

The room was tidy and peaceful. There was a sense of timelessness that was only accentuated by the coral light of sunset.

Dru didn't have to worry about figuring out which bed was Honey's, since each sister had a throw pillow on her bed with her name stitched across it.

Honey's bed was on the right.

Dru slid the bed backward, toward the table. It partially blocked the door to the room, but it didn't sound like the sisters were coming back anytime soon.

A small throw rug under the bed explained why Gert

had never come across the hidden door. It had probably been vacuumed but never removed.

Dru took a deep breath and tried to calm herself.

She knew how Honey's memory seemed to move back and forth between the past and the present. It was entirely possible that there was never a door under her bed.

Or there might be a door, but whatever had been kept behind it was long gone.

Dru pulled the rug aside.

Sure enough, there was a trap door underneath, and below the dark metal handle was a slender keyhole.

Dru pulled the tiny key out of her pocket and slid it into the opening.

She felt the click as soon as she turned it.

But when she tried to pull the handle, she nearly wrenched her shoulder out of the socket.

"Ow," she murmured.

She slid the key into place and turned the other way, but she could hear the lock engage, so she slid it back the other way.

Convinced it was unlocked, Dru grabbed the handle again, this time jiggling back and forth slightly as she pulled. There was a complaining groan of swollen wood and then the thing sprang open.

She let the door rest in the open position, and grabbed her phone to use the flashlight.

The top of a wooden ladder rested against the lip of the opening. It disappeared into a velvet darkness that swallowed up the flashlight beam.

Not this again.

But she was already slipping the phone back into her pocket and lowering herself onto the ladder before she could change her mind. She had begun to unravel this mystery. She had to see it through.

Edgar Allan Crow began to squawk unhappily in his box on the floor when she moved away. She tried to sooth him and assure him she'd be right back, but he wasn't having it. It really seemed like he didn't want her to go.

Was he just lonely, or was he trying to tell her something?

No. That's silly. He probably just wants some food.

Dru sighed and lifted him out of the box, and he immediately calmed. The makeshift bandage dropped away from his wing, but he didn't seem to favor it.

"I guess we're in this together," she said as she unzipped her sweatshirt partway and placed the bird inside, against her chest.

As soon as he settled in, she began to climb down the ladder.

20

Dru felt as if she had been climbing for ages.

The square of light at the top of the tunnel was still visible.

It was hard to imagine Hazel and Honey's homey little room above from the confines of the cold, stony passage she was traversing.

At last, her foot hit stone instead of another rung.

She stepped back and pulled her phone out of her pocket.

She was in a tiny chamber, just big enough to turn around in.

A low, arched passageway led off to the left. She had to duck to fit inside it.

There probably isn't anything down here. Or maybe there's another enigmatic clue. What if I get lost down here? No one even knows where I am, besides the Van Buren sisters.

But she was already on her hands and knees, crawling down the passageway, curiosity winning out over fear.

There were no openings for a long time, which reassured her that she was going the right way, and that she would be able to find her way back.

Dim light appeared ahead of her, and the passage opened up into another room. Soft pink light bathed the space in an otherworldly glow. She glanced up to see the last fiery rays of sunlight reflecting on the walls through an opening in the stone wall somewhere above.

Dru pulled herself to standing and looked around.

She seemed to be in an old maintenance room. There were wooden shelves of fertilizer, bulbs, tools, and other odds and ends. A sack of road salt in the corner had overflowed large, chunky crystals onto the floor. Shovels and rakes were leaned against the walls.

But who would climb all this way to get some road salt?

She spotted a small door on the other side of the shelf. So there was another way in and out. That made more sense.

Dru had completely lost her bearings in the climb down, so she really wasn't even sure what part of the hotel she was in anymore. She tried the door, wondering where it could possibly lead.

But when she swung it open, she was greeted by the sight of a solid brick wall.

Well, that explains why no one ever found it from the other side.

And it also meant that she was in for a long climb on her way back out.

Dru sighed and surveyed the room some more. If there was another clue, it would have to be in here somewhere.

There was a cot set up in one corner with an overturned bucket beside it. She moved to check it out and Edgar Allan Crow wiggled a bit and made a scolding sound as if he hadn't appreciated all that climbing and crawling.

"Sorry, buddy," Dru said, placing him down on the cot, where he settled in immediately.

On top of the bucket was a velvet pouch, covered in enough cobwebs that she almost didn't notice it.

She reached for it, unable to believe her eyes.

She lifted the pouch, testing its weight. It was heavier than she expected, and bulky.

She brushed off some of the cobwebs and then blew on it, filling the dim light with a storm of dust.

When she opened the pouch, its contents glittered in the last bit of light still coming in from overhead.

She poured them out into her palm.

Brilliant red and green stones tumbled onto her hand, their colors flashing crazily.

Rubies and emeralds?

"My God," she murmured.

"Okay, hand them over," a familiar voice said, making her jump.

"Howie?" she said, glancing up in awe.

"I said, hand them over," he said.

For the second time in her life, someone was pointing a gun at her.

Howie's face was a mask of greed and fury. Dru couldn't believe this was the same baby-faced Howie Pembroke who scolded her best friend for wearing black nail polish.

"What are you doing, Howie?" she asked.

"It's my hotel, my treasure," he said.

"Your grandfather said the treasure would belong to whoever finds it," Dru said stupidly.

"My grandfather was an idiot," Howie spat.

"How did you know to follow me here?" Dru asked.

"I've had a plan for a long time," Howie said. "I wasn't going to let you swoop in and steal the treasure."

"What do you mean, you had a plan in place?" she asked, stalling for time.

"I'm the one who leaked the news that the place was being sold," Howie said with a smug smile. "I knew if I did it, the mob would come to try and find the treasure."

"You would have gone up against the mob?" Dru asked, glancing around to see if there was any other way out of the room. There didn't appear to be.

"Those idiots," Howie scoffed. "They think they're tough, but if you sneak up on a person and put a gun to their head, it doesn't matter how tough they think they are. Case in point." He gestured at Dru.

She willed herself not to glare at him. They were so far away from everything, she wasn't even sure anyone would hear a gunshot.

"Anyway," he went on, "I didn't have to go after the mob, did I? All I had to do was follow you."

"Why did you follow me?" Dru asked again.

"You got this job because of something you said in your phone interview," Howie said.

Dru tried to think back to the phone interview, but cold sweat was trickling down her back, and other, more important parts of her life were flashing through her mind.

"You said your grandmother worked here in the sixties," Howie said triumphantly. "I figured you were really coming to look for the treasure, and I also figured you might have a leg up. And I was right."

"I'm happy to hand these over, and tell everyone you found them," Dru offered weakly. "If you will just let me go."

"Oh, I don't think so, sweetheart," Howie said, shaking his head condescendingly. "You've got a journal and a key, and a pair of old ladies to prove me wrong. I think I'm just going to seal you in down here. No one found this place in fifty years. So I think it will be safe to say no one will ever find you. You just got tangled up in some kind of mob murder. It won't be all that strange when you suddenly disappear. And once I "find" this treasure in another part of the hotel, no one will ever have any reason to come snooping around here again."

Wow. Dru wouldn't have imagined Howie was even capable of putting that kind of thought into something. It was actually kind of impressive.

Or it would have been, if it didn't end with her getting *Cask of Amontillado*-ed down here, like a doomed Poe character. Her choice of names for the raven suddenly seemed very appropriate.

Dru glanced up at the fading light reflecting on the wall.

Viktor would be awake soon. She just needed a little more time.

And some way to tell him where she was.

21

"Howie, please," Dru said, stalling for time. "You don't need to kill me. What if I give you an hour's head start and then come out after you? That gives you time to hide the jewels."

He shook his head.

"What else can I do?" she pleaded. "You can't actually kill me over a handful of rubies."

"This is the Hemlock House treasure," Howie said. "So it's rightfully mine. And I can do whatever I want."

Dru glanced around the little room.

There was no place to hide. She could try to grab a shovel, but Howie had a gun. Which, now that she'd had time to take it all in, Dru was pretty sure it was the antique service revolver that usually resided in the display case in the sitting room, along with Howie's grandfather's old uniform.

Antique or not, it was more than a match for a shovel.

Her only hope was distraction.

She lifted her palm.

Howie smiled victoriously.

Dru flung the jewels over her head.

For a moment they seemed to hang in air like glittering raindrops in every color of the spectrum.

Then they scattered on the floor.

Dru prayed that Howie would try to gather them.

But he narrowed his eyes and squeezed the trigger instead.

There was a thunderous crash, and then it felt like she had been hit with a sledgehammer in the chest.

So much for her distraction.

The world tilted sideways, and the ground came up to meet her, slamming her ribcage and knocking the remaining breath from her lungs.

Tears blurred Dru's eyes as the searing hot pain of the bullet's ragged path erupted inside her.

Somewhere far away, Howie was tiptoeing around the room, picking up gem stones.

He bent over her at one point, but it was only to pry the velvet bag out of her hand.

Play dead, Dru.

But you are dead, a little voice in the back of her head replied. *Or you will be soon enough.*

The voice was right. She couldn't make out Howie's words anymore, even though he was right in front of her, and his mouth was clearly moving.

And the room was growing dim.

Howie aimed the gun at her face, but then she sensed movement beside him.

An inky black shadow streaked across the room, accompanied by the rustle of wings. Another shot rang out, but if it hit her, she was too far gone to feel it.

Soft feathers brushed her cheek, then there was a breeze

in her hair as Edgar Allan Crow flapped his way upward to the opening far above.

She was glad he was free.

It gave her some small amount of peace that he would not die with her down here.

Drucilla Holloway was going to die alone. She had to make her peace with that.

But she called to Viktor through their bond anyway, one last time.

She loved him. She knew that now. She didn't care who he had killed, or who he had loved in the past.

She pictured his blue eyes, gazing into hers.

She didn't care if he was a monster.

He was *her* monster.

If only there had been time to tell him.

22

The pain was receding now.

Howie seemed to be gone, and Dru was alone in the darkness, picturing Viktor's face.

Death was kind to her. She swore she could smell his clean scent and hear his voice calling her name from far away.

She closed her eyes, trying to block out what was left of her other senses to hear his voice.

Then strong hands were clasping around her shoulders, shaking her forcefully.

"Drucilla," Viktor cried brokenly.

Something was pressed to her mouth.

She struggled against it with the last of her strength.

Please, just let me go in peace.

But the familiar tangy liquid on her lips cleared her mind slightly, and she let it fall against her tongue.

It filled her senses, like rain in the desert. She wanted to latch on and suck, but she was still too weak.

"Drucilla, I'm sorry," Viktor sobbed. "It's not working."

She longed to comfort him, but she couldn't even open her eyes.

"Please give me a sign," he said. "Tell me that you want me to save you."

She tried to clear the clouds in her mind and understand him. But it was impossible to concentrate over the rush of the feast that was flowing down her throat.

"I have to change you, my love," he told her softly. "Let go of your fears. I will be by your side in your new life for as long as you will have me. For eternity."

He was feeding her a symphony.

She could actually feel her bones and muscles knitting back together.

Her strength began to return to her, and she curled her hands around his wrist and wrapped her lips around his delicious flesh.

"Drucilla," he breathed in relief.

The feeling was beyond relief, it was pure exhilaration. Her chest threatened to split open with the sheer ecstasy of it.

Her heart thundered wildly, then stuttered.

Dru opened her eyes in alarm.

"This is the hardest part," Viktor told her. "Be brave."

But she hardly noticed.

Viktor's eyes were so blue they seemed to throb with color. She could see every minute detail of him, even in the darkness. He was beautiful.

Her heart hammered once more, and then stopped.

A pleasant peacefulness settled over her body.

She let go of his wrist.

"Don't try to get up too fast," he warned her.

But she was already leaping to her feet.

She felt weightless, as if her joy was lifting her up.

Viktor stood too.

She moved to him, placed her hand against his chest and looked up into his inexpressibly beautiful face.

"You saved me," she whispered.

But he looked almost sad.

"Drucilla," he said, his voice choked with emotion. "Do you understand what I've done to you?"

23

D ru couldn't find the words to answer.

Instead, she went up on her toes and pressed her lips to his.

He groaned and kissed her back.

Fireworks went off behind her eyelids.

"Drucilla, you'll never see the sunlight again," he moaned, pulling back.

But Dru didn't care. She was torn with new kinds of hunger. Some of it she didn't understand, but one form was very clear. And she knew exactly how to feed it.

She grabbed his shirt and gloried in the sound of it ripping to shreds as she effortlessly pulled it apart. Buttons scattered on the ground, the sound reminding her of the rubies and emeralds earlier.

So much more precious, the chance to revel in the body of my beloved...

Viktor gasped.

She pressed her lips to his chest, molding his flesh with her mouth.

She'd thought that she would never see him again, that she'd never have the chance to tell him...

"I love you," she whispered into his chest as he tore her clothing from her.

He wrapped his arms around her, swaying as if she were a child, or a delicate treasure to be protected.

But Dru would never be delicate again. And she was *glad*.

"I love you, my angel," he murmured into her hair.

She heard the harmonics in his voice, felt his breath in every follicle of her hair.

It was as if her senses had just awoken, as if she had been wandering the world with dark sunglasses and wool in her ears until now.

He kissed her again and she pressed herself to him, soaking in his scent, and the delicious solidness of his muscled form.

He moaned into her mouth and she pulled him to the floor.

They hit the cool stones and rolled.

It barely registered that she was naked, rolling in her own blood as she drank in Viktor's kiss.

He pinned her to the stone floor, holding her still with his hips.

"I almost lost you," he murmured, pulling back to look deep into her eyes. "I would not have survived it."

"Now you can't lose me," she told him, smiling through the hot tears that sprang to her eyes.

"Don't cry, Drucilla," he whispered. "Never cry."

He bent and licked up the single tear that ran down her cheek.

She smiled as he pressed his lips to her forehead.

But her new body had needs that would not be ignored.

It screamed its demands now with a hunger so piercing she whined out loud.

Viktor smiled and slid his hand down to toy with her breasts.

The sensation flashed through her like lightning.

He bent his head to lash one nipple with his tongue.

An ocean of need opened up in Dru and she arched her back, wrapping her legs around his hips.

24

Dru screamed with the pleasure of anticipation as Viktor pressed his sinful lips in a trail down her belly.

The cold, solid stones pressed up from beneath her. She could smell the tang of recently shed blood blending with the cool, delicious scent of her beloved.

Even the invisible sound of Viktor's lips brushing against her inner thigh revealed itself to her ears.

She sank her fingers into his silky hair, and he rewarded her with a long lick against her sex.

Ribbons of pleasure unfurled inside her. Dru lifted her hips shamelessly to his face, desperate for more.

He roared his approval against her opening, setting off a chain reaction of pleasure that reverberated through her body.

She wasn't sure anymore if she was feeling her own wild desire or his. The room around her was gone, the animal sounds of her desire faded.

There was only Viktor and the pleasure that licked her

insides like a flame, the sensation so big it threatened to swallow her whole.

When she was balanced on the bitter edge of reason, he crawled up to cage her head in his arms.

"Drucilla," he groaned.

"Please," she whispered.

He sank into her slowly and she felt like a meadow in springtime, tendrils of pleasure unfurling, reaching up to touch his light.

"My God, Drucilla," he moaned through a clenched jaw.

She jogged her hips up, urging him on. He didn't have to hold back, he couldn't hurt her now.

As if he had heard her thoughts, he slammed into her, sending sparks through her shivering body.

By the third thrust she was flying, the pleasure nearly splitting her in half.

He stilled for a moment, letting her come down, then began again, building the tension in her, raising her higher and higher until she flew apart again.

"Viktor," she murmured, panting.

He gazed down at her, need burning in his eyes.

When the pleasure disintegrated her for the third time, she felt him let go too and fly with her.

Their cries echoed in the stony chamber and to Dru it sounded like the most beautiful music she had ever heard.

25

W hen it was done, he pulled her onto his chest. She closed her eyes and floated in a sense of satisfaction and peace.

"You dreamed of me, Drucilla," he said tightly.

So he knew that she was aware of his past.

She hadn't been sure how to tell him.

"I did," she said.

"But you still want me?"

"I want you to tell me everything," she said instead of answering. "I want to understand what I saw."

"That's more than fair," he said. "Where shall I begin?"

"I saw what happened here at the hotel, that night," Dru said. "And I think I understand. You had worked for the mob in order to have access to all the blood you needed."

"Yes," he said.

"And you were in love with my grandmother."

He was quiet for a moment.

"Drucilla, that wasn't it," he said carefully.

She waited, wanting him to tell her the truth.

She closed her eyes, trying to hear him through their bond as well as his voice.

"I adored her," he said. "She was like an angel. But I could never really imagine loving her as an equal. I knew that I couldn't deserve her. And I was right."

He was telling her the truth, she could feel it.

"I wasn't the man then that I am now," he went on. "She gave that to me. She gave me the chance to redeem myself, to be a good man, in spite of my... condition. She gave me hope, Drucilla. And then she gave me you."

Dru clung to him, drowning in the depth of his emotion.

"When I killed those men that night, I could see her disgust, feel it like a poison killing everything ugly inside me, forcing me to be reinvented," he said. "She ran, and I did not dare to follow."

Dru recalled that final image of her grandmother, young and beautiful, running away.

"At first, the jealousy nearly killed me," he said. "I fled to the woods and subsisted on rabbits and deer, filled with loathing for the man she ran home to."

Dru felt the hunger in his bones, tasted the bitter flesh of the forest creatures that would soon be her own sustenance, and the bitterness of Viktor's jealousy.

"I decided to follow him to war," Viktor said. "I knew the blood would flow there without me having to kill for it. And I wanted to see him in harm's way. I'm not proud of it, but I thought... I thought that maybe if he never came home, and I appeared at her doorstep, she would change her mind."

It was an evil plan, but Dru understood the lonely logic of it.

"But when I arrived, I could see he was a good man," Viktor went on. "He was kind and had a lovely, self-deprecating sense of humor. I couldn't put him in harm's way. As a matter of fact—"

"You *saved him*," Dru breathed, realizing.

"How did you know?" Viktor asked.

"Grandpa Frank used to talk about his friend, Mike," Dru said. "How Mike pulled him out of a burning building and took a bullet for him, saving his life. He said you looked like an angel with the flames all around you, and that you kept walking with him in your arms, even as the bullets slashed through you. But he never saw you again."

"Mikhail," Viktor told her as he pressed his lips to the top of Dru's head. "It was my middle name, before. Viktor Mikhail Stroika. Your grandparents both knew me as Michael."

"You risked being found out by doing that," Dru realized.

"I did," Viktor said. "But I didn't care. And when it was done, I disappeared again, before anyone could wonder how I'd survived."

He was silent for a moment, as if trying to decide how to explain what came next.

"It sustained me," he said at last. "The idea that I had performed a truly selfless act, if only one time in my new life. It gave me hope that I could be a force for good. And you will be one too, Drucilla. I'm sure of it."

He was gazing at her now with such intensity.

She felt his question before he could ask it.

"I'm glad," she confirmed. "I'm glad you saved me, glad to be whatever I am now, if it means I can go on living, and being with you."

He moved as if to kiss her and make love to her all over again.

"Wait," she said. "There's something you should know, something about my Nana. If you want to hear it?"

He nodded mutely.

"She loved Grandpa Frank with all her heart," Dru said. "You could feel it the minute you were in the room with them. It was the real thing. And she loved that story about the man who saved his life. She knew it was you, Viktor, I'm sure of it."

He nodded, his eyes bright.

"But, Viktor, there's more," Dru told him. "Did you know she came back here every year?"

His eyes widened.

"I think she wanted to thank you," Dru told him. "I think she wanted you to know she wasn't afraid anymore, that she was glad to be your friend."

Tears spilled over Viktor's cheeks and Dru held him close. She felt the waves of relief right along with him as he sobbed, knowing that Jane had been his friend, that she had died knowing he had done what he could to be better.

"I'm still a murderer, Drucilla," he whispered. "I was then, and I am now. I would have killed Little Nicky if Sullivan hadn't done it first. And if you hadn't been bleeding out when I got here, I would have killed Howie Pembroke tonight for what he's done."

"You killed a room full of bad guys to protect my grandmother," Drucilla said. "And you would kill again to protect me."

He nodded, waiting.

"Yeah, I think I'm cool with that," Drucilla said. "I think that sounds pretty good, actually.

Viktor laughed, and the rich sound filled up the cold stone room like a crackling fire.

"So Howie got away," Dru said.

"With the treasure, I'm afraid," Viktor told her.

"Not exactly," Dru said.

"What do you mean?"

"I don't think this was a total Charlie-Foxtrot," Dru said with a mischievous smile. "I think Howie left the real treasure right here."

"Where?" Viktor asked, looking around.

Dru got up again, so astonished at the graceful movement of her body that she almost forgot why she had gotten up.

"Here," she said, heading over to the bag of road salt in the corner. "Look at this."

"It's just salt," Viktor said.

"Maybe," Dru replied. "But the bag is still sealed. Why are there crystals on the ground around it? And why are they so big?"

"Drucilla," Viktor murmured.

She lifted one of the crystals and touched it to her tongue. It was tasteless and solid, and it was almost an exact twin of the crystal that hung on the chain around her neck. The one her grandmother had given her.

"This isn't salt," she said, smiling.

Viktor's mouth dropped open.

On the floor at Dru's feet were more than a dozen, marble-sized, uncut diamonds.

S *ix months later.*

DRU STOOD in the moonlit forest on the edge of the meadow at Hemlock House, with Viktor by her side.

"This is it," Viktor said quietly. "Tonight is the night."

He lifted her hand and they both gazed down at the ring on her finger. It was a simple band of gold holding the diamond that she'd been unknowingly wearing around her neck for so many years.

It wasn't as big as some of the diamonds they'd brought out of the hidden room under Hemlock House, but to Dru, it would always be the most valuable. Besides, she had other plans for the biggest stones in the bunch.

The largest diamond had gone to Honey Van Buren, of course. Eddie "Diamonds" McCarthy had been sweet on the younger Miss Van Buren. That was why he had hidden his treasure under her bed, where she'd kept it safe, all these years, as a true pillar of Hemlock.

The second largest diamond went to Hazel, because she was Honey's best and dearest friend, and Honey would not have enjoyed her own massive diamond if her sister didn't have one too.

Dru had first sent all the diamonds to New York to have them cut, polished and appraised. And it turned out the real value was staggering.

When the stones returned, Hazel and Honey had marched their two right to the little jeweler down in Willow Ridge. He had taken the valuable gems with trembling hands, and set each in a sturdy brooch.

The two women wore them proudly, each proclaiming that she would leave hers to the other, and that the remaining sister would leave both to Drucilla and Viktor one day.

Vampires or no, Drucilla wasn't entirely convinced that Hazel and Honey wouldn't outlive them all.

The days after her transition had been long.

When the ecstasy of her strong new body had worn off, long nights of aching hunger set in. There was a bottomless hollow, right in the center of Dru, that couldn't be entirely filled with animal blood.

But it was staved off with frequent feedings on small mammals.

And Viktor's touch distracted her from her other cravings, too.

In time, Dru's willpower had grown. She was now able to control her hunger, even in large groups of humans. They had been practicing at bars and clubs, to ensure that nothing could go wrong tonight.

"Are you excited to see it?" Viktor asked.

She nodded.

The next largest diamond had been sold at auction, and the proceeds used to restore the abandoned wing of Hemlock House. The general contractor had reported back to them weekly with his progress.

When Howie Pembroke ran away with approximately thirty thousand dollars in synthetic rubies and emeralds, the mob had caught up with him almost immediately.

According to Viktor's old contacts, he and Dru had nothing to worry about from Howie, ever again.

Viktor had bought the hotel out from under the developers as an engagement gift for Dru that made her cry like a baby.

When word made it back to her about the final auction windfall from the other diamonds, she was awestruck.

She had called up Hazel Van Buren, who wanted no parts of it.

"You found it, dear," Hazel said. "The one who finds the treasure is supposed to keep it, the rules are clear. Besides, Honey and I have such a nice life as it is. We have everything we need. Plus our pretty new brooches. Please enjoy the money and try to do some good with it, if that makes you happy."

But Dru had to do something for them. She told the staff to refuse the modest monthly rental payments they had been making. And she issued a decree that there would be a Lasagna Night *twice* a week at Hemlock House, which seemed to tickle the sisters even more than the lavish diamonds had.

Dru and Viktor had spent the quiet months of her recovery researching what to do with the rest of the money. It would be a full-time job, but she was determined to do enough good to put them both clearly in the positive column, so that Viktor could rest easier. Whatever he had done, he was a good man now. He deserved to feel like one.

He took her hand in his and they walked across the moonlit meadow.

Warm yellow light emanated from the windows of the hotel, and Dru could hear music and laughter with her enhanced hearing.

Rich food smells carried on the night air, although they no longer held any interest to her.

"Sorry you won't be able to eat the cake," Viktor said.

"There are plenty of other nice things to put in my mouth," Dru teased.

"Mrs. Striker, are you getting fresh with me?" he asked, arching a brow. "I thought you were my blushing bride."

"I'm not Mrs. Striker yet," she said.

Quick as a thought, he pulled her close and kissed her.

The deep current of his desire tightened around her, sucking her under.

But he released her too soon.

"Let's go fix that," he told her. "Unless you want me to tear that gown to shreds right here in the middle of the meadow."

She looked down at her beautiful gown and considered for a moment.

Viktor threw his head back and laughed. "Come on, Drucilla, the night is young."

"Dru, oh my gosh," Hailey yelled as they approached the front porch.

Dru waved back and then hiked up her gown so she could run toward her friend.

"Human speed," Viktor reminded her.

It was a good point. She'd toyed with the idea of telling her best friend about her new condition, but felt like she needed some more time to come to terms with it herself first.

Viktor ran beside her, and when they arrived at the porch, they both pretended to be out of breath.

"You look amazing," Hailey breathed. "Both of you."

"So do you," Dru said. "Turn around, I want to see all of it."

Hailey spun and her yellow and black lace dress twirled around her knees.

"You look like a haunted princess," Dru said approvingly.

"Nailed it," Hailey laughed. "And you look like an un-haunted princess."

"Got it on the first try," Dru said, giving a very deep curtsy.

"Dru," Zander called as he came out to join them on the porch. "Hey, Viktor."

"Hello, Zander," Dru replied.

"Good to see you," Viktor said.

"Everyone's kind of going crazy in there waiting for you," Zander said.

"We can't have that," Dru said, turning to Viktor. "See you in there?"

"See you in there," he agreed.

"Unless you get cold feet," she teased.

"You won't get rid of me that easily," he laughed.

"Come on," Zander told him.

Dru watched as Viktor and Zander headed for the reno-vated wing.

"Can you believe we've got the old Hemlock House crew together at once?" Hailey asked.

"And we're all awake," Dru pointed out. "How's it been since I left?"

"Weird," Hailey said, thoughtfully glancing inside at the main desk where a brawny looking man was answering the phones. "But we can talk about that later."

Interesting.

"So, I guess this will be a quiet affair," Dru said.

"You might be surprised," Hailey told her with a secret smile. "Viktor's probably in there now. Are you ready?"

"Yes," Dru said.

They headed inside.

The guy at the desk gave Hailey a significant look, which she ignored.

Instead, she led the way to the arch that was now open to the old abandoned wing.

Beautiful chestnut millwork extended down the new hallway, leading the way to the ballroom.

When they stepped inside, Dru gasped with pleasure.

Zander was sitting on a stool with an acoustic guitar in his hands. He began to play as soon as Dru and Hailey entered.

The whole room was filled with roses, and petals covered the wide wood planks of the floor. Tables covered in candles lined the walls.

The previously boarded up sections of the wall had been opened up to reveal tall, arched windows.

It was so new, and yet somehow so familiar.

Her dreams. It reminded her of her dreams. She'd visited this exact place when she'd first come to Hemlock House, before she ever met Viktor.

She scanned the room to find him standing between the windows, waiting for her.

Wooden chairs had been arranged in a semi-circle facing the windows. And the chairs were filled with familiar people.

Dru took a deep breath and began to walk slowly down the aisle to Viktor, with Hailey by her side.

Hazel and Honey Van Buren sat to the left of the aisle, dressed to the nines, with matching velvet hats tied under their chins, and their diamond brooches shimmering in the candlelight. They sighed and clasped their hands together at the sight of Dru as she walked past.

Hugh Channing sat beside them, smiling warmly at Dru.

Jeffrey and Jenna Wilder were on the other side of the aisle, holding hands and looking very smug.

"They came back for this?" Dru whispered to Hailey.

"Yes, and they have their own room this time," Hailey confided.

Dru tried not to giggle.

Melody Young was sitting beside the Wilders with Mayor Tuck at her side. The mayor would be performing the ceremony, and Melody would be taking photos, but Dru figured they would have been each other's plus-one no matter what.

There was a rustling at the open window, and Dru looked over to see an unexpected guest perched on the stone sill. Edgar Allan Crow had returned to watch over the festivities. Dru made a mental note to make sure he got her share of the cake.

Then Dru looked up and locked eyes with Viktor and she could think of nothing else as he fixed her in his azure gaze.

She could feel the fierceness of his love for her, and the wonder in his heart as she stepped closer, ready to join him for all time.

And she could feel him taste the joy that illuminated her, as he took her hands.

Mayor Tuck stepped forward and began to speak, but Dru couldn't hear her words over the sound of Viktor's voice in her head.

Drucilla, I have killed, I have crossed oceans, and I have waited generations to wrap you in my arms. I will never let you go.

She smiled into the eyes of her beautiful monster.

There will never be a need, she told him.

He gazed into her eyes, desire clear in his expression, setting her on fire without even touching her.

"I do," he said aloud.

Dru blushed and waited for her turn.

"I do," she said at last.

"I now pronounce you husband and wife," Mayor Tuck cried joyfully as their friends broke into applause.

Viktor lifted her into his arms and kissed her with all his heart.

I will love you forever, Viktor Striker.

Even eternity doesn't feel like enough.

Thanks for reading **Heart of the Vampire**!

Are you ready for a small-town romance full of sexy shifters, magic curses, and a fiercely independent woman torn between two worlds?

Then keep reading for a free sample of **Curse of the Alpha**!

Or grab your copy right now:
www.tashablack.com/tarkers-hollow-bundle-page

CURSE OF THE ALPHA - SAMPLE

CHAPTER 1

Ainsley was having the dream again.

She had worried that coming home to Tark-er's Hollow would bring it back. Her hands twisted the sheets as she tossed in her old childhood bed. At the same time, she smelled the pine needles crunching underfoot as her dream-self ran through the college woods.

In the dream she was always a teenager again.

Brian Swinton, the new boy at school, ran a few steps behind her, laughing.

Brian had just a few freckles on his cheeks that made you look at his eyes, his big, dreamy, hazel eyes. Once you were done with his eyes, which could be quite a while, you couldn't help but see how his t-shirt hugged his wide shoulders and his Levi's hung from his narrow hips. And even though he was a new kid and quiet, he made Ainsley's heart beat loud, loud, loud.

After school he would walk her home, and sometimes, Brian would try to pull her toward the woods. And Ainsley, who had always been a good girl, would sometimes let him.

There, they would kiss under the pine trees until Ainsley

was dizzy and heated and pushed him away to run as fast as she could back home. He would call after her, both of them laughing.

But the dream wasn't about one of those times. The dream was always about their last visit to the woods.

In the quiet night of her parents' empty house, a more grown up Ainsley thrashed in the sheets and tried desperately to wake up. But her traitorous feet carried her deeper into the woods, deeper into the dream.

As she ran, her own laughter mingled with Brian's, close behind. At last, she stopped, whirled around, and wrapped her arms around his neck, ready for a sweet, slow kiss.

Instead, he spun them both around and pressed her back against a tree.

He'd never done that before.

Before she could react, he slid his hands gently down her ribcage and let his thumbs brush her nipples.

Ainsley gasped as she took in the brand new sensations.

Brian pressed his mouth to hers again and angled his whole lean body against her soft one. She felt his heart pounding in his chest, and the hardened length of him throbbing against her hip.

Her insides clenched in pleasure and she deliberately pressed her breasts against his chest.

He inhaled sharply and stilled for a moment, then devoured her mouth again, fists clenched in her hair now, his hips rocking that mysterious stiff bulge against her.

In that moment Ainsley felt a surge of awareness. Suddenly she could hear every twig snap and every squirrel scamper in the woods. She could smell the wood shavings at the hardware store in the village, and hear the train on the tracks in the city half an hour away, thundering toward Tarker's Hollow.

What was happening to her?

The sensory assault washed over Ainsley in a tidal wave until she felt that her heart could not keep beating.

Even poor Brian Swinton, excited as he was, must have felt the change in her. He pulled away, panting.

"What's wrong?"

"I don't know," she said. "I'm sorry, I..." Tears welled in her eyes.

"Listen, we don't have to make out, Ainsley. I know you have a lot of school work and you're a nice girl..."

From her bed, Ainsley wanted nothing more than to agree with him and walk away. But she knew that was useless. The dream would run its course.

It always did.

Teenaged Ainsley touched a cautious finger to Brian's lips, then cupped both hands around his familiar face, letting her thumbs brush over the freckles on the tops of his cheeks, and staring into his hazel eyes. The smell of anxiety wafted off the light sweat on his brow.

She ran her hands through his sandy hair and he closed his eyes. Her fingers traced the gentle swell of his biceps, and her nails raked slowly down his chest. He leaned into her hands, but she brought them back up to his face.

"Being with you, like this, it might just be my favorite thing," Ainsley breathed.

Before he could respond, she grabbed his lower lip in her teeth and sucked on it gently.

Something was building inside Ainsley, struggling to break free.

Brian moaned softly. His hand cupped her breast, then worked its way down. He fumbled with the button of her jeans while they kissed.

The sounds of the surrounding woods disappeared -

Ainsley could hear nothing over the pounding of her own pulse. At last, the button gave way and Brian slipped his fingers into the waistband of her cotton panties.

There was a blur of movement, and a harsh growl, then everything went black as the air filled with shrill, unnatural shrieks.

Ainsley Connor finally opened her eyes in the safety of her old bedroom, her throat raw from screaming in her sleep.

The dream was over, but the feeling of it still draped her like a thick fog.

Any hope of rest was gone for the night.

CHAPTER 2

Ainsley jumped out of bed, silk pajamas clinging to the cold sweat that covered her. A shiver ran through her at the late summer breeze drifting through the open bedroom window. The familiar trappings of Ainsley's youth surrounded her.

Her parents had never taken down her boy band posters, or packed away the shelves of trophies. Just sitting there made her feel like she was in high school again, her parents asleep at the end of the hall. Like she could run to their room, snuggle herself between the two of them and everything would be all right.

Of course that wasn't the case.

Her parents were dead. That's why she was here, reliving old nightmares in her childhood bedroom.

Ainsley was a very practical person, but this particular dream, one she'd been having for the last ten years, always left her feeling scared and lonely. And now she really was alone – in Tarker's Hollow, and anywhere, if she was being honest.

She decided to head down to the kitchen for tea to

soothe her throat. She slipped on a bathrobe and walked down the narrow hall of the creaky old Victorian.

Her hand instinctively reached for a cell phone in her robe pocket, but came up empty. In New York, she would have found an email from a client or another agent to keep her busy – no matter the hour. But her phone was plugged in downstairs, where she had sworn not to touch it, and she had handed her client list over to a young upstart agent in her firm for the duration of this trip.

Ainsley knew she needed to focus every waking moment on emptying this house so she could get back to New York. Back to her real life. Back to her clients.

And out of Tarker's Hollow before the full moon.

Boiling water hit the peppermint teabag in her mug with a hiss. Ainsley brought the steaming brew to her face and inhaled.

It took her back to after school tea parties with her best friend, Grace Kwan-Cortez, in this very kitchen. Ainsley set her mug on the round oak table, where it rested on a ring stain put there by so many previous cups.

When Ainsley's parents died in the accident, Grace's parents had sent her a card. It read as though no time had passed since the day Ainsley left Tarker's Hollow at age seventeen without looking back.

In the card, Mrs. Cortez told Ainsley that she loved her and that they would always think of her as their daughter and hoped she would think of them like her parents now. Mrs. Cortez also explained that they had set aside a bedroom for her. She could come home anytime to stay for as long as she wanted.

Come home.

The honesty had shattered Ainsley's frozen heart and

she'd immediately stuffed it in the bottom of her underwear drawer, unable to bring herself to throw it away.

The Cortez family home and her own had been the settings of so many happy girlhood memories. She could lose herself wallowing in the past if she wasn't careful.

That's why she was practically hiding out in the house.

If she didn't bump into any of her old teachers or school-mates, if she didn't call Mrs. Cortez, then she couldn't get sucked in. She could get in and get out – just like she planned.

That was sort of the name of Ainsley's game. Since middle school she had been what people might describe as a Type A personality. She liked to ask questions and get things right on the first try. She and Grace had been two peas in a pod.

Until that night with Brian had ruined her life, and ended his.

CHAPTER 3

S he had spent days in her room after Brian's death. When she was finally able to leave her bed and take a shower without breaking down, her parents had told her it was time to have a talk about growing up.

She had thought it ludicrous under the circumstances, and pushed them off again and again, until they cornered her in her room two weeks later, as she packed for college. She'd gotten accepted early, and, like it or not, the summer session was about to start.

It turned out that Ainsley's family had a very different version of "the talk."

"Mom, Dad, you missed the boat. We already talked about the birds and the bees in health class." Ainsley neatly rolled a skirt in plastic and placed it in the blue suitcase they'd bought for her.

"I was thinking more about the wolves," her dad said.

Ainsley froze, thinking of the growl she'd heard in the woods with Brian right before...

"Ainsley, we knew we needed to have this talk with you before you went away. But we hoped you could have a little more time to enjoy your childhood," her dad said. "We weren't even sure if…"

A look from Ainsley's mom made him reconsider finishing his sentence.

Ainsley swallowed and smoothed her hair behind her ears, a nervous habit. She began rolling another skirt.

"I know you're still hurting, honey," her mom whispered and reached to touch Ainsley's face.

Ainsley cringed. The hurt look in her mother's eyes would be with her for a lifetime. Her mom withdrew her hand.

"No matter how you feel right now, it's important for you to learn as much as you can about being a wolf. It is who you are. And you're going to need to know what to do," she said.

A wolf?

There it was. Ainsley had always known she was different. She just didn't realize how different, until that day in the woods. The day she had transformed into some kind of monster and killed poor, innocent Brian Swinton.

Of course she didn't actually remember that part; she had blacked out, mercifully. But Sheriff Warren said it looked like Brian had been mauled by a bear.

It didn't take a rocket scientist.

The realization of what she'd done hit her like a kick in the chest.

"Not to mention that you're very important to the pack," her father added.

Her mother shot him that look again, like he'd said too much. Ainsley seized the opportunity.

"How am I important?"

"Ainsley, our family has been part of this pack for generations," her mother explained. "Your grandfather led the pack as alpha, and now your father has that role."

"A lot of changes are coming to this town, Ainsley," Dad said, "and we will need strong leadership to survive."

Ainsley stared at her father in wonder.

"Is that why everyone in town is so friendly to you?"

"I suspect it has more to do with my effervescent charm, but being the alpha doesn't hurt."

Ainsley ignored his attempt at humor.

"Are they *all* werewolves?"

"Not all of them, but yes, a lot of the people here are wolves. We don't use the term 'werewolf' – it's a little offensive."

Even monsters had to be politically correct, it seemed.

"And *you* are the leader of the pack?" she asked.

"That makes it sound like the old Shangri-La song, but yes, I am the alpha."

Ainsley thought about it.

Her quiet father was always at the center of every party. Their friends came to him for advice. Underneath the old tweed blazers his body was strong and warm. He could still sweep her up and throw her over his shoulder as a teenager as easily as when she was a little girl. His vision was excellent in spite of decades in front of a computer or with his nose buried in an old tome. Even the soft voice he used now vibrated with strength.

She had never really thought about it.

He was her father. He would always be big and strong and brave in her eyes, and she would always want to obey him and make him proud. There was nothing crude and animalistic in that.

Was there?

"I believe you, Dad. But I need to leave. I can't be part of this. What happened was unforgivable."

"It's tragic what happened to Brian, honey," her mother said. Ainsley could tell she wanted to say more.

"He's not the last boy in Tarker's Hollow, Ainsley," her father said. "Another wolf would be the best choice. Until now I've held them back. Now that you know the truth, that can change."

Ainsley had a sudden flash of insight into why the other boys had started being so weird. Lately, she'd begun to actually feel the hungry stares she'd thought she'd been glimpsing for years, and hear the hearts pounding.

When she turned around they always cast down their eyes. She thought that was just how boys were – cowardly. Until the new boy had met her eye and gulped when she looked his way. Her heart turned to ice at the thought.

"The last, the absolute *last* thing on this earth that I want to date is another *wolf*. It's bad enough that I can't get out of this." She paused, considering. "Wait. Is there any way for me to get out of this?"

"No, Ainsley," her father said. "No, there isn't."

"So no matter what, I'm going to turn into a gigantic wolf?"

"Yes."

"Did I turn into a wolf because... because I was making out with Brian?"

"No," her mother said. "Although that sort of... *activity* can draw your wolf to the surface. Your cycle as a wolf has to do with the cycle of the moon."

"Do I have to turn?" Ainsley asked. "What if I don't want to?"

Ainsley shot her a pleading look. Her mom had always been able to make things right. Ainsley wished more than anything that she could go back to being that little girl with the pigtails and the skinned knees, running to her mom for a bandage and a glass of homemade lemonade – to go back to a simpler time, before all this mess.

Her mother sighed.

"You can't change who you are, Ainsley, and turning is part of who you are now."

"There are stories," her father said, slipping into the academic tone he used with his students. "Of wolves that were under duress and couldn't turn. They say the pain was excruciating, both mentally and physically."

"Michael." Her mother shook her head at him.

"So it can be done!" Ainsley said, latching on to the possibility of a normal life.

"It may be technically possible to withhold from turning, Ainsley. But I would advise against it," her father said. "The amount of self control it would take would be monumental. Your mind and body will be consumed with your new life at every moon cycle. You should engage with it, master it, and enjoy it. It is who you are. You can't just run away."

"Watch me," Ainsley said firmly. The teeth of the zipper came together with a satisfying hiss and she swung the suitcase off the bed.

She was going away to college, she had a full scholarship to Columbia, and there was nothing they could do to stop her.

"You're coming home two days before the full moon." Her father's tone made it clear that it wasn't a request.

"Yes, Dad."

Of course she didn't.

She hadn't set foot in the house since that day. Until the

car accident claimed her parents' lives and forced her back into town.

Her parents had hidden the truth from her just long enough to make her a murderer.

And now their degenerate lifestyle meant that Ainsley couldn't just hire an army of ladies armed with boxes and stickers to empty the house. Instead, she had to put her life on hold and risk damaging her career to go through their belongings herself and annihilate any trace of what her parents had been.

CHAPTER 4

Ainsley realized that her cup was empty and she was drifting again, losing herself in memories of a past she'd tried to forget.

She got up quickly, washed her mug, dried it and put it away. When she was satisfied that the kitchen was as tidy as when she'd come down, she headed back through the dining room and parlor to the stairs.

As soon as Ainsley found herself back between the sheets, all her drowsiness vanished. She stared at the stick-on stars glowing on her ceiling, waiting for sleep to come.

At some point, she must have drifted off.

CHAPTER 5

T he next morning, Ainsley woke early to finish sorting the pile of papers on the dining room table. She sat at the table sipping a mug of hot English Breakfast tea - she couldn't bring herself to make coffee using the Keurig that perched on kitchen counter, those little pods seemed insulting, to her and to the coffee.

She set aside any invoices and receipts related to her mother's hardware store. Those would be for the estate attorney to worry about. There didn't seem to be any references to werewolves so far.

Ainsley knew that sooner or later there would be nothing else that needed sorting downstairs and she would have no choice but to tackle her father's study. The prospect both excited and depressed her.

Michael Connor had a perfectly wonderful book collection. Its volumes included all the classics of Russian literature. From Tolstoy to Turgenev, he had them all – in most cases, he had multiple copies.

There were dog-eared paperbacks with copious notes in

his careful handwriting – those had sentimental value and would find their way onto Ainsley's own shelves.

There were also hard backed volumes in shining leather and in paper jackets – some in the original Russian, some translations. Some were gifts from her father's students and colleagues. A few were even yard sale finds, which he bought and gave away if he found the translation acceptable.

And then there were the rare gems. A few of them she would recognize on sight, because she had been with him when he bought them. Each was worth thousands or even tens of thousands.

Michael Connor hadn't believed in locking away rare books. They lived among the rest of the collection. Ainsley recalled the way he used to pull out a volume to pore over it, noting slight differences in the translation. She had even seen him caress their spines in passing with an unconscious tenderness, the way he had sometimes tousled her hair when she was little.

Unless he had made an inventory that she hadn't found yet, Ainsley had no idea which books ought to go to the library sale and which should be sold at auction. Although she knew she ought to ship them all off to a book dealer, it felt wrong to send them away.

She wished that she had someone more versed in rare books to help her with the job.

Ainsley stretched her arms over her head. It was impossible to keep working. She needed a walk, and to open up a conversation with a local real estate agent.

She was going to have to leave the house.

Maybe she would even reward herself with a cup of coffee on the way. Tarker's Hollow had avoided the Starbucks revolution, which was a shame. Ainsley imagined the jolt of a hot Pike's Place with soy as it warmed her chest and belly and brought her to life. Surely there was still a place to get a half-decent cup in town somewhere.

She pulled off her t-shirt and yoga pants and slipped on a sheath dress and a pair of heels. She even remembered to grab a pair of big sunglasses, hoping to preserve her anonymity.

CHAPTER 6

T he walk to town was short but beautiful. Tarker's Hollow had a shade tree committee, dedicated to maintaining the glorious canopy of maples and oaks that met over the streets, dappling the old sandstone sidewalks with soft green shadows.

Each house she passed belonged to a character from her youth. Sadie Epstein-Walker squatted in her garden across the street, big floppy hat and sunglasses in place, harvesting late summer roses just like she had when Ainsley was in high school.

Was she a wolf?

Ainsley studied her back, trying to decide. When Sadie turned, Ainsley shifted her gaze straight ahead and sped up her walk.

A few houses down, Mrs. Hooper's bicycle still sat on her front porch, even though Mrs. Hooper must be seventy by now.

As she turned the corner onto Elm, she could hear a few cars a block over on Yale Avenue. All the streets in town bore the names of either trees or colleges. A gorgeous garden still bloomed in front of the post office, even in the late summer.

She turned the corner onto Yale and passed the flower shop, the toy store, and some new place that sold eco-friendly home décor. Then there it was – the hardware store. There was a lump in her throat when she saw the old sign was still in place.

Selling her mother's family store had been really hard for Ainsley. She remembered how Mr. MacGregor, her high school History teacher, had approached her at the funeral:

"Ainsley, please come home," he said simply, hands pressed against his sides. His blonde hair was still a little long. All the girls at Tarker's High when Ainsley has been there mooned over him.

"Mr. MacGregor, thank you for coming."

"Can we please talk after the service? There is so much I need to tell you."

Ainsley squirmed. "I've really got to get back to New York."

"I'd like to buy the hardware store. Can we at least talk about that?"

Ainsley had resisted the instinct to snarl at him.

Why did she feel so protective of the old place?

Of course she wasn't going to come home to Tarker's Hollow and run a hardware store. Something had to be done about the business and the building.

She agreed to meet him after the service. MacGregor, it turned out, was the beta of the Tarker's Hollow wolves.

He perched on the edge of her father's brown leather chesterfield with his hands clasped in front of him.

"Ainsley, a beta can't lead a pack forever," he said. "It's complicated. The wolves are patient, but something's going to give way soon. We need an alpha."

Ainsley shifted uncomfortably and re-crossed her legs. His heart pounded in response and she froze.

"I'm sorry, Ainsley, I know this isn't the world you chose. But we are your people and we need your help."

"Why don't you just choose an alpha?"

"That's not the way it works. Lineage is important." He twisted in his seat. "We need you to choose."

"Fine. I choose you," she said immediately. "Does that fix everything?"

He swallowed, "Do you know what it means for you to choose?"

"Um, you become alpha, right?"

"The only way for an alpha to emerge is for you to choose a mate."

Oh Jesus.

She studied the face of the teacher she'd fantasized about in high school. He was gazing miserably at her and sweating a little. The scent of his growing arousal was overpowering. A soft, golden haze formed around him. The creases at the corners of his eyes disappeared and his shoulders broadened.

What the hell was going on?

"So, if we just?" she whispered.

His eyes widened and he leaned toward her hungrily. The thundering of his heart vibrated through her whole body as her own pulse struggled to match its rhythm. His face had gone from mildly attractive to dazzlingly handsome; he looked like a young god. The air seemed to crackle with energy, and she moved to bridge the distance between them.

At the last second, he pulled back with obvious effort and sighed, looking away from her.

"We don't just have to couple – choosing a mate means choosing a mate. It's for life."

Ainsley shook her head, and the haze disappeared. The room returned to normal. Mr. MacGregor looked just as he always had – handsome in a rumpled way.

She had only been home three days for the funeral, and already strange things were happening. She couldn't wait to get back to New York.

"Sorry, Mr. MacGregor," she said. "I'm not interested in choosing a mate."

"I know you're not. And even if you were, I shouldn't be on your list." He smiled ruefully. "There are several promising candidates, and one in particular your parents hoped you would choose."

Her parents had a mate in mind for her? Lovely.

"Okay, I'll bite, who's the lucky guy?"

"Erik Jensen."

Ainsley swallowed. The thought of Erik Jensen always made her feel a twinge of regret. Erik had been her best childhood friend. When the boys in school decided that girls were dumb and couldn't play in the woods, Erik had stubbornly insisted that Ainsley Connor was super neat and that they would kick her out over his dead body.

He'd won out over the other kids and Ainsley was allowed to keep her place by his side. By third grade they had ruled the woods and creek and even built a massive tree fort, just the two of them.

But when the school labeled Ainsley as gifted, she had been pulled out of their shared classes. The extra homework cut into her playtime, and she found herself spending more time with Grace Kwan-Cortez and her studious, less "out-doorsy" crowd.

She never exactly had a falling out with Erik. But by

middle school, Ainsley realized that not only did she not hang out with him anymore, he wouldn't even look at her when they passed in the halls.

By high school he was really handsome. His strong jaw contrasted with soft, dark eyes that were framed with long lashes. His hair was so dark it was almost black. He wore a black leather jacket that Ainsley secretly thought was pretty cool.

Although he had "bad boy" good looks and excelled at sports, everyone knew that he was a nice person. He even headed up a group of boys who would shovel out the senior citizens around town in the frequent winter storms.

Realizing now that Erik Jensen was the man her parents wanted for her gave Ainsley a pang of longing. At ten years old, Erik had shown her more respect and kindness than any other man she'd ever met. And like every other person of importance in her life, she'd dropped him like a hot potato.

Ainsley realized Mr. MacGregor was waiting for her to respond.

"Wow, Erik Jensen?" she said.

"That's who your father told me he hoped you would choose. That was a long time ago, but I know he didn't say it lightly."

"Well, I appreciate the insight but I'm not going to be choosing a mate. I'm sure you guys can vote or something. Can we take care of the paperwork for the hardware store?"

CHAPTER 7

Ainsley shook herself out of her reverie and continued her walk. She didn't have time to reminisce. No good would come of that.

Mr. MacGregor had kept up her mom's tradition of putting out some seasonal items on tables out front with silly signs reminding everyone why they needed them. There was a collection of rakes and paper leaf bags laid out with the sign: *You'll be raking in the compliments on your beautiful fall lawn!* MacGregor clearly did not have her mother's wit. But she was glad he tried.

She caught a glimpse of him grinding a key for Patty Loveless, one of the local real estate agents. That reminded her that she had better stop by and talk to Charley about the house. In her periphery she could sense them turning toward her as soon as she shifted her gaze.

Ainsley wasn't about to risk getting pulled into a conversation. She looked both ways and crossed Yale. There was nothing over there except the empty construction site.

No one to bother her.

The construction vehicles seemed out of place, especially for a town that feared change as much as Tarker's Hollow. The former ball field was going to be an Inn and restaurant soon. The town had approved it fifteen years ago, but they were only just now breaking ground because there had been such a fuss.

As Ainsley crossed Yale, she studied the temporary fencing, trying to picture the size of the building and the parking area that would be there one day. Many of the trophies that still lined the shelves of her room featured miniature golden softball players. Ainsley had thrown her share of strikeouts on the field that had already been erased by the heavy treads of the earth movers.

Just as she arrived on the sidewalk on the college side of Yale, a figure appeared behind the fence in the construction area. Tall, dark and handsome didn't begin to describe him. But Ainsley was never the kind of girl who fantasized about Neanderthal types, so she tore her eyes away from his tantalizing shape and headed toward the overpass. She would just walk back over Yale to the café and real estate office.

"Hey!"

She angled away from the guy who yelled at her. Ainsley expected that kind of behavior on the streets of Manhattan, but here? Did construction workers actually think girls liked that?

She turned up her nose and sped up her walk.

"Ainsley!" he called.

She spun on her heel and squinted at him. Did she know this person? She didn't think so. She would have remembered a body like that.

"Ainsley Connor, I didn't know you were in town."

Well, she wasn't going to get out of this. She swallowed a sigh and walked toward him. God, he was good-looking. A white T-shirt stretched over his broad chest. His arms rippled with muscles. Faded jeans hung low on his hips.

Why were these blue-collar types always so hot? It wasn't fair.

"Do I know you?"

"It's Erik. Erik Jensen." His eyes crinkled in a smile. He had the longest eyelashes – that was the only part of him she recognized.

"*Erik*?" Ainsley did *not* remember that incredible body.

"Yeah, I almost didn't recognize you either, Ainsley. We grew up, didn't we?"

Yes. Erik had grown into an underwear model. Ainsley had just grown curvier than she wanted to. But she couldn't help smiling.

"We did," she said.

"I was really sad to hear about your parents." He glanced down and kicked at some dirt with the toe of his work boot. "Sorry. I was out of state for the funeral, or else I…"

"It's okay," she said, letting him off the hook. "I'm dealing with it."

"So you live in New York, right?"

"Yes, I'm in real estate. It's going well." She left it at that. He was still stuck in Tarker's Hollow, and digging holes for a living. How awkward. It would be better to not make a big deal of her success. "How are things with you?"

"They're great, thanks for asking. I just found out I'm on the short list for the highway."

What could that possibly mean? Was he on clean-up duty as some sort of community service?

"I'm not sure I know what you mean."

"Sorry, Ainsley. I guess our small-town news doesn't make it into the New York Times." He flashed a playful smile that made her forget to breathe for a minute. "I own this excavation company. We're working on the Inn project now. And it sounds like we're on the short list to do excavation for the new highway coming in. It's a huge opportunity."

The highway, was that really going to happen? She knew the residents had been fighting it for years, but the highway would finally put the town on the map. Although given the special kind of diversity found in Tarker's Hollow, maybe that wasn't such a good thing.

Ainsley's cheeks flushed at her assumption that Erik was a bog standard construction type. His ambitions had clearly brought him well beyond the role of ditch digger.

It dawned on her that Erik was a wolf, too. She remembered what Mr. MacGregor had told her. Her cheeks flushed even more. She must look like a fool.

"Wow, Erik, that's amazing. I'm really happy for you."

He smiled and looked down modestly, showing off those eyelashes again.

For a moment she allowed herself to imagine what it would be like to be his mate. She let her eyes run down the length of his body, wide shoulders forming a triangle with his narrow waist. His jeans hung just low enough that she couldn't quite see, but could well imagine the silken trail leading down to what just had to be a beautiful cock. Even the jeans couldn't disguise the size of the bulge between his legs.

Plus, he was a wolf. No need to worry about losing control and hurting him. Erik looked like the type that could take care of himself.

He looked up and she met his eyes.

In a heartbeat, the edges of her vision blurred and nothing mattered but Erik. His eyes were luminous; his sweat was an intoxicating musk. His too long hair lifted in an imaginary breeze as his heartbeat strained to match hers. Tiny, golden motes danced along his muscular body.

It was happening again. Just like with MacGregor. Only this wasn't a middle aged History teacher standing on the other side of the fence.

Ainsley licked her lips and moved toward him. Her palms clinked against the chain link fence, just as he crashed into it, clenching the metal in his powerful hands and twisting until several of the links gave way with a pop. God, but he was strong. She had a vision of him tearing down the entire section of fence just to get to her.

A tiny moan escaped her lips and he growled softly in return, his dark eyes flashing a spectacular amber. His wolf must be close to the surface. She could feel her own, begging to be unleashed. Somehow, she tore her eyes from his and the spell was broken.

Thanks for reading this sample of **Curse of the Alpha**!

Want to find out if Ainsley can come to terms with her past and take her rightful place in the pack, even when a sexy warlock comes along to pull her attention away from Eric?

Grab the rest of the story right now:
www.tashablack.com/tarkers-hollow-bundle-page

TASHA BLACK STARTER LIBRARY

Packed with steamy shifters, mischievous magic, billionaire superheroes, otherworldly alien mates, and plenty of HEAT, the Tasha Black Starter Library is the perfect way to dive into Tasha's unique brand of Romance with Bite!
Get your FREE books now at tashablack.com!

ABOUT THE AUTHOR

Tasha Black lives in a big old Victorian in a tiny college town. She loves reading anything she can get her hands on, writing paranormal, sci fi & fantasy romance, and sipping pumpkin spice lattes.

Get all the latest info, and claim your FREE Tasha Black Starter Library at www.TashaBlack.com

Plus you'll get the chance for sneak peeks of upcoming titles and other cool stuff!

Keep in touch...
www.tashablack.com
authortashablack@gmail.com

facebook.com/romancewithbite
twitter.com/romancewithbite

Printed in Great Britain
by Amazon